THE NEW HOPE

Books by Joseph C. and Freeman Lincoln

BLAIR'S ATTIC

THE OWNLEY INN

THE NEW HOPE

Books by Joseph C. Lincoln

ALL ALONGSHORE

BACK NUMBERS

CHRISTMAS DAYS

Books by Freeman Lincoln

NOD

SAM

REBOUND

The New Hope

JOSEPH C. LINCOLN

and

FREEMAN LINCOLN

COWARD-McCANN, INC.

NEW YORK

C.10

MAY 1 '74
BL

This is not a historical novel, in the accepted sense of the term. Although, for its background, we have endeavored to give a faithful and accurate picture of conditions in towns and villages along a section of the Cape Cod coast during the British blockade of 1814, as derived from books and records of that period, we have not confined ourselves within definite geographic boundaries.

The town of Trumet never existed, as we portray it. It was necessary, for the purposes of the story, that the village should have a moderately deep harbor on the ocean side and smaller and shallower ones on the Bay. Orleans, on Cape Cod, has those, but Trumet is not Orleans. Truro is situated about, or near, where we wished Trumet to be— but Truro is not Trumet.

We have exercised, in *The New Hope*, our privileges as writers of fiction. At convenient locations on the Truro shores we have made harbors somewhat similar to those of Orleans. Nearby we set up the purely fictitious village of Trumet.

Point Town, in the tale, is at the tip of the Cape, where Provincetown was, and still is—but that does not mean that the Point Town of the book is actually Provincetown. Writers must be careful to be accurate in dealing with actual communities. With communities of their own crea-tion they can do exactly as they please in the matter of laying out streets and roads, as well as in designating the position of both private and public buildings. Yes, and they can populate their imaginary townships with men and women of their own invention.

All of which is precisely what we have done in this yarn of the *New Hope*. Its characters and their adventures are all fictitious. Certain incidents—such as the capture of the armed sloop, *Gannet*, and her crew by one man—have a basis of historical fact. But even they, as we have told them, differ widely from their pattern.

This explanation is offered with the idea of heading off misapprehension and consequent criticism. The *New Hope* is our own privateer, built and launched by us, and manned and officered by individuals of our own creation. Her story is *just* a story, and pretends to be no more than that.

Joseph C. Lincoln
Freeman Lincoln

Chatham, Massachusetts
July, 1941

CONTENTS

1

In which the blockade tightens, and Captain Dole sees a light in the sky.

Told by

CAPTAIN ISAIAH DOLE

I WOULDN'T CALL myself a nervous man, generally speaking. I have been in some pretty tight places, afloat and ashore—mostly afloat, of course—and I think I can honestly say that, even in the tightest of them, I have been able to keep my nerves from getting the weather gauge of me. I don't say that in a bragging way. It is no credit to me, it is how I am built, that's all. If I have any philosophy, any rule to steer by, it is to take every care to set things going right, do everything possible to make them right, and then—well, then carry on with the job, hoping for the best but ready to tackle the worst if the worst should come. See what I mean?

Which is all right. A good rule. First rate. Only, as they say about every rule, this one was bound to have an exception to it, and, that morning, a Friday morning in late August, 1814, I realized as I came into the dining-room for my breakfast that I was as nervous as a cat navigating a floor that has just been varnished.

I tried not to show it, of course. When Phoebe came rolling out of the kitchen with my plate of fried flatfish in one hand and my cup of blackberry-leaf tea in the other, I pumped up a smile and said "Good morning" in what I hoped was regular everyday fashion. Phoebe answered the hail and then rolled back to the kitchen again to get the ration of rye muffins that went with the flatfish. When I say "rolled" I am not exaggerating a whole lot, for she is

3

about as broad in the beam as she is up and down and her way of moving always reminds me of a barge loaded with salt working through a heavy ground swell.

Her full name is Phoebe Light, and her husband is Ezra Light, the peddler. Jonathan Bangs and I had hired the Light place when we first came back to Trumet, and we had hired Phoebe as cook and general housekeeping roustabout along with it. She and Ezra—when he happened to be at home from his peddling cruises—had a couple of rooms at the back of the house, upstairs, to use for their quarters, and Jonathan and I had the rest of the outfit.

I sat down at my place at the table as if I was going to pitch in and eat. I didn't, though. As soon as Phoebe headed for the kitchen, I got up and went to the window looking towards the southeast. I wanted to see if the *Hawke* was still anchored off yonder. She was. I could see her topmasts over the highest sand hummock at the mouth of the inlet leading through the narrows to Trumet Harbor. I could see the sand breastwork the militia had thrown up on the top of that hummock, and the morning sun flashed on the little, ha'penny brass cannon they had put there with the general hope that it might be of some use in beating off landing parties trying to get ashore in rowboats. I could see the hill and the cannon and the sloping roofs and windmills of Eben Fowler's saltworks. I could see the harbor, with its dories and sloops and one or two small schooners lying empty and useless, same as they had been since the blockade shut down on us in earnest. I could see the little shipyard and our own trim little bark, the *New Hope*, alongside the wharf, and, early as 'twas, there were people working aboard her now. I could see the main part of Trumet, the First Meeting House and the tavern and the Town House and the main road with the houses along it. The Light place is on top of the highest hill in the village, and you get quite a view from there on a clear day.

4

It was fine and clear now, and I *could* have seen all I have mentioned and more, but I didn't, really. I didn't look at them. All I looked for and at were the topmasts of that everlasting British armed brigantine *Hawke* lying off in the blue water back of the outer shoals. Not cruising back and forth, a couple of miles from shore, as she had been doing for the past two months or more, but closer in, as nigh the harbor mouth as her draught would let her lie safe, and anchored there. Anchored! As if she was waiting for something to try to come out. Either that or as if she was waiting for the right minute for herself to come *in*. Either was bad.

Do you wonder I was nervous? Why, yes, maybe you do, for you don't know what was in my mind, and in the minds of almost everybody else in Trumet just then. If you had known you wouldn't have wondered much. In fact, as I stood there, it crossed my mind how many other good folks in our town must be looking off at those same top-masts and worrying to see them in that spot.

I could hear the kitchen floorboards creaking, indicating that Phoebe was lumbering in with her cargo of rye muffins, so I scuttled back to my chair at the table. She had forgotten the butter, of course. A time when she didn't forget something would have been important enough to put down in the log. I reminded her of the butter, and she set sail to fetch it. Butter and milk were things we had a rea-sonable supply of, there being a number of cows in town and pasture for them. Meat, like beef and lamb, we hadn't any—couldn't spare the critters, you see. And quail and partridge and ducks and geese and shore birds we couldn't waste the powder to shoot—not often, although a few were snared. But there were eggs and clams and quahaugs and lobsters and inshore fish by the quintal and corn meal by the barrel. Some molasses and rum still left, but no sugar. Coffee and regular tea, none at all. That is why Phoebe trotted out the blackberry-leaf tea for Jonathan and me. She always had to trot the heft of it back again, for we couldn't drink much of it. Did you ever try blackberry-leaf tea? Well—don't.

Jonathan Bangs came out of his bedroom just as I was sampling my first muffin. I shall have to tell you a lot about Jonathan by and by, as this yarn of his and mine gets under way, and he will tell you his share; so just now I won't say any more than that he was about the closest friend I had in town in spite of the fact that he was only twenty-three, whereas I was forty-one, at this time I'm talking about. He is six foot two, compared to my five foot seven, is light-haired and blue-eyed, husky as a bull and plucky as a bulldog. To see him move in that slow, easy-going way of his, you wouldn't think he would ever get anywhere; but he always did and on time, too.

He came out of his room, shut the door behind him, turned the key in the lock, and went over and hung the key on the hook at the starboard inside end of the mantelpiece close to the wall, where we always kept it. Jonathan's room was, so far as I know, the only locked-up room in that house. Even the outside doors were left open night and day. Except for some apple-hooking boys there had never been any thieving in Trumet.

Since the *New Hope* notion got under way and there had to be some place where important things, papers and such, could be kept, we had locked Jonathan's room door. It had the newest and best lock in the house, that was one reason, and another was that it was on the ground floor and easy for him or me to get at. In a secret drawer that I had contrived and rigged myself back of a regular drawer in his bureau were the papers commissioning the *New Hope* as a regular privateer by the Government, my own papers as her captain, a list of the crew and officers, memorandums showing how much had been spent on her so far, and a private memorandum showing how much money each of the group backing the enterprise had invested in her. This last was only for my own information. Captain Elnathan Berry, who was secretary of the Council—that is what we had fallen in the habit of calling our committee of investors backing the venture—had a list, too, of course.

For the first few days after the locking-up began, Jonathan carried his door key around with him, but Phoebe Light raised such an awful hullabaloo because she couldn't get in to make beds and dust that we decided it might be just as well to have a place to keep the key and leave it there. Nobody but Jonathan and me knew about the secret drawer, anyhow; we had taken mighty good care not to let Phoebe know about it, you may be sure. She was a loyal soul and as honest a woman as ever lived, but she was a great talker and as flighty-minded as a poll parrot. There was never a minute when she wasn't busy, but, if you asked her what she had been busy at the minute before, she was just as apt to have forgotten. Jonathan and I made it our business to see that, every time she took that key down from its hook, she put it back just as soon as she came out of the room. We had a rough time along at first—it was as liable to be in her apron pocket or on the mantelpiece as anywhere else—but, by sticking to it, we finally made her realize that it *must* be on that hook when she, or we, weren't using it. After that it was always there. Shows what perseverance can do, doesn't it?

After Jonathan had hung up the key, and even before he gave me a good-morning hail, he did just what I had done—walked to that southeast window and looked out. I heard him fetch a long breath.

"Um-hm," said I. "I feel the same way. She's there yet."

He nodded, turned and came back to the table. Phoebe had rolled out to the kitchen again after his supply of breakfast, so we had a minute or so to talk in private.

7

"Anchored there, isn't she?" he said, lowering his voice. Coming from that big chest of his even a whisper was more or less of a rumble.

"Yes," said I. "She hasn't moved since four o'clock yesterday afternoon, so she must be."

He nodded again; doesn't waste many words, Jonathan doesn't. Then he said, as much to himself as to me, "I don't like it."

Neither did I and I told him so. "When she was cruising on blockade duty, I didn't pay much attention to her. But for her to quit cruising and drop anchor right broad abeam of the harbor mouth is—well, it does set me to wondering."

"Me, too. Do you think they may be going to attack because we wouldn't pay the ransom? Or is it worse? Captain Dole, you don't suppose they *know?*"

"It is how much they know that is the question. That some sort of a craft is being rerigged and outfitted by us Trumet folks they almost surely know. When the plan first got under way all that was given out was that we were making work for the town men, with the idea of having a vessel ready for the coasting trade again as soon as the war was over. We said that out loud and in public, you remember. I told Ezra Light he better drop a hint to that effect here and there when he was on a peddling trip down towards the end of the Cape. But that we are fitting her for privateering, and, more than all, that we have any notion of trying to run the blockade with her, is something else altogether. I don't see how they *can* know that."

He nodded once more. "Um-hm," he agreed: "but—"

He didn't finish the sentence, so I did it for him. "But, if they don't know—yes, and aren't expecting whatever they know, or guess, to happen pretty soon—why does that blasted *Hawke* come in close and lay there in the very spot where she could make the most trouble? And just now, when we are all but ready?"

8

He took up his knife and fork and played with them. "I suppose the plans for getting the powder down from Tamoset will be settled at Council meeting tonight, won't they?" he asked.

"They certain sure will if I have anything to say about it."

"Yes. And you still mean to make the try to get clear and away right after the powder is aboard?"

"The first decent night after the last keg is stowed—yes sir-ee. The day that powder running is really under way we'll start bringing in the crew. Every man Jack of them has had word to stand by and report for duty when the call comes. They are all picked men, and they won't hang back. Half a dozen of them have had relations or friends pressed aboard British ships, and they are just hankering for a chance to get even. But you know all this as well as I do. Nothing has been changed."

Jonathan leaned towards me across the table. "Captain Dole," he whispered. By the way, I might as well say right here that Jonathan Bangs is about the only man in Trumet who uses my last name when he speaks to me. The rest of them hail me as "Captain Isaiah" or plain "Captain," or, if they are my age and have known me since I was a boy, just "Isaiah." Jonathan, though, hadn't known me so very long, and he was my second officer aboard the *Strong Arm*, so he stuck to the "Captain Dole." Seafaring habits, especially on a fighting vessel, are hard to break.

"Captain Dole," he whispered, "have you ever thought it possible that there might be somebody in this town who is working against us?"

I looked at him. "Against what?" I asked. "What do you mean?"

"Against the whole *New Hope* plan. Trying to hinder it from going through. Somebody on the inside—he would have to be that—who is trying to either stop the bark's get-

9

ting ready for sea or to have her headed off and captured when she tries to get clear of the harbor."

I leaned back in my chair. "What on earth are you talking about?" I wanted to know. "Working against the *New Hope* would be working against the United States of America. The fellow who did that would be a traitor, not only to Trumet, but to his country. Can you think of anybody in this town who isn't for the Stars and Stripes? I can't. Some of them may not like President Madison, and a number think the war was a mistake; but that doesn't make them traitors, not by a long shot. Look here, mister, are you hinting that the reason the *Hawke* is where she is just now is because the Johnnie Bulls have been *warned* that our bark is going to run the blockade pretty soon? If you think that you *are* crazy. Who do you suspect, I ask you?"

I spoke up pretty sharp, for the very thought of such a foolish notion made me lose patience. He reddened up a little, but he kept on, just the same.

"I don't know that I would say I suspect anything, really. I certainly don't suspect any particular person. And maybe the fellow—if there is such a one—isn't working against the *New Hope* plan as a plan. He might be working against people connected with it. Against you and me, say. Or, more especially, against me."

He was making me dizzy. "Now what in the wide world?" I snorted. "Jonathan, boy, the hard work you have been doing lately has struck aloft, and your brain is weakening. Who would work against you? Who has any grudge against you, anyhow?"

"Nobody that I can think of, that's a fact. But, ever since the Council put me in charge—under you, of course—of the work done aboard our vessel, things have been happening. Funny little things, not so much in themselves maybe, but, piling up as they have, to make it look as if they were all my fault, as if I was careless or not attending to my job as

I should be. Oh, I haven't said anything about it before, but it isn't all my imagination, Captain Dole."

He hadn't got me to believing, by any means, but he had got me interested.

"Huh!" I grunted. "Well, for instance—"

"Day before yesterday, for example. You remember—"

"Shh!" I ordered, for I could hear Phoebe clattering towards the door with her hands full of dishes—Jonathan's supply of flatfish, muffins, and blackberry-leaf steepings. She didn't go back either, but, having unloaded her cargo in front of Jonathan, she planked herself down in a chair by the wall and started in to enjoy the passing hour, as the saying is. Phoebe is a good, careful housekeeper, but her notion of a good time is to talk and keep talking. Her tongue always has a full breeze astern of it. When she is alone she talks to herself, and when anybody else is around she talks to him or her or them, as the case may be.

So, after she picked up her moorings in that chair, there were no more whisperings by Jonathan and me. All we were supposed to do—all we could do, as a matter of fact— was to eat and listen. Phoebe was in charge now. She told us all the tittle-tattle going around town. She had been at a sewing meeting the night before—the womenfolks were knitting and sewing stockings and shirts for the men who were signed up to sail on the *New Hope*—and she was loaded to the guards. We heard whose cow had calved and what the Reverend Ichabod Samuels had said to Seth Black when he saw him coming out of the James Otis Tavern, half drunk as usual, and what Seth had said back to the Reverend Ichabod, which was the more amusing of the two. We couldn't laugh at it, though, for Phoebe was so shocked when she told it that she shivered from stem to stern.

"*Where* do you cal'late that Seth Black will go to when he dies?" she wanted to know.

I said I had heard some rumors concerning the port he was supposed to be bound for.

"He won't be doing much drinking down there, I guess likely," she sniffed.

Jonathan agreed that he had always heard it was a dry climate. That seemed to remind her of something, for she left me and opened fire on him.

"I saw somebody at that sewing meeting. Somebody you know," she said, smiling mischievously. When Phoebe Light tries to be mischievous she is something to see—like an elephant making believe he is a kitten.

Jonathan didn't answer, so I did it for him. I knew pretty well what was coming, and I was trying to help him out.

"I guess likely he knows 'most everybody who was liable to be at that meeting," I said.

She giggled, which is one thing a woman of her age and size shouldn't do.

"Oh, I know *that*," she went on. "But this is somebody he knows especial. Somebody he knows very *well*. Guess who it was, Captain Isaiah."

I guessed the most unlikely person I could think of. She tossed her head.

"Oh, now!" she purred. "You know better than *that*. I'll tell you. It was Hope Allen, that's who it was. And she did look *so* pretty. Two or three folks said how pretty she looked. Tamson Weeks whispered to me that she looked just like the pretty English girls she had seen when she was in Liverpool that time when she made the voyage with her father. Tamson never forgets to fetch that voyage of hers in some way or another. There's times when it seems as if I couldn't listen to another word about *that*."

Jonathan was pushing back his plate. I judged he was about ready to run for open water; he doesn't enjoy having his personal affairs talked about by other people, and Hope

Allen was the most personal affair he had. All hands in Trumet knew it, or were coming to know it.

Phoebe didn't pay any attention to his pushing back the plate. She sailed right on.

"I said to Tamson, I said: 'Probably she looks English because she *is* English.' He, he! That was a pretty good one, wasn't it, Captain Isaiah? 'Of course nobody knows for certain,' I said, 'who her father and mother were, or anything, but we do know it was an English ship that was wrecked and that she was the only soul that come ashore alive. A little tiny baby tied to a mattress, just think of it. "The wreck child," that's what folks called her for years and years.' Come to think of it, they don't hardly ever call her that now, do they, Captain Isaiah?"

I didn't make any answer—what was the use?—but I shoved *my* chair away from the table. I knew Jonathan would be heading straight for the shipyard, and I meant to go with him. Just then, though, there came a knock at the door.

Phoebe lumbered over to answer it, but the knocker didn't wait for her, just opened the door himself and came along in. He was Joshua Havens, from the south end of town. He was a member of the militia company and had his militia uniform on then. I judged he had just come off guard duty, either at the breastwork by Fowler's saltworks or on the Bay front by the mouth of Billfish Creek. As it turned out my last guess was right. Billfish Creek was where he had come from.

He acted pretty well upset, too; I saw that right away. "Captain Isaiah," he asked, "have you heard the news?"

"If you mean about the *Hawke* anchoring off the harbor mouth, course I have. Heard it yesterday afternoon, before I left the shipyard."

"No, no, I don't mean that. That's the old news. I've got some new news for you. You know that sloop, that pinky—

Gannet her name is—that the Lobster-Backs have had patroling the Bay for so long?"

"Certain sure I know her. Why wouldn't I? What about her?"

"Well, she came in last night sometime, and now she's dropped anchor, same as the *Hawke*. Only the *Hawke* craft is on the ocean side right abreast the harbor, and the *Gannet* is just in the deep water in the Bay t'other side of the outer bar, right square in front of Billfish Creek. Major Bartlett, he see her when he was making his rounds this morning, and he sent me right off to tell you. Must mean something, he says, but what?"

I looked at Jonathan Bangs and he at me. Phoebe Light started gabbing again, but we didn't either of us pay any attention to her. Joshua's news was news, no doubt of that, and disturbing news, mighty disturbing. No wonder Major Bartlett sent word to me. The Major is getting along in years now, but he served under Washington in the Continental Army at Yorktown, so when Trumet organized its militia company he, naturally enough, was put in command of it. A crotchety old boy, but nobody's fool, and a great one for drills and having his orders obeyed. Our militia company really was a pretty respectable crew of home-made soldiers, not a hit-or-miss squad of rigged-up loafers, like some of the companies in other towns I was acquainted with.

As I say, I looked at Jonathan and he at me. The same thought—or half a dozen thoughts—was in both our heads, I guess likely. Trumet is down along the narrowing section of the Cape. It lies east and west, with the ocean. Our harbor connects onto the eastward, and the Bay is to the west. The main settlement is in the middle, but there are houses and saltworks and fishing shanties along both shores. Billfish Creek is a small stream running out of Hornpout Pond, along through the marshes, and widening out when it empties into the Bay. The tide along our Bay shore ebbs and flows a long stretch, so that, at low water, there is a mile and a half of sand flats. At high tide any craft that doesn't draw much can come right into the creek. At low tide nothing can get in except by following a very narrow and crooked channel.

The *Gannet* was a pink-sterned sloop, carrying a crew of twenty or so, officers and men, that the enemy had had keeping guard in the Bay and cruising up and down, well out in the deeper water, from Ostable to Trumet and back. The head vessel attending to the blockade of our section of the Cape was the frigate *Terror,* Captain Frazier Holt, commanding, and she lay at Point Town; but she was too big to navigate in among our shoals and sand bars, so the *Hawke* and the *Gannet* and one or two barges and small craft did the patroling.

Up to the day before this one the *Hawke* had been satisfied to patrol the ocean side of Trumet. So had the *Gannet* on the Bay side. But yesterday afternoon the *Hawke* had stopped patroling and was lying still opposite the mouth of Trumet inlet and harbor. And, last night, the *Gannet* had quit her patrol and, according to Joshua's story, was anchored in the Bay just past the outer bar, a mile and a half from shore, but directly opposite the mouth of Billfish Creek. It wasn't by accident they both did the same thing at practically the same time, of course it wasn't. It looked as if—well, almost as if the Britishers did know considerable more about our privateer enterprise than we had any idea they knew.

Either that or they were really planning a boat attack on the town, trying to land on both beaches at the same time. I couldn't hardly believe that. It would be too big a risk in lives to make what they would get out of Trumet a paying investment. Even if they won out, which I doubted.

But if it wasn't that it must be—what?

I jumped to my feet. Jonathan was already on his. Phoebe wanted to know where we were going.

"You ain't half finished your breakfast, Mr. Jonathan," she said.

I answered for him. "And he isn't going to finish," I said. "If anybody comes looking for us tell them we'll be at the shipyard. . . . Oh," as the thought came to me, "when do you expect Ezra back, Phoebe?"

She smiled, as placid and calm as a June morning. *She* wasn't disturbed. The *Hawke* and the *Gannet* might have been up on the meeting-house steps for all she realized— or cared.

"There!" says she, as if it was a good joke. "I declare to man if I didn't forget! Ezry got home about two o'clock this morning. Did you ever hear tell of such an outlandish hour to come into a body's house? I said to him, when he come bumping into the bedroom, I said—"

I didn't care what she said. "Where is he now?" I cut in, sharp.

"Ezry? Oh, he's out to the barn, or the yard somewheres, waiting to see you. He told me to tell you he wanted to see you soon's you turned out, but I forgot, I don't know why. I don't often forget things, now do I, honestly, Captain Isaiah?"

I turned to the other two. "Go on down to the yard," I told Jonathan. "I'll be there in a few minutes. Josh, tell Major Bartlett I'll see him pretty soon, but to keep his eye peeled and have those vessels watched, both of them."

Jonathan took Joshua by the arm and led him out of the door. I waited long enough to go up to my room for my cap and watch. Jonathan's sailor's knife, in its sheath, was lying on my bureau. I had borrowed it for some use or other—I don't remember what—the day before and laid it on the bureau, meaning to give it to him. I picked it up, and, when I went down to the dining-room, I handed it

16

to Phoebe. I might have taken it along to him myself, but it was clumsy to put in a pocket, and I was thinking of more important things anyway.

Or what seemed more important just then. If I could have looked ahead—but, there, who can?

I told Phoebe to put the sheath knife in Jonathan's room when she went there to clean up, and she said she would. Then I hurried outdoors, and there was Ezra Light, leaning up against a hitching post, waiting for me.

2.

Ezra was chewing tobacco—he had got hold of a little down the Cape—and was looking mournfully at nothing in particular. That didn't surprise me, for he generally is chewing and he usually looks mournful. He is a little dried-up man, shriveled like a last year's bean-pod, with a one-sided way of talking out of the corner of his mouth and a funny little twinkle in his eye. They say opposites are liable to be attracted to each other, and maybe that is why he married Phoebe, for there couldn't well be two more opposite persons in the world than he and his wife.

He had been peddling ever since he was fourteen years old, and he was all of fifty in 1814. A good many folks up and down the Cape where Ezra did his peddling—yes, and some of them right at home in Trumet—figured him to be a sort of happy-go-lucky no-account, pretty sharp at a trade or dicker, but without much real sense. They would see him jogging by on his mare Selah, his saddle bags full of the knickknacks and notions he peddles—pins and needles and thread and ribbons and women's gewgaws generally— his elbows spread out and his thin little body bouncing up and down when the mare trotted, and they would laugh and ask him how trade was and what he did with all his money, that sort of thing. Ezra always had an answer to

17

make them laugh more, and they would spread it all over town. "What do you cal'late Ez Light said to me this morning? Haw, haw! The darn fool!"

But that's where they made their mistake. Ezra is nobody's darn fool and never was. He is keen and shrewd, could make a living peddling brimstone in Tophet, as the saying is, and when he talks he tells just as much as he wants to and no more. He is as good at listening, too. That is why he was so valuable to our Council, those of us handling the *New Hope* scheme. I honestly don't know what we would have done about having errands run and important messages carried up and down the Cape in those blockade days if it hadn't been for Ezra Light. If Captain Weeks or Squire Bailey or any of the well-known members of our crowd had shown himself in Point Town, with the *Terror* lying off the harbor and the British sailors and marines and officers ashore whenever they pleased, he would have been in the calaboose as a spy or suspicious character inside of an hour. Not Ezra, though—no sir! He was hail-fellow-well-met with all hands, British the same as Yankees. They joked with him and laughed with him and at him, bought his notions and treated him to drinks. He was just Light, the peddler, an "amusing creature" and a standing joke. He a spy or a Yankee agent? Rubbish!

I asked him once how he ever got to be so free and easy with the enemy. "You are as hard and fast a patriot as any of us, Ezra," I said. "I know that, and so does everybody else who knows you well. You couldn't fool me if you wanted to. How is it that those Johnnie Bulls let you come and go and peddle to them and drink and talk with them when they probably would have—well, me, for instance— jailed at sight?"

Ezra grinned, that one-sided grin of his. "Well, I tell you, Captain Isaiah," he said, "I've growed on 'em gradual, as you might say. Fust Point Town trip I made, after the

Terror took station and the town got all cluttered up with Lobster-Backs, they was pretty suspicious of me. Going to have me in irons fust thing, they was. But I kind of palavered 'em, you understand, showed 'em what I was selling and so on, and acted so—so—well, half-way simple, I guess likely you might call it—that they let me go, keeping watch of me, though, for a spell. Now they don't bother to watch, and I vow to man if they don't act as if they was glad to see me. I recollect how, 'long at the beginning, they kept asking me what my opinions about the war was. Ho, ho! Sort of comical, that was, when you come to think of it."

"What did you tell them?" I asked him.

"Eh? Oh, I told 'em that, nigh as I could figger, I was a sort of neutral, with leanings. 'What's leanings?' they wanted to know. 'Well,' says I, 'it's this way: Business is business, and, being a business man, I lean more towards the side where the cash is than to the one where 'tain't. You gentry,' I says—calling 'em gentry don't do no harm, though it's an awful strain in some cases—'you gentry,' I tell 'em, 'have real money, hard cash, to spend. Up the Cape nowadays money is as scarce as good grub, and that's so hard to get that the average family is taking lessons of the cows, so's to learn how to eat hay.' "

"They don't really believe that, do they?"

"They want to believe it, so I take pains to tell 'em what they like to hear. I never tell 'em nothing that will hurt us, you can bet high on that. And my ears are open *all* the time. I pick up more than I drop in the way of news."

He certainly did. He had told me and the Council plenty of things that had helped us and helped the American side, too. He seemed to like me, and I liked him—yes, and depended on him, too. If you keep on with this yarn of Jonathan Bangs's and mine, you will find Ezra Light pop-

-ping up in it every now and again and usually in the places where he does the most good.

When I came out of the house door and saw him leaning against the post, I gave him a hail. He turned his head about half an inch and said, "How be you, Captain?" out of the side of his mouth.

"Have a good trip?" I asked him.

"Eh? Oh, nice miserable trade, same as usual these days. Considering how little I can get aholt of to sell and how precious few of our own folks are buying anything, I do as poor as could be expected, I guess likely. All hands I met was down in the mouth, but healthy. Except the John Bulls and the mosquitos—they was just healthy."

I walked across to where he was standing and asked him if there was any news.

"Not a mite," he said, and walked off towards the barn. I knew what that meant, so I fell into his wake. He went into the barn and leaned up against the end of the stall where his mare Selah was munching hay. Tagging the mare with that outlandish name was just like Ezra. He explained it to me by saying that the Reverend Mr. Samuels told him one time that "selah" was a word in Scripture that nobody seemed to know the exact meaning of. "According to the minister," said Ezra, "some folks cal'late it means one thing and some another. Him and Phoebe had been after me about profane swearing, and it come across my mind that a name that could mean 'most anything ought to come in handy. Does, too. When I holler, 'Git up, you Selah,' I might be calling her a lady or a trollop, and nobody but me would know which. Works fine. Saves an awful lot of breath and damns, that name does."

He leaned against the beam at one side of the outer end of the stall, and I leaned against the other.

"Well?" I ordered. "Now tell me."

20

He shifted his tobacco from one cheek to the other and spoke, lowering his voice a little.

"Captain Isaiah," he asked, "is it supposed to be generally known that you and the Council are cal'lating to get that bark to sea in a fortni't or two? Known by anybody but our own inside crowd, I mean?"

My breath caught in my throat. "Are you trying to tell me—" But he headed me off again.

"I met considerable Johnnie Bulls when I was down yonder," he went on, with a jerk of his head in the general direction of Point Town. "They are about the best customers I have these times, and, besides, I make it my job to foregather with 'em, on account of news. Some of them fo'mast hands and marines aboard that frigate are a loose-tongued lot. Mix up a pint of rum and a sailor, and there's times when it's hard to tell him from a chatterbox! Um-hm —yus, yus. They think I'm Tory anyhow and three parts county fool besides, so they listen while I cuss President Madison up hill and down dale, and then they loosen up and speak out what's on their minds—as much mind as the average run of 'em's got, I mean to say."

He chuckled, and, at any other time, I might have, too; but not then, I was too anxious.

"Go on, go on!" I ordered. "What did you hear? About the *New Hope?* You say the sailors—"

"Hold on! No, no, not the common sailors, not about that part. They know, or think they do, about how fine their blockade is working and brag how many saltworks their fool cannon balls have knocked squewwhiff. I always agree with 'em and give 'em to understand everything is even worse than they say 'tis. That's nothing; that don't do us no harm. The other afternoon, though—Tuesday, 'twas—I drifted into the Point Town tavern, and there was a couple of their officers, all gilt braid and grandness, sitting at the next table. They were having a drink or two when I set down next to 'em, and they'd had a half dozen or so afore, I judged, so they didn't bother to drop their voices none. I was only a common scum Yankee, and they was high and mighty sub-panjandrums of His Britannic Majesty's navy, so what difference did *I* make? If there's one thing special that makes me bile over and spout steam, it's that 'what the devil kind of thing are *you?*' way some of them English officers have of looking down their noses at you. I declare to man, I—"

"Yes, yes, Ezra, I know. They aren't all like that, but some of 'em are. Never mind their manners now, though. Tell me what you heard."

"Well, I couldn't hear it all, but I heard enough to set me to wondering. They was talking about their jobs and how dull they was and how they wished they could be stationed somewheres else, or the Yankees would have spunk enough to fight once in a while, stuff like that. Then one of 'em said he understood there might be a chance for a fight, such as 'twas, afore very long. There was a settlement called Trumet up the coast a little ways, and the poor idiots there had had the dashed effront'ry— What's effront'ry, Captain Isaiah?"

"Oh, cheek, impudence—something of that sort."

"Um-hm. I cal-lated that's what he was driving at. Well, that's what he said they had, anyhow, the effront'ry to be fitting out some sort of craft—Lord and the Yankees only knew what sort of scow 'twas, but something that would float—and they were actually planning to run the blockade with her and go pirating or privateering—which amounted to the same thing—and make the try pretty soon, too.

"'Cording to information received, he said, this Trumet gang had got aholt of some guns and small arms of a sort, God knew how, and had even laid plans to get powder from somewheres. Soon as that powder come, he went on, they would make their try. Did the other fellow ever hear of such dashed impudence in his life?"

I gasped out loud. This was so close to the truth that a near-sighted person couldn't have told the difference, even if he had his spectacles on.

"Information received?" I said over, half to Ezra and half to myself. "What information? And from where? Did this officer say?"

"Um-hm, he did, a little more. The other fellow asked where all this came from, and he said he wasn't exactly sure, but he judged it was pretty close to correct. He said that Forsythe—and who the nation Forsythe is *I* couldn't tell you—had dropped a hint to him which, he judged, must have come straight from the old man. Aboard ship, you understand, the captain is always the 'old man.' "

"Heavens and earth, Ezra," I cut in, impatient, "you don't need to tell me that! I have spent two-thirds of my life seafaring."

"Eh? Yus, yus, so you have. Been 'old man' yourself and intend to be it again afore long. He, he!"

"Sshh! This information came from the old man, eh? That's Holt, of course, he commands the *Terror*. How the devil could *he* have learned about our plans—our powder idea, especially?"

"That's what I wanted to know, and my ears pricked up, now I tell you. But they never said nothing more along that line. Only thing they did say—yes, and agreed on—was that, if either of them was Holt, they wouldn't bother with just laying for dinky privateers, they would send landing parties ashore in settlements—they never forget to call our Cape towns 'settlements,' as if we was half Injuns and lived in wigwams—send them expeditions ashore in settlements that hadn't paid for what they called 'protection' and clean 'em up for good and all. Teach 'em a lesson, so they called it. They went out right after that, so I didn't hear no more."

He waited, expecting me to speak, I suppose, but I didn't, right away. I was thinking, and mercy knew I had enough to think about. One of the ideas that had crossed my mind when I saw the *Hawke* drop anchor the day before and heard about the *Gannet* this morning was that the British might be planning to land and take the town by force. I almost wished they would try it. In the first place I didn't believe they could do it—depending on small boats and men armed with muskets, as they would have to. I believed our fellows on shore could smash those boats with our own cannon and pick off the men with our own muskets before enough of them to amount to anything could set foot on dry land. That is why I had been one of the leaders in our town meetings to fight hard against paying for that "protection" the officers talked about.

Two or three of the other Cape towns had paid ransom money to Captain Holt to be let alone. One of them, whose shores weren't as easy to defend and hard to land on as Trumet's were, paid as much as two thousand dollars in silver. Not because the people were cowards, but because it seemed, under the circumstances, to be the common-sense thing to do. Their best buildings and their biggest stretch of saltworks were within big gun shot from the *Terror*, if she moved across abreast of them, and she could lie there and play William Tell and the apple without getting a scratch in return. So they paid up.

But Trumet wouldn't pay up. Sent word to Holt that if he wanted the cash he better come in and try to collect it. The *Hawke* and the *Gannet* moves had made me wonder if there wasn't to be a collecting party, after all.

But our bark and our powder plans! Those were the frightening things. How *could* they have heard about them?

Ezra Light, I guess, was thinking along with me on the same lines, for he said:

"Sounds almost as if there was a sift-through among us somewhere, don't it, Captain Isaiah?"

It did. When Jonathan had hinted at the same notion I called it silly and put it out of my head. Now, though, it did look as if there must be a leak, and a dangerous one. The only place such a leakage could spring from was right among us Council members, and, if *they* weren't true blue patriots and loyal to our country, who was? And, besides, every last one of them had money invested in the *New Hope* enterprise.

I pumped Ezra dry, but he had told me all he knew or had heard. I ordered him not to whisper a word, even to his wife, about any of it, and he laughed.

"Well, what do *you* cal'late I'll do, Captain Isaiah?" was all he said. It was enough.

As I turned to go out of the barn he asked me where I was bound. "Down to the shipyard," I told him.

"Um-hm. Cal-lated that's where you'd steer for. That little bit of a Bangs shaver is down there ahead of you, I shouldn't wonder."

"Yes."

"Um-hm. Sticks to the job like hot glue, don't he? Smart fellow for his age—and size—I call him. Ho, ho! Don't talk too much neither. Never seemed to me he did."

I swung around towards him. "What do you mean by that, Ezra?" I asked, pretty sharp. "You aren't hinting that Jonathan Bangs had anything to do with that 'sift-through' you were talking about?"

"Eh? Oh, no, no! Not knowingly. Sartin he ain't."

"Knowingly? Now what is behind that?"

"Why, nothing, nothing, Captain Isaiah. Only when a young feller his age is chasing a petticoat his tongue is liable to slip cable once in a while. I recollect when I was

25

courting my Phoebe I used to tell her considerable more than I meant to."

He stopped, grinned, and added: "I don't do it now. It ain't needful; she does the heft of the telling in our family."

I grinned, too, even though I didn't feel like it. "Jonathan wouldn't tell Hope anything of what went on at our meetings. If he did she wouldn't repeat them, for her father's sake, if nothing more. Henry Allen's money is in the *New Hope* like that of the rest of us."

"Um-hm. That's so. Jonathan's been having a little trouble down there to the yard lately, ain't he? Things kind of going wrong with his work, or his watching, or something."

I hadn't really paid much attention to what Jonathan started to tell me at the breakfast table, but now here it was again, and from somebody else.

"Ezra," I barked at him, "what's this you're saying now? Who told you rubbish of that kind?"

"Why, Solomon Fletcher was passing by while you and Jonathan was eating. On his way to work down to the yard, himself, he was. I asked him how things were going, and he said fust rate, only that young Bangs seemed to be getting a little mite careless lately. Nothing to amount to much, he said, but it slowed up the rest of the crowd, sometimes. . . . I didn't believe it, but—well, I thought you ought to know what was being said, so I told you."

"Humph! Glad you did. . . . Oh, Ezra, there is a Council meeting tonight at the Town House, and you may be wanted. Keep within hail, will you?"

"I'll be close aboard. . . . Keep your eye peeled, Captain Isaiah."

"I shall, and you do the same. Much obliged, Ezra."

As I said that there was a dull flat "boom" from over to the eastward. I knew what it was and so did Light. The *Hawke*, since she took up her new station the day before, had fired a cannon shot every three or four hours or so during the afternoon and evening, and now she was beginning again. Just a reminder to Trumet that she wasn't there to catch codfish, I presume likely. The balls didn't do any harm—flung up a little sand, that's about all.

"Hoping to give Eben Fowler's saltworks a dyspepsy pill, I presume probable," said Ezra. "Oh, well, powder and ball's cheap when it's the King paying for 'em, and blockading must be dreadful tedious work."

I left him then and started on my walk to the harbor and shipyard, walking fast and thinking even faster. As I came down off the hill and swung along our main road through the center of the town, I noticed—even as distracted as my mind was I couldn't help noticing—how many more folks were out of doors at that early hour in the morning than I had been used to seeing out of doors since the blockade shut down on us. Mostly old men and women they were, of course, for practically every able-bodied man who could drive a nail or handle a rope or work iron, or even lift and haul and carry, was busy aboard the *New Hope* or getting the stuff out of the storehouse.

There would be three or four of those older men and women standing by a kitchen door, talking, or a couple leaning over a gate or a fence—and talking. When I went by their answers to my good-morning hail were—or it seemed to me they were—sort of half-hearted or, at any rate, absent-minded. I didn't need to be a smart guesser to know what they were talking about. The news about the *Hawke* and the *Gannet* had spread around, and every man, woman, and child in Trumet knew where those vessels were at that minute and were exchanging ideas as to why they were there. Wondering if there was to be an attack, of course, but more worried for another reason.

And our privateer was that reason. Practically every family in Trumet had some sort of a stake in the *New*

Hope, either money or men signed on to sail when she sailed. They had banked on that little bark of ours—and theirs. And they were looking sideways at me now and whispering among themselves after I passed, because the *New Hope* had been my idea in the beginning, mine and Jonathan Bangs's. Jonathan thought of it first, but I was the one who went around talking it up with our leading citizens, folks like Captain Elnathan Berry and Captain Elkanah Davies and Captain Jeremiah Weeks and Eben Fowler and Squire Bethuel Bailey, solid people of Trumet. I had talked and argued until they swung into line and agreed to buy shares. As the thing got under way more and more had come in, with money or work or both, until the enterprise had got to be almost what you might call a town affair, a community enterprise.

A town affair, yes—all but the responsibility for making it a go. The money and the hard work, those were share and share. But the responsibility, the bulk of it anyway, stayed right where it was at the start, on my shoulders. Jonathan's too, perhaps you will say, but Jonathan was only a young fellow, and Trumet would never have followed him alone into any such venture.

I was Trumet born, my folks had lived in Trumet for generations, I had had experience, had even commanded a privateer that made money for her backers and a little for me. I knew—or ought to know—what I was getting all hands into. Hopes had been high—that's why we named our brig the *New Hope*—but, if those hopes were smashed, the end of the drop would be, as it always is, a whole lot lower than before the rise, and the blame would land where the responsibility had been, right on those same shoulders of mine.

Do you wonder I was thinking hard while I was hurrying down to the shipyard that morning in August, Year of Our Lord 1814?

I am Isaiah Hamilton Dole. As I have said, I am Trumet born and brought up, but my father died when I was thirteen, leaving Mother with precious little except the small house we lived in and about enough money to pay for our rations and clothes, such as they were. I went to school until I was fourteen, then I went as cabin boy on a brig out of Boston, bound for the West Indies. I learned navigation under Captain Barnabas Salters, an Ostable man, and went on up to be second and then first mate in one craft or another until I got to be captain—I was twenty-one then. I used to come home between voyages for my shore leaves, but Mother died when I was twenty-four, and I gave up Trumet altogether and, when I wasn't cruising hither and yon, stayed in Boston or, sometimes, in Salem.

My quitting Trumet wasn't because I was sick of the place. It was just one of those things that come into the lives of young men and young women, and because they *are* young men—and women.

Even when I was in school I knew Martha Allen—Henry Allen's sister, she was—and we two liked each other well. By the time I was twenty she and I had come to what you might call an understanding; we were going to get married some day or other, when I had enough shot in the locker to pay the bills. But it didn't work out that way for us. I had the chance to go in command of the barkentine *Swift* on a long voyage clear to the other side of the world, and I was liable to be gone a couple of years. Martha didn't like the idea, and she wanted me to give it up. I wouldn't do it, so she said I cared more about going to sea than I did about being with her, and I said she cared more about having her own way than she did about my chances in life. So, after that, she—well, she said I could go where I pleased and stay there, and I said I would go—and did. Foolish? Certain it was. I know it now, and I have often wondered if—but there, that was the end, so what's the use wondering?

Two years afterwards—I and my ship were in the Indian Ocean somewhere—she married Eben Fowler, a man some years older than she was—three years older than I, so far as that goes. Eben was a land owner and a money maker who showed every symptom of being able to make more. He was after Martha even when she and I were so thick, and I guess likely a good many people thought him, with his prospects, a considerable better catch for her than ever I was. She didn't though—not then. The poor girl didn't live long after her marriage. She died three years and six months after the wedding day. Eben kept on making money. He was one of the first in Trumet to see what profit there was in making salt from sea water, and his saltworks, with their rows of sheds and windmills, were about the largest in our part of the Cape.

When the war broke out I was in Salem, and the Peabody brothers, struck with the privateering fever like about every other shipping firm, offered me command of the topsail schooner *Strong Arm*, an able craft, well armed and well manned. Jonathan Bangs was my second officer, that is how he and I first met. The *Strong Arm* did pretty well, and so did her owners and those aboard her, including me. We took considerable many prizes and did our share of fighting. Early in 1813, though, a grapeshot knocked me endways and smashed my left leg, two ribs, and my collar bone. They got me back to Salem, and I was laid up in sick bay there for a long spell.

Even when I was up and around the doctors told me I wouldn't be fit for duty for months. I was blue and down-spirited, and they seemed to think that a change of air and different things to look at might do me some good. I didn't know any place to go except Trumet, so for Trumet I headed, aboard the packet from Boston, which, as the blockade hadn't yet bothered our coast much, was running regular at that time.

Jonathan Bangs, who had been slightly wounded in the same fight I was, surprised me by saying he guessed he would go along. He and I had got to be close friends.

"What on earth do *you* want to go to Trumet for?" I asked. "I'm going because it used to be my home town, but it isn't yours. You was brought up somewheres in Maine, I remember your telling me."

He grinned, that slow grin of his. "Oh," he said, "I never met a Caper yet who didn't swear that the Cape was the nighest thing to Heaven on this earth, so I thought maybe I better take my chance while I could. Nothing like getting prepared, you know, Captain Dole."

"Humph!" I grunted. "If our old First Meeting House parson, Reverend Ichabod Samuels, ever hears you talk like that he'll figure you are pretty well prepared for the other place."

But to Trumet we went together, hired the Light place, with, same as I said, Phoebe Light to housekeep for us, and settled down for what we called "the present." Then the British decided they could spare more ships for work on this side of the big water and that the New England coast needed as much attention as anywhere else, so Trumet, like all the rest of the Cape, was shut in—locked up, as you might say. Our "present" looked as if it was liable to stretch out into nobody knew how much future.

I don't quite know how to give you an idea of what that locking up meant to us Cape folks. Trumet had been prosperous, with work and living for everybody. Fishing boats and schooners going and coming all the time; a small shipyard, where a good many sloops and some larger craft were built every once in a while, which meant work for carpenters and joiners and blacksmiths and riggers and sailmakers; men going on coasting voyages or fishing to the

Banks; saltworks going full blast—making salt from sea water, you understand; the Boston and New Bedford packets making regular trips. A lively, up and coming town.

But now, with the enemy frigates and sloops and barges policing our coasts, we who had depended on the sea for our living and our goings and comings were cut off from it practically altogether. No more deep-sea fishing, no more coasting, no more shipbuilding. What was the use of building and launching craft that couldn't be sent out of the harbor without risk of being sunk or captured? No more saltmaking, for why make what you can't get to market?

There was plenty to eat. You can't starve a population that lives where the bays and coves squirm with fish, the beaches are plugged full of clams and quahaugs, and ground that will grow 'most any of the common vegetables. Starvation—no; but stagnation—yes, indeed.

There is no use mincing words or making believe, the war wasn't a popular war with the majority, rich or poor, in our section of the country. Not that we Down-Easters aren't as good Americans or as patriotic as anybody else, but the general feeling in our part of the North—the 'long-shore part, that is—was that declaring war wasn't, under the circumstances, good judgment on the part of the Government. It wasn't liable, all considered, to do the United States much good, and it might do the Lord knew how much harm. Now that it is all over and we are at least as well off as we were before, that kind of talk isn't heard at all. It—what the history books call the War of 1812—was, so they teach our children, a grand and glorious popular triumph. All right, that is what ought to be taught, I guess likely, but the "popular" part wasn't true at the time I'm yarning about.

"Madison's War," "Farmers' War," "Teamsters' War":

that's what the opposition papers and a great many people called it; it was so called all up and down the coast from New York to Maine. Those who got their living from and by the sea felt and said that it was only the landlubbers and inland folks who brought it on and *they* wouldn't have to suffer from it. Not true, of course—or only a grain of truth here and there—but it was said and thought and printed.

Well, Jonathan and I stagnated along with the rest. We had our shares of the *Strong Arm* prize money, so we didn't suffer for ready cash, and we had enough to eat and to wear. The loafing around day after day, or sitting in the James Otis Tavern listening to the grumblings of the folks who dropped in for a glass of rum and molasses and water, was dull—terrible dull. I didn't see how I could stand it much longer. I even went so far as to consider hiring or buying a horse and setting out for Boston overland on horseback. That was the only way of getting there—that or by ox-cart, which would be almost as slow as sitting still. There I was, only just past forty and in the prime of life. I'd be blessed if I meant to loaf that prime away sitting on my stern and calling the Government names.

Oddly enough, it was Jonathan Bangs who gave me the big idea. He wasn't having quite as dull a time as I was, for he had found a real interest. Her name was Hope Allen, and, according to town talk, she was interested in him, too.

Well, he and I happened to be down at the shipyard together one day, and that yard, like everything else in Trumet, was dead as Nebuchadnezzar's grandmother. Nobody working, not a hammer falling or a rope being hauled. There was a two-hundred-ton bark lying at the wharf that had belonged to Eleazir James, one of the well-to-do men of the town. He had had her built for coast voyaging, and she had made only a couple of trips to the Spanish West Indies and back when two things happened—

Eleazir died and the blockade closed down on us. Mrs. James, the widow, wanted to sell her, but who was buying vessels just then?

Her name was *The Flyer* and a flyer she was, according to report, and could be made to fly faster with a little rerigging and overhauling below and aloft. Jonathan Bangs, standing alongside of me on the wharf, put his hand on my shoulder and pointed towards *The Flyer* with the other.

"Likely looking craft; eh, Captain Dole?" he said. "Make a pretty good privateer, if she was rigged for it, don't you think?"

I nodded. "I would ask nothing better," I told him, "than to be in command of her, refitted and armed, somewhere in the trade latitudes. No Johnnie Bull merchantman would sail clear of us, I'd lay my share on that."

The fingers of his big hand on my shoulder tightened. "Thought so myself," he agreed. "Well, why don't you do it?"

I didn't understand—and no wonder.

"Do what?" I asked, looking up into his face—most folks have to look up when they talk to Jonathan Bangs.

"Why not see if you can't get up a company here in Trumet, buy her—I know she can be bought cheap—refit her and rig her for privateering, and go after those merchantmen you were talking about? You as captain and I as first officer. Eh? Why not?"

I laughed. "Sounds good—as a joke," said I. "Our privateer would do a big business. British merchantmen are kind of scarce in Trumet Harbor. And outside—well, this coast is supposed to be blockaded."

He snapped his thumb and forefinger.

"Blockade be darned!" he said. "You could run *any* blockade, Captain Dole. I know it, and so does every other man that ever sailed under you."

Still I couldn't believe he meant it. He should have been grinning, but he wasn't.

"Have you gone adrift up aloft?" I snapped, impatient. "Besides the rerigging and fitting and the rest of it, there are a few other things that the average privateer finds handy. Carronades and small arms and—"

"Wait a minute, sir. What about the cannon and muskets—yes, and the pistols and cutlasses—that came off the *San Jose?* They are still up in Reuben Gifford's shed; I took pains to go and look at them yesterday noon on my way home to dinner. They are rusty, some of them, and maybe a little old-fashioned, but they would do for a start, and we could get newer and better ones from the prizes we took. *You* took, I mean; I wouldn't dream of starting on such a cruise—no, nor of trying to put through such a crazy scheme—without you in charge and in command of the whole thing."

I breathed hard. "Meaning that I am even crazier than you, I judge. Well, if this is just a joke I'll laugh when you pass the word. If you're serious—"

"I am serious," he broke in. "I've thought about it a lot lately. If you can get the cash together to buy that bark and the stuff from the *San Jose*, the refitting and rigging could be made almost a town affair. Trumet is full of men with nothing to do, and most of them would, I believe, take a share or two in the venture and pay for their shares with work, carpentering or blacksmithing or what not. Why— Oh, don't look at me like that, Captain Dole! You think it over, that's all."

Well, I thought it over. Then I began talking it over with a dozen of Trumet's ablest and most well-off menfolks. Each one of them began, as I had, by calling it crazy, and each one of them ended, as I had, by coming into it, not only with money, but heart and soul, as you might say. And the joiners and sailmakers and riggers and ironworkers came into it, too, just as Jonathan said they would, taking shares to be paid for with the work of their hands. The *New Hope*, that was the new name for our bark, was just what Jonathan had called it, a town affair.

Mrs. James sold the vessel to us at a very reasonable figure. The buying was left to Captain Weeks and Squire Bailey, a good business man and a good lawyer. In the end they got her for a sum in cash and the rest in shares in our profits—if any. Buying the old cannon and small arms, solid shot, grapeshot, bullets, and such, was an all-cash transaction. The *San Jose* was a Spanish armed brig that drove ashore on the shoals a half mile or so to the westward of the harbor inlet in the big winter gale of 1810. She piled up on Big Flat Shoal and banged to pieces there before the winter was over. Not a soul aboard her was saved. Whatever was in her hold was lost for good, of course, but, during the low tides and fair weather that followed the gale, a good deal of her deck stuff was salvaged and carted ashore. There were some big guns and a lot of solid shot and grapeshot, eighty or ninety muskets, some cutlasses, and I don't know what all.

The notion of the salvers was to ship the stuff to Boston by packet and sell it there—for junk, if it was good for nothing else; but it was awful heavy to handle, and, when old Reuben Gifford made a bid for it in one lump, they finally let him have it. What Reuben wanted it for nobody could ever seem to find out from him. He was a queer stick, anyhow—a little bit foggy up aloft, folks thought—and the idea was that he figured there might be another war some time and he could sell the arms then for a big price. He died before the war he was looking for came, and the whole collection was lying where he had had it carted, in the old shed astern of the house, now vacant, where he had lived. His cousin and only kin was an Orham man, and he was only too glad to sell the "old iron," as he called it, for whatever he could get. You may be certain that Squire Bailey, who handled the deal, didn't tell him what *we* wanted it for.

The cannon were kind of old-fashioned, and everything in the pile was more or less rusty, but the rust could be cleaned off—and was. The powder aboard the *San Jose* had been soaked and ruined, of course, and where and how to get hold of enough for our use we didn't know. At last, though, we made connection with some people, friends of ours, up in Tamoset—fifty or sixty miles to the southwest—and they agreed to have a certain number of kegs of good powder ready for us, provided we could arrange some way to get it down from there. Carting it overland, by ox teams, would be an awful job and even more risky than trying to run it through by water, for there were bound to be enemy sympathizers along the route who might carry the news to the wrong quarters.

At last, after I don't know how many Council meetings, we had all but agreed on a plan to try to run it down along the Bay shore, in a shallow-draught vessel—or vessels— waiting, of course, for a black night and the right tide, and having a gang ready to take it off the vessel the minute she showed her signal off the Billfish Cove shore. The final details of the plan hadn't been quite settled, but I expected they would be at Council meeting that very night.

So that was the situation on the morning of the day when the *Hawke* and *Gannet* upset everything by taking up their new stations. The *New Hope* was practically ready to go. I had superintended her making over and re-rigging myself, and, to be honest, I was pretty proud of my job. That she could pick herself up and sail I knew. As to making her over for a fighting vessel, we had done as much as we could about that. Carronades set in place; ports cut; shot lockers and powder lockers built between decks; stores almost all aboard; a picked crew of eighty men—all able-bodied, smart sailors and, some of them, men who had fought the British before in the early days of the war—ready on call. I was to command her; Jonathan Bangs was to be first officer; Abel Snow, who had been aboard the *Constitution* when she licked the *Guerrière*, second officer. A good bos'n, a good cook—yes, even a surgeon, a young fellow from Wellmouth who had just finished his doctor schooling in Boston and had been caught by the blockade when he came down to see his family.

All ready and itching to get away as soon as that powder was stored. But now—what?

There! Now, at last, I can heave ahead with my yarn. When I got to the shipyard that morning the first person I looked for was Jonathan, but I didn't see him anywhere. The workmen were hard at it, doing all sorts of finishing-up jobs, and a gang was carrying bundles and barrels from the wharf storehouse and stowing them in the hold and between decks. I walked around, looking at this and that, making sure that the last gun was in place, the round shot and grape in their lockers, everything made fast and shipshape. I found nothing wrong. Even the slow matches for touching off the guns were ready in the right places.

When I came on deck, after my round of inspection, Henry Allen and Eben Fowler were just coming aboard from the wharf. Henry is Hope Allen's adopted father, or Hope is his adopted daughter, whichever way you want to put it. He was a man about fifty-five, a fisherman by trade, and as cranky and cantankerous as they come. Except with Hope, that is; he idolized her and, so folks said, would have spoiled her if he could. He had been a widower for years, and he and Hope lived together in a small house at the west side of the village, abreast of where Billfish Creek widens out into Billfish Cove.

Eben Fowler was Henry's brother-in-law and one of Trumet's big men. Besides his saltworks he was supposed to be interested in a half-dozen different business affairs up and down the Cape. He was the one, you will remember, who married Martha Allen after she and I had our foolish quarrel and broke off keeping company. A tall man, gray-haired—the Fowlers always turned gray early in life—with heavy dark eyebrows and a pair of sharp black eyes. Pretty dignified, careful in his choice of words, and a habit of dressing younger than his age.

Henry was first to see me, and he came across, walking brisk as he always did, and gave me a hail.

"Where's Hope?" he wanted to know.

I told him I had just got there myself, and, if Hope was anywhere around, I hadn't seen her.

"Humph!" he grunted. "Well, where's that young Bangs sprout? He ain't here either, is he?"

"Doesn't seem to be, that's a fact. And, Henry, if you call him a sprout I'd like to know your notion of a tree."

I thought that was a little bit funny, but Henry didn't seem to. He just grunted again and scowled. Eben Fowler joined us then.

"Good morning, Captain Isaiah," he said. "Is everything going well?"

"Seems to be—aboard here."

Just then there was another one of those "booms," from the westward this time. The *Gannet* had caught the cannonading disease, I judged.

All three of us looked in the direction the "boom" had come from. Eben Fowler smiled, that dignified smile of his.

"Looks as if they were attending to you as well as me, Henry," he said.

Henry Allen swore. "Let 'em bang away," he sniffed. "Nothing aboard that pinky that'll carry within a half mile of my house this stage of tide ... Say, look here, Isaiah, what do you cal'late this is all about, anyway? Those two craft anchoring where they are?"

39

I shook my head. "I wish I knew. What you think, Eben?"

Fowler looked pretty solemn. "I can't imagine," he said. "Unless—well, perhaps our not paying that ransom may have been a mistake. You may remember I wasn't sure our —er—defiance wasn't a little too loud. We might have made it a little less cocksure. Are they going to land and take the town, Captain?"

Somehow the way he said that made me turn and look at him. "You don't think that is what they are planning for, do you, Eben?" I asked.

He hesitated, just a second. "No-o," he said. "We debated that chance pretty thoroughly in the Council meeting. The general feeling was, you remember, that they would probably feel it was not worth the risk. However—"

"However—what?" I snapped. As I said in the beginning, my nerves were pretty much on the ragged edge that morning. "If they try it they'll learn how much risk it is before they get through. Eben, you don't think Trumet should have paid that ransom, do you?"

Before he could answer Henry Allen had a word to say. "Might have been cheaper in the long run," he growled. "Might have saved us more money than this risk of yours," stamping on the deck of the *New Hope*, "is liable to earn, Isaiah. Providing she ever gets to sea at all, that is to say."

I was beginning to get mad all the way through. "Who says she won't get to sea?" I asked. "Who says that? Tell me their names; I want to know who is talking that way."

Henry's lip twisted. He pointed with both hands, one towards the east and the *Hawke*, the other towards the west and the *Gannet*.

"Looks as if there was two sets of folks trying to say it this minute," he sneered. "And as if they might know something of what they was talking about, too, don't you think?

40

What fetched them in to lay where they are if they haven't found out something is up?"

It was exactly what had been worrying me, and it made me madder than ever.

"Found out?" I snarled. "How could they find out? Who would tell them? Answer me that."

Eben Fowler leaned towards me and spoke low. "Ezra Light has been in Point Town lately, hasn't he?" he asked. "I understand he has just got back from there."

I whirled on him like a flash. "Ezra is one of the squarest patriots we've got," I vowed. "He has learned more for our side than any other man in Trumet. I would trust Ezra anywhere."

Henry laughed. "That's part of your trouble, Isaiah," he said. "You trust too darned easy, maybe." Then, his tone changing, he grunted. "Hum! There's that girl of mine now, and look who is with her! Just what I expected. What did I tell you, Eben?"

Hope Allen was coming down the wharf with Jonathan Bangs close astern of her. He had been showing her the stuff in the storehouse, I judged; at any rate, they seemed to be coming from there. Hope isn't a big young woman, rather undersized, if anything, and, in company with Jonathan, she looked like a rowboat alongside a ship of the line. He could have picked her up and carried her under one arm, if he had needed to—and she would have let him. That last sentence is important, because she had a will of her own.

First thing I noticed about them was that she was looking sort of flushed and excited and uppish, and Jonathan, although he was flushed, too, looked kind of down in the mouth. They came over to where we were standing. She said good morning to me and then turned to Fowler.

"Eb," she said—sometimes she called him "Uncle Eb" and sometimes just "Eb," because, of course, they weren't really relations at all. "Eb," she said, smiling and those bright eyes of hers sparkling, "I have changed my mind about not going to the party tonight. I will go, after all. Call for me, will you?"

Eben said he would be delighted. Henry kind of glanced at Jonathan and said he guessed he would be getting along. Hope said she must go, too, she was going up town on an errand. "Are you going that way, Eben?" she asked. Eben said he was, and the three went away together, she walking with Fowler.

Jonathan and I watched them go. I turned to look at him.

"What's the matter, boy?" I asked.

"Matter? Matter with what?"

"Why, with you. You look as if somebody had stepped on your sore toe."

He laughed, or tried to, for he didn't make a very good job of it.

"I am all right, toe and all, so far as I know," he told me. "Well, I must get to work. Nothing you want of me just now, is there, Captain Dole?"

"Why, no, nothing more than usual." And then, as the thought came to me. "What about those—what did you call 'em?—little happenings that made you wonder, or suspect, or guess that somebody, or somebodies, might be working against the *New Hope*, or against you in particular? You were going to tell me about them at breakfast when Phoebe broke in on us. Now might be as good a time as any to heave aboard with the telling, mightn't it?"

He kind of hesitated for a minute or so, seemed to be thinking it over. Then he shook his head.

"I don't believe I will tell you, after all, Captain Dole," he said. "Not just yet, anyhow. If it is all right with you I had rather wait until I'm a little surer. You see—"

He stopped there, in the middle of his sentence.

"No," I told him, "I don't see. If anybody is working

42

against our scheme I want to know it. It is part of my job to know it."

He hesitated again. "If I were certain it was against the *New Hope* I should tell you, no two ways about that. It would be your job then, of course. But if they are working against me—why, then it is my job, isn't it? If it is all the same to you, Captain Dole, I'd like to fight my own battles."

He looked able to fight them. His jaw was set square, and there was a fighting look in his eyes. Something had happened to him, and I couldn't imagine what. He had acted anxious to tell me when we had our breakfast talk.

"But you seemed to think—" I began. He didn't let me go any farther.

"Do me a favor, Captain Dole," he said. "Let me wait—well, and watch—a little while longer. If these things are real I want to know, not guess, about them. Let me work it out by myself for another day, anyhow."

"Humph! Look here, Jonathan—"

But just then one of the workmen—Peleg Bounderby, the blacksmith's son, seems to me it was—came aboard from the wharf and broke in on our talk to tell me there was somebody out by the shipyard gate who said he wanted to see me.

"Who is it?" I asked.

Young Bounderby grinned. "It's Seth Black," he said.

Seth Black was a good-for-nothing old fellow who lived alone in a little pigsty of a shanty over on the sand bluff bordering Shad Cove, which is not so far from Billfish Creek and about a half mile or so from where the Allens lived. Seth did some day fishing and clamming, some lobstering—and a whole lot of drinking when he had money or could find anybody to pay for his rum.

"Seth Black!" I snapped. "He will be a great help—just now. Is he drunk?"

"Only a little mite aboard, I judged, Captain Isaiah. I wouldn't have bothered you only he said it was important."

"Important nothing! He probably wants to beg a shilling for more drinks. Tell him I am busy now, but perhaps I'll see him later on—if I think to remember it."

Peleg went off, laughing. I stayed where I was. A good many times since then, I have wondered how much of this yarn of Jonathan's and mine might have worked out altogether different if I had gone to Seth Black then. I did run across him later in the day, as it happened, but by that time he had found somebody with the extra shilling.

4.

That was a day, take it by and large. One of those days that didn't have hours enough in it to go around, if you know what I mean. I stayed aboard the *New Hope* long enough to make sure the stuff from the storehouse was going aboard as it should, and then I went into the storehouse to see how that end of the work was being pushed. I couldn't see anything to find fault about. Jonathan was superintending and doing a hustling job of it, and most of our crowd didn't need to be hustled anyway. This was their vessel and their venture, same as it was the Council's and Jonathan's and mine. Their hearts were in it as well as their arms and shoulders.

Next I tramped across lots down to the top of the sand bluff overlooking the mouth of Billfish Creek. Major Bartlett was there, in charge of a crew of his militia who were digging in, deepening the breastwork they had thrown up there, as they had the one at the harbor entrance on the ocean side of town. The heft of the able-bodied young fellows in Trumet—all the skilled trade workers, practically—were busy on or about the *New Hope* at the shipyard, so the Major's squad was mainly older men, and half-grown

44

boys off the laid-up fishing boats. They were working though. Major Bartlett saw to that. He was marching up and down behind them, giving orders and waving the gold-headed cane the selectmen had presented to him when he came back from Yorktown as if it was a sword. He had his men jumping for him, I will say that. Made a first-rate mate on a vessel, the Major would.

He showed me the *Gannet* laying off back of the outer bar, pointed at her with his cane. He didn't need to, I could see her plain enough. Just a pinky she was and not very large, but she was armed and probably had a fair-sized number of sailors and soldiers aboard. Major Bartlett was hopping around telling me what he and his company could do to those Redcoats if they tried to send boats ashore.

"We would make them think they were named Corn-wallis," he chuckled. "Let 'em try to land. I wish to the Lord they would!"

I was coming to be more and more certain that the *Gannet* was where she was, not to get British on dry land, but to keep us Yankees from getting off it. What Ezra told me he overheard in that Point Town tavern kept coming back to me. Captain Holt had had "inside information." It was that word "inside" that worried me most. As I have said before, only the members of our Council knew about the powder at Tamoset. I went over their names one by one in my mind.

No, no—and no again! Not one of them would have let out that inside information. I would as soon suspect myself —or Jonathan Bangs. And then—which shows how ridic-ulous a person's mind can act when it gets into the state mine was—it struck me once more how odd Jonathan had acted when I asked him to tell me what he meant about those "little happenings." He had been keen to tell me up at the house; then, later on, down at the yard, he didn't want to tell. Why had he changed his mind? He and Hope Allen were away together somewhere when I got to the shipyard that morning, but, of course, that didn't mean anything. They were together as often as she would let them be, which wasn't more than half as often as Jonathan would have liked, I imagined. Queer how a big man like him would take orders from a little woman like her.

And then I remembered Ezra Light's hint about the fellow who was courting being liable to tell his girl a good deal more than he meant to. But what could Jonathan tell Hope that she didn't know already? Unless it was about the powder—and *that* we members of the Council had sworn never to tell *anybody*, not even our own wives and families.

And that set me thinking about Henry Allen. Henry was Hope's father—all the father she had, anyhow. And Henry was in the Council, and it was Henry who had said—Eben Fowler and I heard him say it—that it might have been cheaper in the end for Trumet to have paid ransom to the British.

And Fowler had suggested that perhaps Ezra Light wasn't as square as he pretended to be.

Heavens and earth, this wouldn't do! I would be suspecting Phoebe next. Time to stop such craziness and think of something sensible. I left the Major and his crew to their digging and went back to the shipyard.

Everything was going all right at the yard, so I took another long tramp, to the eastward this time, out to the other breastwork by the harbor mouth. Phineas Burgess was in command there, and he told me that nothing special had happened since the *Hawke* cast anchor the afternoon before. "We get a bang once in a while," Phineas said, "but they haven't hit anything but sand and salt water so far. They'll get sick of it pretty soon."

It was almost seven bells, half-past eleven o'clock, when

I got back to the village, and it was then, as I was passing the James Otis Tavern, that I ran afoul of Seth Black. It had been only a little while, three hours or so, since he was down at the yard asking to see me, and you wouldn't hardly think so much could have happened to him in such a short spell. If it had been money for rum he had hoped I might let him have—which would have been about as vain a hope as a body could think of offhand—he wasn't hoping it now. His hope had been realized somewhere else, I judged, for he had had the rum, plenty of it. I didn't notice the state he was in when I saw him coming out of the tavern, so I gave him a hail. He made a fairly straight course across the road to where I was, but he had to grab at my arm to steady himself when he got alongside. He looked at me as if he wasn't quite sure who it was he had hold of.

"Here we be, all taut and right side up," he crowed. "Rugged water in the channel, but a safe landing and not a plank started. Trust old Seth to— Huh! Eh! Why, it's Captain Isaiah, ain't it? Well, well, how be you, Skipper? What would you think of a little dram? Just to keep your bilge sweet, eh? How's that notion strike you?"

It didn't strike me at all. I realized what I had let myself in for. Seth Black was precious little help to anybody when sober, but drunk he was a nuisance.

"I should say one of us was sweet enough already," I told him. "I understood you were looking for me this morning, Seth. Something important to tell me, they said. Well, what was it?"

He didn't hear that, didn't pay any attention to it, anyhow. He patted my coat sleeve.

"Don't mistake me now, skipper," he said, purring like a cat and smiling like a basket of chips. "This is my treat. I'm paying for what I buy you. Yes sir, I be! Don't you believe it? Look a-here."

He fished into his starboard breeches pocket and came

47

up with a fist full of money. He had it clutched so tight that I could only guess how much, but there must have been four or five dollars anyway. I was surprised. When Seth Black had three shillings all at the same time, he figured himself rich.

"Where did you get all that?" I asked. "There can't be any strangers in town, and all the rest of us know you."

He chuckled to himself. "Maybe there'll be more cash than that in my hands some of these days. Yes siree, bob!—consider'ble more! He, he! Now we'll splice the main brace, eh?"

"We will not. What was this important thing you wanted to see me about? Or can't you remember?"

He kind of pulled himself together, or seemed to. Jammed the money back in his pocket, almost as if he wished he hadn't shown it to me.

"Remember?" he said, solemn. "Why, sartin sure I remember. . . . What was it?"

This wasn't getting me anywhere, so I tried to pull away from him, but he stuck to my arm like a barnacle to a wharf spile. He leaned towards me and whispered in my ear; it was like having that ear close to the bung of a rum keg.

"How's things going aboard that bark of yours, Captain Isaiah?" he whispered. "Going to run her out pretty quick, they tell me."

"Who told you? You mustn't believe all you hear, Seth."

"Is that a fact! Well, sometimes I do and sometimes I don't. If I was to tell you one or two things I *know*, maybe you wouldn't believe them, either. He, he!"

"What do you mean by that?"

"Oh, nawthing, nawthing. Might cost anybody consider'ble to know as much as your old Uncle Seth knows. Maybe that Council crowd of yourn would pay. Yes, or the Britishers. They would stump up, I guess likely. Anyhow," with another one of his chuckles, "somebody's going to stump. That I *do* know."

My patience had pretty well gone through the scuppers. "Look here, Seth," I said. "If you go around Trumet talking this way, you will land in jail or with a rope around your neck. They hang traitors in wartime, don't forget that."

I said it as if I meant it, and, tipsy as he was, it seemed to get inside his skull. He stopped his chuckling and went on a new tack.

"Now, now, now, Captain Isaiah," he said, "don't you get silly notions about good old Seth. *He* ain't no traitor. He's a free-born American, that's what he is. 'Yankee Doodle come to town,' that's *his* tune, you bet ye. Ask any of them fellers over to the tavern, they'll tell ye. Why, they just about pray to me to sing it to 'em. That and the one about the *United States* and the *Mashdonee*"—"*Macedonian*" being what he meant, of course.

He started to sing it right there on the main road.

> " 'Bold Carden thought he had us tight
>   And so did Dacres, too, sirs,
> But Hull 'n' Decatur put 'em right
>   With Yankee Doodle Doo, sirs.
> They thought they see our ship aflame
>   Which made 'em all huzzaw, sirs,
> But when the second broadside came
>   It made 'em hold their jaw, sirs.'

"Eh, how's that? And that's only the first verse. Wait till you hear the next."

But I didn't wait. People were beginning to come to doors and windows, and I wasn't particular about giving a show. I jerked my sleeve away from him and walked off. Which, as I look back at it now, was another one of my mistakes. It might even have been worth while to go into the tavern with him and let him stand treat. I don't often

49

drink in the forenoon, but— However, I didn't—and after-wards I was sorry.

I went home for dinner around noontime, but I ate alone, for Jonathan didn't get there until I was through. I didn't ask any more about the little happenings, thinking perhaps he might mention them, but he didn't. One thing he did say, though, which kind of surprised me. I was just going out of the door, and Phoebe was in the kitchen.

"Captain Dole," he said, lowering his voice. "I shan't be at home tonight—no, nor any night from now on. Until that powder is loaded and the *New Hope* is ready to sail, I am going to sleep aboard her."

"What for?" I asked him, for this idea was brand-new. His answer was prompt enough.

"Because I don't think she ought to be left after dark without a guard," he said.

I nodded; in fact, I had been thinking pretty much the same thing myself. "That's probably true enough," I agreed. "Although I don't see why you need to take on the job yourself. You are working like a horse all day, and you need your sleep. I can hire any one of a half-dozen old fel-lows to stand watch for a couple of shilling a night."

"I know, but I should feel safer if I did it, myself. Oh, I don't mean to do sentry go. I'll turn in in one of the berths, probably. I sleep with one ear open these times, anyhow."

I thought it over. "We-ll," I said, finally, "I don't see why you shouldn't, if you're set on it. But—say, Jonathan, what put you up to this? Nothing new and troublesome has happened since this morning, has there?"

There was a flash in those blue eyes of his. "No," said he, "and I don't intend anything shall, either. Just explain to the Council why I'm not at the meeting tonight, will you, Captain Dole?"

I did explain after the meeting was called to order at eight that evening with Captain Jeremiah Weeks presiding. All hands seemed to think it was all right for Jonathan to sleep aboard the bark if he wanted to, although the majority felt it wasn't really necessary. Henry Allen, always on the off side of the fence, was the only one who made any objection, and his objection, I judged, was mainly because he wasn't strong for Jonathan at any time. He had notions of his own about who Hope ought to marry, and Jonathan's name wasn't rated high on the list, most folks thought.

"Umph!" grunted Henry. "According to tell, your Bangs pet hasn't done too careful a job of running things daytimes. Don't see why we should take him on nights, too."

That stirred me up, of course. "Now what do you mean by that, Henry?" I wanted to know. "I am in charge of this *New Hope* enterprise—you fellows put me there—and I am responsible for Jonathan, along with the rest of it. I haven't heard of any carelessness he is to blame for. If you have I want to know what it is and know it now, so spit it out. What are you hinting at?"

My tone wasn't too pleasant, maybe, and Weeks and two or three others started in to smooth my feathers. Captain Jeremiah said he could imagine what Henry referred to; there had been a little undercover talk here and there about things going wrong, the work being slowed up and so on, but he had looked into the matter, and he couldn't find anything of importance behind it.

"Jonathan is one of the youngest men in the crowd," he said, "and there is bound to be a little feeling among the older ones at being ordered around by him. Petty jealousy, that's all, and natural enough, I suppose. Pay no attention to it, Isaiah."

"Henry Allen seems to have paid attention to it," I said. Eben Fowler took his turn at the feather smoothing.

"This is an important meeting, gentlemen," he put in, "and we shouldn't waste valuable time on trifles, it seems to me. The fact is that Isaiah here has already—with our approval, of course—intrusted young Bangs with much, and if he thinks he should be intrusted with more I see no reason to criticize or object. His spending his nights aboard the bark can't do any harm and may ease his conscience—if you care to put it that way."

It wasn't the way I cared to put it, and I said so. "You think his conscience needs easing, I should judge. Well, if it does I haven't heard why yet. Why not talk plain?"

But Captain Jeremiah thumped for order, and I stopped. Fowler laughed.

"Mercy on us, Isaiah!" he said, good-naturedly; "you *are* full of red pepper tonight. I am not accusing Jonathan of anything. I used that 'conscience' without thinking. So far as I know his conscience is as clean as your shirt—and, from what I can see of the shirt, that's clean enough."

Well, Phoebe had handed that shirt to me after supper and vowed it was just off the ironing board. Everybody laughed and I had to join in. Even Henry Allen grinned, in spite of his grumpiness. The Council went on to take up the arrangements for meeting and landing the powder when it came from Tamoset, which was the real business the meeting had been called for.

We had talked it all over before, back and forth and from stem to stern. We couldn't ox-cart it sixty-odd miles, we had settled on that. It would take forever and be full as risky as trying to fetch it by water. The water way was risky, too, Lord knew, but, given the right weather and the right tides, we all believed it could be done and done quick. Our Tamoset friends had undertaken to get everything ready at their end. They had agreed to have some kind of craft, or crafts, to load it on and to man it, or them, with trustworthy and able men who knew the Bay waters and channels. What we had to do was to let them know when to start and to arrange to meet the boat—or boats—at some safe and agreed-on place along our Trumet bay shore. This wasn't so easy, now that the *Gannet* was picketing Billfish Cove, but it had to be risked, or our whole scheme would come to nothing.

After a whole lot of talk we settled on the place, another inlet about a mile above Billfish. Hauling the stuff across lots and over to the shipyard and harbor would be a tougher job than from Billfish, but we all agreed it could be done—had to be, in fact. The exact date would have to depend on the weather, of course, but we decided to ask the Tamoset crew to make the start on or about the middle or latter end of the next week. We would be watching and waiting for them until they came. A fair wind would help a lot, of course, but they would have oars, and hands enough to row, if and when rowing was needful.

The next thing was how to get the word to them. Somebody would have to go to Tamoset on horseback and go right off because it was Friday evening now and he would have to get back with the word that the folks there understood and would be working with us. Besides, they might have worked out a plan that was better than ours, and, if so, they must get the details of that scheme to us, so we could conform to it.

"Be sure to have them write it all out, times, places, and everything," said Squire Bailey, always the careful one. "We can't trust anybody's memory, I don't care how good it is. Let them give this writing to our messenger for him to fetch back with him, and, for heaven's sake, order him to hang on to it, not give it up to anybody but a known man—one of this Council."

Everybody nodded, this was sensible enough.

"Who is that messenger going to be?" asked Captain Elkanah Davies. "You, Isaiah?"

I shook my head. "I can navigate a ship better than I can a horse—yes, and make better time, too. Besides, I've got plenty to do here. To my mind there is just one man fitted for that job, and that's Ezra Light."

Some of them agreed I was right, but there were some that looked pretty dubious and some that objected. Henry Allen, of course, was one of the objectors. "I never could see why you are so soft on that Light mess," he growled. "Fur's I'm concerned he never had more than a spoonful of brains to start with, and the most of that spoonful has slopped out."

The Reverend Ichabod Samuels was another of the doubtful ones. He told us he feared that Ezra Light was not a man of high moral character. "A scoffer," he said. "I have heard him say things which were almost atheistic. I cannot believe him to be a person in whom a trust such as this should be placed."

I stood up for Ezra, of course. Also and moreover I said that he was the one person who could leave Trumet on horseback in these times, be gone a couple of days, and not be asked about.

"No, nor be bothered along the way, either." I went on, "either by our own side or by British hired men and tattle-tales. He knows everybody from one end of the county to the other, and everybody knows him. He will take his peddling packs along with him and just be on another peddling cruise, that's all. It has got to be Ezra; he is the only one that fills the bill every way you can think of."

Argument? Good land, yes! But it was Eben Fowler who had the last word.

"Why not let Isaiah handle this?" he said. "He is satisfied with Light, just as he is with young Bangs. If all goes well, he should be given the credit. If it goes badly, why—"

"I'll get the blame," I put in. "I know that, Eben, you needn't remind me of it. All right, I'll be on hand to take it. As for the credit—well, that can go to anybody that wants it."

So we took a vote, and Ezra and I won out. Even Allen didn't vote against us. Then the Reverend Ichabod made a long prayer asking for the Almighty's blessing on our undertaking, and the meeting broke up.

I saw Ezra before I turned in. I told him just what he was to do and that keeping mum and making speed were the two main items in his manifest.

"Better borrow another horse, hadn't you?" I suggested. "Yours must be pretty well beat out after your Point Town cruise."

He wouldn't hear of it. "What? Selah?" he said. "Captain Isaiah, you don't know that mare. She'd undertake to go to Jerusalem if I headed her that way. I'll start early tomorrow morning, peddling packs and all. . . . Huh! Speaking of Jerusalem, one of them Johnnie Bulls told me t'other day that that was where anybody that drove as hard a bargain as I did must have hailed from in the beginning. He said he'd swear my first name was Israel, not Ezry. Israel Light! Ho, ho! That wa'n't bad, considering who said it. I come down a cent in my price to pay for the laugh."

He got away about five next morning, and I watched him from my bedroom window.

Nothing out of the common run happened all that Saturday forenoon, nor afternoon either. Jonathan, when he reported for breakfast, said he had had a quiet night down at the yard. I asked him if anything unusual had happened there since yesterday morning, and he said no. Still didn't offer to give me any particulars about what had happened before that, either. He was very quiet and looked, or so I thought, even more down in the mouth than when I said good night to him. Something was worrying him, sure. I rather guessed the something was named Hope Allen, but I couldn't very well ask. Subjects like that are a man's own business, and the other fellow better keep out of it if he wants to stay healthy.

That night, though, something did happen. Ezra was on his way to Tamoset; Jonathan was down aboard the *New Hope*; Phoebe had gone out to sewing meeting at the Poundberry house; I was alone in the sitting-room, smoking my pipe. It was about half-past eight, or thereabouts.

I heard steps hurrying up to the side door, and somebody knocked. I opened the door. Washy Rogers—Joe Rogers's eleven-year-old boy, he was, and his first name was Washington, although Washy was what all hands called him— was standing outside. He was puffing and out of breath.

"I've got a—a letter for you, Captain Isaiah," he stammered. "Seth Black, he give it to me to fetch to you. Here 'tis."

He handed me a piece of paper, dirty and all crumpled up. I looked at the thing and then at the boy.

"Seth Black gave it to you?" I said. "What is it?"

"I dunno. He told me to be certain sure you got it. Said 'twas awful important, he did."

"Humph! Was he drunk?"

"No, sir, I don't think he was. He was all of a twitter, though."

I unfolded the scrap of paper. It was as dirty and smudged inside as it was out. Written or scrawled there, with a quill that Noah might have used aboard the Ark and with ink that looked as if it was made of tar and water, was this:

If you want that *New Hope* of yourn to get a goin for god sakes come See me rite orf. Bad work up tonite. Trater and i know who tis. *Come Now!* Seth.

It took me a minute or so to make it out. With the shaky handwriting and the smudges and blots, to say nothing of the spelling, it was considerable of a puzzle.

"Humph!" said I. "Where was Seth when he gave you this?"

"Down to his shanty, Captain Isaiah. He must have seen me going by, I cal'late, 'cause he come running out with it."

"And you're sure he wasn't drunk?"

"Yes, sir. Didn't talk that way, anyhow. Acted all kind of trimbly, as if he was sick—or scared—or something."

"How long ago was this?"

Washy kind of hesitated. "Oh, about six or so, I guess likely. I'd been jobbing eels over on the Shad Cove flats, and I was on my way home to supper."

"Um. Must have late suppers at your house, son. Why didn't you bring it before this? Put it in your pocket and forgot it, I guess likely, didn't you?"

There was more stammering here, but I could see that my guess was right. I gave him a few coppers for his trouble, and he scampered off. I read the thing over again.

Of course, I didn't put much faith in it. So far as Seth Black's being "all of a twitter" and trembling were concerned, I could imagine why. A person who put away as much rum in a day as he did was liable to begin seeing all sorts of scary things, to say nothing of "traters." However, I decided maybe I had better go down and look at him. I would be making a fool of myself, probably, but—well, I would go.

It was a dark night, and I had to go across the fields and through the pines, so I took my candle lantern and started. It was a mile trip, and wet and stumbly through the bayberry bushes and briars, but I made it, by main strength and wasting a lot of bad language.

The Black shanty—not much bigger than a henhouse it was—was on the top of the high sand bank at the inner end of Shad Cove. Seth had a rickety clam shed and a battered-up old dory down on the beach at the foot of the bluff.

He lived all sole alone. His nighest neighbors were the Allens, and their house was a half mile off, the other side of the big pine grove.

There was no sign of a light in the shanty when I hove in sight of it. It was just another blacker blob against the blackness of the night sky beyond the edge of the bluff, that was all. I stumbled up to the door and knocked on it. No answer, no sound of any kind. I knocked louder.

"Seth!" I sung out. "Hey, Seth!"

Still not a move or a sound. I gave the door a shove with my foot and went in.

Seth Black wasn't there, and it looked as if he hadn't been there for quite a little spell. The shanty had only two rooms in it, and the one I was in was a sort of combination sitting-room, dining-room, kitchen, and general pigsty. By my lantern light I could see a patched-up old table against the wall with dirty dishes on it. The chair nighest the table was upset, lying on its back on the floor. There was a loaf of bread and a knife on the table and a slice with a bite taken out of it on one of the plates. A candle stuck in a bottle was there, too, but it had burned down to the edge of the bottleneck and quit. The tallow had run down onto the table, so I judged Seth must have left it lit when he went—wherever he had gone.

I looked into the only other room. Seth's bedroom it was, and about as big as the galley on a three-man fish boat. Nobody there, either. I came to the conclusion that the red, white, and blue sea serpents that Seth was probably seeing when he wrote me that note had gone out of doors where there was more room for him and them to exercise in.

I went out, too, pretty well disgusted with myself for taking the long walk down there, and mad because now I must tramp home again. I had taken a step or two when I saw something that made me stop and stare and catch my breath.

I was facing eastward as I came out of that shanty. My back was toward the Bay, and the village and harbor in front of me. I could see nothing of them, of course, only the dim shapes of the pine tops against the sky. And, all at once, those shapes stopped being dim and began to stand out clear and plain.

That eastward sky was lighting up, was turning red, a red that kept getting brighter and redder yet. The meeting-house steeple showed against it, but the brightest part of that redness wasn't behind the steeple, it was to the left, considerably more to the left.

It was about where—where—good Lord Almighty! It was over the shipyard—the shipyard and the *New Hope!*

I began to run.

2

In which Jonathan shoots at shadows
and is captured by the militia.

Told by

JONATHAN BANGS

I.

THE SKY in the east was red with fire.

That is the place, in this yarn of ours, where Captain Dole's first watch on deck ends. It is the place where I, Jonathan Bangs, must take over.

I wish it was a real watch on a real deck of a real ship. I'd feel better then. Even if the weather was dirty, and getting dirtier, I wouldn't be scared—the way I'm scared now at the blank sheets of paper lying under my hand. I know less than a little about the spinning of yarns. Worse, my mind isn't a quick, sure mind like Captain Dole's. It's a mind that works like a man in heavy boots trudging through deep dry sand. It sweats. And it takes a long, weary time to get wherever it gets. I'm slow. I'm slow to think, speak, eat, love, and hate. If I'm just as slow to write, the Judgment Day will find me still chewing the big knuckles that Hope likes to tease me about, my trick far from done.

The sky in the east was red with fire.

Where was I when I saw that glow—a bad unnatural thing in the black August night?

I was not where Captain Dole had trusted me to be at that hour. I was not where I, myself, had expected to be. I was not in my place as new night watchman of our little bark, the *New Hope*. I was not on the privateer's deck, but ashore, and more than a mile from the harbor side.

Around me were the dark, ragged shapes of close-growing scrub pines. Their long-fallen needles formed a silent carpet underfoot. Ahead, in a little clearing, two men stood in guarded talk. I did not know the names of those men or the look of their faces or their business together.

In my right hand was a pistol, loaded and cocked. In my mind was indecision.

Should I challenge those men? Should I step forward, pistol raised, and demand to know who they were and what they were about? I most surely should have, but—and may the Lord forgive me—I didn't. Instead, I stood stock-still, like the great blunderbore that I am, and wondered what was the wise thing to do.

One of those men I had first seen only a few minutes before, from my post at the starboard rail of the *New Hope*. As merely a shadow he had separated himself from the darker shadows of our storehouse near the wharf, and had moved away towards the town.

No honest man could have had business at such a place at such a time, and it is obvious to me now what I should have done. I should have ordered him to halt. Had he refused to obey, common sense should have made me fire my pistol, either at him or into the air as a warning. Any of those things might well have changed the course of events.

But, being Jonathan Bangs, I did nothing that a quick-witted man would have done instantly. I did not shout or fire. Instead, I forgot my job on the bark, climbed down to the wharf as silently as I could, and set off in pursuit.

As I just said, my pistol was ready, my target near, and my duty plain. Even so, it was not I who decided the shape of what followed, but the eastern sky behind my back.

The man I had trailed was the first to see the spreading blur of crimson just over the horizon. In the midst of his urgent talk with the shadowy figure he had just joined, he suddenly stopped and turned about so that he faced me, one arm stretched out.

"Look!" he cried aloud. "You insist on proof, so I'll give it to you! She's on fire now! Look!"

Crouching low, in the momentary belief that I had been discovered, I turned my head and looked to the east. There I saw the glow and needed no help to know what it meant. The *New Hope,* and with it all my and Trumet's hopes, was burning. Just as surely, the man I had followed into this grove of pines had set the fire.

"Stop!"

For once Jonathan Bangs didn't pause to think. I burst from the screening pines like a charge of grape from the muzzle of a carronade.

"Put up your hands, you—"

Of course they didn't put them up nor stop. Instead they ran in opposite directions for the edge of the clearing, giving me a choice of targets. I picked the likeliest, held my breath to take steady aim, and fired.

The flash blinded me so that I couldn't tell if my shot had been lucky. I swore, flung down my pistol, and ran forward, yelling.

A low-growing bayberry bush stopped my rush. Its branch caught my foot and sent my hulking body crashing to the ground. As I lay there, gasping, the sounds made by the running men grew fainter and then faded away altogether.

Bayberries and pine needles! They were close to my big nose, and I remember thinking, as I lay there, that I would always associate their clean, pleasant odor, with one of the most unpleasant moments of my life.

But I was wrong. The moment was bitter, but I was to know others that were more so. I was to know them very soon.

Some people like to say that when trouble happens there's sure to be a woman in the immediate vicinity. Well, I won't go so far as to say that Hope Allen was responsible for the trouble I've just finished telling about. But I *will* say—just before I duck and run for my life—that Hope Allen was certainly in the vicinity that particular night, and that except for her the trouble would never have happened quite in the way it did.

I had first laid eyes on Hope soon after my arrival in Trumet, on a day when, our noon meal done with, Captain Dole asked if I would like to walk with him over to the Bay side for a visit with his old friends, the Allens. "Henry Allen," observed the Captain, "is a queer stick, but you might like his daughter. Hope was just a mite when I left Trumet to go to sea, but, from what I heard since I got back, looking at her is a guaranteed cure for most any ailment—particularly for sore eyes. That's the opinion of the young bloods in Trumet, anyhow. Would you like to try it out?"

"I'm game for anything you suggest, Captain Dole." I was feeling as good-natured as a cat full to the whiskers with rich cream. "But I give you warning I won't be bowled over by your beautiful Miss Allen—if that's what you're hoping. At this stage I haven't any interest in females."

"Humph!" Captain Dole darted me a sharp glance from his black eyes as he turned towards the door. "Show me a man, eighteen or eighty, that isn't interested in a handsome female, and I'll show you a man that's sick! Avast talking foolishness and come on!"

I laughed and followed him out into the warm sunlight.

The Allens lived about as far from the James Otis Tavern and the Town House and the center of things in general as anybody could and still stay within Trumet's boundaries. To get to their house Captain Dole and I struck off south, across the moors, until we came to a four corners, formed by the crossing of Bay and Point Roads. Both sandy ways came from the village and led to the Bay shore. Bay Road, however, ambled southward, while Point Road brought Captain Dole and me straight to the Allens' doorstep.

The Allen house was much like other Trumet houses, with shingles weathered a silver gray, windows only at eye level since there was no second story, and a kitchen wing that ran parallel to, and was a smaller copy of, the boxlike main body. It was backed at a little distance by a semicircle of the usual pitch-pines and faced on the west by the spread of Massachusetts Bay. At the foot of an easy slope and not far away I could see the mouth of Billfish Creek, which connected with Hornpout Pond further inland.

At that time, Billfish Creek, Hornpout Pond, Bay and Point Roads, Shad Cove, and the rest were no more than pleasant-sounding names to me. A little later on, each was to have an association—unforgettable but not always pleasant. Even now I can't hear the name of Hornpout Pond without a little shiver. For it was in the saltmarsh at its edge that I was later to find, his face an unnatural white in the pale light of early dawn, the body of a murdered man.

But that was still part of the future. I had no premonition of what might be ahead of me as I glanced at the pleasant view and followed Captain Dole to the door of the kitchen wing, where we knocked and were let in.

The Allen kitchen was a wide, cheerful room which gave the feeling of being a place for living as well as cooking. To be sure, the broad fireplace, the ovens, the shelves and cupboards full of bright metalware and pottery, the scent of baking and of spices, the sound of a kettle boiling were all there.

But there were other things. There was sunlight through four broad windows. There was a rag rug full of bright colors on the scrubbed floor. There was a round pine table with three or four wooden chairs around it. There were candles on the table, a few books, a pair of spectacles, a piece of unfinished knitting. Under the table was a big pair of frayed carpet slippers, beside which a tortoise-shell cat lay sleeping in a compact ball.

Henry Allen, who opened the door to our knock, gave me an impression of grievance that might at any moment flare into anger. He was a tall, angular man, so thin that any breeze would make his clothes flap about him. He had heavy black hair, a strand of which kept falling down across his forehead, and was quickly tossed back by an impatient jerk of his head. Henry Allen's eyes were bright and never still. His face was so thin that the high cheek-bones cast shadows. His mouth was strong but discontented.

Hope Allen, his daughter, was also there, and in describing her I must be careful.

When a man is warned that a girl he is about to meet is a beauty, the picture of her that he forms in his mind is sure to be more or less inaccurate. For no good reason at all I had decided that Hope would be tall, dark, dignified, calm, and have regular features. Hope, when I met her, was such a complete opposite to my imaginings that she took me by surprise.

She was a tiny thing, hardly taller than a growing child, but never for a moment to be mistaken for one. Her twenty-odd years declared themselves in every move that she made, and in every line of her young body. In seeing Hope I felt as though I were looking at a grown woman, but through the wrong end of a spyglass.

She certainly was not dark, dignified, or calm. Her hair was red—a deep mahogany shade, to be sure—but red. Such hair is always beautiful in itself, but it seems to be the sad fact that so many women who own it fail to have beauty. I can only say that Hope succeeded. Her features were not regular, if only because her nose turned up at the end. But she more than made up for this supposed fault by her dark blue eyes and the warmth of her mouth. Her physical movements were light and swift, and to complete the upsetting of what I had expected, it was obvious that no person of Hope's coloring could ever be suspected of calm.

She and her father had evidently been interrupted in the midst of a rather hot argument when we came in, for no sooner had Henry Allen greeted us than he pointed his long forefinger at her and shook his head. "Take a look at this girl of mine, Isaiah," he said gruffly. "People tell me I'm lucky to have her, and in some ways I cal'late they're right. But she has crazy, tom-fool ideas like the rest of the young-ones her age. I'm glad you weren't here just now to hear her tell me that the British are as nice folks as anybody else! From the way she tells it, I ought to kiss the next Britisher I see instead of kick him! The British!"

"That's not quite what I said, Father." There was respect in Hope's tone, but stubbornness, too. "I just said I couldn't see why we should *hate* the British just because this country is at war with theirs now. After all, isn't our blood really as British as the blood in the reddest Redcoat that walks? Just because the English live on the other side of the water and have had bad rulers, are they actually very different from us?"

"The English!" Henry Allen said the word angrily. "The English are no better than dogs. If I could cut myself and drain out every drop of English blood I have, I'd do it mighty quick!"

69

"Maybe so, Henry," said Captain Dole drily, "but, since both your mother and father were English born, I doubt if you'd be much good to yourself afterwards. I've generally understood that a man needs blood in his business, and there's been considerable mighty good British blood, here and there, around this world. Can't dodge that fact, any of us."

Hope looked for a moment as though she would like to continue the argument, but suddenly the bright light died out of her eyes. "It's silly for Father and me to be squabbling this way, and it's my fault. I ought to be feeding the hens instead of preaching about something I don't really understand. Perhaps Mr. Bangs will help me with my chore."

Without words I followed her through a door into the connecting woodshed and then to the sunshine outside. There Hope sat down on a low bench that ran along the shingled wall of the house and closed her eyes with a sigh. I stood beside, staring down at her with real interest. At last I heard my voice say, "You pick a peculiar time, Miss Allen, to feed hens."

"Perhaps ours are peculiar hens." There was a gleam of blue as she half opened her eyes to look up at me. "And, for that matter, what does a sailor know about feeding hens?"

"I was raised on a Maine farm, where I fed hens every day for fifteen years. I always tossed them their grain at sundown."

"Really? How strange. But I remember now that the people of Maine are said to have savage customs." She smiled to take any sting out of her words. "But you're right, of course. The Allen hens, like the Maine ones, eat at dusk. Still, I didn't lie just now, for a lie is supposed to deceive, and I fooled nobody. Father knew I was just trying to get away from the imp that pesters me."

70

"Imp?"

She nodded. "I love my father and understand him fairly well, but I have a devil inside that makes me argue with almost everything he says. I ought to be ashamed, because I usually argue just for the sake of arguing."

"Then you didn't mean what you just said about the English?"

"Perhaps not, but I thought I meant it at the time. Perhaps you can put me straight. You must have met a lot of English people in your travels, and they say you've travelled over all the world. I hear that you've even fought against the British in a battle. It that true?"

"Yes."

"Then tell me."

"If I can. What do you want me to tell?"

"Tell everything." She made an impatient little movement. "Tell me all about the battle, all about yourself and your life."

I shook my head. "I'm afraid my life story would make dull listening."

"Bosh!" There was no doubt now about her impatience. "False modesty annoys me. You've seen the world and fought in a battle. I've done nothing but live in Trumet, where salt from the sea and fish from the same place are the only things that count. If your story bores me I promise to stop it soon enough." She smiled. "I'll end it by saying that I must feed the hens—sundown or not."

I did my best, which wasn't very good. Most of the things I had seen and done were so close behind me that I couldn't see them very clearly. It makes me uneasy, also, to talk about myself, so I blundered along, and probably would have soon come to an end except for Hope. She asked one question after another until she finally hit on a subject that I was glad to discuss. That subject was Captain Dole. When I finished with Captain Dole, and paused to

71

take breath, I realized that the sun was a lot nearer than it had been to the western horizon and that Hope was looking at me with amusement.

"I thought you might be tongue-tied," she said, "but I was wrong. You can be talkative, Jonathan Bangs, when you talk about Captain Dole. It's a funny thing—the worship one man can have for another one."

"Worship?" I frowned. "I doubt if the word describes the way I feel about Captain Dole. It's true that I like him more than anybody I have met, or am likely to. He's everything that I would like to be myself."

She was watching me. "And why not?"

I laughed at the thought. "And am not! If you knew me better you wouldn't have needed to ask."

"I've heard a lot about you, and I've listened to you talk. Perhaps I know you better than you think." She hesitated. "Perhaps I know you well enough to guess that one of your big faults is your habit of belittling yourself."

I felt a stir of annoyance. "A man might have a worse fault. He could boast."

"He could." She nodded. "And perhaps he would be wise—if he could live up to his boasting. I think the world gives people the value they give themselves. A man who waits for recognition is likely to wait. The strong take what they want."

The words were without offense but for some reason seemed to demand that I defend myself. "Perhaps I'm not so easy-going as you think. Perhaps even I wouldn't be slow to take what I really want."

She looked me full in the eyes. "And what do you want?"

I had an answer ready for that, and didn't pause in giving it, even though I knew it would sound a little silly. "I want to make my home here in Trumet—to make myself a part of Trumet."

Her eyes, widening in surprise, were the sudden, glinting

blue of the sea when the sun comes out from behind a cloud. "Trumet!" She laughed softly. "Wonders will never cease! The one wish of this man is to live in a forlorn little fishing village." There might have been scorn in her voice. "There, for certain, is ambition!"

"You asked a question," I told her resentfully, "and I answered it—to your amusement. Perhaps you'll do the same for me. What is *your* dearest wish, Miss Hope Allen? What do *you* want out of life?"

"What do I want?" Her firm little chin came up then, eagerly, and she gazed past me, not seeing the Bay before her eyes, but daydreams. "I want all the wonderful things that there are! I want to see the world—all of it! Most of all I want to get away from washing dishes and scrubbing floors. I want to get away from this dreary, self-centered, gossipy little place."

"Oh." Her way of talking about Trumet annoyed me. "So you want excitement. Just how are you hoping to find it?"

"You know my story?" She was almost fierce. "Then how do you know that I'm not somebody important in England? I *might* be. My father might even have a title! Perhaps I belong in a big house! Perhaps I should have a lot of people to wait on me! Perhaps, oh, perhaps all sorts of grand things! Who knows?"

Her childishness should have made me laugh, but instead I felt a perverse wish to hurt her. "Who knows? On the other hand, who knows but what you are the daughter of some Liverpool innkeeper, destined to wash dirty glasses? That's just as likely as your being the daughter of an earl."

Hope looked me in the eyes. "I think," she said slowly, "you could teach me to hate you pretty quickly. Is it your idea of fun to take the romance out of other people's daydreams?"

"No, and if I've done that to you I'm sorry." I was, gen-

73

uinely, a little ashamed. "I was just trying to point out that you might be a lot worse off than you are. The grass isn't always greener on the far side of the hill. Perhaps, right here in Trumet, you may still find what you're looking for. Who knows?"

"Trumet! Romance in Trumet!" She was scornful. "And you've been to Hong Kong, Capetown, Calcutta!" She shrugged and tilted up her nose. "But I forget. Perhaps you have had too much of the glamorous Far East. Tell me, Mr. Bangs, are the ladies there really so *very* beautiful?"

"I don't know." I knew she was making fun of me, but didn't know what tone to take. "I've kept away from oriental women. I've heard they are dangerous for American sailors."

"I see." Hope put her chin in one small hand, cocked her head, and looked up at me innocently. The imp that she had spoken of was in full possession of her then, but I had not yet learned to read the signs. "I suspect, Mr. Bangs," she said sweetly, "that you are a noble man—solemn and bulging with morals. I'm almost willing to bet you've never sinned—even to the tune of stealing a harmless kiss."

I should have run, then and there, for I was out of my depth. My growing peevishness, however, was enough to hold me, in spite of being helpless in this kind of verbal fencing.

"Perhaps you admire thieves," I said shortly. "I don't."

Hope considered the matter with a fine judicial calm. Then she shook her head. "I don't respect thieves. No. But I respect chicken-heartedness even less."

The red blood was now in my cheeks, and no mistake. "Let's not quibble. What you're saying is that you despise a coward. And a coward, in your mind, is a man who doesn't grab what he wants in this world, whether it belongs to him or not?"

74

She glanced at me out of the corner of her eye. "Strong men don't ask for things."

I drew a little breath, my mind made up. "Then take a look," I said in the casual tone of someone discussing the weather, "at a strong man."

Before she could guess what I was up to, I leaned down, cupped her chin in my hand, and kissed her—full, and at some length—on her mouth.

Codfish do not fly through the air, nor does the sun shine at midnight in these parts. But I could say that either thing had happened with more feeling of telling the truth than I feel in telling what I have just told. The fact remains that I kissed Hope Allen; kissed her uninvited, deliberately, and with, I flatter myself, a fair degree of efficiency.

Nor did the skies open and the stars fall to earth. Hope didn't move or cry out. She sat still until I had let her go and stepped back, but as I did so every trace of color drained from her face, leaving it the clear white of porcelain.

"You wouldn't dare," she murmured at last with slow and complete disbelief. "You couldn't possibly *dare!*"

I knew that I had just done an inexcusable thing, but I didn't care. To the contrary, I felt a sense of pride. I felt strong again, and master of the situation. I laughed with real pleasure. "I wanted to kiss you, so I did! Strong men take what they want; that's your own gospel, Miss Allen. And now, what would you like to say or do to punish me? If you like, I'll offer my face to be slapped. Or I'll confess to your father and let him shoot me dead. Which would you like?"

The color had now come back to her face with a vengeance. It was bright scarlet. "I'd like," she said in a small, strangled voice, "you to get out of my sight. At once!"

"I will." I bowed but felt no dismay, though my face was

solemn. "But may I say I'm sorry if I've insulted you? No insult was intended. I just answered a challenge."

"You mean I invited you to kiss me!" She shivered. "You're a brute!"

"No." I shook my head, smiling, sensing that she wasn't as angry as she wanted me to believe. "You know better than that. Tell me the truth. Did you, or didn't you, dare me to do what I just did?"

She pulled an absurd little square of linen from the neck of her dress and touched the corners of her eyes, watching me closely. Then, suddenly, she nodded. "But I didn't think you'd dare. I never dreamed it!"

"You agree that you asked for it?"

"I just said so." She drew a long breath. "It was my imp again. My imp betrayed me. But I baited you, all the same, and deserved what I got. I'm ashamed, for really I am not the kind of girl you must be thinking."

"I'm thinking nothing you wouldn't like. May I see you again tomorrow—if only to prove that my manners aren't always bad?"

She seemed, for a moment, to be considering her answer, but when she looked up at me it was with a twinkle of amusement. "Will I be safe in your hands? You are, you know, a most dangerous man."

"You are laughing at me again. . . . Well, never mind. "You'll be quite safe. May I come?"

She nodded. "Yes, Mr. Bangs."

"Please call me Jonathan."

"No." She gave her head an abrupt little shake, so that the sun glinted in her red hair. "I had much rather call you Jon. I mean, of course, Jon with no *h*. I will call you Jon, but not John. Do you notice the difference in the sound? It is faint, but it makes a great change. Not John—*Jon*."

I could see no difference in the wide world, but I didn't care. "Very well—Hope."

We were smiling at one another, and then, for no good reason, we both laughed out loud.

3.

The details of vacation days aren't easily called back to mind, but to my best remembrance I divided my laziness, from then on, about equally between Hope Allen and the people of Trumet. I tried to make friends with both and thought I succeeded.

For her part, Hope lost no time in leading me to believe that she wanted nothing more than friendship from me. I was content with that; perhaps I was even a little relieved, since in my innocence I believed that I didn't want any sort of romantic tangle.

As friends, she and I met more and more often, until finally we were together for some part of almost every day. Hope knew Trumet by heart, and as she showed it to me, I quickly came to realize that she loved her little village—that all her silly talk about Trumet being a forlorn fishing village was idle chatter.

We walked together through the woods and over and down the rolling slopes, which must be very like the moors of Scotland that I have read about but never seen. We sat on the edge of the sand cliff on the Bay side and watched the tide ebb until the flats were bare and dry, except for scattered little pools, for more than a mile from the shore's edge. We took food with us and ate it on the clean, broad beach facing the Atlantic. We sunned ourselves in the windless, cuplike hollows between the dunes. Sometimes we talked about little things, tentatively exploring each other's minds. Sometimes we were silent, Hope with her chin upon her closely hugged knees, I sprawled beside her, with a knife in one hand and a four-inch model of the *Strong Arm* in the other.

I looked up from my plaything once to find Hope looking at me with a little smile. "Such a tiny ship," she said softly, "for such a big man."

My old annoyance stirred at the mention of my size. "Am I honestly," I inquired crossly, "such a freak of nature?"

"No." She gave her head that quick little shake that I had come to know. "You are no freak of anything, except maybe in your own mind. I sometimes wonder what kind of picture you have of yourself. But don't tell me, because it would only make me cross. Let me tell, instead, what I see when I look at Jonathan Bangs."

"I'm afraid," I said, grinning, "that my head will be turned."

"I see a big man," she said thoughtfully, ignoring me, "but one whose bigness is noticeable only when he stands beside smaller men. He isn't clumsy, lumpy, or out of proportion. He seems to move slowly, but moves much faster than that. I see a man with light hair and eyebrows; with nice blue eyes and a good mouth, and a jaw that is a *man's* jaw. I see a man with an education and brains that are better than he knows, or will admit. I see a man who will go a long way, once he gains confidence in himself."

"Well." I sat staring. "Well! Is there more?"

"No." There were little spots of color in both her cheeks. "I think I've already said more than enough, but not to flatter you. It was just—but no matter. It's your turn, now. Would you like to tell me what you see when you look at Hope Allen?"

"Yes." Seeing that she had no intention of fishing for compliments, I told her honestly what was in my mind. "When I look at Hope Allen I see a girl who tries to make others think that she is a brainless young thing with flighty notions. She tries hard, but she fools nobody—least of all Jonathan Bangs."

"Oh!" She scrambled to her feet. "I think I hate you!"

"Why?" I grinned again. "Because I say you are a fraud?"

"You accuse me of having no emotions," she declared, hotly, stamping her little foot. "Do you think I'm a placid cow?"

"Heaven forbid! I should hate to face your anger."

"Then don't ever again hint that I'm a sensible person." She was half in earnest. "I hate sensible people!"

Such were our hours together. Their harmlessness was so firmly fixed in my mind that it never once occurred to me that others might think differently. It took Captain Dole, himself, to shake me from my complacency.

I was busily brushing myself off before leaving our quarters at the Lights' house one afternoon when I looked up to find the Captain looking at me with his bright, dark eyes. "It strikes me you're a busy young fellow these days," he said quietly, "especially for somebody that hasn't a thing in the world to do. What's on the docket for this afternoon? You wouldn't be seeing that little red-head, Hope Allen, would you?"

"Why, yes, it just happens that I am." There was something about his tone that made me frown. "We're going over to Rogers' Pond to catch some perch. Why?"

"Oh, nothing, nothing! I just wondered." Captain Dole brushed a fleck of dust off the knee of his breeches. "Hope's quite a nice girl, isn't she, Jonathan? Good-looking, too. Seeing quite a lot of her, aren't you?"

There was no mistaking his tone now, and it made me angry. "Perhaps I am—and why not? I like her, and she likes me. We're friends, and we have a good time together. That's all there is to it, and if anybody tells you anything different, Captain Dole, you can say, from me, that he's a liar!"

"There, there! Keep your hair on, Jonathan, my boy. There's no call for you to get all heated up. If people think, and say, that you're courting Hope Allen, it's only the natural thing. You see her every day. You're both young, healthy, and one of you—mind, I'm not saying which—is fairly good-looking. What else would you expect people to think?"

"I don't know or care! What I'm telling you is that Hope and I are good friends and nothing more."

"I see." He nodded. "Well, perhaps that's the best way to have it, since one of these fine days you and I will have to haul up into the wind and run for some other port."

"What?" I looked at him blankly. "You mean we're leaving Trumet?"

"What else?" He shrugged. "Neither one of us is rich, and we've got a living to make. We won't make it here. Not with this war on, we won't. We'll have to be moving soon, and the Lord only knows if we'll ever be back."

"I'll be back," I told him stubbornly. "I'll be back if it's the last thing I do."

"Maybe," said Captain Dole, "and maybe not. Nobody can say anything for sure in this world."

I was disturbed and peevish when I flung myself out of the house a few minutes later. It annoyed me that people were mixed up in their minds about my friendship for Hope. It was like throwing dust on a clean thing. Why couldn't the world mind its own affairs and leave Hope and me to ours? Why, also, in the midst of my fun, must Captain Dole talk about leaving Trumet—and soon? I wouldn't leave Trumet, I told myself savagely—but knowing that I was lying—until it suited me to leave.

I was so wrapped up in my own thoughts that I hardly glanced at Hope when I met her on the path near her house. I merely said a brief good afternoon, took the long fishing poles out of her hands, and would have set off in the direction of Rogers' Pond without another word if she hadn't stopped me.

"Wait a minute, Jon. I don't know about fishing. I—I don't know that I ought to go."

I turned back to her, at once, my own troubles forgotten. For Hope's voice was one I did not know. It was strained and shaken. Her face, too, now that I really looked at it, was a little pale, and I thought she had been crying. "Hope!" I was startled. "What is the matter? What has happened?"

"Nothing much." She shook her little head. "It's just that I've just come from a quarrel with Father. A really hateful quarrel."

"With your father?" I was surprised, knowing Henry Allen's love for his foster-daughter. "What on earth about?"

"About something silly." She looked down at her fingers, twisting them. "Father doesn't want me to go fishing with you today. He doesn't want me to see you so often. He said he'd like it much better if I didn't see you at all."

"What do you mean?" I was slow to understand. "He doesn't want you to go fishing with me? He doesn't want you to see me? Why not? What have I done?"

"You've done nothing—except see me."

"Then what is his objection? Doesn't he like me?"

Hope managed a smile. "He *says* that he doesn't like you at all. But I don't think that's the truth. I think—I think it's something else altogether."

"What else could it be?"

"Can't you imagine?" She did not look at me but at her hands. "My father loves me—quite a lot. I've been with you almost every day for quite a long time. Father doesn't like— he's afraid that—"

"I see what you're trying to say. Your father is afraid I'll steal his daughter! He thinks that you and I may be in love—may be planning on getting married!" For the second time that day I was indignant. "What blasted nonsense!"

She looked up at me then with a little gleam of laughter in her eyes. "Am I so ugly, Jon, that it is nonsense for Father to think you may have fallen in love with me?"

I brushed the remark aside. "You know very well what I mean. The fact is that you and I are friends—not lovers. Did you tell him that?"

She nodded. "I told him that."

"And he didn't believe you?"

"Not at all. He said that a girl and a young man could not be friends—that they were lovers or nothing."

"Poppycock!" I clenched my big hands into fists. "Complete poppycock, and this is the second time today that I've heard it!"

"The second time!" It was Hope's turn for surprise. "What do you mean?'

I told her then what Captain Dole had said, and we sat down on a nearby stone for a half hour of quite enjoyable mutual self-pity. We told each other that we were misunderstood and ill-used. We said quite gravely that people in general had small and nasty minds, that they judged the conduct of others from their own, and that they were constitutionally unable to mind their own business. We assured one another, more than once, that we were friends in the same way that two men can be friends and that there was no mawkish sentiment between us. Not being satisfied with all that, I finally turned my pettishness on Henry Allen.

"You say your father has taken a dislike to me because he's afraid you and I may be in love. What of it? Does Henry Allen think he has to hate every man who comes to the house courting his daughter?"

"I don't know."

"Well, in any case he won't have to bother his head long

about me. Captain Dole has just had the goodness to tell me that we must soon be away from here."

"No." Her blue eyes widened as she looked at me. "You are leaving Trumet?"

I scowled. "So the Captain says. He says that we have to make our fortunes and that they can't be made here."

"He's right, of course." Hope's voice was very small and gentle. "A blockaded fishing village is no place to earn a fortune. You must go away—perhaps far. Oh, well." She smiled faintly. "Father, at least, will be happy."

"Perhaps," I said with sudden tense determination, "and perhaps not. Not if I have my way. I believe that a fortune can be made in Trumet—blockade or no—if the right way is found and taken. I intend to find and take it!"

Those were just words when I said them, but a little later they had meaning. For it was then, as we walked along the harbor shore, that I suddenly put one hand on Captain Dole's arm and pointed with the other. "There lies an able ship," I said, or words to that effect. "And lying idle, too. Why not fit her, arm her, man her as a privateer, and run her to sea past the blockade? If she had a lucky cruise there'd be fortunes in it—fortunes for everybody in Trumet! Fortunes for ourselves!"

Captain Dole looked at me as though I had finally taken leave of my poor wits. That was, nevertheless, the beginning of the *New Hope* enterprise.

4.

Hope alone knows the anxiety and suspense I endured while my pet idea was being considered by the people of Trumet, and before the money was raised to put it into operation. I thought of nothing else, and the actually few days seemed endless. Still, when the big decision was finally reached, it took me completely by surprise.

I had agreed to meet Hope that afternoon at Doane's Hollow to pick blueberries, and I was already late when I came charging angrily into the Lights' dining-room, where Captain Dole was sitting at work on some papers. He took off the spectacles that he uses for close work and would have spoken, but I was too full of my own affairs to heed. "That walking rum puncheon, Seth Black, is a nuisance!" I growled, struggling to get out of my jacket. "He cornered me at the Tavern, half drunk as usual—"

"Why, Jonathan, you surprise me! I thought you didn't drink much of any."

I grunted with surprise. "What makes you think I was drunk? Black was the drunken one—but not drunk enough to suit him. He—"

"Got time to talk to me for a minute, Jonathan?"

"Of course, if it's important. The thing is that it's three o'clock now, and—"

"You might call it important," said the Captain with a drawl that was unusual for him, "and you might not. Just thought that you might like to know that it looks as if your crazy idea was going to go through."

I was halfway to the door of my room, but his words stopped me short. "What!" I spun about and stared. "What are you saying, Captain?"

"Nothing much. Except that Squire Baily finally gave up the fight with his law common sense and said that he'd go along with us. That just about fixes it so far as money goes, I guess, so that we can heave ahead. There's a meeting for all concerned at the Town House tonight to discuss why and wherefores. You're invited—unless you're too busy."

It took a while for his meaning to sink in. When it finally did, I whirled my jacket around my head and threw it on the floor. Then I jumped on it with both feet so hard that the things in the whatnot rattled and Phoebe Light screeched from upstairs to know what had happened.

I paid no attention to her at all. "Just say that again, Captain Dole," I begged, breathing hard, as though I'd run a mile. "Please just say it once more!"

He said it again, and a lot more, with the result that I was more than an hour late in reaching Doane's Hollow. I was breathing hard, too, when I got there, for this time I *had* run a mile, and as hard as I could run.

I bellowed Hope's name at the top of my lungs—which was silly, since she must have heard me crashing through the bushes—but I got no answer. The hollow was quiet and apparently deserted, and it was only after a frantic search with my eyes that I spied her sitting in the shadow of a boulder not far off.

"Hope!" It never occurred to me to question her silence or to look at her face. "You'll never believe it, but it's all fixed!" I executed a lumbering imitation of an Indian war dance. "It's done, I tell you! The deed is done!"

"If you mean that the blueberry picking is done," she replied in a tone completely icy, "you may be right. I've worked until my back is almost broken, but I think I have enough! Yes, the blueberry picking is all done. A lot of other things are all done, too!"

I knew then that she was furious and knew the reason, but I was so full of my wonderful news that I could not take her anger very seriously. "I'm late, Hope, and I'm sorry. I'm very late, but I couldn't possibly help it. Do you realize what I'm trying to tell you? The privateer plan is going through! Squire Bailey decided just this afternoon that he would put in his share of the money, and that fixes everything! There's to be a meeting later on today, and—"

"In that case you'd better start for it now, so you won't be late." She got to her feet, her eyes hot. "I'm sure you wouldn't be late to your precious meeting for anything!

85

It's a different thing if you're late meeting me! It doesn't matter if you promise to help me pick blueberries at three and appear at four, babbling about privateers! It's of no consequence if my head is spinning and my hands scratched and my dress torn and my back broken into little bits! It doesn't bother you at all! Very well. In that case, Jonathan Bangs, you just get along to your meeting, and hurry up about doing it!"

"I'm sorry, Hope. I'm really sorry, but you must understand." I was confused by her fierceness. "First, I was held up in the village; I couldn't help it. Then Captain Dole met me at the house with the news about the privateer. I *had* to talk to him about a thing as tremendous as *that*. I thought you'd understand. The minute I could get free I ran every step of the way, just so that I could tell you. I thought you'd be glad."

"Oh, Jon." Her anger ebbed away as I watched. The glow died from her blue eyes, the color faded from her cheeks, and her tense muscles eased. "Of course I'm glad. Of course I understand. I think I must be a little crazy these days, Jon, so please forgive me. It was my pride. I hated to think that you valued our friendship so little that you didn't come when you said you would. You couldn't, of course, and I should have known. Forgive me."

"I'm the one who should ask to be forgiven," I said roughly, shamed by her meekness. "I did wrong, and I'm sorry. If it will help, I'll pick so many blueberries for you, here and now, that you never again will be able to look a blueberry in the face."

"Oh, never mind the blueberries!" She motioned me to sit down beside her in the shade of the boulder. "Tell me about the privateer, Jon. Is it really settled at last? How wonderful! How wonderful for everybody—for you. Tell me."

I told her what I had had from Captain Dole. Now that

enough money had been promised, events would march. The bark would be purchased, and the guns from the old wreck to arm her. A privateer's commission would be got in Boston. There were rumors of powder to be had in Tamoset. The crew would be gathered from men in the neighborhood. The refitting would begin at once. Captain Dole would be the master of this Trumet craft of war, and I was to be her first officer! It was a fine story to tell, and I felt in telling it as though it were a miracle.

"And so," said Hope gently, at last, "the dream that you and I have dreamed has come true. Our privateer will sail and come back full of treasure. All of us in Trumet will be rich and happy. The thing is done."

"No." I shook my head. "It's far from done, and that, of course, is what you are saying. Many things might happen. The British might learn of our plan and send a raiding party. We might be captured attempting to run the blockade—though I don't believe it. Once at sea—"

I stopped there, not wishing to remind her of the dangers of war. Nor did she press me. She had become very quiet and thoughtful, and her eyes had an expression I could not fathom. "How long will it take, Jon, to make the privateer ready for sea?"

"No one can say, since it depends on so many things." I laughed. "But I can promise you one thing. Jonathan Bangs won't be leaving Trumet to seek his fortune for a number of long weeks! I've fooled Captain Dole there, though he doesn't know it."

"But those weeks will pass—and end. And then you will go to sea."

"We'll go to sea—if it is the will of God, and the misfortune of His Britannic Majesty's fleet."

"And then?"

"What happens after that is up to Captain Dole and what hunting he finds. We may cruise these waters or south to the Caribbean. We may slip across the South Atlantic to the latitude of the Azores. We might even raid the English Channel itself! Who knows?"

"Who knows?" She nodded. "But one thing is certain. You will be gone a long time. A year? Two years?"

"Again I don't know. Why do you ask?"

She did not look at me. "Because, for those of us who must stay here in Trumet, the days will drag. We'll be lonely while you are gone."

I felt a lump in my throat. "We'll come back, Hope, my dear, remember that. We'll come back."

"Can we be sure of that?" she asked in a voice so low that I could barely hear it. "There will be the ocean to struggle with—and the enemy. There'll be storms and battles. It's a certain thing that not all those who go will come back."

"You mustn't talk that way," I told her as sternly as I could. "You mustn't think that way, either."

"I'm sorry." She looked at me, then, and I saw that her eyes were full of tears. "It is just that I am selfish, and a coward. I don't want you to die, Jon. I want you to come back to Trumet—and to me."

"And to you."

Even as she spoke the words, I knew.

My knowing was no revelation. It was more as though someone had reminded me of a well-known fact that I had temporarily forgotten. I reached out and took one of Hope's berry-stained little hands in mine.

"Must we keep on playing this silly game?" I asked her gently. "Must we go on pretending and believing that we are dear friends, when we aren't friends at all? We aren't friends at all? We aren't friends, are we, Hope?"

"No." She shook her head, almost whispering. "We aren't friends."

"And I love you, don't I? A great deal?"

She did not take her eyes from mine. "Yes, Jon."

"And you love me?"

"Yes." Her lips trembled, but she did not pause. "Yes, Jon. More than life."

That moment when I took her in my arms was, beyond all doubt, the one that marked the full flood of our tide of happiness.

5.

Yes, that was the very peak.

I can say that now, for in looking back I can see that the markers standing beside my path after that all pointed in one direction. And that direction was down.

The possibility of trouble ahead would have seemed more than unlikely at the time. Hope and I loved each other. My plan for the privateer had been accepted and would be used. My leaving Trumet had been indefinitely put off. With the exception of Captain Dole I was the most popular and sought-after man in the village. I had everything I wanted, and the future looked bright.

But just a few short weeks later that brightness had faded. Hope and I were walking a road that led straight towards trouble. It seemed likely that the *New Hope*—that was the name decided upon for our bark—might never leave her dock in Trumet Harbor. Captain Dole and I, far from being local heroes, had come to be looked at with reproach, and even a certain amount of suspicion.

Perhaps some of our loss of popularity was only natural, for once the first excitement and hope of the new venture had passed, the dangers and risks that went with it became more and more apparent. Could the powder be brought in successfully? Could the blockade be run? The more Trumet worried about those things the more it began to wonder whether Captain Dole and Jonathan Bangs were really showing the way out of the wilderness, or whether the leading was in the other direction.

But when the *Hawke* anchored opposite the mouth of one harbor and the *Gannet* just off the mouth of the other, the thing really came to a head. Some of the people who had invested all they had in the *New Hope* decided, then and there, that their money was as good as lost. And they didn't hesitate to let everybody know who they thought should take the blame. The scowls, dark looks, and even the outspoken remarks that greeted Captain Dole and me that morning were ample proof of the general feeling.

Since the new situation was no fault of ours, I was indignant that we should get the blame. Captain Dole, however, was calm. "Human nature, boy," he told me that afternoon when I protested, "is something you and I won't ever be able to change, no matter how hard we try. You and I started this privateer notion. If it works out all right we may get *some* of the credit. If it doesn't work out, we're certain to get *all* of the blame. Just now the prospects don't look so good, so we're just a couple of salt-water loons that ought to be locked up out of harm's way. That's the way some Trumet folks are feeling, and I don't hate them for it. They're just human."

"Is it our fault if things have turned bad?" I demanded hotly. "How were we supposed to know that the British would suddenly tighten their blockade? Maybe the privateer isn't the reason they're doing it. Maybe it's because Trumet wouldn't pay the ransom. But suppose the British *have* found out about the bark? Is that your fault, or mine? Everybody who put a penny in the company knew from the start that we would have to take that chance. Why should you and I be blamed for a piece of bad luck?"

"Why?" Captain Dole smiled. "Why, because it happened. See here, Jonathan: When a man bets on a horse to win a race, he knows that he's gambling—that he's as likely to lose money as win it. Sure he does. But when the horse comes in last, and his money is lost, does the man blame himself? Not by a jugful! He blames the horse. That's mere human nature."

I said something profane about human nature.

"Don't take it so hard, boy. It's just part of the game."

"Look here, Captain Dole," I put in, frowning. "Do you believe anybody in this town passed the word to the British about the *New Hope?*"

"No." He shrugged. "If the English have found out, there's a hundred ways it might have happened besides that one. I don't think anybody in this neck of the woods has been low down enough to tell 'em on purpose."

"Neither do I." I was grim. "But some people seem to. I heard a bunch of the men talking nonsense about a 'traitor,' this very noon hour."

"Let 'em talk if they want to." He shrugged. "It'll take their minds off you and me."

I said sourly, "I'm not so sure it will."

"Phew!" Captain Dole whistled and looked at me sharply. "So that's the way of it! You think some of our kind charitable town folks have decided that you and I are the dirty dogs!"

"They trust you, all right. If anybody gets the name of traitor tied to him, it'll be me. Wait and see."

"You're dreaming, Jonathan." He was scornful, but I could see that he was a little worried. "You're having nightmares! What call have they to say that you're a turncoat—any more than me or anybody else?"

"I don't know. I just think it's in the wind."

I listened while he told me not to get into a stew about things that weren't so—and weren't important anyhow. "Your conscience is clear, so you shouldn't give a continental, no matter what they say. If they pick on you it'll be just because they've got to find somebody to blame. It won't be personal."

I didn't agree, but I said nothing, having a fondness for fighting my own battles. All the same I was willing to bet some people were already saying that I had sold them out to the British. And if they were saying it, it wasn't just by accident. There was more to it than that.

Somebody in Trumet, though I couldn't give him a name, had been working against me for weeks. If he wanted to make me out a turncoat now, he could do it fast enough, and without taking half the trouble that he had used in making me appear careless, bungling, and untrustworthy in my job at the shipyard. And by that time I seemed to be all of those things.

On the face of it, it would seem hard to hurt a man's reputation by staging a series of seemingly trivial little incidents, but from recent experience I happened to know that it was extremely simple.

One of my duties as first officer had been to see to the safe-keeping of all stores, supplies, and tools used in the refitting. To that end I made a careful tour of inspection each night after work was done, making sure that any material likely to be damaged by the weather was safely stored in a dry place. The job was easy and I had done it faithfully, but my pay was unusual, to say the least.

One morning, for instance, a master carpenter named Dave Bassett came up to me with a troubled expression on his usually pleasant face. "Kind of forgot something last night, didn't you, Jonathan?" he inquired tartly. "That promise you made me yesterday afternoon must have clean slipped out of your mind."

"I don't think so, Dave."

Bassett had been forced to knock off work the previous day when he got word his wife was sick and needed him. I had been standing near when the message came, and had offered to save him the time and trouble of putting his tools away. I had done the job personally, too, so I had no misgivings.

"If you're talking about your tools, Dave, they're safe below decks. I put them there myself, and you'll find them if you look in the right place."

"I found my tools," said Dave grimly, "but not below decks. I found 'em on the forecastle deck, right where I laid 'em down when I quit work yesterday. Last night's rain found 'em before me, too, from the way they look!"

"But that can't be so!" I felt as though I must be having a bad dream as I looked at the rusted saw he handed me. "I'm telling you, Dave, that I put your tools away not ten minutes after you left yesterday afternoon! I did it myself!"

"You did, eh?" Dave looked at me, and if ever a look shouted "liar," that one did. Then he shrugged with disgust and turned away. "Well, if that's the case, I guess I ain't the loser. My tools may be ruined as far as carpentering is concerned, but they ought to bring me a pile of money at auction." He winked meaningly at the group of workmen who were listening. "Them tools are something extra-special, ain't they, boys? Why, them tools can *walk!*"

His listeners laughed, which was natural enough. It was also natural that my good name didn't take on any added polish when the story spread through the town. People thought, and I can't blame them, that I had been caught in a piece of rank carelessness. They thought that, once caught, I had tried to save my skin by telling a silly lie.

There was absolutely nothing that I could say or do to help myself. I knew that I hadn't been careless and that I had told no lie. But I had no proof except my own word, and even my closest friend would have had a hard time believing that, considering the evidence. "But, Jonathan,"

93

such a friend would have argued, "if you put those tools away, as you say, who took them out again? And why? Why would a person do such a senseless thing?"

There was only one answer to that question—an answer as simple as it was puzzling. After hours of thought I was forced to the conclusion that there must be somebody in Trumet who disliked me to the tune of taking a lot of trouble to do me harm. The fact that I knew no such person and could give no reason for his malice made no difference. His existence provided the only sensible explanation for the thing that had happened.

If I had any lingering doubts about the matter they were soon quieted, for the affair of Dave Bassett's tools proved to be only the start. In spite of everything I tried to do I was soon made a fool of again—and then again, and again.

As a matter of routine, one evening, I locked the door of the storehouse, at the dockside, and hung the key on the hidden hook where it belonged. But in the morning the door was found unlocked and wide open—a plain invitation to thieves and apparently another sure proof of my carelessness. Two days later, as part of my regular job, I used sand to put out a fire that was used during working hours for heating water. But the first man on hand the next morning found that fire burning dangerously, a pile of finished lumber only a few feet away. This time, having learned my lesson, I did not even try to defend myself. The third attack came within the week, and the method used was the same. Fearing rain during the night, I made it my final chore at the end of the day to cover a pile of exposed perishables with a tarpaulin, weighing down its edges with heavy timbers. Again I might as well have saved myself the trouble, for when the storm had passed the perishables were ruined—my tarpaulin had vanished during the night.

Vanishing, too, were the remains of my good reputation.

Captain Dole now rather blames me for not having come to him at once with the truth of those incidents as they happened. He says he would have believed my story and that together we would have found out who was making the trouble. Perhaps he is right, but at the time I never thought of asking for help. I felt that the purpose of the dirty work was to hurt me and not the *New Hope* enterprise. I felt that a personal fight was my personal business.

For all that I had been able to find out or do, however, I might just as well have swallowed my pride. The things had kept on happening, while my reputation got worse until I had become, in the eyes of almost everybody connected with the *New Hope*, the worst kind of first officer.

And now there was this new thing. If people were already talking about possible traitors, I would have been willing to bet it wouldn't be long before my name was mentioned as the most likely candidate for the honor. I would have bet—and two hours later I would have won my bet.

I was walking along the main street, taking an urgent message from Captain Dole to Eben Fowler at the saltworks, when I noticed that a small boy was keeping me company on the opposite footpath. He would get a little way ahead, wait for me to come up, and then go ahead again, staring all the while. Finally he gathered up his courage.

"Spy!" cried this youth suddenly in a frightened treble. "Dirty turncoat!"

Before I could take a step in his direction he had fled out of sight around the corner of a house.

Spy and turncoat. Those weren't easy words to swallow, I can promise you, even though they came from a boy of ten. For the boy was obviously not speaking his own opinion but that of older people whose talk he must have overheard.

My state of mind just then was pretty bad, and was made worse by the fact that I realized Hope Allen and I were daily drifting further and further apart. Indeed it seemed that unless something happened very quickly to prevent it, she and I must soon come to a final parting of the ways.

It is a hard thing to try to explain what had happened between Hope and me. It is even hard to believe that it happened at all, when I think of the happiness we had found together, only a few weeks before in the warm stillness of Doane's Hollow. During that hour I had been sure that our newly found love would last. At that time I would cheerfully have risked everything on my belief that no circumstances, or chain of them, could ever shake our belief in one another.

That's how little I knew, then, about the uneven path of love.

I woke up a week or two later, when Hope's attitude towards me changed completely—without explanation or apparent reason—in the course of a single twenty-four hours. When I kissed her good night one evening it was with the knowledge that she and I were as close to being completely happy as two people can ever be. When I met her again the next afternoon I met a stranger. This new Hope let me hold her in my arms but seemed to shut me away from the intimate places of her mind. This new Hope and I were ill-at-ease and out of tune.

I wasn't particularly upset at first, knowing that girls were subject to strange moods and believing that, in a little while, things would be all right again. But time only made things worse. There were no more companionable silences between us. With me Hope was talkative, on edge with some sort of strange excitement, unnaturally gay. Sometimes I caught a look in her eyes that might have been one of fear. Sometimes I wondered if she was truly happy when we were together and if perhaps she was not faintly relieved when I said I must go. Finally I asked her point blank if something had happened—if something was wrong.

"Of course not, Jon. What a silly question!" Her tone was sharp. "What could be wrong?"

"I don't know," I replied uncomfortably. "It has seemed to me lately that you have been—strange."

"Strange!" She mocked my seriousness. "When you have known me longer you'll discover how strange I truly am!"

"I don't care. There's only one thing I really care about. Do you love me, Hope, as I love you? Do you truly care?"

"Must you ask?" She was suddenly somber. "Can you doubt?"

"I must ask. Lately—for some reason—I've wondered."

"Don't wonder, Jon." She looked at me full, and for a moment her eyes were tender in the old way. "I'm truly yours, and always will be. If I've seemed strange lately, it's been nothing but a mood. It will pass."

"And nothing is wrong?"

"Nothing!" Her voice was sharp again, and unnatural. "Nothing!"

But somehow I felt that she was not telling the truth, and was frightened.

6.

By this time the work of refitting the *New Hope* was nearly finished. Ezra Light was to set off for Tamoset to make final arrangements for smuggling in the powder we must have. It had been agreed to run the blockade on the first favorable night and tide after that powder had been stored aboard. The British maintained their newly established watch at the mouths of both harbors, and our militia, in turn, never took their eyes from the British. I had decided to spend my nights from then on aboard the *New*

Hope, as a self-appointed watchman. The fear of calamity hung over the town like a cloud. It was a period of lull, but all knew that an explosion of some kind was not far away.

Tempers were at such a razor edge in Trumet that it did not surprise me to hear, Friday evening as I walked morosely along the main street towards the shipyard, sounds of angry commotion coming from the taproom of the James Otis Tavern. There were shouts, scuffling noises, and the sound of an overturned chair. Then the big front door was flung open, and a man came flying out. He came so fast that, when his feet hit the ground, he lost his balance. He lurched, and staggered in my direction, finally falling heavily not a yard from where I stood.

The door of the James Otis had already been slammed shut once more, but I needed no light to help me identify the man at my feet. The rich odor of rum, and Seth Black, were always together.

"Get up, man." I had little love for the poor sot, but I reached down and helped him to his feet. "Are you hurt?"

I doubt if Seth even heard me. He shook off my hand and took a step back in the direction he had come, his fists raised above his head. "You—you skunks!" His voice was shaking but with anger and not grief. And if he had been drunk a few minutes before, as I had little doubt, he was fairly sobered, now, by his rage. "You can't do this to good old Seth Black! Not and get away with it, you can't! I'll git ye yet—just you wait and see if I don't!"

"There, there, Seth," I said soothingly, "take it easy. Don't mind the boys. They just think they're having fun."

"Fun!" Seth was still unconscious of me, and talking only to the men inside the James Otis. "I'll show ye what kind of fun you'll have! You'll be laughing on t'other side of your faces pretty quick when your darned *New Hope* is at the bottom of the harbor! Think you're smart—think you

98

know everything! Make fun of me, will ye, when I tell you that the traitor in this town ain't no Jonathan Bangs! Heave me out on the road, will ye, when I tell you you're barking up the wrong tree! Just wait a while you—you sculpins! Just wait!"

I, for one, didn't wait. I stepped forward, grabbing Seth by the collar of his ragged jacket, and shook him until his teeth should have rattled. "What's this? What's all this talk about traitors? Answer me, Seth! Speak quick, or I'll—"

"Jonathan! Jonathan Bangs!" Seth was aware of me now, all right, and if ever I saw a man half scared out of his wits he was that man. "Don't be mad, Mr. Bangs, please! *I* didn't call you no traitor—I swear I never. I'm your friend! It was them fellers in the tavern! They—"

"I know all about that," I said grimly. "I can guess what the loafers in the tavern are calling me. And I don't care. What I want to know—and what I'm going to find out— is what you meant when you just said they were barking up the wrong tree. If you think somebody besides me in this town is a turncoat I want to know his name! Spit it out, Seth!"

"I didn't mean nothing, Mr. Bangs." He was more scared than ever. "I was just mad, I guess, and talking wild. I didn't mean a thing I said. Please let me go, please. I ain't done you no harm. Why, I'm your friend!"

"Wait a minute." I did some pretty quick thinking in a very short time, but, while I was doing it, I kept a firm grip on the Black collar. Unless my guess was wrong, his recent talk hadn't been nonsense altogether. He knew some- thing or other, and what it was I intended to find out. Nor was I in any mood to care what means I used. "Don't get mixed up about things, Seth." I deliberately made my tone as soft and soothing as I possibly could. "You say you're my friend. Well, I'm *your* friend, too, and don't forget it. You won't come to any harm from me."

"Then let me go, Mr. Bangs." He wriggled feebly. "I'm in an awful hurry. I—I got to meet a man. Let me go!"

"In a minute, Seth. You and I have got to have a little talk first." I held his collar tighter than ever, but, from the way I spoke, butter wouldn't have melted in my mouth. "You and I are friends, and friends ought to help each other. They ought to stick together—particularly when they're both in trouble, the way we are. We're both getting a pretty dirty deal in Trumet, it strikes me. I'm being called a traitor, when I'm not one, and I don't like it. I guess you don't like being thrown out of the James Otis on your ear, either. I guess you'd like to get even."

"The skunks," said Seth bitterly. "Darned dirty skunks!"

"Then why not get even? How would you like for me to walk into that tavern right this minute and knock those skunks' heads together? I can do it. I can make them get down on their knees, and kiss your shoes, and beg you to let them up. How would you like that? I'll do it this minute, if you'll tell me one thing."

He shivered. "What is it?"

"Just tell me the name of this traitor you're talking about. Just say his name!"

"No! No, no, *no!*" Seth seemed to shrink inside his clothes. "Don't ask me nothing like that, Mr. Bangs. Don't! He'd kill me if I told! I wouldn't never live to see the sun come up! Maybe I won't live that long, anyhow. Maybe I've said too much already! Let me go!"

"Wait." I had no intention of setting him free. There was no pretense behind the fear in his voice. I realized now that he was actually afraid for his life. The interview, which to me had begun as a nuisance, had developed a deadly seriousness. I tried another tack. "Never mind who the man is, for now. Tell me what he's up to. Is the *New Hope* really in danger? What is going to happen? Is there anything I can do to help stop it? You'll tell me those things, if you're my friend—and if you're not a traitor yourself!"

"I ain't no traitor! That's one thing I *ain't*." He was still badly frightened, but he must have had a certain amount of courage, for he finally came closer to me, and spoke in a rapid, slurred whisper.

"I'm a fool for saying a word, but I'll tell you this much. There's a traitor in this town, all right, and it ain't you, neither. The real traitor's in cahoots with the British. Between 'em they mean no good to your vessel, though what 'tis they're scheming to do I don't know yet for sure. But this much *is* sure, Jonathan Bangs. Your *New Hope's* in danger—real danger. If you don't want her to go up in smoke or down to the harbor bottom you better be on watch every minute! Just watch. Don't tell nobody or trust nobody! Don't trust your nighest friends—or maybe even them that are closer'n friends!"

"What's that you're saying?" I went cold all over. "Be careful, if you want to stay in one piece. Are you hinting that—"

"No!" He was scared again, but this time of me. "I don't mean what you think. I ain't saying nothing about Miss Hope Allen. She's a real nice girl, and, whatever she's up to down at Shad Cove, you probably know already. But the traitor—"

"His name! Tell me his name!"

"Look!" Seth suddenly stretched out his arm and pointed over my shoulder. "Look there!"

Well, it was an old trick, but it worked. I turned my head, relaxing my grip on the fellow's collar. In another instant he had jerked free and had vanished into the dark, where I knew that he was safe from me.

I didn't try to find him. Instead of that, and instead of going down to stand guard at the shipyard, I struck off in another direction. My pace was so fast and my thoughts so tangled that it seemed no time at all before I found myself pausing for breath at the edge of the clearing where Hope Allen's house stood.

It was very clear in my mind, at last, what I must do, and do at once. I must see Hope and force her, no matter what, to explain herself. She must tell me the exact shape of the shadow that had come between us. She must explain the things that Black had just said, and hinted about her, as I held him by the collar in front of the tavern.

For, if I had frightened Seth Black in insisting that he tell me the name of his real or imagined traitor, Seth had in turn succeeded in scaring me. He had done it in spite of the fact that I knew he was an inveterate liar. It was possible, though I didn't believe it, that all his talk about a "traitor" had been a tangle of lies. But it was not possible that his hints about Hope had been invented or even embroidered. In view of the way they were sure to strike me, as Hope's lover, Seth could only have made them honestly, and by mistake.

Seth had told me that the bark was in danger, and warned me not to trust my friends, or even *those closer* than friends. By the last he was referring to Hope. He must have been—who else? Why did he warn me against her? What did he mean about Hope's doings at Shad Cove? She had not, as Seth suggested she must have, told me of those doings. She had not told me anything of any importance for several long weeks.

That was a state of things that I was determined to change immediately; yet I had no real fear, as I stood there, that Hope might be mixed up in anything actually bad. But the seeds of doubt must already have taken root in my mind or I wouldn't have done what I did a moment later, when the Allens' kitchen door opened, was softly shut again, and Hope herself came directly towards me across the grass.

Ordinarily I would have called to her at once, but this time I did not. Instead, I held my breath and stood still, hidden by the shadows of the pines. Hope did not see me, though she passed so close that I could almost have touched her. Almost running she was, as she started down the little-used wood road that led to Shad Cove, and an instant later, I followed.

I followed just as quietly as I could, and with the hope that she wouldn't hear me. I might have been following an enemy instead of the girl I was supposed to love. And if, as I half knew at the time, I was doing a thing to be ashamed of, it wasn't long before I got my punishment.

There is a large boulder that stands near the top of the bluff overlooking Shad Cove and the Bay, and that boulder was Hope's destination. When she came opposite it she left the road and took a step or two across the grass. Then she paused, and I heard her whistle one long low note. The whistle was answered, and I saw a tall figure appear from behind the rock and come in her direction. I heard the rumble of a man's voice, and the gentler sound of Hope's reply. I saw the two dim figures join and walk slowly back to the boulder. There they began a conversation that came to me only as a meaningless mutter.

Since I am as human and proud and jealous as anybody else, I will leave it to be imagined what I went through during the next half hour. So many explanations came to me, all of them unpleasant, for the thing that Hope was now doing, that it is a wonder I did not make a complete fool of myself, then and there, by confronting the pair and playing the injured lover. But somehow I managed to keep silent, though fuming, until the conversation finally ended.

I watched the two leave the boulder and walk to the

place where a narrow path wound down the face of the bluff to the Shad Cove shore. When they had followed it out of sight, I sneaked after them till I came to a spot where I could look down on the beach.

I don't know what I expected to see when I peered over the edge of the little sand cliff. But what I saw, in point of fact, made me forget everything that had happened earlier.

On the calm waters directly below lay a longboat. Her shape was vague, but I didn't need a light to know that she wasn't a local craft. She seemed to have a considerable crew, and I thought I could make out rows of oars on either side. Only her stern was touching the shore, and she was ready to shove off at a moment's notice.

As I stared, the man who had just been with Hope walked towards her swiftly and alone, across the narrow beach. "All right, Adams, cast off. Look alive, now!" His quietly spoken words were clear. "This might not be the healthiest place in the world for the like of you and me!"

"Aye, aye, sir!"

The tall man found his place in the stern sheets. The oars dipped silently into the water, and the longboat moved away. As quietly as a ghost it disappeared from sight.

I shook my head, as a man will when his eyes have seen something that his brain finds hard to believe. For there wasn't the faintest doubt in my mind that the longboat was British, or that she had come from the blockading fleet. She couldn't be anything else, yet the scene had been so unexpected and so quickly ended that it had seemed unreal. Then I heard the faint sounds of Hope's footsteps as she trudged back up the sandy path, and I knew that it had been real, indeed.

I waited for her at the top, blocking the way with my body. But before she had seen me, or walked into me, she halted. Almost within reach, she turned about to face the

Bay. If she was looking for the longboat, there was no sign of it. I heard her sigh.

"Don't worry, Hope. Your British officer is quite safe!" In the silence my voice sounded unnaturally loud and harsh. "And perhaps now you'll be willing to explain a few things to *me!*"

Hope didn't cry out. She merely turned so that I could see the outline of her white face. "Jon," she said faintly, at last. "Jon!"

7.

At last I have nearly finished the long voyage back to the place where I began my part of this tale, for I am not going to give the details of the quarrel that Hope and I had before we parted that evening.

I am sorry to have to recall it at all, for both of us will always be ashamed of it. For my part, I was as near to being out of my mind that night as I have ever been. Hope's case was not much better. The things that we said to each other were senseless, and bitter, and took us nowhere.

As I recall, I accused Hope of being either faithless or a traitor, or perhaps both. Hope raged at me for spying on her, and for damning her without giving her a chance to speak. She told me that, since I had done so, she wouldn't give me so much as a word of explanation. She said that I could think whatever I liked, and do whatever I chose.

"Since you're so easily convinced I haven't any common decency, Mr. Bangs, go right ahead and be convinced! If you believe I'm being paid for spy work by the British, keep right on believing it! What you're convinced of, or believe, is the least of my worries!"

"What I ought to do is plain enough." I was just as bitter as she was. "Ever since this morning, this whole town has been convinced that there's dirty work going on. They've been scared to death that something might happen to the

New Hope. What will they say when I tell them what I've just seen in Shad Cove? What will they think if you won't explain what you were doing talking with an officer from the British fleet? Do you expect me to protect you? Do you think I can be quiet about all this?"

"I don't expect anything! Go talk your precious head off, Jonathan Bangs! Go tell Trumet everything you can think of to tell about me! Do you think I care? Do you think I'm afraid of you, or what you may do? Well, think again. I'm not afraid of you, and I won't explain one single thing! Now hurry up and get on with your tattling! Only go!" She clenched her little fists. "Go, and don't come back as long as you live. I never want to see you again!"

Needless to say, I went. And needless to say I did no tattling, as Hope would have called it. When Captain Dole asked me at breakfast the next morning if everything was all right with the *New Hope*, I said yes. But I couldn't look him in the eye when I said it, for I knew what I was making myself by keeping still about what I had learned from Seth Black and what I had seen at Shad Cove. I also knew that even if Hope hated me as much as she said, and was as guilty as she seemed, she was still safe from me. I'd never be able to say the words that would get her into trouble as bad as that would be.

It was a blessed relief when the work required of me that day, which was a Saturday, was finished and I was allowed to be alone. Having no appetite, I did not even go near the Lights' house for supper. I stayed on the bark, pacing her decks with only my black thoughts for company, until the summer day had faded away into a dark, still night.

My mind was anywhere but on my job of guarding the privateer, and it was only by chance that I happened to discover the prowler at the storehouse door. My mind was far away, but my eyes were staring in the right direction when on the dock a shadow moved that should not have moved.

I have already written what happened after that. I have told how I failed to fire my pistol or to cry for help; how, instead, I followed the prowler to a far clearing in the pines where another man was waiting. There, on turning my head, I saw that the sky behind me had turned red with fire, and knew what the fire must mean. Then and there, for the first time in my life, I felt the real wish to kill.

That I did not kill was not because of any lack of desire. I surely had killing in mind when I burst from cover and fired my pistol. If my rush, afterwards, had enabled me to get my fingers on either of those men, I honestly believe that he would have been spending his final mortal minutes. But a bayberry bush prevented. It caught my foot and sent me sprawling to the pine needles, where I lay gasping while the sounds of flight dwindled and died away.

I could not have stayed there for a very long time, although it seemed forever before I could get back my breath. At length I scrambled to my feet and began a hasty search for my discarded pistol, thinking only that I must find it before running back to warn the town and to do what I could towards saving the *New Hope.*

But the pistol escaped me in the darkness, and the delay gave my thoughts time to calm themselves and to take some sort of order. Already I could hear hoarse shouting in the distance and the brazen clang of an alarm bell. That meant that the fire had already been discovered and that scores of men would be fighting it before I could get there to help. Perhaps my real job just now was not at the harbor but trying to capture the man, or men, who had wrecked Trumet's hopes. It was the thing I most wanted to do, at any rate.

But how? I gave up the search for my pistol and stood quite still for a minute of hurried thought. The man I had followed from the harbor was as surely the man who had set the fire as he was surely the man who had pestered me for weeks. But he had gotten away without giving me so much as a glimpse of his face. He had led me to this spot where another man had been waiting. What was the reason for their meeting, and who was the second man?

Suddenly I remembered the words the first man had cried as he pointed to the glow in the east. "You ask for proof, and I give it to you! She's aflame! Look!"

When those words were spoken I had listened to them with my ears and not my mind, but now their meaning seemed plain. In coming to this clearing, the man who had set the fire must have been reporting to his master—to the man on whose orders he had set it. He had probably come for his pay, and had pointed to the glowing sky as proof that the work was done. Who had the best reason for wishing the destruction of the privateer? Who would be most willing to pay for having her burned?

The answer to both of those questions was obviously the British, and in that case one of the two men I had just fired at was almost certainly a British agent. Perhaps he was an officer come secretly ashore to see that the work had been done and to pay for it. Perhaps, even now, he was hurrying to the place where a boat waited to take him out of danger.

That last thought had no more than flashed through my mind before I, too, was hurrying. A British longboat had landed in Shad Cove only the night before. Perhaps one was there now! If I ran every step of the way I might possibly get there ahead of the man the boat was waiting for. It was only a chance, but it seemed a bright one, so I set off at a gallop for Shad Cove.

A little later I had come for the second time in twenty-four hours to the great boulder, and was once more peering over the edge of the sand cliff near it. This night was much blacker than the previous one, but I was able to see enough to make me breathe a prayer of thanks. For the longboat was again lying at the water's edge, and I was in time. My guess had been a good one.

The waiting period that followed was long, and one of growing misgiving. For one thing, it didn't take me long to remember, after I had regained my breath and had started to make my plans, that I was unarmed. My pistol lay somewhere in the clearing a mile or two back. Even my sheath knife was not in its usual place, for I had loaned it to Captain Dole several days before and he had forgotten to return it. If, therefore, I was to subdue a man who was undoubtedly armed, I must do it with my bare hands.

That was bad enough, but when I came to look over the ground and to weigh my chances of getting even within stone's throw of that man my heart sank. The odds against me were at least two to one, for, if he approached his boat from either direction along the open beach, he would be quite safe. Unarmed I might be able to handle a lone man but hardly an entire boat's crew. The one egg that remained in my basket was that my man would approach by way of the steep path he had used the night before. And even that egg developed a slightly bad odor when I discovered that anyone coming to the top of the path must come across open ground that offered no trace of cover for ambush.

The plan that I finally adopted was not made from choice but from sheer necessity, since it was the only one possible. Its success demanded that my man take the path down the cliff and that he did not see me should I crouch in the scanty cover of some bushes on the beach at its lower end. If he granted me those two things it was possible that I might be able to knock him out as he passed with a single blow of the piece of stone I picked up for the purpose. Even then the blow had to be struck just so, for, if my man cried out, the nearby boat's crew would come quickly to his aid.

That this wild-eyed project would meet with no more success than it really deserved I was practically certain. But it was at least a project, and having made it I settled myself down to wait with a certain sense of relief. I was quite sure that the wait would be short, but the fact was that nearly two long hours passed before anything happened.

It must have been after midnight when the guard on the beach suddenly spoke sharply to his crew. "Quiet, men! I think he's coming—up the beach from the south. Look sharp, bos'n. Can you see something moving down there?"

There was a brief pause and then an answer. "Aye, sir. That must be the lieutenant—at last!"

Groaning, I stretched my stiff muscles to stand up in honor of a meeting and escape that I was helpless to prevent. I saw a dim cloaked figure come out of the darkness to join the guard, and was fighting an impulse to rush down upon them, armed as I was with nothing but my piece of stone. I was actually getting myself together for just that senseless bit of heroics when suddenly the quiet night was shattered by a loud, familiar voice from overhead.

"Let 'em have it, boys!" The voice was the voice of Major Bartlett, the militia captain. "Fire!"

There was a pause that lasted no longer than it takes an eye to wink. Then came the roar of a volley of musket fire.

I must have been nearly as stunned with surprise as the poor devils in the longboat, my brain not instantly responding to what my eyes saw. The water about the boat was briefly flecked with white where bullets struck. I heard the yell of a wounded man. I dimly saw the man who had been on guard leap for his place in the stern, his young voice calling the order to shove off. I saw the longboat move towards the open water. But most remarkable of all, I saw the man I had waited for being delivered straight into my hands.

For, instead of jumping to safety in the boat, he hesitated for a second and then turned in the opposite direction. The sound of the volley had hardly died from my ears when I saw him running straight up the beach to the place where I stood.

Something prevented me from bringing my stone down on his head as he came within reach. Instead, I flung myself bodily upon him, so that we both fell heavily to the sand.

"Take it easy, my friend! Your goose is cooked!"

But the words had not left my mouth before I realized my mistake. The body lying limply under mine was not a man's body, and even before she whispered my name I knew that I had captured no British spy but Hope Allen.

"Oh, Jon—Jon!"

Things happened much more rapidly after that than I will be able to tell them, but their sequence is very clear in my mind.

Hope and I had hardly untangled ourselves when the urgent voice of Major Bartlett again came loud and clear from overhead. "Never mind the boat, boys! Let her go. Grab that man they left behind. Get down on the beach and grab him!"

"Save me, Jon! Don't let them find me here!" Hope was tugging at my arm, her voice the most desperate I had ever heard. "I swear to you I'm not what you think! I'll explain it all to you—but don't let them find me! If you ever loved me, Jon, help me get away!"

I didn't think about the rights and wrongs of anything, because there wasn't time. I just knew that Hope was in trouble. I acted instinctively, half lifting and half dragging her to the bushes where I had been hidden. "Stay here!" I said roughly. "They don't know there are two of us down here. Stay there and don't move!"

Then I turned from her and ran straight up the path so fast that I had actually reached the top of it before I met four militiamen coming in the opposite direction. Their charge smashed me solidly to earth almost at the feet of Major Bartlett.

"So!" said the Major a few minutes later with satisfaction. "We had to wait a long time on the top of this bluff, but it looks as though it had been worth while. Just look, boys, what we got!"

The boys didn't have to look very hard, because there was a burning torch not a foot from my face. The glare hurt my eyes, but I couldn't shield them with my hands, for those were tied tightly behind my back.

"We got Jonathan Bangs," the Major continued grimly. "Mr. Bangs set fire to the ship he was supposed to be guarding, and then tried to get away to his friends, the British. But something slipped up, seems so. Yes! Well, I'm told that a hangman's noose slips up, too. For men like you, Mr. Bangs, it slips up a durn sight too tight for comfort! Bring him along, boys. He'll be a sight for sore eyes to the folks in Trumet!"

3

In which Jonathan bids Solomon Snow
good-by and meets
Lieutenant Jermyn Forsythe, R.N.

Told by

JONATHAN BANGS

I.

WHEN MAJOR BARTLETT and his militia took me back to Trumet that night, I was in a pretty bad situation, but at the time I did not realize just how bad it was. Instead of being greatly worried or frightened, I was almost cheerful.

For one thing, I knew that I had not done the things I was accused of. I had had nothing to do with setting fire to the *New Hope*, and when they pounced on me at Shad Cove I hadn't been trying to get away to the British fleet. My conscience was clear on those counts, and I was trusting enough to believe that my innocence would soon make itself known—one way or another.

A further cause for good spirits was the news that the *New Hope* had not been burned to the water line as I had feared. The militia boys, thinking that they were doing me a bad turn, lost no time in telling me about that. They said that a sudden change of wind had blown the flames from the blazing storehouse away from the vessel instead of towards her. That piece of luck, they gloated, had spoiled the traitor's plans and had saved our bark. The storehouse was gone, but there hadn't been much left in it that was of value.

"So you're not so tarnation smart, after all!" said the youth who was marching on my left, with satisfaction. "The *New Hope* ain't hurt a particle, Mr. Johnnie Bull Bangs, and you're headed straight for I don't know what.

I wouldn't be in your boots, this minute, for all the rum in Jamaicy! It'll take a bigger piece of luck than a shift of wind to keep you from getting your comeuppance, and don't you think 'twon't."

I didn't make any answer because there wasn't any use, but I still wasn't greatly concerned. I realized that the next hour or two would probably be unpleasant, since Trumet had had a bad scare and would think that I had been the cause of it. I would probably be in for a lot of hard looks and hard words, but scarcely anything more. For these people weren't hotheads. No matter how angry, they wouldn't do me any actual harm until I had had a hearing, and at such a hearing Hope Allen would come forward to clear me.

Yes, I was confident enough about that, for I had no doubts about Hope's coming to my rescue. Nor had I yet calmed down enough to ask myself disturbing questions about what she had been doing on the Shad Cove beach at midnight. I merely knew that she had begged me for help and that I had given it to her—at once and without argument. I was glad—and inside of me a little proud—that I had.

"Do you mind telling me where I'm being taken and why?" I asked the question of Major Bartlett, who was marching along just ahead of me as perky as a little bantam rooster. "I don't understand any of this business, remember. I don't know what you mean by calling me a traitor or by tying me up as though I'd been caught robbing a hen yard, either. Perhaps you'll tell me."

"Tell you!" The Major snorted with angry disgust. "If there's any telling to be done, Mr. Bangs, you're the one to be doing it. You might tell, for instance, what you were doing on the Shad Cove beach talking to the officer of a boat from an enemy's ship! That'll take a lot of plain and fancy telling unless I miss my guess!"

"Then you've missed your guess," I said calmly. "I wasn't doing anything I'm ashamed of down there. I'll explain myself all right, when the time comes—if I get a chance."

"You'll get a chance," said the Major shortly. "You'll get more chance than you deserve and get it quick. I sent one of the boys ahead with the word that we're bringing you in, and unless I'm way off the mark there'll be folks waiting for you at the Town House. You can tell your story there, Mr. Bangs, and, if tempers aren't any better than they were a couple of hours ago, it had better be a mighty good one!"

The Major was right. Late at night as it was, the crowd waiting for me in Trumet seemed to consist of every grown-up man in the town, and the reception it gave me sent a tiny chill crawling down my back. I don't mean that the men shouted or threw stones or even called names when they saw me. They acted just the other way around, at first—quiet and grim and as businesslike as though they knew just what they wanted to do and how they wanted to do it.

When I was hustled into the room where the town meetings are held, there was a little rumble of male voices and then quiet. Faces, most of them belonging to people that I knew, turned to stare, but the faces weren't friendly or even familiar. I tried to tell myself that it was their being covered with black streaks of soot from the fire that made the faces seem so strange and forbidding, but I knew better.

Major Bartlett marched up front to where the Council was seated back of a long table. When he halted, his heels clicked together as though he were the commander of regular troops instead of a band of untrained country militia. His words, however, weren't very military.

"I'm glad my word got here before you men had turned in for the night," said the Major in his harsh voice, "because I've brought you a present that'll make you sleep

117

easier. The present's name is Jonathan Bangs, and if you ask him polite enough he might be able to tell you some interesting things. Maybe he'll tell you something about who started that fire down at the harbor! Maybe he'll tell you why he was being so chummy with a British longboat on the Shad Cove beach a little while back when we laid him by his traitor's heels!"

"Wait a minute, Major!" Captain Dole pushed back his chair and stood leaning across the table. His linen was soiled, there was a big burn on the shoulder of his blue coat, and his dirty face was strained and tired. "I know you won't take it the wrong way if I ask you to be very careful what you say, just this minute, and just how you say it. All of us in this room have had a pretty tough time since supper, and maybe our judgment and tempers aren't quite as calm as they might be. If we don't watch out we may say things, and do things, we'll be sorry for later."

"All I'm doing is telling the truth." The Major bristled. "You can't blame me if that truth hurts somebody. And I won't be sorry later, either—not having a taste for crying over turncoats!"

"I'm no turncoat or anything like it." I looked straight at Captain Dole, but I spoke loud enough so that all could hear. "I don't blame the Major for thinking what he does, but it's all a mistake."

"If you didn't set the fire, who did?"

The angry question was shouted from somewhere in the body of the hall, to be followed by others in rapid succession.

"Who told the British about our bark? Who sold us out?"

"What kind of a watchman do you make yourself out to be?"

"Where in Tophet were you when the blaze broke out?"

"Why didn't you holler for help?"

"How'd you like a dose of tar and feathers?"

"Where were you all the time the rest of us were fighting the fire?"

"Don't ask him that, boys! Ask me, and I'll tell you!" The Major had turned about and in his excitement was practically hopping up and down. "I'll tell you where the scut was! He was running like a rat for the British longboat that was supposed to take him safe away! He'd be out there with his friends now if it wasn't for my boys. They damn near blew that English craft clean out of the water, and they scared Johnnie Bull Bangs so bad that he ran right square into their hands. If Bangs isn't a turncoat, then I'm a Chinaman! Hanging's too good for him!"

Almost anything might have happened after that, for the crowd was in a mood to welcome almost any excuse for violence. The men were on their feet, and most of them were shouting unpleasant suggestions as to how I should be rewarded for my patriotism, or lack of it. Those nearest me seemed to be coming nearer because of pressure from behind. I strained to free my bound wrists so as to be a little less helpless, and out of the corner of my eye saw Captain Dole move as though to come to my side. It looked like real trouble for a moment, but then Mr. Eben Fowler made himself known.

"Quiet! Don't be fools! Silence!"

It was surprise, I think, more than anything else, that made the men forget me for the moment and that saved my skin. For Eben Fowler, owner of the town's largest saltworks, was the last man in the room who could be expected to bellow in that fashion. Fowler was a quiet, reserved man whose influence was due to his business ability and not to his lung power. As a matter of fact, he had a reputation for never raising his voice, even in the most trying of circumstances. Yet suddenly here he was standing on his chair and shouting like a bucko mate. The crowd gaped at him in astonishment, and tension relaxed.

"I'm sorry, gentlemen." When the room had quieted, Fowler got down from his chair and straightened the set of his coat with a hint of embarrassment. "I usually don't make quite so much noise, but perhaps it's better to have one of us make a fool of himself than to have all of us do it. Captain Dole was right when he said that we must be careful what we say and do tonight if we don't want to be sorry later. We'll surely be sorry if we act like a mob instead of like sane citizens. A criminal, no matter how guilty, is entitled to a fair trial. I suggest that we hear what Major Bartlett has to tell us. After that, Bangs can say whatever he thinks will do him the most good. After *that* we can act with a clear conscience."

"It won't take long for me to speak my piece." The general murmur of assent had hardly died down before Major Bartlett took the floor. "When the fire started my boys were doing their regular turn of guard duty near Billfish Creek and so forth, but I wasn't with them. As Squire Bailey can tell you, the pair of us were at his house, making final plans for defending this town if the Redcoats should send a raiding party. We both heard the alarm bell go, which goes to show I'm not as deaf as some folks like to make out. We both heard it, together, and—"

"Hold on a minute, Major." Henry Allen was leaning across the Council table with his long arm stretched out and the lock of black hair falling over his eyes. "I'm sorry to shove my oar in like this, but I just had an idea that seems to me sense. If you say your say first, Major, there's nothing to stop Bangs from listening. And then, if he's smart as he thinks he is, he'll see to it that his lies jibe enough with the truth to sound more like it. Why not have him spin *his* yarn first—before he can make it fit with the others?"

"That's a good idea, Henry." Captain Weeks jerked his gray head in strong agreement. "It's fair, too. If Mr. Bangs is telling the truth, he hasn't got anything to be afraid of."

"That's perfectly agreeable to me." I had no choice but to speak with a great deal more confidence than I felt. "So long as you'll let me tell my side of this business, I don't care when I tell it."

"That's the stuff, Jonathan!" There was relief in Captain Dole's voice. "If you talk first, we'll get this mixup straightened out in a hurry, and that's what we all want. That and a little sleep."

"All right, Bangs. Give us your story." Eben Fowler was watching me closely. "Tell us everything you've done from supper time up till now. And, if you're wise, you'll take my advice. Don't lie."

That was just the thing that gave me a funny feeling in the pit of my stomach as I took a deep breath and began to speak. I knew that I had to lie, and I knew myself to be a very poor liar.

The beginning wasn't so bad because I didn't have to use my imagination. I just told the exact truth the way things had happened from the time in the late afternoon when I began my watch at the *New Hope* up to where I fired my pistol at the two men in the clearing near Doane's Hollow. It was plain sailing so far, with nobody in the hall interrupting me with so much as a cough. But I knew that breakers lay dead ahead, and I instinctively paused to get myself together before tackling them.

In the brief silence, Henry Allen, behind the Council table, suddenly laughed. "That's about as likely a yarn as ever I heard!" He jerked his head to get the lock of hair out of his eyes and turned to me. "According to your tell, you saw somebody sneaking around the storehouse where he hadn't ought to be. Why didn't you holler at him? Why didn't you give the alarm? Why didn't you tackle him, then and there, instead of trailing him miles, more or less, out into the bushes? Why did you let him get away?"

"I don't know." I shrugged, suddenly very tired. "I don't know why I didn't do a lot of things. Unless it was because—"

"Unless it was because the whole thing is a pack of lies!" Allen glared at me with angry contempt. "Which it is. Any fool can tell that!"

"Maybe a fool can tell it." I glared back at him. "A fool doesn't know the truth when he hears it!"

Eben Fowler stopped our bickering by slapping his open hand sharply on the table top. "May I make a suggestion, Captain Jeremiah? This sort of thing doesn't get us anywhere. Let Bangs get back to his story; but let him answer me one question first. Bangs, you say you followed a man to Doane's Hollow. Have you any idea who that man might be? Did you get a glimpse of his face? Did you recognize his walk? How about his voice?"

I shook my head. "It was dark, and I couldn't come very near. His voice was just a man's voice. All I know about him was that he wasn't a small man. I couldn't even swear to that, I suppose. It was pitch dark, I tell you."

"I see." Fowler smiled politely but in a way I didn't like. "How about the second man? I suppose you haven't any notion who he might have been, either. No? Too bad. You seem to have had bad luck." He looked meaningly at the others at the table. "Well, never mind. Get on with whatever else you have to say."

"He's got plenty to say," remarked Major Bartlett grimly. "The fire started about nine-thirty or so, and it was after midnight when we picked him up on the Shad Cove beach. He's got to tell everything he did in between and tell it mighty careful. Can't say I envy him the job!"

Well, I wasn't looking forward to that job, either, now that I was really faced with it. I realized for the first time just how clever Henry Allen had been. If he had not prevented Major Bartlett from telling his story first, I would now have something to steer by. As it was, I was like a sailor in shoal, uncharted waters, except that I did not have the sailor's privilege of dropping anchor. I had to pick a course and run it blindly, trusting to pure luck that I didn't run hard aground.

My beginning was, I still think, a stroke of inspiration, for I said that when I tripped over the bayberry bush in the clearing near Doane's Hollow, I had been knocked senseless by the fall. "I must," I told them, marveling to myself at the brilliance of the idea, "have hit my head on a stone, or a stump, or something like that. Anyhow I was unconscious."

"For how long?" snapped Captain Elnathan Berry. "How long was it before you came to?"

"Bet you I can answer that." Henry Allen laughed sarcastically. "That bump on the head laid him out for a full couple of hours. When he came to, he couldn't have come more than half way, for, instead of racing to the harbor to help us fight the fire, he went barging off in t'other direction. When he'd come to the other half there he was down at Shad Cove with the militia tying him up and calling him naughty names! That's the way 'twas, of course. Just as easy and simple and innocent as falling out of bed! Sartin! Of course! Bah!"

Captain Jeremiah was banging for order, but it was Squire Bailey who put a stop to the general laughter and uproar. "If you hit your head hard enough to get knocked out, Jonathan," he said quietly, "you ought to have a cut or a bump to show for it, I should think. Where's the bump?"

Luck was with me then, for I was able to find, and present for inspection, a satisfactory lump on the right side of my skull under the hair. I hadn't the faintest idea when, during my adventures of the night, I had received it, and I did not care. All that I knew was that I was trembling a little from the narrowness of my escape and that I felt a warm glow of hope. If things kept going the way they were, I might still come safely to port.

I went on with my yarn.

To the tune of more sarcastic laughter from Henry Allen I said that I did not know how long I had been unconscious in the clearing; that when I came to I decided to hunt for the two men I had just shot at. How long did I hunt for them? I couldn't say, exactly. I just thought it was my job to hunt. Where did I hunt? Why, everywhere. I searched the woods and the fields until I finally came to the Bay shore.

"Didn't I tell you?" asked Allen in disgust. "Sure and sartin! All 'twas he just took a nap and woke up at Shad Cove! Sound sleeper, this fellow. Ha, ha!"

I looked Henry in the eyes, hating him just then even if he was Hope's father. "I have told you how I happened to take that 'nap,' Mr. Allen, and what I did afterwards. It is a fact that my hunt finally took me to Shad Cove. I came to the bluff at the edge of it and saw a boat down on the shore. I didn't know it was British. I just knew it was a boat."

"Where?" said Major Bartlett with sudden sharpness. "Where were you on the bluff?"

"Right above where the boat was beached. Not very far from that big boulder by the path."

"So." The Major took a step nearer. "What time of night was that?"

"I told you I didn't know the time. I'd been knocked out."

"All right, all right! What did you do then?"

"I went down the path to see what the boat was. It was so dark that when I crossed the beach I walked right into a man who was standing there. And that was a bad mistake

124

because the man was a British naval officer! He pushed a pistol into my belly and took me prisoner. Then—"

"What then?"

I shrugged, glad that my stint of story telling had come to an end at last. "Then your militia fired from the top of the bluff. The British officer ran one direction, and I ran the other. You know the rest."

"But, Major! Major Bartlett!"

It was one of my militia guards who had cried out in sudden excitement. He stepped forward and grabbed his officer by the arm, only to find himself pushed rudely away. "You keep out of this, Warren! Step back, and don't speak till you're spoken to. I'll handle this!"

The Major came over to me and looked me in the face, which is to say that he tilted back his head. "So that's your story, Mr. Bangs," he said very softly for him. "Well, well! Just let me see if I get it exactly straight. You saw the boat at the edge of Shad Cove from the edge of the bluff a little way from the big boulder. Then you walked straight down the path to the beach and into the hands of a British officer. He had no sooner taken you prisoner at pistol point than my militia boys fired their volley. Is that the way it was, Mr. Bangs?"

I nodded dumbly, sensing trouble but not knowing how it would come.

"All right!" The Major turned to face the Council table. "Bangs has told his yarn, gentlemen, and now I'll tell mine! It won't take long. At half-past ten tonight one of my patrol spotted that British longboat in Shad Cove and was smart enough not to scare it off. He reported to me, and twenty minutes later I and a dozen of my men were posted on the top of that bluff by Shad Cove. The British didn't know we were there, and that suited me. We knew they were waiting for somebody, and whoever it was was the one we wanted to catch. We waited for more than an hour, and now here's the thing that's important. Bangs says he saw that boat from the top of the same bluff. Funny thing he didn't see us or we see him! He says he walked down the path to the beach. Well, that's a funny thing, too. Why? Why, because I'd been planted right square in the middle of that path for a whole hour! If he used that path when he says he did, he walked right through me— and I didn't feel a thing! Not a thing, and that's the gospel truth! If Bangs isn't a liar then I must be one. And if he isn't a sneaking traitor, too, then— Well, then what is he?"

There was uproar behind me at that, but I hardly listened. All I could do was look at the sick, bewildered expression on Captain Dole's face. I'd like, some day, to be able to forget the way he looked.

2.

The rest of what was left of that night, I was lucky enough to spend in the lockup at the back of the Town House. And I mean just what I say. I was lucky. For, if more than half of the men who were at the Town House had had their way, after Major Bartlett exposed me as a liar, I'd have spent it a lot less comfortably.

And the odd thing is that I couldn't have blamed them if they had decided to take me out then and there for punishment. They had provocation enough, and they had what seemed to be conclusive proof of my guilt. They had given me a fair trial, and during it I had damned myself with my own clumsy lies. This was war time, remember, when the slow processes of law are more often ignored than followed.

But the wind, together with the day of the week, pulled me out of as bad a hole as I ever want to be in. If the breeze of the preceding evening had not suddenly changed from west to east, the *New Hope* would have gone up in smoke, and tempers would have been just that much worse than they were. They would have been enough worse so that my goose would have been royally cooked. That same goose might have sizzled, anyhow, if I had made my dismal attempt at telling fairy stories a couple of hours earlier than I actually did.

For it was Saturday night when the fire started at the storehouse, but by the time I had been captured, brought in, and given my hearing, it was Saturday night no longer. It was Sunday morning!

The great majority of the men in the hall at the Town House were pious, church-going, and God-fearing, but, if a tar-and-feather or a hanging party had been decided upon, I doubt if one of them would ever have realized that he was breaking the Sabbath. The Reverend Ichabod Samuels was the important exception. As was expected from the minister of the First Church, he was sternly devout, preaching and enforcing to the best of his ability, not only the spirit, but the letter of the Scriptures.

It was he who rose from his place and put a swift end to the hot argument as to whether I should be boiled in oil, so to speak, or thrown to the lions. In his booming pulpit tones he told the men of Trumet that they were thinking of doing a violent and, perhaps, a lawless thing upon the one day of the week that belonged to the Lord alone. He did not argue against such an act. He merely dwelt at some length on the punishment that would surely come to those who thus violated the Sabbath, and then flatly forbade the said breaking. Needless to say, he was obeyed.

And so I owed my good health to a whim of the evening breeze and to an accident of the calendar. There is doubtless a very fine moral to be drawn from this if I only had the wit to imagine what it could be.

Before I was led away to my cell, reserved heretofore for the likes of Seth Black, I asked if I might be allowed to have a word alone with Captain Dole. But that was instantly refused, with Henry Allen expressing what was probably the general feeling.

"Isaiah Dole we've known for a long time," said Henry, his black eyes smouldering, "and we trust him. He hasn't given us any reason not to trust him. Not yet. On the other hand, he brought you to Trumet, and, from the way he stuck up for you when the rest of us began to see what kind of a critter you are, it seems that he is still your friend. That being the case, he might let friendship make him forget what's right and proper. We'll save him from that, just the way we'll save you in the lockup till the Sabbath is over. No, Johnnie Bangs, if I have my way you can't talk to Captain Dole alone. If you've got anything to say to him, say it out in front of all hands."

I looked at the Captain and forced myself to keep on looking in spite of the expression on his tired face. "I'm not guilty of this thing, Captain. I swear it before God. Things look bad, but—"

There wasn't anger in his eyes as he looked at me. It was plain, nevertheless, that he was puzzled and hurt and disappointed. "Yes, Jonathan, things do look bad enough. It beats me, that's a fact. *I* can't make it out."

"You'll understand tomorrow," I told him doggedly. "Don't damn me for good before tomorrow night. Please try to have faith in me that much longer."

"Take him away." It was Eben Fowler who gave the order, although he had no especial right to do so. "They say the devil can quote Scripture, so I suppose a lying hypocrite may be expected to preach faith. Take him out before we forget it *is* the Lord's Day."

It wasn't bad in the lockup, but perhaps that was because I was in a mood to be grateful for small favors such as an unstretched neck and a skin free from black tar and white feathers. The cell surely wasn't over-large, being about as long and wide as it was high. It had a small, heavily barred window at one end and a strong door at the other. Its furnishings consisted of a bucket in one corner, a rickety stool in another, and a wooden bunk that was covered with a blanket which had probably been clean a long time ago.

When the door slammed behind me I realized all at once how thoroughly done in I was, both in mind and body. I knew at the same time that I had no hope of sleep, since a thousand thoughts were churning around in my head like so many bees in a hive. That being the case, I merely took off my shoes before spreading the upper six feet of myself on the surface of my hard bed. My remaining few inches stuck out over the bunk's end, but that was no new experience for them or for me.

When I closed my eyes I saw big rings of bright light that contracted slowly into pin points and vanished, only to be replaced by others. I was watching them when I fell into a deep and dreamless sleep.

It was broad daylight before I woke, and the sun was much higher in the sky than it usually was when I climbed out of my comfortable bed at Ezra Light's house. I was stiff and sore, and ached in an extraordinary number of places at the same time, but my spirits were much better. It seemed as though all the things that had happened the night before must have been part of a bad dream. But, even if they were true, there was surely much more reason for encouragement than I had been able to believe when they locked me in. After all, the sun still shone, and the *New Hope* lay unharmed at her dock. And even if I stood convicted and condemned as a turncoat, my real danger must be past. Before very long Hope must surely hear from her father about the trouble I was in. She would surely come forward to save me. Yes, I told myself, before noon I would be walking the streets of Trumet, a free man.

Which shows what a few hours' sleep can do, even for a prisoner in a town lockup.

But the time dragged, and, although it was not yet eight, it seemed much later when I heard footsteps in the passage outside. I was on my feet when the door opened, half expecting to see Hope. Instead, Captain Dole, Eben Fowler, and Henry Allen walked in. From their expressions it didn't seem as though they were bringing me good news.

They were all grim, but Captain Dole was perhaps the grimmest of all. He hung back of the others by a step or so, staring at me with peculiar intentness. I saw him shake his head quickly, from side to side, as though he were trying to give me some kind of warning.

"Good morning, gentlemen." I didn't want them to think that I was afraid or even worried. "Have you found out yet that you've jailed the wrong man? Has anything happened since last night? Is there any news?"

"No." Henry Allen's expression did not relax at all. "There ain't any news, and won't be till tomorrow morning, when we have a free hand to attend to you!"

"That's where you're wrong." I looked him square in the eyes and spoke confidently. "Something will happen today, just wait and see. By night I'll be out of here, and you'll be asking my pardon for thinking a lot of things about me that aren't true."

"Bosh!" Allen laughed shortly. "More big talk, Bangs, that's all that is. You had one fine piece of luck last night, but you won't have another. You're going to get what's coming to you, just as sure as tomorrow's Monday!"

"Mr. Allen is right, Bangs." Eben Fowler's voice was just as neat and precise as he was himself in his black Sunday clothes. "You tripped yourself up with your own lies and impossible excuses, and every man in that Town House heard you do it. We are all certain that you are in the British pay, that you set the fire last night and then tried

130

to get safely away to your paymasters. It isn't a case of are you a double-dealer or aren't you, because that's all settled. If you're smart and know what is good for you, you'll give up and confess. I can't promise anything, mind you, but there is just a chance that, if you tell the three of us the whole truth, you may get off lighter than you will if you don't."

I shook my head. "I haven't anything to say."

"Wait a minute, Jonathan." Captain Dole stepped forward. "You know well enough that I'm your friend. And, being your friend, I want you to know that I agree with Eben in what he has just said. I ask you to tell us the truth—the whole truth. If you'll do that, I'll work my hardest to get you out of this mess as—well, as easy for you as I can. And I may still have a few backers left in Trumet, even after everything that's happened."

I hated to do it, but I had to shake my head. "I'm sorry, Captain, but it's no use. I haven't done anything. My hands are clean."

He looked at me then as though he thought I had gone crazy. "Boy, boy," he said, sharply, "don't start that again. It is as plain as the sun that you've been lying. Why, they caught you at it flat-footed last night. You know they did."

I shrugged. "All I know is that talking has made enough trouble for me, already. I'm through with it except to tell you again that I'm no traitor. I'm as honest and loyal as the rest of you. That's the truth, and, what's more, you and everybody else in Trumet will know it's the truth before this day is over."

"We're just wasting our time. This critter is as pig-headed as he is crooked!" Henry Allen turned to Captain Dole. "Go ahead, Isaiah, and tell him about that note in your pocket. Tell him about that and see what he says."

Captain Dole seemed to be rather taken aback. He didn't

like it, I could see, but he finally told me about the note he had had from Seth Black the night before—the note warning him of a double-dealer in the town and of danger to the *New Hope*. "The main thing in that piece of writing," said the Captain slowly, "was this: Seth said that he knew the fellow's name. He asked me to come to his shanty right away, so's he could tell it to me."

"You went, of course!" I was excited, for this was help from a quarter that I should have thought of but had entirely forgotten. "What did Seth say?"

"He wasn't home." Captain Dole shook his head. "His shanty door was open, but he wasn't there. Then I saw the light of the fire in the sky, and I forgot all about him and ran."

"But you've seen him since! You must have! What does he say? Who did he say the traitor was?"

Captain Dole didn't answer, for Henry Allen cut in ahead of him. "We've seen Seth, all right," he declared, "and he's told us everything we need to know!"

"Wonderful!" I could have shouted in my relief. "Who did he accuse?"

Captain Dole was scowling. He swung around to face Allen, but again Allen spoke first. "Who do you *think?*" he sneered.

The tone of his voice made me understand what he was driving at. I put an unbelieving finger on my chest. "You aren't trying to say that he named *me!*"

"Who else would he be liable to name?"

I took a long look at Allen and another at Fowler. Then I put back my head and laughed. *"You're* lying now! The whole business is an out-and-out lie!"

"Be careful, you scut!"

"I'm sick and tired of being careful, Allen!" I was really angry now, which is a thing that is too rare with me. "And I'm sick and tired of you! You've been riding me as though I were your worst enemy, and I've had enough. I tell you, you're lying! If Seth Black accuses me, why don't you bring him in here and have him do it to my face? Why not? Because you don't even know where he is! You've made up this yarn just to try to scare me into confessing something I didn't do!"

"That's the way I like to hear you talk, Jonathan," vowed Captain Dole. "I didn't know they were going to try this on you. As a matter of fact, nobody's seen hide nor hair of Seth Black since before supper last night. He's dropped clean out of sight—seems so."

"Then find him!" My urgency made me forget my anger. "If you are my friend, Captain Dole, you'll find Seth Black if it's the last thing you do!"

There was a new gleam in the Captain's eye. "I'll try, Jonathan, I'll promise you that. It's just what is going to be done. I'll do my level best. And, if I do find him, you aren't afraid of what he might say?"

"Afraid?" I laughed again. "See here, Captain Dole, if Seth Black puts a name to the scamp who is working against us that name won't be mine. I know what I'm saying because *I* had a talk with Seth Black in front of the James Otis only a couple of nights ago! Listen!"

They listened while I told them, almost word for word, about my talk with Seth Black. As I went along it seemed to me that Eben Fowler and Henry Allen grew more and more long in face, while Captain Dole became more cheerful. When I had finished, the Captain looked at his two companions with a new briskness.

"This changes things a little, don't you think so, boys? Jonathan doesn't seem to be afraid of what Seth Black may say. He's asked me to find him just as quick as I can, and I believe he means it. That's the last thing he'd want if Seth knows anything against him. If that was the case, he'd pray that Seth was on the bottom of the Bay and that he would stay there."

"Maybe," said Eben Fowler slowly and coldly. "And maybe the bottom of the Bay is just where Seth is!"

"What?" Henry Allen stared at Eben. "What are you driving at, Eb?"

"Why, nothing, I suppose." Fowler shrugged. "Only it struck me that, maybe, Bangs isn't afraid of Black because he knows that Seth won't do any more talking—ever. Maybe Seth knew too much, and Bangs knew he knew it— so— Just an idea, that's all. I'm not accusing him."

"The devil you're not!" I doubled up my fists. "So now I'm a killer as well as all the rest! Why, you—"

"There, there, Jonathan." Captain Dole quickly stepped between me and the other two men. "Hush! Eben didn't really mean anything like that, of course. Don't get excited. Keep your head. That's what we've all got to do."

"All right, Captain Dole." I swallowed hard. "I'll behave, but you'd better tell these fellows to watch their tongues! I've had about all I can stand. Just to keep things straight, I'll remark that I don't know anything about Seth Black. I don't know why he's gone or where he is, and I'm asking you to find him just as quick as you can. Don't do it for my sake because I don't need Seth Black to get me out of this mess. Somebody—something else will do that. Find Black for the sake of the *New Hope*, that's all. You may not believe me, but the man Trumet ought to be scared of isn't in this cell! He's still loose, and while he's loose the bark isn't safe for a second, or our powder-running plans, either! Ask Seth! Promise me that you'll find Seth Black!"

Captain Dole promised, and also promised that I'd be told the minute Seth turned up. After that the three men left me and went about their business. My trouble was that I had no business. All I could do was trudge back and forth in my little coop, and think—and wait.

Waiting is never an easy or an enjoyable job, no matter if the one who is waiting is as easy-going as I am. Waiting makes every minute stretch into an hour and makes every hour seem forever. My waiting that day was something I don't like to think about, because it was waiting that didn't end anywhere.

At first I expected Hope to come to me at any moment. At each faint sound that seeped through the thick cell door my heart jumped, and I strained my ears to hear her footstep or her voice. But the hours dragged by, and nothing happened. I was merely impatient in the beginning, but, by and by, impatience turned into anxiety and worry. Was Hope ill or injured? Had her father locked her in her room so that she couldn't get out of the house? Was it possible that she didn't care enough to be bothered about what happened to me? Was she so selfish that she didn't know even the feeling of ordinary gratitude? It seemed so, it truly did. Could it be that she was mixed up in this mess so deeply that she couldn't help me without getting herself into bad trouble?

The path that my feelings took can be imagined. Doubt finally turned into anger, and anger into bitterness.

By the time that the long slanting rays of the sun told me that it was late afternoon, I was coldly resigned to the knowledge that I had been sold out by Hope and that Captain Dole had failed me by not finding Seth. I also had a clear knowledge of what I must do.

If I stayed in this cell until the following morning I would be brought again before the Council, which would show me short mercy. If I was to confront Hope and to drag from Seth Black whatever he might know, there was only one thing to do. I must get out of that lockup, somehow or other.

I was determined to do it, and in the small dark hours of Monday morning I succeeded. It was about four-thirty, as

135

near as I could guess, when I walked unnoticed out of the Town House.

I was a fugitive, but free.

3.

The way of my jail break was no cause for pride. As a matter of fact, I felt a certain amount of pity for jolly old Solomon Snow, my guardian appointed for the night, who lay snoring in a blissful drunken sleep on the bunk inside my locked cell. Solomon was undoubtedly in for a bad time with the Council the next morning, but it was my guess that they would go a lot easier on him than on me.

Solomon's trouble was that he had an understanding heart and a fondness for rum, whereas a good jailer should have neither.

To Solomon's way of thinking it was only Christian charity to procure rum for the easing of what he called my few remaining hours in this vale of tears, and only common civility to bear me company in soaking it up. Nor had he any way of knowing that, each time we tipped our mugs, the water in mine was only faintly colored while the rum in his remained undiluted.

I must say that it took a prodigious amount of both spirits and time to bring Solomon Snow to the desired state. We began our little party in my cell soon after midnight, but it was nearly four hours and more than a full quart later before I could roll his fat little body onto my bunk with any feeling of assurance that it would stay there until morning.

Even then he managed briefly to open his pale, un-focussed blue eyes and to, smile up at me with infinite sadness. "You're a good frien', Jonathan," he whispered. "A fine frien'. I guess likely—when they feather you—or tar 'n' hang you—I'll cry, I guess likely." By way of proof he shed a few tears in advance.

"There, there." I poured out what little was left of the rum in a cup and held it to his lips. "Drink this. It'll cure your sorrows."

Most of the stuff dribbled down the folds of his triple chin, but some found the mark. He hiccoughed violently, closed his eyes, and began to snore.

I covered him with the ragged blanket, took the key from his pocket, locked the cell door from the outside, and tiptoed out of the deserted Town House. The main street was dark and empty, but I could take no chances. I left it immediately, at a fast dog trot, in the direction of the fields and pine groves. Perhaps it was my imagination, but I thought that even from this distance I could still hear the comforting rumble of Solomon's snores.

Seth Black's shanty was my first port of call, but the trip down to the Bay shore was wasted. The shanty was empty, as I should have expected, and its emptiness made me realize the difficulty of the job I had set for myself. If Seth was lying somewhere in the open, drunk or dead, I could not search for him in the daylight, for then I would myself be hunted. In the dark, my chances of stumbling across him would be small, indeed. And, if Seth was well and able to navigate, Captain Dole would certainly come up with him before I did.

I cursed softly, knowing that I was completely at a loose end and knowing that I must stay that way for some hours. The second part of my program called for my having a few words with Hope Allen, and I couldn't have those until her father had had his morning meal and had left for the village and the shipyard.

The sensible thing, meanwhile, of course, was for me to find a dry place somewhere in the bushes and to get some sleep. But somehow, tired as I was, I could not bring myself to lie down or even to stay in one place. My stirred-up state of mind demanded that I keep going, so I spent what was left of the night hours wandering the woods with one eye out for Seth Black and the other for patrolling militia.

I saw neither, and the damp gray dawn found me in a thicket of scrub oaks near Hornpout Pond.

Between me and the pond's northern edge lay a stretch of brown salt meadow, covered now with an uneasy blanket of waist-high, cold gray mist. And as I peered across its lonely expanse I saw, in the strengthening light, a flock of circling black crows.

At any other time I would not have given those common birds more than a passing glance, but under the circumstances their actions caught my instant attention. They were hovering and dipping and jawing at one another in a way that showed more than ordinary interest in something in the marsh directly below. Something or somebody was disturbing them. Who could be in this spot at this hour? I thought of Seth Black. At last accounts he hadn't been located. Was it possible that he was hiding, as I was myself?

I set off to find out, with my boots squashing noisily in the wet marsh, and the mist curling weirdly about my legs. The crows were my guide, and the crows led me—just as they later led Captain Dole—to the same spot.

Seth Black was there, sure enough.

He lay in the tall grass and among the cattail flags. He was half in and half out of the shallow water, and something about his sprawled position told me that he was neither asleep nor in a drunken stupor. From where I stood, on a dry hummock above, I could see that Seth had had his last tot of rum at the James Otis. Or anywhere else.

He was dead and had been dead for some time.

I don't remember feeling horror or pity or any of the things I normally would have felt. Perhaps that was because I had reached a state where my emotions were numb, or perhaps it was because I had half come to expect that something like this had happened. In any event, I was quite calm as I jumped down the little bank and bent over the body.

Then I sucked in my breath.

There was an ugly stab wound at the base of Seth's neck, in the back. I didn't need a surgeon to tell me that it had been the cause of his death or that it had been made with a broad-bladed knife, struck when his back was turned. I couldn't find the weapon or see any signs of a struggle. It was murder, of course.

"So he got you," I spoke half aloud. "You knew too much for somebody's good, and he knifed you. Who was it, Seth? Who did it?"

Who did it? Neither Seth nor I could answer that question. But as I stood there shivering, half from cold and half from fatigue, I realized very clearly what Trumet would think when it heard of this killing.

Who killed Seth Black? Why, the evidence fitted together as neatly as the pieces of a broken china cup. The evidence said that Jonathan Bangs was the killer. It said it just as loudly as Trumet would say that Jonathan Bangs must be captured and hanged for his crimes.

All that ran through my mind in less time than it takes to tell it, and I'm not ashamed to say that I was suddenly and desperately afraid. I turned tail and fled, splashing across the salt meadow like a rabbit with a dog at his heels, nor did I pause for breath until I was safely hidden in a tangle of bushes on a slope back of the Allen house.

There I stayed for some time while the sunlight broadened what turned out to be a beautiful summer morning and while I struggled to bring order out of the confusion of my thoughts. In some ways the forced wait was a good thing, for it gave me time to recover from my panic and to look the whole situation squarely in the face.

By the time Henry Allen finally went out to the barn, hitched his horse to the cart, and rattled off in the direction of the village, I was master of myself again. I had made up my mind about a lot of things and had a plan of campaign. The carrying out of my campaign would require rigid self-control and the complete hiding of my true feelings, but I felt that I was capable of both. I felt that a man could do almost anything when he knew that his life was at stake.

I gave Henry Allen about a five-minute start before I came out into the open and made my very cautious way to his house. The door of the kitchen wing was open, and, when I crept up to it and peered in, Hope was standing at the hearth with her back towards me. I seem to remember that she had on a dress of some blue, unstarched stuff. I remember, too, that in spite of my bitterness the sight of her gave me a peculiar feeling in the back of my throat.

I didn't speak. Somehow I could not. I just waited until she happened to turn in my direction. Then, all at once, we were looking straight into each other's eyes.

"Jon! Why, Jon, they've let you go!"

It must have been a real shock to her to turn and suddenly see me standing there in her doorway—rumpled and dirty and unshaven and grim. I half expected her to scream or to fall in a faint, but nothing like that happened. Frightened as she must have been, she gave no sign except to stand there motionless with her eyes opened wide.

"No, Hope. They haven't let me go." I stepped into the kitchen and shut the door behind me. "I got away, and they'll be after me. I can't stay here long, but I've got to talk to you."

"Of course." Still she did not move. "You look tired,

Jon, dear—terribly tired. You must be hungry, too. Let me get you something to eat."

"There isn't time for eating," I said harshly. "I've escaped from the lockup, I tell you, and they probably know it already. They'll search the town from stem to stern, and they won't come here last. I've got to hurry."

"I don't understand. I don't see why you bothered to escape. Didn't you believe what I told you in my note—the note I sent yesterday?"

"Note?" I looked at her, wondering if she was lying or telling the truth. "I had no note from you yesterday—no note and no anything else!"

"Oh!" Her hand came quickly to her mouth. "But I wrote you! I told you not to worry and that I'd explain everything to the Council this morning. I wrote, and father promised to give you the letter!"

"I got no letter." I felt a quick, hot desire to believe what she said. "Perhaps your father forgot his promise. Perhaps he wanted to forget it, since he has no love for me. In any case, I had no word from you."

"Oh, Jon!" There were suddenly tears in her eyes. "You stayed in that filthy lockup all day yesterday, thinking that I had deserted you after all you've done for me. How you must have hated me!"

"It doesn't matter."

"But it *does* matter. It matters terribly!" She came swiftly to my side and took my arm in her two hands. "You must listen to me, Jon, no matter whether you hate me or not."

I tried not to look at her. "I don't hate you, Hope."

"I think you do." She spoke softly, nodding. "There's something in your voice that makes it different from the voice of the Jon I know."

"Does it matter? Do you really care, Hope, how I feel?"

"Yes." She nodded her head swiftly, so that her red hair glinted. "I care—and I'm ashamed. Perhaps it's too late to do

141

any good, but I want you to know that I'm ashamed of the way I treated you Friday night at Shad Cove. You had a right to question me, and I should have told you the truth. But because I felt that you should believe in me no matter how things seemed, I lost my temper. I'm sorry, Jon, and it isn't easy for me to say that I'm sorry. I'm grateful, too, for what you did Saturday night when the militia would have caught me. I'm more grateful than you'll ever know—and I hate myself. I shouldn't have trusted a letter yesterday. I should have come to the lockup, myself."

"It doesn't matter, Hope." She had shaken me more than she could possibly guess, but being stubborn I refused to give in. I had made up my mind once and for all about her, and about the course I must take. "A day in the lockup didn't do me any harm. I was able to get out before it was too late."

"Your running away was a bad mistake, Jon, you must see that." She was intensely earnest. "People will think now that you really have a guilty conscience. You must give yourself up at once!"

"No, thank you," I said grimly. "I have no desire to hang!"

"Hang!" Hope shook her head impatiently. "What a silly way to talk. Even if I didn't tell the Council the truth— which I will—they'd never hang you. What on earth would they hang you for?"

"For murder," I told her brutally. "For sticking a knife into Seth Black when his back was turned! That's what they'll hang me for—if they catch me!"

"Seth Black! Murdered!" She gasped and paled. I had only to look at her to realize that, however nasty the business she might be mixed up in, she knew nothing about Seth's death. She listened in frightened silence as I told her about Seth's note to Captain Dole, about his disappearance after the fire, and about my discovery of his body in the salt marsh. When I had finished, she seemed bewildered. "But, Jon, I don't understand! Not any of it. Who killed Seth? What does it all mean?"

"I don't know." I shrugged. "I only know that if I'm caught I'll hang for killing a man I never harmed. The evidence is all there. It's so strong that I wouldn't blame them for hanging me."

"Don't talk that way." She shivered. "What are you going to do? There must be something."

"Yes." I was able to smile. "There's something I can do. It's as easy to tell as it will be hard to carry out. I can find the man who killed Seth Black. If I can do that, I can clear myself. Not otherwise."

"Yes. I see what you mean, of course." She was frowning in thought. "But have you any idea who he is? Do you know why he killed Seth?"

I said, "Seth was killed so that his mouth would stay shut. Seth knew too much about traitors for somebody's good, so he had to die. Who knifed him, I haven't the faintest idea—but I've got to find out."

"How? Have you any plan, Jon?"

"Perhaps." I had no intention, just then, of telling my plans to Hope. "Would you like to help me?"

"Of course!" She looked suddenly glad and made a little move as though she would come to me. But something, perhaps it was the look in my face, made her pause. "I'll do anything," she said in a subdued voice. "I'll do anything I can."

"Good. Then tell me what you were doing at Shad Cove with that enemy officer Friday night. Tell me what you were doing on the same beach twenty-four hours later. Why did you ask me to save you from the militia? Those are the things I want to know. Will you tell them?"

She caught her breath. She looked, I thought, a little frightened but more bewildered. "Of course," she said, "I'll tell you everything, but that won't help you to find the man who killed Seth. It can't."

"I think it will," I said quietly. "Anyhow, I'd like to hear the story. Tell it quickly, please. My time is short."

She paused for a moment before speaking, as though putting her thoughts in order. "It won't be easy to tell, Jon. It will be hard for a number of reasons. For one thing, I'm not very proud of myself for what I've done. For another, you may misunderstand when you hear what I've got to say. Perhaps you'll be so angry that you'll be through with me for good." She nodded soberly. "But I'll have to chance that. In any event, you'll stop thinking what you thought when you saw me with that British officer the other night, and that will be something. I'm no traitor, Jon. Lieutenant Forsythe and I have met quite a few times during the past few weeks, but I swear to you that we haven't so much as discussed the war. Our business has been entirely—personal."

"I see." I stared at her in honest amazement, hardly believing my ears. "So it hasn't been treason, after all, but just a little innocent romance! How very damn reassuring!"

"You see?" She made a little motion of hopelessness with her hand. "You're angry with me already, and I haven't really begun."

"I'm sorry, Hope, I really am. I won't interrupt again. What was your personal business with this Lieutenant— what's his name—Forsythe? How did you happen to know him at all?"

"That's just it." The color suddenly flooded her face in the way I knew so well. "I've known him for years—ever since I was seventeen. At that time I was visiting a friend in Boston, and he was a young officer on a British warship that happened to be in the harbor. We met and I—we—"

I laughed grimly, suddenly understanding what she was trying to say. "So my idea about the romance wasn't so far

144

wrong, after all! You and this man Forsythe met in Boston, and fell in love! That's it, isn't it?"

"Yes, Jon," said Hope quietly. "That's what happened. We met, all those years ago, and we fell in love. It doesn't seem real now, but it was real and desperate enough at the time. I was only seventeen, remember, and he—"

"Spare me the details." My sudden, angry jealousy made my voice hard and sarcastic. "I can imagine the handsome and dashing young British naval officer! You loved him and he loved you. What happened. Was marriage part of the plan?"

She looked down at the floor and went on in a colorless, even voice, as though determined to finish an unpleasant task as quickly as she could. "We wanted to get married, but it was impossible. I was very young, and Jermyn was in no position to support a wife."

"Jermyn!" I laughed with spiteful derision. "What a name! How completely and utterly British! Is he as sweet as he sounds?"

She looked up at me then in a pleading sort of way, as though asking for my help. "Don't, Jon! It's hard enough to tell you all this without your being hateful."

"I— Oh, well, I'm sorry." I felt a little ashamed of myself. "Go on."

Hope shrugged. "There isn't much more to the story. We swore to be true to each other forever. Then Jermyn's ship sailed out of Boston Harbor, and—"

"And that was the end of love's young dream?"

"Not quite." She bit her lip. "We wrote to each other for a long time, and often. But it took months for me to get an answer to any question that I asked Jermyn by letter, and we were separated by thousands of miles of ocean. The waiting seemed hopelessly long to me, and after two years had gone by without my once seeing his face, I finally came to realize that I—well, that I wasn't in love any more."

I must have smiled or have shown somehow by my face what I was thinking, for Hope's eyes suddenly blazed with anger. "Don't tell me what's in your mind," she said hotly, "or I'll scream! I know what you think. You think that if I were a true woman I would have waited for Jermyn until I was old and all my hair had fallen out. Well, in that case, I'm not a true woman! I'm human, and I want to live and be happy—the way other people do. There's no living, or happiness, in being alone. Never mind. I won't waste your time by trying to defend myself. I'll just keep to the facts. The facts are that I wrote a letter to Jermyn, years ago, saying that everything was over between us and asking him to forgive me. I never had an answer to that letter, and I never saw Jermyn Forsythe again until—until just lately."

I thought I was beginning to see the pattern of things. "And then your long-lost lover came back?"

"Yes." She nodded. "A man on his way through here from Point Town brought me a letter one morning. In it Jermyn said he was on the frigate, *Terror*, in Point Town Harbor. Apparently he had never received my letter breaking our engagement. From what he said, his feeling for me was unchanged. He said that he must see me—that, no matter how great the risk, he was coming ashore at Trumet to talk with me."

"When was this?" I asked sharply. "Were you and I—?"

"Yes, Jon." She lowered her head. "It was after our afternoon in Doane's Hollow. I was promised to you."

My contempt must have shown in my voice. "And you didn't think it worth while to tell me anything about this letter? You kept quiet about it?"

"I was afraid." She looked up, begging me with her eyes to understand. "I was afraid that, if you heard about Jermyn and me, you would be jealous."

I laughed unpleasantly. "Jealous? About such a mere trifle? Why, Hope!"

She nodded. "You'd have been furious, but I should have told you, just the same. I should have been honest about it. Instead, I did the weak thing. I didn't answer his letter, but when he wrote me another, asking me to meet him at a certain hour on Shad Cove beach—I went down there."

"Of course! What else could a lady do?" I bowed with elaborate irony. "And how was Lieutenant Jermyn Forsythe, of His Britannic Majesty's navy? Was he just as dashing and handsome as ever?"

Hope looked me squarely in the eyes. "I'm not going to lie. The truth is that Jermyn Forsythe is a very attractive man—but that doesn't make what you're thinking the truth. The first thing I told him about was you and me. I said that I was sorry, but that he had come back too late."

"Really? Honest girl! And what did he say to that?"

For just an instant I thought her angry resentment was going to end our interview. But it didn't. Her cheeks flushed and then paled, but she went on doggedly in spite of my bitterness. "He said a lot of things. He said that he loved me. He said that I had belonged to him long before I had ever met you and that he would never let me go. He said that he would make me forget about you. He reminded me of my promise to be true to him always, and asked me if I was going to be false to it."

I nodded, speaking sweetly but with mayhem in my heart. "I can understand perfectly how the lieutenant must have felt. How about you? What did you think—and feel? Could it be that you fell in love with your old sweetheart all over again?"

"No." Hope drew a long, uneven breath. "You're making this very hard for me, Jon. I'm trying to be honest, and I'm trying not to lose my temper when you bait me. I didn't fall in love all over again with Jermyn. But I like him, and I'm sorry for all the unhappiness I've caused him. I'm ashamed of the whole mess."

I shook my head in wonder. "So that's the explanation! How altogether lovely! You've been meeting your former lover from time to time on Shad Cove beach for reasons that have nothing to do with war or privateers! Your business together has been personal, and was personal Friday night when I stumbled on you."

"Yes." She looked me in the eyes. "That's the whole truth. It may have made you hate me, but it must make you see I'm no traitor. Do you believe my story?"

"I believe it."

And that was so. With one possible reservation, everything that Hope had told me carried the ring of honesty. I believed that, in her meetings with the British officer, Forsythe, Hope had been treasonable to no one except possibly to me. There should have been tremendous relief in that thought, but I was still far from happy. For, even though she might be no conscious traitor to her country, it was still quite possible that she cared more about the Englishman than she admitted. If so, a lot of things could have happened.

"Did it ever occur to you," I asked, expressing one of them, "that your lieutenant might have come ashore here for some purpose other than just to see you?"

"No." The color was suddenly high in her cheeks. "He wouldn't have deceived me like that. He wouldn't have dared! If I had thought he had—"

"Somebody," I told her coldly, "has been coming ashore from the British fleet to deal with a traitor. Somebody made the arrangements to have the *New Hope* set afire. Somebody met the traitor near Doane's Hollow after the fire had been started. I know because I saw the man with my own eyes."

"Then you didn't see Jermyn," said Hope with rapid intensity, almost as though she were trying to convince herself as well as me. "He wouldn't do a thing like that. He wouldn't sink so low!"

"No?" I looked at her. "Well, if you want my honest opinion, Hope, I think he would. What's more, I think he *did*. It stands to reason—as you would quickly see if you weren't blinded by your—well, whatever it is that you feel for this man. Love, as I have reason to know, makes fools of us all."

"Stop! You're hateful!" She raised her little open hand as though she would slap me with it across the mouth. "I could really hate you, Jon, if I didn't know what it was that makes you talk this way. You're jealous! Jealous! In the next breath you'll be saying that Jermyn murdered Seth Black!"

"Perhaps he didn't," I said evenly, "but perhaps he knows who did. I intend to find out. But never mind that. You haven't yet finished your story. What about Saturday night? What were you doing at Shad Cove beach? What was the reason for that piece of play-acting that you and I staged down there? For one reason or another, I think that I'm entitled to know the facts about that."

It was a simple request, but it had a strong effect on Hope. All the anger went out of her, and all the animation. She dropped her hand and took a half step backwards, staring at me. "Saturday night?" she said faintly. "Why, of course, I'd almost forgotten." There was something new in her eyes. It might have been fear. "I must tell you about Saturday night."

Well, she told me, and the story was simple enough. Saturday night, she said, she had had an appointment with Forsythe at the usual place. But Forsythe had not kept it. After waiting for him a long time, she had walked to the beach, found the longboat, and asked the midshipman in charge where Forsythe was. The midshipman told her that Forsythe was detained by duty on the *Terror*. Then Major

Bartlett's troops had fired their volley. Hope ran up the beach and into my arms.

"I was afraid to have the militia find me," she said uncertainly. "I was afraid they might—think things. That's why I asked you for help. You must understand, Jon. You must! I was frightened!"

"I understand."

We looked at each other, and then Hope suddenly covered her face with her hands. "You don't believe me," she said slowly, her voice muffled. "You think I'm lying."

"That's right." I didn't raise my voice in anger, because I felt no anger. I was bitter past all telling and coldly sure of where I stood. Another might easily have deceived me with such a simple story as Hope's, but it was foolish for her even to try it with me. She and I had been too intimate in spirit for that. Every word she had spoken about Saturday night was false—and I knew it. "You *are* lying, and the reason speaks for itself. You love this man, Forsythe, and you're trying to shield him."

"No!" she said desperately. "No, Jon! That's not so!"

"The whole thing is quite plain." My voice, I think, showed little of the emotion that was shaking me. "You're infatuated with Forsythe—perhaps enough so to have been a party to the dirty work he's been encouraging in Trumet. I'm not sure about that, but I'm pretty sure about Saturday night. Forsythe came ashore then to see his scheme for burning our vessel put into effect and to pay for the doing of it. He had the bad luck to run into me. I fired at him. I think I wounded him. I think that he came to you for help. I think that you hid him—and that you're still hiding him! I think that yesterday you were afraid to come to me in the lockup because your story might prevent your Englishman from getting safely away. I repeat that I think you're still hiding him! You're hiding him in spite of the fact that his arrest might prevent me from being hung for the murder that I didn't do! That's what *I* think, Hope Allen, about what happened Saturday night and after!"

"No!" Hope backed away, her face white. "No, Jon!"

"Where's your English lover?" I said brutally. "Where have you got Forsythe hidden away? You might as well tell me, for I'll find him anyhow."

What might have happened then, I don't know. Perhaps Hope would have told me the truth—I am inclined to believe so. But, as it was, we were still staring at each other wordlessly when through the open window I heard the sound of men's voices.

Hope was across the room to the window and back again before I was able to move. "Three men!" she said breathlessly, tugging at my arm. "They're coming here! They mustn't find you, Jon. Quick!"

She half pulled me across the kitchen and into the little sitting-room that lay beyond. This offered no hiding place and no way of escape except through the single, closed window. She pointed to that window. "There," she whispered; "but be careful! It's apt to squeak when you open it."

Then she was gone and the door was closed behind her. As for me, I was tugging at the window, which squealed indignantly in protest, when I heard excited voices in the kitchen demanding Henry Allen. Those voices I knew well. They belonged to Elnathan Berry, Eben Fowler, and Captain Dole, and the reason for their excitement was soon plain.

The men spoke loudly, and I could hear every word. I listened until I heard one of them—it was Captain Berry—roaring about a murder. They had found the body!

I pulled up the window the rest of the way. I waited, a hand on the sill, until I heard Captain Elnathan, his voice shaking with rage, declare they had absolute proof that I —I, Jonathan Bangs—was the murderer and that he, for one, wouldn't rest till he saw me hanging by the neck—or words to that effect.

I didn't wait for any more. I half climbed and half fell out of that window to the grass outside. Then I scuttled off into the safety of the bushes without once looking behind.

I should have been afraid, but I was not. Jealousy and anger had driven fear into the back of my mind. Jermyn Forsythe, indeed!

4.

What I did after that was plain common sense. To move about to any extent would be to ask for capture, and to watch Hope would be the quickest way to find Lieutenant Jermyn Forsythe. For those reasons I took a place in the thick underbrush which was not only moderately safe from prying eyes but which gave me a clear view of the Allen premises.

My talk with Hope had swept away any doubts that I might have had about the whereabouts of her Englishman. If I knew anything I knew that he was lying hidden, and most probably wounded, in a place close by. I also knew that Hope must go to him sometime very soon.

My anxiety to come face to face with this lady-killing ornament to the Royal Navy was such that the knuckles of my big hands almost itched. For him I had by this time conceived a very healthy hatred. I promised myself that, even if I was denied the pleasure of flattening his aristocratic nose with my fist, I should surely find some other means of making him suffer for coming between me and the girl I loved.

Luckily for me—and I was sane enough, even then, to realize it—not only jealousy but good policy would be served by my meeting with the man Forsythe had dealt with, and therefore knew, our "traitor." The traitor was almost certainly the murderer of Seth Black. So if Forsythe was willing, or could be forced, to give me the man's name, my personal danger and my personal troubles might very swiftly be brought to an end.

The more I thought, the more I realized how much depended on what this Lieutenant Forsythe did and said when I confronted him. He was a British officer and presumed, therefore, to be a gentleman—from Hope's say-so he was a most fascinating gentleman indeed. Such men, judging by what I had read and knew, had rigid codes of honor. Would it come within the bounds of that code to tell me the thing that I wanted to know? He would never, of course, tell me the name of the traitor he had dealt with, no matter what arguments I used. His contempt for such a creature might be complete, but he would still feel that he was honor-bound to protect him to the end from the consequences of his treachery. Murder, however, was a very different thing, and one with which a man of Forsythe's stamp could have no dealings. If I told him that his hired turncoat was a murderer of an old man and that the murderer had succeeded in pinning his crime on me, I might get some sort of favorable response. I might—and yet again I might not.

Nose-punching, I realized then and there, would be out of the question when my would-be rival and I faced each other. To the contrary, I would be forced to display considerable diplomacy, persuasiveness, and tact. For the Forsythe fellow would be holding most of the high cards in the game. If he told me what I wanted to know, all would be well. But suppose he flatly refused to tell anything. How could I find my murderer then? How could I give him a name?

During my time in the lockup I had spent more than one fruitless hour in trying to decide who in Trumet I might logically suspect of having committed the crimes that had been laid at my door. Aside from the obvious facts that he was a traitor and a killer, there was only one thing of any significance that I could bring to mind about this nameless individual. And even that thing had an "if" tied to it.

Someone in Trumet had contrived and executed a series of incidents, during the refitting of the *New Hope*, for the purpose of discrediting me. If that man—and it was a big "if"—was also the traitor and murderer, then I knew something that might be of value. That something was that he had a personal grudge against me. But who could have such a grudge and why?

The only person who seemed to fill the requirement was Henry Allen, Hope's father, the man who had adopted and reared the "wreck child." Henry Allen disliked my attentions to his daughter. He had more than once, and in public, quite openly shown his aversion to me. I could easily imagine Henry Allen as the man who had methodically made a fool of me in my job at the *New Hope*, but there my imagination balked. Was Henry Allen capable of selling out his friends to the enemy and of slipping a knife into drink-sodden old Seth Black as well? I couldn't picture it, somehow, for Henry, though rough and crotchety, was a man of known character and one of the town's most ardent patriots as well. It was barely possible, on the other hand, that his loudly voiced hatred of the British was sheer playacting. Perhaps Henry Allen was secretly a British-lover. Perhaps he knew all about Hope's and Forsythe's one-time romance. Perhaps he approved of Forsythe as a son-in-law. Perhaps all three of them were in the plot.

Perhaps— But, no, in my heart I believed no such things.

Who else then, in Trumet, could be suspected? Eben Fowler? I was quite sure that he did not like me, and I knew that he was very friendly with Henry Allen, but that was the feeble all that I could summon up against him. Fowler was a respected business man in the town and had a heavy investment in the *New Hope* enterprise. To think of the dignified saltworks owner, with his precise speech and ever-present dignity, as a cold-blooded killer seemed absurd. Such thoughts about Elnathan Berry, Elkanah Davies, Jeremiah Weeks, or Squire Bailey were equally ridiculous. It would be just as sensible, I reflected sourly, to start sniffing on the trail of the Reverend Ichabod Samuels. The minister of the First Church was no less likely as a knife-wielder than any of the rest.

No, the powers of reasoning would never lead me where I wanted to go. As I crouched in the bushes waiting for the men who had found Seth Black's body to leave the Allen house, I realized quite clearly that my only hope of salvation lay in the willingness of an enemy officer, and a rival in love, to give me aid. It seemed a faint hope.

Captain Dole and his three companions did not linger long in Hope's kitchen. After about fifteen minutes they came out and set off in the direction of the village, walking fast and deep in earnest talk. I wondered whether they would be the ones to discover that Solomon Snow was now the only inmate of the lockup or whether the news would meet them on the way. I listened carefully for a moment, half expecting to hear the harsh notes of the alarm bell in the village, but all that came to my ears was the muted rumble of the surf on the ocean shore.

The men were hardly out of sight before Hope, herself, came out on the grass, where she shaded her eyes with her hand and peered intently in my direction. I could not tell if she wanted me or if she was just making sure that I was no longer in the neighborhood. In any event, though I was tempted, I made no move or sound that would show where I was hidden.

The reason for that was that I no longer trusted Hope completely, and myself not at all. Hope's power over me was still very real, and I was afraid that, if I allowed myself to look into her blue eyes or to listen to her voice any more than I already had that morning, I might in the end find myself acting upon the dictates of emotion rather than reason. For all I knew, a part of the story Hope had told me earlier might be true. It had sounded so. On the other hand, I *knew* that her account of Saturday night had been sheer fiction. Since she had seen fit to lie to me in part, perhaps she had done so in full.

My desperate need at the moment was to hear whole truths—not half truths or lies—and I felt that I knew a better way of filling that need than of talking any further with Hope Allen. For that reason I kept still in my hiding place until Hope had given up her scrutiny of the pine woods and had turned away.

Not three minutes later I knew where the British officer, Lieutenant Jermyn Forsythe, lay hidden.

Hope showed me the place, of course, as I had reasoned and hoped that she would, but she showed it to me much more quickly and easily than I would have believed possible. I had thought to be led a long and difficult chase along wood roads and across the rolling dunes, but instead I was not forced to move a single step to learn the thing I wanted to know.

There was a group of outbuildings on the far side of the clearing where the Allen house stood, and towards these Hope ran lightly and swiftly, holding her skirts out of the way with both hands. She passed the low gray henhouses without slowing down, nor did she turn in at the open door of the new barn where Henry Allen kept his horse and cart. The pines began just beyond, and as she seemed to be about to vanish among them I half rose to my feet to follow.

Then, almost as the running girl turned off in its direction, I caught a glimpse of, and remembered, the half-collapsed and unused old building—part of an abandoned salt storehouse—that stood just beyond the edge of the clearing. It was partially hidden by the branches of a dead pine that had fallen across its sunken roof, and approach to it was made difficult by a tangle of thorny blackberry vines.

I caught my breath. Could Forsythe be hidden there— within easy call of the Allen house itself?

Hope made her way through the brambles with a quick sureness that, to my suspicious mind, suggested recent familiarity with the path. When she came to the wall of the building I caught a glimpse of white as she turned her head for a brief survey of the clearing behind. Then a black rectangle suddenly appeared as the shack door was pushed open. It vanished again, and Hope with it.

She was gone, and I knew where. She was gone to her English lover. It was possible, and even probable, that at this very instant she was in his arms.

I cursed, bitterly and aloud. My reasoning had been proven correct, and I knew the thing I most wanted to know; but my vivid mental picture of a lovers' meeting more than overbalanced any satisfaction I might otherwise have found in that knowledge. It took real will power, I can swear, to remain in my clump of scrub oak while that meeting went on for minutes that dragged by with agonizing slowness.

It must have been a half hour later, at least, before the door of the old shack opened once more and Hope came hurrying back towards the house. Her head was down as though she were in deep thought, but in the middle of the clearing she suddenly came to a halt and for the second time that morning searched the surrounding woods with inquiring eyes. That she was looking for me I felt fairly sure, but I felt no inclination to go to her. By that time I was so wretchedly bitter against her and her obvious faithlessness to me that if she had called my name, asking for help, I think I should not have answered.

"Hope! Hope Allen!"

The sudden harsh voice, unexpected and close by, startled me as it did Hope. She spun about in the direction from which it came, and I saw her hand go swiftly to her breast. Almost at the same time, I saw Major Bartlett.

The Major had appeared from the place where the wood road led off in the direction of the village and was coming forward with his slight limp made more apparent by the fact that he was waving his stick. He looked hot and tired as well as excited. "You haven't seen anybody skulking around in the bushes, have you?" he demanded, puffing. "Jonathan Bangs, the skunk, got Sol Snow drunk last night and then walked right out of the lockup! Unless he got away safe to the British, he must be hiding somewhere close by. We've got to catch him if we can. He isn't only a traitor, Hope, he's a murderer! He killed Seth Black! It isn't safe for you to be here all alone by yourself. The critter will be dangerous if he's cornered! How do you know he isn't hiding out in your own barn right this minute? I'll search it for you—and the henhouses, too. Mustn't take any chances!"

If Hope was frightened for the safety of the man she had hidden—as she must have been—she gave no sign. She asked the questions that the Major expected her to ask and assured him that she had been all through the barn and the other buildings that morning without seeing a sign of me. When he still insisted that they make a further and more careful search, she was clever enough to pretend to agree. But before she would take a step in that direction there was something, she said, upon which she must insist. The Major must first come into the house with her for a cooling drink. In view of the heat of the day and the perspiration on the officer's brow, she would not take no for an answer.

Well, the Major growled and protested that he had no time to waste, but he finally went inside for his drink. He not only went inside, but he stayed in the Allen kitchen for at least thirty minutes, while I could imagine Hope practicing her wiles, as I twiddled anxious thumbs in my thicket, not daring to move in any direction.

When he came outside again, the veteran soldier seemed to be much refreshed, for his back was straighter and I heard him laugh as he said good-by to Hope. He seemed also to have forgotten his idea of inspecting the outbuildings, for he merely waved his gold-headed cane in salute to his hostess and stumped off in the direction of the militia emplacement near Billfish Cove.

Hope hardly waited for him to get out of sight before she, herself, was on the move. She set out briskly, and with evident purpose, towards a place that I could not guess. It must have been somewhere in the Shad Cove direction, however, for she took that way through the pines and was soon out of sight.

I made no move to follow, nor did I think of such a thing. I had pressing business to attend to, and knew that, if it was ever to be accomplished, now was my time.

The blackberry bushes twined themselves about my feet as I approached the abandoned storehouse on the far side of the clearing, and my thrashing to free myself from them must have given ample warning of my coming. When I got to it I found that the ancient door of the gray building had no lock and that it opened inward under my hand with no more than a low moan of protest. I stepped inside.

To my unaccustomed eyes the interior of that place was as dark, I remember thinking, as the inside of a cow. I sensed, as much as saw, that all around me were piles of broken and rotting barrels reaching nearly to the ceiling. The air was cool and damp and carried a not unpleasant scent of dry wood.

"I'm just around here to your right, if you don't mind." The sudden deep voice out of the dark was calm, cultivated, and completely British. "And mind the holes in the floor as you come along, or you'll dashed well break your neck!"

There was a prickling sensation just above my collar where the hair begins, but I did not speak. I felt my way cautiously along until I came to a corner. Around that, in a tiny room with old barrels for walls, was my man.

He was half sitting and half lying in a wooden armchair with his bandaged right leg propped up in front of him on a box. On another box at his side burned two large candles. Their flickering light was reflected from the braid and buttons of a British naval officer's uniform. It gleamed also on the barrel of a large pistol that was pointed squarely at my chest.

"Good morning, Mr. Bangs." The deep voice was lazy and amused. "Hope you won't mind my not rising; no discourtesy intended, I assure you. Rather, we might call it a compliment to your skill in the use of small arms. But perhaps I had better introduce myself. My name's Forsythe. To be more formal, I'm Lieutenant Jermyn Forsythe of His Britannic Majesty's ship, *Terror*." His pause implied a polite bow. "At your service, Mr. Jonathan Bangs!"

5.

I stared at him, wordless, like a country boy at his first glimpse of a great city. But if the officer thought that the expression on my face implied awe, he was greatly mistaken. I was merely surprised, and somewhat confused, by a number of unexpected things.

It had been my thought that when I finally came face to face with Forsythe I would find a man frightened and cringing and more or less ready to beg for mercy. This man's attitude was the reverse. He seemed unsurprised, fully at ease, and genuinely affable. He was in uniform, whereas I had expected some sort of disguise. He called me by my full name, though he had never seen me before. His words implied the knowledge that it was I who had shot him in the leg.

My bewilderment showed in my face, and I was angry at the knowledge. To cap my humiliation the Lieutenant was holding me at the point of his pistol, while I was as defenseless as a baby. Rushing in to make my capture, it had never once crossed my mind that I might be the one to be captured.

"I'm a fool!" I said harshly, with angry contempt for my own stupidity. "I'm a complete damn fool!"

He laughed. He laughed not in a way to give offense but because he found real amusement in the situation. His teeth flashed white as he did so, and on looking at him I realized that another one of my imaginings had been quite wrong. This was not the arrogant, oily, sophisticated man of the world that I had pictured. His body was almost as big as my own, and unless I greatly missed my guess it was equally strong. His face was not dissipated or sly. It was open, humorous, and young. Topped with a mop of badly mussed blond hair it looked as young, surely, as my own.

"Of course you're a fool, Mr. Bangs!" Forsythe nodded approvingly. "We're all fools. If we weren't, we wouldn't do the silly things we do!"

"I'm the greatest fool of all," I told him, still bitter. "I walked into this place unarmed!"

"The devil you did!" The Lieutenant laughed again and laid his pistol carelessly in his lap. "Well, I suppose that does show a certain lack of discretion. And yet I don't know, after all. Tell me this, Mr. Bangs. Suppose our positions were reversed. Suppose you had the pistol and I had none. What would you do? Would you shoot me dead?"

"Probably not." I shrugged. "I'll admit that I'd like nothing better, but I probably wouldn't."

"Of course you wouldn't." The Lieutenant appeared satisfied, as though he had proved a point. "No gentleman would."

"So?" I felt that this was more like it. This was the way that Englishmen talked. "What makes you think so?"

"I don't have to think about it." He made an impatient movement, as though I were wasting his time. "Gentlemen don't shoot sitting birds, that's all."

"I'm just a Provincial, you know," I told him sourly. "I wouldn't trust my gentlemanly instincts too far if I were you."

"No?" He cocked his head, looking at me. "Well, I'm trusting mine and suppose we prove yours. Here! Catch, Mr. Bangs!"

Quick as a flash he picked up the pistol on his lap and tossed it lightly in my direction. My gesture in catching it was entirely instinctive, for there was no thought in my mind except blank astonishment. When I looked up again Forsythe was grinning delightedly.

"Who's the silly fool now?" I demanded, unbelieving. "Are you completely out of your wits?"

"Not at all, old boy." It was evident that he was pleased with himself. "I'm quite content to have you take charge of the weapon. The fact is, Bangs, that I don't like firearms —as a part of a personal interview like this. Dangerous things, eh? Make me nervous, though I'll grant you that they're useful at times. I was glad to have that pistol when I heard you scratching around outside this place, but I only wanted it for self-defense. I was afraid you might be the hot-headed sort, and take a pot shot at me before we could talk. Now that I've seen you, I know better."

"I see." I spoke quite gently. "I understand."

"No you don't." Forsythe shook his head. "You think

I'm mentally deranged—slightly mad, eh? I'm not. See here, Bangs. Now that you've got the pistol what are you going to do with it? What *can* you do that you couldn't do without it? Nothing, as I see it."

"No?" I stared at him. "May I ask why not? There's a war on, Forsythe, whether or not you remember. You're my enemy. Last night there was an attempt to do my country harm, and you were responsible for it. I've caught you, and you've been—er—deranged enough to give me your gun. Having the gun, what's to prevent me from marching you·up to the village and handing you over to the authorities?"

"Why, Bangs, old fellow, I'm surprised." Forsythe whistled. "There are so many reasons why you won't do the unpleasant thing you suggest that I won't even bother to mention them now. Not a word will I say until I've done my duty as a host."

He reached down beside him and picked up a plate on which rested a whole chicken, roasted a golden brown. "A noble bird," said Forsythe, sniffing, "and worthy of our attention. There's rum, too, to wash it down—and milk." He made a little face. "Some people *like* milk."

"No thank you," I said stiffly. "I won't eat."

"Don't tell me, Bangs." Forsythe sighed, half closing his eyes. "Don't tell me that you're going to be stuffy and refuse to eat with your enemy. That's poppycock!"

"I'm not hungry," I told him, lying.

"Come, come! You disappoint me. There's time for everything. It's obvious that you must be half starved, and yet you won't eat! When a man's belly is empty he can't keep his wits about him, now can he? And you'll need your wits, I promise you, before this little chat of ours is over. I'll tie you up in knots, otherwise." He stretched out his hand. "Just let me have that pistol a moment, will you? Word of honor I'll give it straight back again."

And I gave it to him—God knows why. At his casual request I handed over the weapon. He accepted it with a little bow and then pointed the muzzle in my direction.

"Now eat, Bangs!" he commanded with pretended ferocity. "Eat, or I swear I'll blow out whatever few brains you may really have!"

What could I do in the face of such absurdity? I laughed, of course. I had not eaten since the night before, and the smell of that roast chicken was— Well, the next thing I knew I was downing famished bites of the said chicken and swigging his rum and milk as though the man were my long-lost friend instead of what he was. In the midst of the procedure, I paused long enough to express some of the wonder that I felt.

"I ought to hate you, Forsythe, you know," I told him with a shake of my head. "God knows I've got reasons enough. I don't understand myself at all, except that— Well, the truth is, you're different than I had expected."

"I know." The Lieutenant nodded, quite serious for once. "All that you knew about me personally—forgetting the enemy business—was that I happen to be fond of your promised wife. In your mind that made me a low breed of snake. Only natural way for you to feel." He took an appreciative sip of his drink. "The fact is though, Bangs, that I'm really not such a damn bad sort. I drink and play too much, of course, but that's about the sum of my sins. I'm not poison to women, the way you probably think. It's an awkward thing to talk about, but I want you to know that my intentions in regard to Miss Hope Allen have been aboveboard all the way through. Honorable and all that."

All of a sudden I stopped eating, but not because my appetite was gone. It may have been Forsythe's use of Hope's name, but, for whatever reason, I no longer wanted food. I was suddenly aware of the desperation of my position and of the tremendous risk I was running in sitting where I was when at any moment the militia might come thundering at the door. There was more to my feeling, even, than that. It was almost as though a little bell had sounded in the back of my brain, warning me against this British officer. Up until the time the man had started to talk about Hope, I had sensed his honesty, but now it seemed as though I caught a false note. I told myself that I had better be on guard.

Forsythe, his eyes fixed on a wingbone of the chicken, went on with what he had to say. "After all, you shouldn't blame me too much, old boy, for this business about Miss Allen. As she has told you, she and I were promised to each other years ago. I didn't know that that promise had been broken when I saw her again only a few weeks ago. She told me then about you, but I couldn't believe her. I told her that she was mine and would always be in spite of everything. You can't blame me for that, can you? You can't hate a fellow for trying to get his own again."

"No," I said shortly. "But we won't discuss it."

"Very well." He showed genuine irritation for the first time since I had seen him. "I just wanted you to know that I wasn't consciously doing an underhanded thing. But what difference does it make what I did—since I failed?"

"You failed?"

"Looks like it, doesn't it?" He laughed impatiently. "I know now that I came back to Miss Allen several weeks too late. By that time she belonged to you. She still does. You're a lucky man, sir. I congratulate you, Bangs."

I was sure then, in my own mind, that he was insincere. I did not for a moment believe that he meant one word of what he said about Hope's belonging to me.

"How do you happen to know that my name is Bangs?" I demanded sharply. "You never have laid eyes on me before. How do you know that it was I who shot you in the leg Saturday night?"

"How do I know?" Forsythe blinked in apparent surprise. "Why, tut, tut, Bangs! I know for the same reason that I know there is no real thought in your mind of marching me up to the village and turning me over to the local authorities!"

"And why do you think I won't do just that?"

He rubbed his blond head in puzzlement. "Would you mind telling me something, old man? Exactly what did Miss Allen say to you just now before she sent you here to see me?"

"Hope?" It was my turn for astonishment. "Hope send me here? When I last saw Hope she denied that you were anywhere about. I knew she was lying and watched her. I saw her come to this place and knew where you were to be found. When she went away, I came here. Hope didn't send me. You may be sure of that!" I added bitterly.

"Ah!" The Lieutenant leaned back with a satisfied sigh. "Oh, yes, yes; I see it now, of course. A natural mistake on both our parts, Bangs. You came here as a result of your own deductions and observations, while all this time I've been thinking that Hope sent you."

"Humph! If you did think that, you *are* mad, Forsythe. Hope is hiding and protecting you, isn't she? That being the case, the last thing in the world she would do would be to tell me where you were, much less send me to see you. Not being out of her mind, herself, she would know what I'd do when I did see you."

Lieutenant Forsythe smiled. "Really? Oh, I say, Bangs! You terrify me. And just what would you do?"

I half got to my feet. "I'd take you to Trumet and hand you over to the Council. That's what I'd do—and that's just what I'm *going* to do!"

The Lieutenant slowly shook his head. His look was

almost sorrowful. "Don't understand the situation at all, do you? Not at all. Let me ask you something, dear boy. Suppose you did as you suggest and took me to this so-called Council of yours. Would you be greeted as a hero? Would a medal be pinned upon your manly breast?" He spoke softly. "Why, I think not. I think it much more likely that you'd be clapped into your cell again as a traitor and a murderer!"

This cool, common-sense statement hit me with the suddenness of an unexpected blow in the face. "I'm no murderer," I said harshly, "and you, yourself, know that I'm no traitor."

"Of course, old fellow. You and I both know that. But what does Trumet think *it* knows? And how will it act, if it can lay hands on you?"

"How do *you* know what Trumet thinks?" I asked him woodenly. "Can it be possible that—?"

"Of course it's possible." He was growing more impatient. "I learned it just the way I learned your name and the fact that you are the one who put this uncomfortable slug of lead in my person Saturday night. I learned it from Hope Allen, naturally."

"I can't believe it." I rubbed my eyes wearily with my hand. "I can't believe Hope would sink so low."

"For God's sake, Bangs!" Forsythe slapped the box beside him so hard with his open hand that the candles on it jumped. "Don't be such an *abysmal* ass! You're thinking that Hope has betrayed you, when all she's done is try to get you out of the foul mess you're in! If you'll listen for a minute, you'll understand."

I listened, and, in spite of myself, I believed.

According to Forsythe, Hope had come to him as soon as Captain Dole and the other discoverers of Seth Black's body had left her house. She told him that she couldn't shield him from arrest a minute longer for the reason that

I—Jonathan Bangs—stood accused of murder and would surely hang unless the real murderer was caught.

"The young lady was entirely logical," said the Lieutenant, smiling faintly. "She said that the murderer of this Black person was obviously the man with whom I had made arrangements for a—er—a certain fire Saturday night. That being the case, she said, I must know the murderer's name. She demanded that I give her that name, forthwith, so that her beloved Mr. Jonathan Bangs would not hang by the neck for a crime he had not committed!"

"And you?" There was little hope in my heart. "I can imagine your answer. You told Hope that the quicker Jonathan Bangs hung by the neck, the better you would be pleased!"

"Why, Bangs! Dear me, dear me! You're unkind." His eyebrows arched. "You may not believe it, but from my way of looking at things it would hardly be honorable for me to let an innocent man suffer if I could prevent it."

I felt a sudden surge of excitement. "You told her the name?"

"Not quite, Bangs." Forsythe gently shook his head. "I told Hope to find you and to send you to me. I told her that you and I might very possibly be able to do business together."

"Business? In what way can you and I do business?" I frowned. "I'm afraid I don't understand."

"It's really quite simple," he said easily. "You want to find a murderer, and it so happens that I'm in a position to help you find him. *I* want to get back to my ship without—er—troubling the local authorities, and it happens that you're in a position to help me get there. Do you see? It's a matter of give and take. To put it another way, it's an affair of business. You Yankees are all for business, or so I'm told."

It took a little time for what he was driving at to sink

into my skull, but it finally did. "I think I understand quite clearly." I laughed, but not pleasantly. "You will tell me the name that I want to know if I, in turn, will help you to escape to your ship. To save my neck, in other words, I must give aid to the enemy. I must really *be* a traitor!"

"Oh, Bangs, I was afraid of this! Afraid you might feel the urge to be noble!" He closed his eyes and groaned as though in anguish, but when he opened them again I noticed that he was brisk enough. "See here, old man, do you mind if I point out a few things to you? And do you mind not interrupting until I'm done? Thank you. Now, let's suppose that you do the noble thing and have me arrested. What will happen to you, personally? You'll never get the information I can give you—so if you're caught you'll hang. What service will my arrest do your country and cause? None, Bangs, none! I'm in uniform, remember, so they can't hang me as a spy. All they can do is make me a prisoner of war, and as such I'll be nothing but a nuisance. And when Captain Holt hears of it he will demand my instant release on pain of burning your town to the ground. You know that Holt has the power to carry out any threat he makes. Trumet would let me go fast enough, I haven't a doubt in the world about that."

"All that may or may not be true," I admitted, "but tell me one thing more. Since arrest means so little to you, why are you going to all this trouble to avoid it?"

"A sound question, Bangs." He laughed. "Not so noble, but much better. You deserve an honest answer. First of all, there's my pride. To tell you the truth, I don't fancy being laughed at. And I will be laughed at if I go back to my fellow officers having to admit that I let myself be captured by—"

"By a gang of country bumpkins?" I completed his sentence for him.

"Put it that way if you like." He shrugged. "Anyhow,

there it is. My pride would be enough to make me take this trouble, and more, but there's still another consideration. If I'm taken, Bangs, I'd be afraid for Miss Allen's sake. Naturally, I'd never breathe her name. But still something might get out. People would wonder where I'd been hidden for two days and who fed me. You see what I mean, don't you?"

I saw. I should have foreseen, but I had had little time, since I learned that there was a Lieutenant Forsythe in the world, to think clearly or look ahead and consider possible developments. Now, however, he was forcing me to consider those developments, and their not only possible, but probable, consequences. Probable? Why, they were inevitable! If I did my duty as an American and a patriot— if I carried out what had been my firm determination when I came into that ruined building—namely, to seize this man and deliver him to the town authorities—if I did that, what would happen? What would happen to me, to the *New Hope* enterprise, to Trumet, and to Hope Allen?

What Forsythe had said about Captain Holt's probable action was undoubtedly true. If no word came from his lieutenant after any appreciable length of time, Holt would infer that the latter had been captured, would demand his release, and would back that demand with force of arms. Trumet would resist, of course, but for how long could it resist? And a successful attack upon the town would mean the capture or destruction of the *New Hope* and the end of all our dreams.

All this was true, and, even furiously angry and chagrined and desperate as I was, I was obliged to realize its truth. It was true, but—

Now that I am dealing with the truth I may as well come out with the whole truth. And the whole truth is that, crushing and baffling as the reasons I have just given were to me at that time, the most compelling was what would happen to Hope if this British officer were to tell his story of her protecting and harboring and hiding him. In the eyes of Trumet that would be—

What *would* happen to her?

She had deceived me, had tricked and lied to me, had—had—

Foolish, of course. Treasonable, perhaps. But she was Hope, still my Hope, in spite of everything. Yes, and by the Lord, so she would always be! And for her sake, more than all the rest, this patronizing Britisher must be permitted—yes, even helped—to get away from Trumet before it was too late.

All this was pouring through my head like water through a mill sluice. Forsythe was watching me, that irritating half smile on his face. He repeated his question. "See what I mean, Bangs, eh?"

I nodded. "Yes," I growled sullenly. "The meaning is plain enough.... Well, what do you want me to do?"

Forsythe's ideas were very definite. His main concern, he said, was lest Captain Holt become alarmed at his subordinate's continued failure to return and make demands of Trumet concerning him. Such demands would start the manhunt that he—Forsythe—was most anxious to avoid.

The part the Lieutenant wanted me to play was simply that of a messenger between him and the master of the *Terror*, Captain Holt. "Could you get to Point Town, Bangs?" he asked. "Without being seen or held up, I mean?"

"I probably could if I had to," I told him. "If there was any good reason why I should."

"Known thereabouts, are you?"

"No."

"Good. Well, this is my idea."

The idea was that I was to go to a place in the Point Town neighborhood that night with a letter to Holt—which was to be written, shown to me, and sealed by

Forsythe under my eyes. Details as to the manner of delivering it were plain, and, once it was delivered, my half of the bargain would be complete. Forsythe said that he would attend to his escape without any aid from me.

"Why don't you escape now?" I asked. "You got here somehow or other."

He smiled and patted his bandaged leg. "Can't just yet, thanks to this little souvenir of your regard, Bangs. Nothing serious, just a flesh wound, but I know enough about such things to realize I must favor the condemned thing a few days longer. Couldn't have a doctor—reason's obvious —but I fixed it up myself, with Hope's—er—Miss Allen's help. She's a very good nurse, Bangs. Tell you that for your future reference, eh?"

I could have choked him, slowly and with great enjoyment.

"No," he went on. "Must hang about this—er—mansion a bit longer, I'm afraid. You take the note to Holt, and I'll attend to myself. Shan't enjoy the Allen hospitality long, I promise you."

He certainly wouldn't if I could think of a safe way to prevent it—safe for Trumet and Hope, that is. I thought it over.

I said, "I seem to remember there was to be a—well, call it a payment for my taking this Point Town trip. You said we could do business together. How about your half of the bargain?"

"I've had that in mind ever since I foresaw the possibility of our meeting, my dear fellow. I think I have it rather neatly worked out. It's this way. The delicate business that brought me ashore Saturday night was all started by a letter from a man in Trumet to Captain Holt at his ship. This letter—a sneaking, miserable piece of business if I ever saw one—offered to sell certain information and certain services. The letter was signed, and Captain Holt knows the name as well as I do. My suggestion is that I tell the Captain that I have given you my word of honor that he will repeat the name to you as soon as he has received my letter. Neat, don't you think?" Forsythe was pleased with his notion. "If we do it that way, you'll get your reward the moment your job is done!"

I thought the thing over carefully but could find no convincing fault with that course of action.

"There *are* two things, Bangs," said Forsythe slowly, frowning, "that I feel honor bound to tell you. The first is that I can give you absolutely no guarantee that the worm-in-human-form I have been dealing with is your murderer as well."

"I'll risk that," I said promptly. "I haven't much doubt."

"Good." He nodded. "The other thing I must warn you is that I can't promise that the name signed to the letter is the traitor's real name. I've seen the creature several times, to be sure, and I've always called him by that name, but that doesn't really signify. It is quite possibly a false one."

"That's another chance I'll have to take." I shrugged. "Just so long as the letter wasn't signed 'Loving Friend' or 'Heart Aflame' or—"

"No." The officer laughed. "The name on the letter is a real one. It's as real as Jermyn Forsythe—or Jonathan Bangs."

"All right. Then I'll take the chance."

"Splendid." Forsythe rubbed his hands and sighed with relief. "Then all that remains is for me to dash off the screed to my commanding officer. Thank goodness all the talking is over. I'm positively hoarse—and, unfortunately, the rum—er—flagon is empty."

The Lieutenant produced quill pen, paper, ink, and even a bit of sealing wax—all of which had been provided, I was informed, by Hope for the very purpose. So far as the pen was concerned, Hope apparently might have done better, for it caused Forsythe to do an astonishing amount of cursing while he struggled with it.

At length, however, the blond young man sat back in his chair with a gusty sigh, waving the paper to dry the ink. "It's done, no matter how badly," he said ruefully. "I'm no scholar, I'm afraid, and my spelling is apt to play foul tricks on me when I least expect it. Never mind, perhaps it will serve. Read it, Bangs, dear boy, and pass judgment."

I read the brief note carefully, and while the spelling was, as promised, decidedly unique in places, the sense was clear. Forsythe told his commanding officer that he had met with a slight misfortune but that he was quite comfortable and safe. He would return to duty very shortly, he promised, and he begged vehemently that no uproar be made about him in Trumet. He pointed out that any inquiry at all would certainly stir up a most unwelcome wasps' nest. And, at the end, was the promised paragraph in which Forsythe solemnly enjoined Captain Holt to uphold his lieutenant's honor by giving the bearer the name signed at the bottom of the traitorous letter from Trumet. Knowing the British character I had no doubt that Holt would comply.

"It seems all right to me." I handed back the paper with a smile. "What's that scrawl at the bottom of it?"

"Scrawl, Bangs? What scrawl? Oh, you mean my signature. It does look as though the cat had fallen in the inkwell, at that! Never mind. Old Holt-Holt will know who it's from, all right. Just to make sure, I'll seal the thing with the sacred old family crest."

He tugged a massive signet ring from his finger and busied himself with the sealing wax and a candle. He stuck out his tongue like a small boy, in the process, and managed to make a general mess of the job, but in the end he finished it.

"So that's that! Everything shipshape. I'd give you my

blessing and send you on your way except for one thing. I'm perfectly sure that there's something I ought to have told you—but haven't. Some message or other from Hope. Most annoying!" He scowled fiercely for a long moment in deep thought. Then suddenly he snapped his fingers in triumph. "I have it, Bangs! It was about that knife that was found by the body of the Black fellow—the chap that was murdered."

"You're wrong." I shook my head impatiently. "There wasn't any knife by the body. I know because I was there first, and I looked very carefully. There wasn't a sign of a weapon."

"Natural mistake," said Forsythe calmly, "but not mine. The error's yours. Extremely likely that there was no knife by the corpse when you found it, but when your three cronies from the village made the official discovery—there *was*. Bad luck, Bangs, because that knife makes the case against you look blacker than ever. You see, it was *your* knife!"

"No!" I shook my head with a total lack of under-standing. "It wasn't my knife. *Mine?* Of course it wasn't!"

"Don't I make myself plain?" Forsythe asked patiently. "Well, I'll try again. The men who found the body found a knife lying beside it. They described the knife to Hope. She swears that she knows that knife well—that it's yours. Why, see here, Bangs, Hope says that the initials J.B. were burned on its leather scabbard as plain as plain. Would that make it your knife—or wouldn't it?"

"J.B.? Burned on the scabbard?" I stared at him in com-plete amazement. "Why—why, yes! That's my knife, of course! But—but—" I put out my hand. "Wait a minute, Forsythe, let me think! Don't say anything, please."

I turned my back, trying desperately to think.

A knife had been found near Seth. It hadn't been there at dawn, that much I knew. But, according to this story, it

175

was there a couple of hours later when Captain Dole and the rest came along. And it must be my knife—not a doubt in the world of that! But how did it get there? Where had it come from? Why, I hadn't laid eyes on that knife of mine for nearly a week! Sometime or other I had loaned it to somebody. Who?

"Think, Jonathan, think!" I said the words to myself fiercely. "This is terribly important! Who did you—?"

"Come, come, Bangs, don't take this so hard." Forsythe was speaking from behind me with another hint of impatience. "Too bad you dropped your knife when and where you did, but it doesn't really matter so much, does it?"

"No." I knew that I hadn't dropped my knife beside Seth, but I also knew that there was no use in telling Forsythe that. I turned back to him. "I guess it doesn't really matter. Let me have that letter, will you? I'll be going."

"Presently." Forsythe was looking at me with a curious expression. "I'd like to ask you one question. It's about my pistol here. Did you realize—"

"I'm not quite so stupid, Forsythe, as I look," I told him quietly but with satisfaction. "Your pistol isn't loaded, of course. Men that know firearms as well as you do, don't toss them carelessly about the way you did. That gesture gave your little show away. Do you think I'd have handed it back to you if it had been loaded?"

"Unquestionably, no." He passed me the letter with a little sigh. "You're clever, Bangs, I admit it. . . . You aren't *too* clever, are you?"

"No. Just now I don't feel clever at all." I held the letter to Holt in my hand and turned to the Lieutenant. "Good-by, Forsythe. Maybe, everything considered, I should say good luck."

"Good luck, old man."

I left him then, after stowing that letter carefully in an

inside pocket of my jacket. And the strange thing is that, even as I made my way out of that tumbledown old store-house, I was aware of a very definite feeling of uneasiness—an uneasiness that had nothing to do with Seth Black or my sheath knife. I wondered at the time if it could be the letter to Holt that was bothering me, but I pushed the idea impatiently aside, as a whim.

I'm sure now that it was no whim—or premonition either. I've thought about the thing a lot, off and on, and though I have no shred of proof I've come to the conclusion that at the time my fingers were vainly trying to send a message to my brain.

The message? Well, as I reason it out, the letter I had watched Forsythe write had been sealed not sixty seconds before I had handled it. What my fingers knew, and were trying to tell me, was that the wax of that seal should have been warm—and not stone cold!

4

In which the Council sends one letter,
and Captain Dole finds another.

Told by

CAPTAIN ISAIAH DOLE

I THINK MAYBE that, before I take my trick at the wheel and begin this next part—section—whatever you mind to call it—of this two-sided yarn of Jonathan Bangs's and mine, I ought to ask anybody having the patience to read it to remember always that it *is* two-sided. In my parts I am trying to tell of the happenings I, myself, was mixed up in. In Jonathan's parts he tells of what happened to him, of what he did, and why he did it. Generally speaking, neither of us knew the other's actions and thoughts, the whys and wherefores governing them, until quite a while later, although the happenings and thinkings were going on at the same time.

For example, take the doings of the day after the fire at the shipyard. The fire was on Saturday night. Jonathan was arrested and brought to the Town House by Major Bartlett and his militia on Saturday night. Now the last words I wrote about *my* Saturday night told of my going down to Seth Black's shanty in answer to that crazy note of his, finding nobody in that shanty, coming outdoors, seeing the red light in the sky, and starting to run. That was when I put down my quill and Jonathan took up his.

Since then, though, his pen has been scratching hard and fast, and he has told all about *his* Saturday night and Sunday and more besides. I am away astern and I have to catch up. So I must ask the reader—again taking it for granted that there is or ever will be a reader—to go back to the Saturday night and keep me company for a spell.

When I got to the yard the worst of the scare was over. The *New Hope* wasn't even scorched, but the storehouse, what was left of it, was just a mass of smouldering timbers and smoke. That change of wind had saved our bark, and, if ever I felt like getting down on my knees in thankfulness, it was right then.

But my happiness didn't last long. Before it had had a chance to really soak through my skin, as you might say, the news of Jonathan's arrest, after being caught in direct communication with the enemy, was yelled into my ears from no less than half a dozen pairs of lungs. They had marched him off to the Town House, and, as soon as I made sure that the bark and the yard would be properly sentineled and guarded every minute from then on, I hurried up there myself.

I had to practically shove my way into the room where they had taken him. This wasn't any everyday dignified, regularly called Council meeting, you understand. This was a get-together which had called itself. It was Trumet's meeting, and a good half of grown-up Trumet was packed into that room, a few women along with the men. The Council members were seated at their regular table, it is true, with Captain Jeremiah Weeks in his presiding officer's chair, but his thumpings for order during the proceedings didn't amount to much more, so far as getting attention was concerned, than the shake of a baby's rattle might get in the middle of a hail storm over a tin roof.

I had come there with the full intention of ridiculing the whole business, telling Bartlett and his toy soldiers that they were making fools of themselves; Jonathan Bangs was no more responsible for the shipyard fire than I was—or the Reverend Ichabod was, for that matter—and that, if he had been caught near a British boat, it was because he was trying to catch the fellows in it. In fact I was about to say something along that line, but Captain Jeremiah asked for order, so that Major Bartlett could tell his story, so all I did then was to warn the Major to be careful and say nothing he wasn't sure of.

Jonathan has already told what went on at that mass meeting, so I shan't tell it again. I did my best to let him see that I was standing by him and didn't believe any of the stuff they were charging him with. Henry Allen was the worst of the lot and the bitterest. He had never been reconciled to the idea of Hope and Jonathan pairing off, and his spite showed now in every question he asked, and every time he laughed it was a mean laugh. I shouldn't have blamed Jonathan much if he had punched Henry's head, and there was one time when I didn't know but he was going to.

It wasn't Henry, though, nor Fowler, nor any of the others who were condemning him offhand, who worried me. It was Jonathan, himself, and the tangle he got himself into when he undertook to answer Bartlett and explain how and why he happened to be on the beach where the militia caught him. The Major's story was straight as a string, no kinks or knots in it anywhere. Jonathan's—all that part about tripping in a bayberry bush and knocking himself out so completely that he didn't come to for more than an hour—was so nonsensical that even I knew it was a lie. And the Major, when he got after him about where he was on the path and all that, snarled the silly story up like a wet fish line. I kept thinking to myself: "Oh, boy, boy, *what* are you doing this for? What is behind it all? You're no turncoat or traitor, course you aren't. But what *have* you been up to?"

His asking to be let have a word with me, just the two of us alone, was encouraging. He would tell *me* the truth, I was certain of it. But Allen put his foot down on that idea. On the whole, considering the state of town feeling that night, it was a sort of relief to my mind when Jonathan was taken off to the lockup. He would be safe there, anyhow, and I would make it my business to see him the first possible minute after sunup.

Nothing especial happened after he had gone. Captain Jeremiah Weeks notified us Council members to be on hand in that same room at nine o'clock on Sunday. He made it early so we could be through before church time. With the Reverend Samuels present he felt he had to put this in, I presume likely. The minister strained his own conscience enough to say that he, himself, would try and attend that meeting—which, considering what he was and his cast-iron scruples against Sabbath breaking, was, of itself, something to remember.

It was away along towards two when I got home. I had been afraid that Phoebe might be sitting up for me, ready to talk herself and me crazy about the fire and all the rest of it, but she had gone to bed, so I tiptoed up to my room and turned in. I didn't imagine I would be able to sleep any, but I did, and it was after six when I woke up. My first thought was to get to that lockup and see Jonathan and talk with him, if I could, before anybody else did. Breakfast could wait until I came back

Phoebe wasn't up yet—at least I didn't hear her in the kitchen—so I slipped out by the side door. I was a little surprised to find that door swinging open, not wide open but ajar. Of course I hadn't locked it when I came in—nobody locks his house door in Trumet—but I did think I had shut it tight. Maybe Phoebe had come in later than I had, although that didn't seem hardly possible. I shut it carefully this time, went out of the yard, and took the short cut across the fields towards the village.

As I came out on the main road, at the corner by the church, where the Bay Road joins, I saw two men come out of the Bay Road and walk on ahead of me in the way I was going. They were walking slow and talking very earnest so I was close aboard when they turned and saw me. I had recognized them before this—Henry Allen and Eben Fowler. I wondered what they were doing out so early and why they were together. Eben was dressed for church, dignified and precise from maintop to keelson. Henry had on his Sunday rig, too, but he couldn't look dignified even if he was starched and ironed.

"Ahoy there," I hailed. "Well, well! Haven't you fellows been to bed at all? Where are you bound?" Then, as the thought struck me: "What is it? Nothing more gone wrong, has there?"

Eben would have answered, I think, but Henry stopped him. "Huh!" he grunted. "Where are *you* bound? Suppose you tell us that first."

I didn't exactly know why I should tell them anything, and I didn't fancy his tone too well. My own was a little bit crisp, I shouldn't wonder.

"I'm bound about due south just now," I said. "Any objections?"

Henry looked at Fowler and Fowler back at him. "*I* told you!" said Henry. "The good friend trying to get in ahead of the rest of us. Well, he didn't quite come it, did he?"

Eben motioned him to hush. "Isaiah," he said to me, "am I right in supposing that you are on your way to the lockup to talk with Bangs?"

"And, if I am, what of it?"

It was Allen who answered that. "What of it?" he said over after me. "Well, just this of it. At the meeting last night it was decided by all hands present—except you, maybe, and Bangs for certain—that you and he weren't going to have chances to talk things over together by yourselves. Now mind you, Isaiah Dole, I ain't accusing you of anything, nobody is, but—well, we *know* this Bangs turn-coat sold us out first and then tried to burn us out. He was caught at it. Now he has always been your pet, and even last night you were trying to favor him. So—well—"

I think he saw that my right hand was getting ready to go into action. Anyhow, he stepped back out of range. Eben Fowler stepped in between us.

"There, there," he said. "Henry, your temper is running away with your common sense. You ought to be ashamed of yourself. Isaiah, I apologize to you for him, and he will do it himself later, I am sure. This is the situation, and I rather wonder that you haven't recognized it yourself. The meeting last night *did* decide that Bangs must not be allowed to talk with *anyone* for the present. He is a con-victed criminal, a traitor to all Trumet, and—"

"Not convicted yet, by a darned sight," I broke in. "And he won't be until I hear better evidence than I did last night."

"What more do you want?"

"I want him to have a chance to tell the truth, all of the truth. Oh, I know a part of what he told there at the Town House wasn't true. He was making it up as he went along, that was plain enough. He is hiding something, something he doesn't think the whole town ought to know—yet. And he probably didn't realize last night what a mess he was getting himself into by holding it back. He has had time to think it over now and—"

"And you were cal'lating to get to him early and help him think himself out of that mess? Uh huh! Well, you're not going to be allowed to. That's so, isn't it, Eben?"

This was from Allen, of course, and once more I took a step towards him and again Fowler stepped in front of me.

"Henry," he said, impatiently, "I do wish you would use the upper part of your head more and your tongue less. All the same, Isaiah, Henry is right, in a way. After Bangs was taken to the lockup last night it struck some of us—Captain Elnathan Berry for one and myself for another—that it would be very dangerous to let him see or talk alone with anybody, for the present, at least. If he is a traitor he may not be the only one. So, with Captain Weeks's approval, Henry and I saw Snow before we went home and gave him orders to let nobody in to see Bangs—nobody at all. And, if anyone comes there, trying to see him, to tell us who that person is. We are on our way there now to hear whether or not anyone has tried."

That was plain enough, and it was just as plain that I was the "trier" they expected to hear about. If I had asked them if they suspected me of being in the traitor gang they would have said no, that they never dreamed of such a thing, but I didn't give them the satisfaction of saying it. I didn't ask.

"Hum," said I. "Yes, yes, I see. Well, I am going to see Jonathan, and I am going to see him right away. If Sol Snow tries to stop me he'll be making a big mistake."

Solomon Snow was the special constable whose job was to watch the lockup, nights, at the rare times when there was anybody in it. He was fairly old and more than fairly fat and took his rum full as regular as he did his meals. Sol was one of the town jokes, as you might say.

When I made my declaration about seeing Jonathan whether or no, Fowler and Allen looked at each other. Eben shook his head.

"All right, Isaiah," he said. "Snow couldn't stop you, I imagine, and Henry and I shan't try. Only"—bearing down heavy on the word—"*only*, if you see him, we shall be there when you do. You—or anyone else—can't see him alone. Those were Captain Weeks's orders, remember."

For just a second I hesitated. I was so mad that my voice shook, I guess likely, but what could I do? A fight in the middle of the main road on Sunday morning wouldn't help

Jonathan any, and it certainly wouldn't help me. I gave in.

"Just as you say," I growled. "Then we'll all see him. Heave ahead."

We walked on. The Town House was only a little way ahead. Fowler said something about what a mercy it was that the fire had been put out before it did any more damage. I didn't say anything, nor did Henry. And then, all at once, he did.

"You didn't get to that fire soon as the most of us, Isaiah," he said. "What kept you? Didn't you hear the bell?"

I stopped short in my tracks. It seems queer enough as I tell it, but it is the living, honest truth, I hadn't thought of Seth Black, nor the note he wrote me and which had sent me down to his shanty the night before, since I came out of that shanty and saw the firelight over the shipyard. The fire and Jonathan's arrest and all the other excitement had driven Seth and his letter clean out of my head. My only excuse—if it is an excuse—is that I had never really taken that note in dead earnest. Nobody took Seth Black in earnest—or hadn't up to that time.

"Good God!" I swore. The note was still in my pocket, and I reached in and took it out. "That's where I was," I said. "This thing is responsible for my being late getting to the fire. I give you my word I'd forgot it altogether."

Eben took the note from my hand. He read it, and Henry, looking over his shoulder, read it, too. He was the first to say anything.

"Huh!" he grunted. "Drunk when he wrote it, most likely. Seen him since you got it, Isaiah?"

I told him of my trip to the shanty and of finding no one there. Allen didn't pay much attention, but Eben seemed to be sober and, for him, a good deal upset.

"The *New Hope*," he muttered to himself. " 'Bad work up tonite.' 'Trater and I know who 'tis.' . . . Lord above!

188

the fellow *did* know something. He must have.... But why did he write to you, Dole?"

"Because I happen to be the head of the *New Hope* enterprise, in a way. I suppose that was the reason. It is the only one I can think of."

Henry was scowling. "Cal'late I might think of another one if I tried," he growled. "Considering that Isaiah here is the closest chum of the traitor we were lucky enough to nail, it might be that Seth thought of Isaiah as the one to tip off. Sounds reasonable, don't you think?"

Eben was thinking, but not of just that, I judged. "I want to speak with you a minute, Henry," he said. "Excuse us, won't you, Isaiah?"

Without waiting for me to say whether I would excuse them or not, he took Allen to one side, and they whispered together. I heard Henry say: "Good idea" and "Sartin." Then, when the whispering was over they came back to me.

"Now we'll go in and see the fellow," said Eben, leading the way up the Town House steps. He still had Seth's letter in his hand so I reached across, took it, and put it back in my pocket.

Solomon Snow, looking half asleep, unlocked the door of the lockup when Eben knocked and let us in. Jonathan looked glad enough to see me but disappointed, I thought, when he saw that I hadn't come alone.

He has told all about what was said at that lockup talk between the four of us. I hadn't meant to say anything about the Black note just then. I wanted to think the whole thing over before I let anybody know that I was paying too much attention to it. If I had thought, I don't believe I should have mentioned it to Allen and Fowler until later. But my remembering it took me by surprise, and I out with it and now it would be public property—unless, as I hoped, I could get it before the Council before anybody else learned of it. Then I meant to beg them to keep it a secret, at least until Seth had been located and questioned.

Henry's shooting that stuff about Black's having been found and talked with already took me by surprise. That is what he and Fowler were whispering about, of course. Jonathan hit it right when he said it was a try at scaring him into confessing something. The way he came back at them tickled me and bucked me up, too. And his insisting that Seth be hunted up was just as heartening. He wasn't afraid of anything Seth could say, that was a sure bet. As for Eben's hints that Black was dead and Jonathan had killed him—that was child's talk, and I was surprised that as sensible a fellow as Eben Fowler should have said such things. He seemed to have almost as bitter a spite against Jonathan as Allen had, and I couldn't quite see why. Henry and he were relations, by marriage; perhaps that was it.

It was getting on time for the Council meeting, and, when we came out of the lockup, we went right into the meeting room. There were no outsiders at this meeting, just the Council and nobody else, but it was a lively session just the same and a pretty irritating and uncomfortable one for me.

There was a report about the fire damage, and that was encouraging. Thanks to that shift of wind and the fact that most of our supplies and stores were already aboard the *New Hope*, we had come through without enough damage to hurt us badly. A bunch of loose boards and straw and litter had been piled against the storehouse wall and whale oil poured over it—a hurry-up job it looked like. It flamed up quick and run up through the gable of the roof, making a great show of blaze and sparks for a few minutes, but it wasn't hard to put out.

When that report was disposed of, the real trouble began. The minue Jonathan Bangs's name was mentioned the guns began to pop. Captain Elnathan Berry's blunderbuss was the loudest. Elnathan is a fine man and an honest, square citizen, but he is considerable of a hothead. In his mind there wasn't any question that Jonathan Bangs was the firebug and the traitor and our first duty was to make an example of him, whatever that meant. Elkanah Davies was inclined to feel the same way. *And* Henry Allen, of course.

When I got a chance to say something I asked permission to call the Council's attention to one or two points that struck me.

"If Jonathan Bangs set that fire," I began, "as Captain Elnathan and you others seem to take it for granted he did, why on earth did he make such a half-way bungle of it? He was all sole alone there at the yard from right after supper time on. He could have laid a regular Fourth of July bonfire if he had wanted to and laid it aboard the *New Hope*, too. *That* fire would have cleaned us out completely. The bark is the one big thing in our scheme. If *she* burnt we were gone, that's all. If, as some of you are so certain sure, Bangs is a traitor drawing British pay, why didn't he make certain of earning his money by getting rid of the privateer—not a shed with only a little of importance left in it? Bosh and fiddlesticks! If the young fellow is a traitor—which I don't believe for a minute—I *know* he isn't a damn fool."

Well, that stirred things up. The Reverend Ichabod had something to say about profane language and might have said more if the others hadn't been too interested in worldly matters to give him the chance.

Henry Allen growled, without getting to his feet, that he judged I was so anxious to clear my blue-eyed boy's coattails that I was almost ready to swear the fire had set itself. Squire Bailey, always level-headed, stopped the rest of the sneering by saying that there was something in what I had just said. "Setting that fire, as and where it was set, would have been, for a person with Bangs's opportunities and time, a foolish and slipshod job, I should say. And I agree with you, Captain Dole, young Bangs never struck me as a fool."

"Except when he told that string of lies in this room last night," grumbled Davies. The Squire nodded. "Yes," he said, "that was foolish enough—and pretty surprising, too, coming from a young fellow with at least the average amount of common sense. He couldn't have supposed we would believe him."

Captain Weeks asked me if I had any idea why Jonathan had lied. "You know him better than any of the rest of us; you've known him longer, anyway."

I shook my head. "I was hoping to see him alone," I said, "and that he might, perhaps, tell me more than he would the whole town. I wasn't permitted to do that, so I know nothing—except that he did lie."

Allen laughed out loud. "Something to hear you say that much, Isaiah," he crowed. He would have said more, probably, but Eben Fowler stopped him by asking the Chair's attention.

"Captain Dole has just told Henry and me something which may or may not be important. If he had told it last night—but he didn't. He forgot it—he says."

Everybody looked at me and kept looking while I told about the Seth Black note. The note was passed from hand to hand. There was a buzz of whispering, and a half-dozen questions were fired at me. Captain Jeremiah rapped for order.

"This is—is queer enough, for certain," he said, looking at the piece of paper through his spectacles and then at me over them. "Captain Dole, you forgot this last night you say. Why?"

When an old friend like Jeremiah began calling me "Captain Dole" instead of by my first name, it showed plain enough the change that was coming across those Council members so far as complete trust in me was concerned. I don't suppose I should have wondered at it. Jonathan Bangs was already condemned as a traitor in the eyes of most of them. I was the one responsible for bringing Jonathan to Trumet. I had backed him for the position he held in our *New Hope* enterprise. And even now—as they saw it—I was taking his part and pretending still to believe in him. Why, in a way, I was pretty close to being under suspicion myself.

I realized this, and I suppose it should have made me more careful, but instead it made me mad. I explained that I had forgot Black's letter because I had other things to take up my mind after I saw that fire blazing in the shipyard. "Considering who had written it I didn't give much heed to it when I got it. I don't know as I do even now, far as that goes."

The rest of them did. The Reverend Samuels asked if anybody had noticed Seth around the yard at the time of the fire. Nobody could recollect his being seen at all. "That's funny," grumbled Elkanah Davies. "About everybody in Trumet who was able to walk was there."

Squire Bailey suggested that, remembering Black's habits, it was quite likely that he wasn't able to walk by that time.

"I do think, though, that he should be located and questioned at once," he said. "I suggest, Jeremiah, that a committee be appointed to hunt for Seth Black and bring him before a meeting of this Council to be called as soon as he is found."

All hands of us thought that was a good notion, so Captain Jeremiah appointed Elnathan Berry and Eben Fowler and me as the committee. I had to say I'd serve, of course, though I wasn't what you'd call eager. I was liable to be busy enough without any extra job.

Squire Bailey asked me when I saw Seth last, and I told

of meeting him by the tavern. "He offered to buy me a drink and started to sing songs. If there was any hints about traitors in that performance I didn't get it."

And yet, as I said it, it came to me that Seth *had* said some queer things. That about the British being willing to "stump up" for something or other. Yes, and I remembered, too, that he had tried to see me down at the shipyard that morning. I think likely I should have mentiond this, but Captain Elnathan and Elkanah and Henry were whispering together, and now Elkanah bobbed up with another motion.

This was that a committee of two or three "responsible, unprejudiced" Council members be appointed to go to Jonathan Bangs's room at the Light place and search it carefully.

"If he has been having dealings with the enemy," Elkanah went on.... "Yes, yes, I know you don't believe he has, Isaiah, but I'm only saying 'if.' ...*If* he has, there is a chance that there might be some evidence, papers or letters or something, in that room that we ought to see, and see right off. So I move it be attended to."

Henry Allen seconded the motion. Squire Bailey asked me if I saw any objection to the idea. I told him no. "Only," I put in, "you want to remember that Jonathan hasn't slept in that room for two nights. He has been down aboard the *New Hope.*"

Allen sniffed. "He wasn't aboard her at the important time last night," he pointed out. "When they caught him he was way over by Shad Cove. And why? Don't ask me, because I haven't heard any satisfactory explanation yet."

Weeks named Captain Elkanah and Allen as room-searching committee. That ended that session. It was church time, anyway.

Another meeting was called for eight o'clock that evening. Fowler and Berry and I hadn't been able to locate Seth Black by that time. We had been down to his shanty and around to the two or three shacks up and down the beach where he sometimes dropped in on the few cronies he had, but nobody had seen him since the day before. Captain Elnathan, who is considerable older than Fowler or me, was pretty tired by this time, so he was in favor of our calling the hunt off until Monday morning. "If he hasn't shown up by that time," he said, "we'll make a good, clean daylight job of it. I, for one, don't fancy tramping through pines and briar patches in the dark. By tomorrow Seth will have got over his attack of the 'horrors,' most likely, and will be finding himself."

I didn't know but what Eben Fowler, after his wild talk about Black's being dead, and his more than halfway hints that Jonathan had killed him—all that spiteful, silly chatter he had tossed off there in the lockup—might want to keep on, but he didn't. He seemed to have got over what ailed him and be sensible again.

"I guess you are right, Elnathan," he said. "We'll leave the fellow to his 'horrors' till tomorrow."

So we went to the evening Council meeting. There nothing much of any account was done. Plenty was said but not much of that was important, either. And, although Elkanah Davies and Allen had given Jonathan's room at the Light house a thorough ransacking, they had found not so much as a scrap of paper that was in any way suspicious. A squad of militia were standing guard on the *New Hope* and the shipyard, and their orders were to let no one inside the gates without orders from the Council heads, and not even then unless they were under escort.

So we adjourned, subject to call on Monday.

2.

It was almost eleven that Sunday night when I opened the side door and found Phoebe Light and the cat sitting up for me; that is, Phoebe was sitting in the rocking chair, and the cat was sitting on her. The cat was sleepy but Phoebe wasn't. I had eaten—what little eating I had done since the fire—at the tavern, and this was the first time I had been home. Phoebe had been at that fire, of course, with the rest of Trumet, and her tongue, I judged, had been running steady about every waking minute from then on. It was all set to run now.

Oh, wasn't it dreadful? Wasn't it awful? Could a body ever believe such things could happen? Did I ever in my born days hear tell of such—

"Yes, yes," I agreed, to save time. "Now I am turning in, Phoebe, and I shall turn out again pretty early, so don't bother about cooking my breakfast. I'll eat somewhere and somehow—if I happen to think of it."

"But, oh, Captain Isaiah! About poor Mr. Jonathan— Ain't it terrible? Captain Elkanah and Henry Allen coming in the house and tromping all round his room and pawing his clean things all over. Why, I'd just washed and ironed them shirts of his, and now—"

"Um-hm. I know. Well, good night."

"But they say he's been took up by the milishy and put in the lockup. In that awful lockup! Everybody knows how dirty *that* place is. I declare to man I wouldn't put a— a skunk in there."

"Um-hm. Well, Jonathan probably is glad you didn't put one there. Good night."

"But, Captain Isaiah, you know what they are saying he did?"

"Who did? The skunk?"

"No, no! Skunk! The idea! No, what Mr. Jonathan done. He set fire to the vessel—our bark—and was running off to join the British when they caught him."

I turned on her. "Do you believe that, Phoebe?" I asked.

"Eh? Why—why, no, course I don't, really. Only—"

"Then, if you don't believe it, don't say it."

"But I wasn't saying it. I was just—"

I shut the door. She beat me. I never knew anybody else so set on having the last word. Yes, and the first word, too—so far as that went.

Eben Fowler and Captain Berry and I had planned to meet at Eben's house at eight Monday morning to start hunting for Seth Black in earnest—that is, providing Seth hadn't turned up somewhere by or before that time, which I thought he probably would. I turned out early, heard Phoebe in the kitchen but dodged outdoors before she saw me, and hurried down to the shipyard to see how things were there.

They were all right, thank goodness. Abijah Doane, who was sergeant of the militia guard aboard the *New Hope*, reported that nothing out of the way had happened during the night. I asked him, careless as I could make it sound, if he had seen anything of Seth Black lately. He said he hadn't and didn't know as he was especially hankering to.

"What's all this fuss about old Seth?" he laughed. "Heard Captain Elnathan was asking about him yesterday afternoon. Seth must be getting popular all at once. Generally speaking, folks are more anxious to keep clear of him than they are to run across him. Haw, haw!"

I ate a mouthful at the tavern and hustled on over to Fowler's. Eben and Captain Elnathan were in the front yard waiting for me. Elnathan, it seemed, had been around asking more questions since he had his half-past-six breakfast, but nobody he asked knew anything about Black.

"It seems as if nobody got a sight of him all day yesterday," he said. "Funny, too, for he's generally batting around. I wonder if anything *has* happened to him. Maybe he sobered up after he wrote that letter to you, Isaiah, was scared when he realized what he'd done, and ran away."

"Eben, here, thinks he's dead, I believe," I said with a

grin. "Thinks he talked too much about traitors and things and was killed to keep his mouth shut. That was your notion, wasn't it, Eben?"

Fowler didn't like that. Even the mildest kind of joke, with him on the wrong end of it, was as hard for him to take as a dose of dock-leaf bitters. His back straightened.

"I said that to watch its effect on a—um—particular friend of yours, Dole. I did *not* say that I believed it."

That, and the look that went with it, put me in my place, of course. Back in the days when Martha Allen and I were keeping company I had often seen him look at me in that high and lofty way, and, if I had had any decent respect for dignity, I ought to have wilted, I guess likely. I'm afraid I didn't, though; rather enjoyed giving him a jolt now and again.

We were undecided just where to begin our hunt this time, whether to go down to Seth's shanty again or to take a trip down to the Bay beach and search the clam shacks there. Finally we thought we would try the Bay shore first.

We started off down the Point Road.

We had got within sight of the roof of the Allen house, ahead and over to the right, with Hornpout Pond on our left, when—just as Jonathan Bangs has told you he did earlier that morning—I noticed the flock of crows swinging and cawing over the clump of pines the other side of the narrow stretch of salt marsh. Crows are common enough, but they don't usually act that way unless something is disturbing them. I shouldn't have paid attention to them if we had been on any other errand than the one we were on, but as it was—well, I did, anyhow. I presume Phoebe Light would say it was a spirit hand pointing them out to me.

Captain Elnathan asked me what I was looking at.

"Those birds," I said. "They are fussed about something."

Fowler wasn't interested. He suggested a blacksnake might be responsible. Well, birds do hate snakes—they steal their eggs and young-ones—and that little bunch of high ground the other side of the marsh was famous for snakes. The explanation was reasonable enough, but, somehow, it didn't satisfy me this time. "You fellows wait here a minute or two," I said. "I'm going across for a look."

Berry said I must enjoy getting my feet wet and Fowler looked impatient, but I went just the same. At the far side of the hummock the little bank sloped sharp down to the pond. It was all high grass and cattail flags at the edge of the water.

And sticking out from among the flags and roots was a pair of boots. The boots weren't empty—there were feet and legs in them. I suppose I must have jumped down that bank, although I don't remember jumping—don't remember getting down at all. I stooped to the body lying there and pulled the grass away from the face.

Oh, well! You know whose body it was; Jonathan has already told you how *he* found it. I was terribly upset, but I don't seem to recollect being really surprised at all. I had known the minute I sighted those boots that this was the end of our hunt for poor old Seth Black.

I bent over him, and then I saw how he had been killed. His shirt was pulled down from the neck, and I could see plain enough. He had been stabbed from behind, and whoever did it did a thorough job.

The thought flashed to my mind: Eben Fowler was right, after all! Seth Black *has* been killed—and, probably, to shut his mouth for good and all.

I ran up the bank and yelled at the top of my lungs. "Come here!" I hailed. "Come quick!"

They must have judged it was something serious, for they

199

didn't call back but came on the run. Fowler ahead, and Elnathan, who must have been making his first run for a good many years, surprisingly close in his wake. They looked where I pointed. Then they saw, too.

I don't know who spoke first after that minute when we all three stood and looked. Seems to me now that we all spoke together. I recollect Berry's saying something about taking the poor devil out of the water. "For God sakes, don't leave him there!" he begged.

So we lifted what was left of Seth Black out onto dry land. I was kneeling over him, with Elnathan at my elbow, when I heard Eben Fowler speak quick and sharp. I looked up. He was standing by the water's edge pointing down into the grass close to where Seth had been.

"Look!" he was saying. "Look there!"

Berry and I both looked. In that grass, where it had been dropped or thrown, was a knife, a sailor's knife made to be worn in a sheath at the belt. I had seen hundreds like it, had owned a half dozen myself. Captain Elnathan picked it up. "That's what it was done with," he snarled. "Oh, the blasted, murdering swab!"

The sheath was close alongside it in the grass. I was the one who picked that up, and, the minute I held it in my hand, I saw something that made me catch my breath. On that sheath, burnt into the leather with a hot iron, were two letters—J. B. Even without those letters I would have known that sheath anywhere, just as, when I had a real look at the knife, I knew that I, myself, had had both sheath and knife in my own pocket considerable less than a week before.

They belonged to Jonathan Bangs.

The others saw the initials, too. They didn't need to be told whose they were. Fowler growled in his throat. Captain Elnathan spoke his thoughts out loud.

"J. B.," he said, slowly. "Jonathan Bangs! Blast his black soul!"

Eben nodded. "I wouldn't have believed it!" he said in a kind of whisper. "When I said that yesterday morning in the lockup I—I had no thought of its being the—the truth. Good Lord Almighty! I can't believe it now!"

Berry was shaking all over. "Don't be a fool, man!" he snapped. "It's proved, isn't it? Hanging is too good for him, but I'll see that he gets that much, anyhow. Oh, the dirty dog!"

I hadn't said a word. Eben Fowler laid a hand on my shoulder. "This is tough on you, Isaiah," he said. "It isn't your fault, of course, but—"

I pulled away from him. "Oh, shut up!" I snarled. And then, after a minute or so, "Well, what next?"

The next thing was to get Seth's body away from there. We couldn't carry him, of course. There was a little talk about just what to do, but Elnathan and Eben did the talking, for I was in a kind of fog. Still I didn't believe—couldn't—wouldn't believe. Two thirds of my mind kept saying: "I know better. It's a lie," and the other third was telling me that it must be true, there was the knife to prove it.

Henry Allen's was the nearest house, so Berry and Elnathan decided to go there and get Henry to come, with his horse and truck cart, for the body and take it up to Sylvanus Wixon's. Wixon was the Trumet undertaker, and, as poor old Seth didn't have any relations so far as anybody knew, he would be buried from there—after the doctor had looked him over, of course.

"You wait here till Henry comes, Isaiah," said Captain Elnathan. You will notice he didn't ask me what I wanted to do, just gave the order, same as a skipper might give it to a foremast hand. I don't know as it struck me at the time—I was too upset and foggy to think clearly even yet—

but it was one more sign of my changed rating in the town and Council. That change, that I had got a hint of in Sunday's Council meetings, had really set in. Jonathan Bangs was convicted of treason and murder, and I, myself—although I doubt if any of them suspected me of being mixed up in the murdering—wouldn't be wholly trusted from then on.

As I say I didn't realize this at the time, but, when Elnathan ordered me to stay there and wait until Allen came, I asked a question.

"Are you two coming back with Henry and the cart?" I asked.

Fowler didn't answer, but I saw him look at Elnathan. Elnathan didn't hesitate at all.

"No sir-ee, we're not," he said, sharp. "We're going straight from Allen's to the lockup. I, for one, want the chance to tell that damned Bangs cutthroat that he is going to hang—and soon, too. Come on, Eben."

But that I wouldn't stand for. Jonathan might hang, he might even deserve hanging, but at least I meant to be among the first to tell him why and hear what he had to say for himself. According to my law and gospel, you don't desert a friend until you are certain sure he ought to be deserted. I wasn't sure of that yet—not even with that devilish knife in front of me, I wasn't.

"If you are going to the lockup I am going with you," I told him.

"You'll wait right here," snapped Captain Elnathan.

"You try and make me," I snapped back. "You aren't going to bully that boy without my being on hand to listen to both sides."

I don't know how it might have come out—the old Captain was savage mad and he wasn't used to being contradicted—but just then we heard somebody whistling over on the Point Road. I scrambled up the bank and through the bushes and saw Issachar Atwood walking along that road. He had been digging clams down by the creek mouth. I sang out to him, and he came splashing across the salt marsh.

It will take too long to tell you how he looked and what he said when we showed him Seth Black's body lying there. It doesn't matter, anyhow. What did matter was that, without asking Eben or Elnathan to say aye, yes, or no, I ordered Issachar to stay in that place until the cart came and then the rest of us started for Henry's. Elnathan scarcely spoke to me on the way, although Fowler might have if I had let him. I didn't, for I didn't want to be spoken to—or to speak either. The fog in my head was clearing up a little mite, and I was getting able to think. There were some queer things about that knife being left where it was, there certainly were.

Nobody answered when we knocked at the Allen kitchen door, so we opened the door and went in. Nobody in the kitchen when we got there. A minute later, though, the door leading from the sitting-room opened, and Hope Allen came in. She looked very white and stirred up. Stirred up as I was, myself, I noticed that, and I wondered if she could have heard about the murder. She couldn't have, of course; I realized it as soon as the thought came to me.

Eben Fowler must have noticed how she looked, for he spoke first.

"What is it, Hope?" he asked quickly. "Is anything the matter?"

She acted almost as if she didn't hear him, as if she was thinking of something else.

"What?" she stammered. "What? Matter? No, nothing is the matter with me. Why do you ask that?"

Before Eben could say any more Captain Elnathan cut in. "Where's your father?" he asked.

"Father? Oh, he went up to the village some time ago with the horse and wagon. There was some carting to be done at the shipyard, I believe."

Berry grunted. "Funny we didn't meet him," he said. "We came straight along the Point Road. I didn't see him anywhere, did you, Eben?"

Eben Fowler shook his head. "We weren't on the road all the time, Elnathan," he reminded him. Then, as if it didn't matter, anyhow, he went right back to the question he had asked first.

"You are sure there is nothing the matter, Hope? It seemed to me—you look—"

She didn't let him finish. "Oh, no, no, no!" she broke in, impatient. "I am all right. A little—er—headache, that's all. What are you three here for? Why do you want Father? . . . Has anything else happened? Anything since the fire, I mean?"

And then Captain Elnathan, who has about as much notion of tactfulness as a bull, had to come bellowing in. "Happened!" he snorted. "I should say something *has* happened! Murder is what has happened—bloody, sneaking, cowardly murder! And we know who did it, too. Yes, by the Almighty, we do!"

The blundering old jackass! He had forgotten that this girl and Jonathan Bangs had been close friends—yes, and unless all Trumet was wrong in its guessing and gossiping considerable more than friends—for months.

"Hush, Elnathan!" I ordered. "Hope, Mr. Fowler and the Captain and I have just had a good deal of a shock, and we are all upset. You see—"

"Wait! Please wait, Captain Isaiah! You say—you say someone has been murdered. Somebody here in Trumet?"

"Well—yes. I—"

"Wait! Why do you want to see my father?"

I began to realize that maybe I had been almost as blun-

204

dering as Elnathan. Eben Fowler took charge now, and his quiet, soft-spoken words helped to smooth down the situation—like pouring sweet oil in it, so to say.

"There, there, Hope," he told her. "There's nothing for you to be alarmed about. Your father has nothing to do with the—the dreadful affair. We came to him because this was the nearest house to—to where it happened, that's all."

I expected, of course, that her next word would be to ask who the murdered person was. She couldn't have known. If anyone else had found that body before we three did, it wouldn't have been left lying there; and half of Trumet would have been on its way to the place by this time. No, she couldn't have known, and yet she didn't ask. Fowler went on.

"There, there, Hope," he said. "Don't be frightened. "It is not one of our friends, thank goodness. Poor old drunken Seth Black is lying dead up here by the pond. We found his body a few minutes ago."

You couldn't keep Elnathan Berry gagged any longer. His kettle lid blew off then and there, and the steam spouted.

"He was stabbed in the back with a knife," he all but roared at her. "And we found the knife, found it lying right alongside, where the murdering villain had dropped it. And we know whose knife it was—all hands of us knew it soon as we saw it. Why, the dog's initials were there, right on the sheath. J. B., that's what they were. And if those letters don't stand for Jonathan Bangs, what do they stand for?"

I could have choked him. I thought Eben looked as if he could, too. I stepped forward, didn't know but she might faint or something. She didn't, though. She had been pale when she first came into that room, and, for just a second, she whitened still more. And then the red came

205

flaming back into her face. Her shoulders squared, and she faced the three of us, her eyes shining like fire coals.

"It's a lie!" she vowed. "A lie! I don't believe a word of it. Of course it isn't true. You ought to be ashamed to even think such things."

I was ashamed. Ashamed of my thoughts and more ashamed of myself for thinking them. There was no shaming old Captain Elnathan, though. He flew right back at her.

"Ashamed of nothing!" he thundered. "I tell you we found the scamp's knife with his name on it, right there by the poor devil he killed. I tell you—"

She held up her hand. "Hush!" she flashed at him. Then, turning to Fowler and me, "*You* tell me, Uncle Eb. You or Captain Isaiah."

So Eben told her what we had found and how we came to find it. He even went so far as to explain why we had come to her house—after Henry and the horse and cart. She heard him through, didn't interrupt once.

"Is that all?" she asked scornfully. "Is that what you call proof? Nothing but that?"

Captain Elnathan looked at her as if he calculated she was crazy. "Nothing but—but—" he sputtered. "Nothing! For heaven's sakes what more do you want? If that ain't proof—"

"Oh, hush!" she broke in again. "Eben, do *you* believe Jonathan is a murderer?"

Fowler hesitated. "Well, my dear," he stammered, "I—I can't tell you how I hate to believe it. I have always had a high regard for the young man. And I know, too, that you and he—"

She didn't let him finish, either. She swung around to me. "Captain Isaiah, you know Jonathan better than anyone else—except—well, better than anybody, perhaps. Do *you* believe he would do a thing like that?"

I tried not to hesitate; I don't think I did.

"No, I don't," I said.

She drew a long breath. "Of course you don't! I knew you couldn't. I am glad someone has common sense—yes, and loyalty."

That was too much for Elnathan.

"Loyalty!" he snorted. "Talk about loyalty and that Bangs cutthroat at the same time! He was a traitor in the first place; we knew that before we found out about the murdering. He all but burnt up our bark and was sneaking off to join the enemy, the gang that hired him, when the militia caught him at it. And poor Seth Black knew he was a traitor and so—"

"Oh!" She stamped her foot. "Oh, that is another wicked lie! He isn't a traitor. He never was. I know it."

Captain Elnathan started to break out again and then gave it up. He turned to Fowler.

"Come on, Eb," he said, disgusted. "She's crazy. So head over heels crazy about that Bangs blackguard that she would swear black was white if he told her 'twas. If I was her father—if I was Henry—I'd shut her up in a dark closet or somewhere till she came to her senses. Come on, come on! No use wasting breath here."

Eben looked anything but comfortable as he moved towards the door.

"Are you coming with us, Isaiah?" he asked.

Elnathan was more disgusted than ever.

"What do you want him tagging along for, Fowler?" he asked. "He is as soft-headed about Bangs as she is. Heard what he just said, didn't you? Didn't believe he was guilty! Lord sakes alive! Come *on!*"

He was at the door by this time, with Fowler a few steps astern of him. Hope asked where they were going. Eben answered.

"Why—why, Hope," he said, "we are going to the

lockup to see Jonathan Bangs. Oh, my dear girl, I can't tell how sorry I am that— Why, what is it?"

It was the expression on her face that made him ask that, I guess likely.

"The lockup?" she repeated slowly. "Why, he—"

And then she stopped short.

"What were you going to say, Hope?" asked Eben again.

"Nothing. . . . Captain Isaiah, you—you will—you won't let—"

"I won't let him be hurt—no, nor condemned as a traitor or murderer, either—until I am a whole lot more sure than I am now that he is either one. As I said in the Council meeting yesterday, Jonathan Bangs is a long, long way from being a fool. And nobody but a driveling idiot would stab a man with a knife with his own initials on the sheath and then leave that sheath in plain sight where anybody but a blind man could find it the first time he looked. Bosh! Now," turning to Eben and Elnathan, "I'm ready to go with you. You aren't going to that lockup without me, so don't imagine you are."

We went out and left Hope standing with her back against the door to the sitting-room. I never was more sorry for anybody in my life.

We headed back up the Point Road on the way to the village and the lockup—but we never got there. A couple of hundred yards from the Allen house we met Henry himself, on the seat of his truck wagon, driving home. He looked excited, and he hailed us before we did him.

"Where you been? Where you bound?" he sang out. "You've heard the news? Course you have!"

There was only one item of news in our minds just then, but I couldn't understand how he had heard that yet. I spoke before Elnathan or Fowler did.

"What news?" I asked.

"Why, about that Bangs fellow. He got out of the lockup

sometime along in the night; got old Sol drunk and cleared out. When they went there this morning there wasn't a sign of him. What do you think of that? Guess there ain't much doubt now that he set the fire, is there? Off aboard one of those John Bull boats this minute, he most likely is, collecting his pay for doing it."

3.

Oh, well, Henry had a lot more to say, but I didn't pay much heed to it. All I could think was: Oh, Jonathan, Jonathan, how *could* you? The boy was in a bad enough pickle before, but there might have been somebody besides myself to take his part—two or three somebodies, maybe, if he had only stayed where they put him, faced the music, and told a true, straight story—*all* of his story.

But now! Why, his running away would be proof enough of guilt to convince even the few that might still have wanted to believe in him. If he wasn't guilty why did he run? Oh, Jonathan, Jonathan! I'll take back what I said about your not being a fool. You are one—either that or something a good deal worse.

These were some of the things that kept whirling through my muddled head while Henry Allen was talking. I didn't ask a question or make any remarks. Eben Fowler was about as quiet as I was. Captain Elnathan, though, was spitting fire like a volcano. He was for wasting no more time. Jonathan Bangs must be caught and tried and strung up before the day was over.

Henry Allen sniffed at that. "Cal'late you didn't hear all I said, Elnathan," he put in. "You've got to have some-body to hang if you want to make the show worth going to. Nigh as can be guessed—and guessing is all there is to go by—the rascal got out of the lockup sometime last night. This morning the militia guard down by the mouth of the harbor thought they sighted a boat rowing out from the beach a half mile or so to the south'ard. It was too far out for them to do anything by the time they got there, but the general belief is that friend Benedict Arnold Bangs was aboard that boat. That's the general guess, anyhow."

And then, of course, we had to tell Henry about Seth Black and listen to all his "God sakeses" and "You don't tell mes." Finally we sent him over to help Issachar Atwood collect what was left of Seth and cart it to the under-taker's. Captain Elnathan hurried off to see Jeremiah Weeks and have another Council meeting called first thing. I went straight to the Lights' house, for I had something I wanted to ask Phoebe. Where Eben Fowler went I don't know.

Phoebe was in the kitchen when I got home. She hadn't heard about Seth yet, the Lord be thanked, and I didn't tell her. She had heard, though, from somebody, about Jonathan's getting out of the lockup, and she was in a state halfway between crying and fighting mad. It seems that the person who told her—Melissa Timson, seems to me it was—had declared it proved Jonathan to be a firebug and a traitor in pay of the enemy and Phoebe had flared up and given Melissa fits. If you will remember, she, herself, had said something of the same sort to me only the night before—Sunday night, that is—and when I asked her if she believed it, she said no, she didn't. The fact is, I presume likely, that she didn't want to believe it, and so the oftener it was said to her the more she got afraid it might be so and the madder and more weepy she got.

Anyhow, my coming in was a blessing for her because it gave her a chance to ease her mind and fire some of the broadsides she had been thinking up since Melissa left. All I could do for the first few minutes was say yes or no, and I had to say those quick.

"The very idea!" she wheezed—she had been talking to

Melissa and herself so much that she was hoarse already. "The very idea! Just because poor Mr. Jonathan broke out of that lockup, folks are calling him—er—er—a treason and a—turnstile."

I judged she meant "turncoat," but telling her so would have been too much of a job just then. She blazed right along.

"Saying his running away proves it! I never heard such silly talk. I said to that Melissa T., I said: '*Anybody* would break out of a lockup like that, wouldn't they? Any clean person, I mean. And I will say this for Mr. Jonathan, he was one of the neatest, cleanest souls ever I did washing for. And careful of his things! Why, there was hardly even a button off his shirts or underdrawers—' There now, Captain Isaiah, you see the state I'm in. You know me well enough to know I never would have called those—er—garments by name in your presence if I wasn't *so* tittered up I don't realize what I'm saying. . . . Well, anyhow—"

After a while—and it was quite a while, too—I smoothed her down enough to ask the question I had been waiting to ask. "Phoebe," I said, "do you remember Friday morning, just as I was leaving here to go down to the shipyard, I gave you that sheath knife that belonged to Mr. Bangs, the one I had borrowed of him, and asked you, when you went in to clear up his room, to leave it on his table? You remember that, don't you?"

She bobbed her head. "Remember? Of course I remember. I hope you know by this time that I ain't the kind to forget things."

"Oh, certain, I know that. You put the knife in that room, didn't you?"

"Sartin sure I did. Why—"

"Just a second. When did you put it there? Right off, that morning? Or next day? Or when?"

"Eh? I put it there right straight off, of course. You told me to, yourself."

"All right, all right. I just wanted to know, that's all."

"Well, you ought to have known in the first place, I should think. Seems to me I've housekeeped for you and Mr. Bangs long enough for you to know I *always* do what you tell me to. Of course, if you ain't satisfied—"

"There, there! Never mind."

"But I do mind—"

She was in one of her stubborn conniptions by this time, and I gave it up. I meant to ask her more about the knife later on, but I had had experience enough with her to realize that this was no time to do it. The state of mind she was in now—especially after her flare-up with the Timson woman—meant that the more she was asked the more obstinate she would be in sticking to what she had said in the beginning. I hadn't much doubt that she had put the sheath knife in Jonathan's room Friday morning; it would have been the natural thing for her to do. If she hadn't—

What was in the back of my mind was this: When Fowler and Berry and I came out of the Allen house, after our talk with Hope, the memory of my leaving Jonathan's knife with Phoebe to be put on the bureau in his bedroom came to me all of a sudden, and I had been thinking about it, now and again, ever since. I asked Henry, in our talk with him a few minutes before, if he and Captain Elkanah Davies —the committee sent by the Council to search Jonathan's room and dunnage on Sunday—had seen the sheath knife when they did their searching. He hadn't. There was no knife of any kind in that room, he was ready to swear to that.

"We would have seen it if there had been," he vowed. "We combed that room thorough, now I tell you."

Phoebe had told me that Jonathan had come back to his

room on Friday to get some of his things to take down to the *New Hope* where he was standing night watch, so, of course, he must have taken the knife along with the other things. She had put it there, and it wasn't there Sunday afternoon, so that was the only answer. I may as well say here that Doctor Blodgett reported to the Council, at the meeting that followed right after this, that, as near as he could figure from the condition of the body, Seth Black had been dead more than twenty-four hours when we found him. "I can't be too definite," said the doctor, "but I should figure that he must have been killed sometime Saturday evening or night."

The night of the fire, you see. Well, I got to his shanty at half-past ten, or thereabouts, and he wasn't there then, so it sounded probable.

And Jonathan had got his knife back on Friday. If he only hadn't—but he did, so that spark of hope for him was squelched. It was a mighty faint glimmer, anyhow, but I was chasing glimmers. I wouldn't even yet believe he was a traitor and a murderer.

I was the only one in town—except Phoebe Light, maybe —who didn't believe just that. The Council meeting that Monday was the grimmest, ugliest one I had taken part in up to that time.

And, too, it was the first one where, during the biggest part of it, I felt so all alone, as you might say, with no-body—not even Squire Bailey—to take my part; where what I had to say was listened to grudgingly. They let me talk, but, when I had said my say, they went right ahead as if I had been keeping still. I don't suppose I can blame them much. Every man there had put his spare dollars in the *New Hope* enterprise. And now it looked as if all that had gone for nothing. If Jonathan Bangs was a traitor, if he had been working against instead of for the Trumet people, if he had sold them out to the enemy—why, well, you can understand the feeling.

And I, as I have said before, was Jonathan's backer. I had brought him to Trumet. He had taken them all in, had made fools out of them, had stuck his knife into their backs just as he had stuck it into the back of poor old Seth Black. Of course, if what they believed about him was true, my back was just as full of holes as theirs, but they didn't stop to think of that.

There was bitter talk, plenty of it. And frightened, discouraged talk, too, from a few. Henry Allen and Captain Elnathan Berry were as bitter as anybody. Elnathan was speaking about our scheme for getting the powder down from Tamoset. "Bangs knew as much about those plans as anybody," he said. "And what he knows the British know by this time. A grand chance that powder will have to ever get into our hands. May be aboard the *Terror* already."

Henry Allen laughed, sarcastic. "Don't forget who we sent to Tamoset to help with those plans," he sneered. "Ezra Light, that's who. Another one of Isaiah's pet trusties. I'll sell out my share in this *New Hope* fizzle for four shilling, cash. Anybody offer to take me up?"

That was a little more than I could stand. I jumped to my feet.

"*I'll* take you up, Henry," I said. "And here are the four shilling, right in my hand. Bah and bosh! What is the matter with you—yes, and some of the rest of you, too? The *New Hope* fizzle, as you call it, isn't a fizzle yet by any manner of means. The bark is ready, the stores and guns are aboard, the powder is either on the way, or soon will be. As for the plans for getting it here and Jonathan's knowing about them, you forget that he doesn't know what those plans are any more than you or I do. Our Tamoset friends were the ones to settle the details of those plans. Light will tell us those details when he gets here."

"If he ever does." This was from someone at the back of the room; I couldn't turn around quick enough to see who. Captain Jeremiah Weeks pounded for order.

"That will do, Captain Dole," he ordered. "I think I can safely say that this Council doesn't intend to surrender while there is a plank afloat to cling to. We've gone into this thing whole-hearted, for better or for worse; our fellow townsfolk have trusted to our leadership and gone into it, too. We tried to figure against every possible block and hindrance from the outside, but we didn't figure on dirty work from the inside. Well, now we'll just have to figure how to fight that—yes, and beat it. As Captain Dole has just said, we've got a crack vessel, armed and rigged and ready for sea. We've got a hand-picked crew ready to step aboard. We've got a first-rate captain—"

He stopped and looked around the room.

"I'll say that again," he repeated. "We've got a first-rate captain. He may have made a bad mistake in his choice for first officer, but, after all, we are partly to blame for that choice ourselves. I don't believe there is one of us here who would want to put the *New Hope* under anybody but Isaiah Dole. If there is now is the time for him to speak up."

He waited. How many of them might have wanted to speak up I can't tell; what I do know is that none of them did. As for me, I couldn't scarcely believe my ears. I had been feeling like a leper in the Bible; it had seemed to me that all hands pulled their coat skirts to one side when I passed them for fear of catching the disease. And now, to hear the head of our Council come out for me this way was —well, it was like getting a pat on the back when you are expecting a punch in the jaw. It didn't mean that Captain Jeremiah Weeks wasn't as down on Jonathan as anybody else; it didn't mean that he wasn't still holding me responsible for trusting Jonathan and giving him the chance to play traitor. What it did mean was that he—Weeks—was square enough and broad-minded enough not to let his spite and hate of one man interfere with his honest rating of another. He knew I could navigate and command and fight a ship, and he was big enough to say so.

He waited a full minute—it seemed longer to me. Then: "I judge you all feel as I do—" he began; but Eben Fowler was rising to his feet.

"Captain Weeks and gentlemen," he said in that quiet, soft-spoken way of his, "I am sure that we all agree with our chairman in his estimate of Captain Dole's ability as a seaman and commander of a vessel. I should like to ask him one question, however. Circumstances have changed greatly in the past few days, as we all know. I'm not referring to the treason in our own town, nor to the likelihood of our powder-running plans being discovered and wrecked because of that treason. I am not touching on the cowardly murder of a helpless old man, for that, of course, is a part of the same traitorous plot. What I mean by the change of circumstances is the fact of our harbors, our ways to open water on both shores, the Bay and the ocean, being now closely guarded and watched by armed craft night and day. It means—Captain Dole himself has heard and brought us evidence which seems to prove that the enemy knows of our privateering scheme and is prepared to block it. I should like to ask Captain Dole if, in spite of that knowledge and close watch, he still believes he could get the *New Hope* out and away? I should like to hear him answer that question."

There was a kind of low rustle of whispering all around the room. Everybody was looking at me when I stood up. I didn't take much time with my answer.

"Yes, I do," I told them. "It will be a tougher job, it may mean a chase and, perhaps, even a fight; but, give us the right kind of night and the right wind and that powder safe aboard, I'll undertake to get her out and clear. I'll even go so far as to bet Allen here another four shilling on it."

It looks pretty boastful to me as I write it down. And, to be honest, I am afraid it was more confident than it ought to have been. There was another rustle of whispers when I finished, but nobody—not even Eben or Captain Elnathan—spoke out loud, so I sat down.

The meeting lasted until one o'clock in the afternoon; nobody thought about dinner, I guess likely. Somebody suggested that a new first officer ought to be appointed in Jonathan's place, but that matter was put over till later. In the regular run of things I would have been let pick my own man, but, in spite of Captain Weeks's talk about my capability, that idea wasn't mentioned. There were limits to their trustfulness, that was plain enough to see.

One other important thing was done, and it was so odd—or must seem so crazy to anybody reading this—that it may need a little more explaining. I must say again, what I am sure I have said three or four times already, that this war we were in—this War of 1812, as they call it now—was a queer kind of war, especially in our alongshore section of New England. Our people fought in the war: Ostable County men had been aboard our navy frigates and manned and officered ever so many of our privateers; Trumet men had been killed or wounded in those fights. But they were fair, stand-up fights, you understand, and no hate in them, so to speak—no personal hate, that is. Fighting was what they were there for, and, when the job was done, each side respected the other. Is that plain? I don't know as it is, but—well, I know what I mean, even if I can't say it right.

And since the blockade really got us we had seen a good deal of the English officers and men. In certain towns, where the harbors were deep enough to be used as stations for the bigger vessels, those officers and men were ashore every day and often in the evenings. They stopped in at the taverns, bought fish and clams of the fishermen, danced with the town girls at parties—things like that. They made themselves as agreeable and decent as they could, considering everything, and, although they were not loved, they weren't hated—man by man, that is. And the money they spent helped out, too. In fact, one of those places—you'll find it in the town records, although the history books may not mention it—passed a resolution in town-meeting to be "as friendly with the enemy as possible under the Constitution."

What that kind of friendliness might mean exactly I wouldn't undertake to tell you, but the resolution was passed—or so I've heard on good authority.

And so, with that little bit of explanation breaking the ice under my bows, I'll risk going on to tell of the action which was taken at our Council meeting that Monday afternoon. Captain Jeremiah Weeks, himself, was responsible for the action being taken. He made quite a long speech. I remember it well enough, but I won't set it down here. The general talk had switched for the minute from Jonathan Bangs's sell-out to the killing of Seth Black; how cowardly it was, how dirty mean it was, how Jonathan must be caught and hung for it. Captain Elnathan Berry, I judged, would have hung him three times—once for playing traitor and twice more for butchering Seth. I tried once to say a word, to hint that, after all, we weren't certain sure yet that Jonathan was guilty on either count, but I might as well have saved my breath. Perhaps I didn't make it sound earnest enough. I realized, only too well, that, if it had been anybody but Jonathan, with the proof of the knife and his running away and all, I might have been as strong for hanging as they were.

I did say one thing that caught their attention.

"You say 'catch him,' " I told them. "How are you going to do that when you don't know where he is?"

Captain Jeremiah answered that. "I think we do know," he said. "The boat which the militia believe they saw this morning was sent out from the *Hawke,* of course. It was going from the shore towards the vessel, so the guard think. If Bangs broke out of the lockup before that, and there is no reason to suppose he didn't, he was aboard that boat. That is as good as proved, I should say. Now then, gentlemen, I have a proposal to make, and I should like your backing in carrying it out."

Captain Holt, commanding the British frigate *Terror,* was an officer *and* a gentleman. He was in the service of the enemy, of course, but that was his duty and didn't affect the "gentleman" part of his make-up. "I have met Captain Holt personally," said Jeremiah. "I met him in Halifax before the war broke out, and I liked him and respected him. Everything I have heard since about his conduct of affairs in Point Town has been to his credit. He *is* a gentleman. Now I can understand his sheltering a spy; that would be his duty, too, although he might hate it as much as I should. But I do *not* believe he would shelter a blackguard who would stab a helpless old man in the back. I propose that we write a letter, signed by myself and the officers of this Council, to Captain Holt and that in that letter we state exactly what Bangs did, the proof we have that he did it, and ask Holt to surrender him to the justice of the outraged citizens of the town of Trumet. The letter can be sent under a flag of truce to the *Hawke* or *Gannet,* with the request that it be forwarded to Captain Holt at once."

That was his proposition. Did you ever hear anything so ridiculous in your life? And coming from sane, common-sense Jeremiah Weeks, of all people! And that Council voted it, too. Two or three didn't vote, I noticed, but mine was the only no vote, and the looks I got when I said that no proved—if proof was needful—that, so far as helping

Jonathan was concerned, I hadn't helped him and had done myself more harm. A committee was chosen to draw up the letter, and then the meeting adjourned, subject to call at any time.

I went home. Phoebe had had dinner waiting for me a good while, but I don't know what she had cooked or how it tasted. She talked all the time, but I don't know what she said. I went straight to my room and shut the door astern of me. My head was pretty foggy, but there was an idea somewhere in that fog, and I wanted to be alone and try to think it out into the light—if there was any light anywhere.

4.

The idea wasn't much more than a glimmer, sort of a guess at a shadow, you might call it. It had come to me when Fowler and Berry and I were at the Allen house talking with Hope. Hope had—the very first minute I laid eyes on her, and before we told her of Seth's murder—looked and acted very much excited and upset about something. I wasn't the only one who noticed it; Eben Fowler's first words to her had been to ask what was the matter. She tried to make believe nothing was the matter, pretended she was surprised at his asking such a question, but I, for one, didn't think the make-believe made a very good show. She was pale, her eyes looked almost as if she had been crying, or was ready to cry, and when she came through that sitting-room door and saw us there in the dining-room, she looked—well, sort of desperate, that's the only word I could think of.

When Captain Elnathan blurted out the news about Seth Black and made his accusation of Jonathan Bangs her defense of Jonathan was real enough. There was no make-believe in the way she flew at Elnathan and called him a liar. I wasn't quite so sure, now that I had had a little time to think it over, that the story of Black's being killed was news to her, although I didn't see how in the world she could have heard it. If anyone had found that body before we did, the yarn would have been all over town by then, and the body certainly wouldn't have been left lying. But, all the same, it wasn't Berry's blowing off that made her so white and strange-looking. She had been that way before we spoke at all. As for her having a headache—well, that was a woman's excuse, too old even to waste a thought on. I'll bet that Eve told Adam she had a headache when he wanted to know why she tempted him into eating the apple.

If Hope had heard about Seth, who told her? And the finding of Jonathan's knife *was* new to her, that I would swear to. And the way she blazed up at the notion that Jonathan was a killer was a comfort to me. She and Jonathan had squabbled about something; I remembered how cool she was to him that day at the shipyard when she walked off with Fowler and left Jonathan biting his nails. And Jonathan had acted blue and out of sorts afterwards. That I had judged then, and still did, to be just a fellow-and-girl spat, one of those things that happen when two young folks are keeping company.

It hadn't stopped her from flying at Captain Elnathan, like a mother cat at a strange dog, when he called Jonathan a murderer as well as a traitor. She even went so far as to say she *knew* he wasn't either one. "Knew"—that was a strong word. Did she know? Or what or how much might she know that even I didn't? I was going to try and find out. I was going to have a straight talk with Hope Allen before that afternoon was over.

I didn't go down the regular roads when I headed for the Allen place. I knew how many hang-over-the-fence gossips I would have to pass, how many half-whispers I would be likely to hear, and how many questions I would have to answer or dodge if I did that. I went out through the Light

221

back yard and across the fields and through the pine and scrub oak woods. It was the late middle of the afternoon when I got to the Allen house. A gray-shingled, spread-out old place it was, with a couple of tall silver-leafs in the front yard and a big lilac bush by the side door. Henry had inherited the place from his father, but he had built on an extension here and tagged on a shed and outbuildings there, until the whole establishment was as out of the common and cantankerous and "go-my-own-way" as Henry was, himself.

I was afraid Henry might be at home, although I hardly thought he would be with all there was going on up town. And I was almost as much afraid Hope might be out. She wasn't though: she came to the side door when I knocked. If she was glad to see me she hid her feelings well. "Father isn't here, Captain Isaiah," she said. "I think you might find him up at the shipyard if you went there."

"I know," I told her. "That's one of the reasons I'm not going there. It is you I've got to see, Hope. May I come in?"

She couldn't very well say no, although I was sure she wanted to. She held the door open, and I walked past her into the dining-room. She didn't ask me to sit down. We faced each other.

"Hope," I asked, "when did you see Jonathan last?"

It took her by surprise, my putting it as blunt as that. It must have sounded to her as if I knew a whole lot more than I did. She was standing by the table, and she put one hand on it almost as if she needed a prop, something to hold her steady.

"Jonathan?" she repeated after me. "When did I see him? Why—why, I don't know—exactly. When was it?"

"That is what I am asking you? Have you seen him today?"

"Today? . . . Why, how could I? He was in the lockup."

"He *was* in there, but he hasn't been there since sometime late last night or very early this morning. He got away. Have you seen him since he got away?"

"Why—why, no. . . . No, I haven't."

It was a brave try, but to lie so that it sounds convincing takes a good deal of practice. To do that a person has to lie all over, so to speak: with the face and eyes—yes, and hands —as well as just with the mouth.

"Haven't, eh?" I said. "Are you sure?"

"Yes . . . Why—why, of course I am sure. No, I haven't seen him."

She was doing better now; still a long way from good enough, but better. I tried a new tack.

"Hope," I went on, "you are a friend of Jonathan Bangs's, aren't you? A real friend, in foul weather as well as fair? I took it for granted you were."

She didn't hesitate this time. "Certainly I am," she said.

"Good! Well, so am I, and that's why I've come to you. You and I are about the only friends he has left in Trumet. Neither of us want him to be hanged."

She caught her breath. "Hanged!" she gasped. "Hanged? Oh—"

"He will be, if Elnathan Berry and the majority of the Council have their way. Hanged as a traitor and a murderer. I heard you say that you didn't believe he was either of those things. You said more than that. You said you *knew* he wasn't. How did you know?"

She tried to answer, but the words wouldn't come. Both of her hands were on the table now, and I could see the ruffles at the edges of her sleeves trembling.

"How did you know?" I asked again.

"I knew— Oh," with a sort of burst, as if she couldn't hold on any longer, "I knew because I know him. I know he wouldn't do such horrible things. You know it, too, Isaiah Dole! You say you are his friend. Well, if you are, you *must* know it."

She rather had me there. I hoped I knew it, you may be certain of that.

"All right then, Hope," I said, "we'll leave it that way. We'll say we both know it. Now, that being so, we must work for him, try to find ways to help him. And we've got to work together. You see that?"

"Yes . . . Yes, I suppose so . . . What can we do?"

"We can begin by one not holding back anything from the other. I may be wrong, but I believe you are holding back, Hope. I believe you—"

Her hands were off the table now, and she was holding them out, palms towards me, as if she was pushing me away.

"No—oh, no!" she begged. "Don't ask me any more questions now, Captain Isaiah. Please don't. I have told you—"

"There, there! You haven't told me anything. And you must, if we want to save Jonathan. Tell me this much: do you know where he is this minute?"

"No—no. Please—"

"Jeremiah Weeks and the rest are sure he got away in a boat before daylight this morning and has joined up with the British. Do you know whether or not that's true?"

"I—" she began, and then stopped. I had the notion that she was going to say that it wasn't true, but, if so, she changed her mind.

"No," she said. "No, I—I don't know anything. Won't you please go away, Captain Isaiah? I—I don't feel very well, I—my head—"

If she was going to fall back on that headache again, I might just as well go. She never seemed to me like the kind to have hysterics, but she might if she thought they would help any. Hysterics, for a woman, are mighty handy to have in the house, sometimes.

So I turned to the door. "I am going, Hope," I told her. "I want you to think over what I said about neither one of us holding back. And," putting on a little more emphasis, "if you *should* run across Jonathan anywhere, you might tell him the same thing. You might tell him the truth doesn't usually hurt an innocent man—much."

I walked straight away from the house, for, as I passed the gate post, I caught a glimpse of her watching me from the window. I didn't walk very far, though—only to the edge of the woods, where I picked out a thick bunch of beach-plum bushes and briars and scooched down behind it. I could see the Allen house from there and anybody who left it by any one of its doors.

Young woman, I thought to myself, you didn't say much, but, unless I'm more mistaken than I think I am, you *have* seen and talked with Jonathan Bangs today and, if he hasn't gone to the *Hawke* or *Gannet*, you may be planning to see him again. Well, *I* want to see him, and I'm going to, if it is possible. He's one young fool, and, I judge, you are another. It is high time somebody sensible took charge.

I waited in that bunch of bushes for a good long spell. I don't know just how long, but long enough for those briars to make me realize that I wasn't sitting on a feather bed. At last, though, the side door of the house opened, and Hope came out. She was bareheaded, so I judged she wasn't going far. She didn't turn towards the village, either. She looked up and down the road, and then headed off around the corner of the barn and towards the path through the pines that led over to Shad Cove. It was that path I had taken when I went to Seth Black's shanty Saturday night after the boy brought me that note from him. Only two nights ago, that was; it seemed no less than a month.

I followed her, staying in the woods all the time and never getting near enough for her to hear or see me. She didn't look back once, just hurried right ahead. About a hundred yards from the Black shanty and not very far from the edge of the high, steep sand bank that pitches down to the beach along there is a big rock, one of those rocks that are scattered all over the north side of the Cape, like raisins in a Thanksgiving pudding. The woods are thick around that rock, and I had to move careful, so I lost sight of her for a minute or so.

When I caught up and peeked out at her, she had climbed up on the rock a couple of feet and was doing something with her hands, I couldn't at first make out what. That rock, like so many of them, had a big split in it, and the split, in the course of time, had filled up with trash and earth, with weeds and huckleberry bushes growing in it. She was reaching into one of those clumps. She grabbed there a second, and then she lifted out a flat, thin sliver of stone—one that had been part of the big rock in the beginning—lifted it out and laid it to one side. Then, from underneath where the stone had been, she took out something. I couldn't see what it was then, but when she got down to the ground she still had it in her hand and then I could see. It was a folded paper. It looked like a letter.

She tucked the paper into the waist of her dress. Then she climbed up on the rock again and put the stone sliver back in the place where she found it. Another minute and she was hurrying back along the woodpath the way she had come, with me as close at her heels as I dared to be. When I caught up with her this time she had taken the letter, or whatever it was, from her dress and was stopping to look at it. It was then I spoke to her.

"Hope," I hailed.

She jumped as if I had shot at her. The hand with the paper in it clenched tight. When she whisked around towards me, her face was flour white.

"Oh!" she breathed. "Oh—who—"

"Just me, that's all, Hope. Nothing to be scared about. Only—well, don't you think I might be interested in that letter, too? You and I agreed to work together, didn't we?"

She didn't speak a word, just looked at me, her eyes wide. I went on.

"The letter is from Jonathan Bangs, of course," I said, "and he hasn't run away to the Britishers. Well, I never really thought he had. And you and he have seen each other since he got out of the lockup. I suspected that, too. And now he has written you, telling you, I suppose likely, what he is doing and what he calculates to do. All right, I haven't any objections to any of that; if he knows he can trust you that's fine—that's the way it ought to be. But—*but*"—I made this sound as emphatic as I could—"he ought to know he can trust me, too. And, if he's got any common sense left at all—which I'm beginning to doubt—he must know I am trying to help him. If he is where I can see him and talk with him, that's exactly what I must do and right away. Let me read that letter, Hope. After you have read it yourself, of course."

I never took my eyes off her face while I was saying this, and I must own up that what I saw there surprised me, in a way. The first part of my speech seemed to—well, ease her mind a little, as you might say. She didn't act quite so frightened, which maybe was natural enough. But, when I asked for the letter, the scare seemed to come back. Her clutch on that paper didn't loosen one bit.

"No," she said, kind of low at first and then louder. "No—no—*no*!"

"But, Hope, can't you see? . . . Come now, that letter *is* from Jonathan, isn't it?"

She waited, swallowed, and then said: "Well—well, suppose it is."

"Why suppose? I know it is from him."

Another little wait. "Well?"

"Isn't it from him?"

"Well. . . . But I can't let you read it."

227

"Why not?"

"Because—oh, because it is mine. It is—it is personal."

I never had any doubt of that, and I said so. "The trouble there is," I went on, "that the time for 'personals' among us three has gone by. He ought to realize that; you ought to realize it. . . . Oh, for the Lord sakes!"—my temper was dragging anchor—"for the Lord Almighty sakes, must I go all through this again? Let me see that letter."

"No—no, I can't."

"Then you *want* him to hang for a traitor and a murderer? You'll enjoy it, along with the rest of Trumet, I judge."

And now again she burst out at me, just as she had in her own sitting-room a little while before. "He isn't—he isn't—he *isn't*, I tell you!" she flared. "He isn't a traitor! He isn't a murderer! If—if"—she seemed to be groping for the right thing to say—"if you would only trust him—yes, and trust me—for a little while. . . . No, you can't read this letter. Go away! And—and don't spy on me any longer. . . . Oh, Captain Isaiah, *please!*"

Well, I went—like a soft-headed fool, I went—knowing all the time that I was one. I could have taken the letter from her by main strength, I suppose. Maybe I should have done just that; if I had, as I look back at it now, it might have saved a lot. I didn't because—oh, I don't know why, except it might be that the word "spy" stuck in my craw. I *had* spied on her and—oh, let it go at that! Just a soft-headed fool, and not for the first time in my life, either.

As I tramped back along the path I was still trying to find excuses for myself. I stopped in at the shipyard and found things all right there, a strong guard set and the last of the stores aboard. I went home, ate a little supper, and turned in, still thinking hard. I made up my mind to give Hope Allen and Jonathan Bangs until the next day noon.

Then, if neither one of them made a move I would make one myself. I would get that letter and—and—

But, blast it all, the letter would be burnt up before that, probably it was in ashes already.

And the next morning—Tuesday, that is—when I came out of my room, Ezra Light was in the dining-room waiting for me. He had had his breakfast and was standing by the window, chewing his tobacco and looking as mournful and natural as life, as if he hadn't just ridden horseback to Tamoset and back.

He turned his head to look at me. "Hello, Captain Isaiah," said he. "Nice morning, considering the kind of weather 'tis, as the fellow said."

To see and hear him anybody that didn't know would have judged we had said good night a few hours before. I crossed that room in not more than three steps and slapped him on the back. "Lord Almighty, man," I crowed, "I'm glad to see you! Did you—? Is everything all right?"

He nodded. "Um-hm. All right up yonder, where I come from—or was when I left. From what *she* tells me," jerking his head in the general direction of the kitchen, where Phoebe was clicking dishes and rattling pans, "most of the wrong is down here. Poor old Seth! Considering how no-account he was when he was alive it's sort of strange how important he is dead. Ridiculous sort of world, ain't it?"

I didn't want to talk about Seth Black just then. I leaned towards him. "Ezra," I whispered, "what about the—the powder? Is it all arranged? When—"

He shook his head to stop me. "Tell you what let's do, Captain Isaiah," he broke in, with another look towards the kitchen. "You eat your breakfast, and then you and me'll go out in the barn and take a look at Selah. The old girl's been stepping along considerable lately, and she ain't used to being broke of her rest. I'm some worried about her nerves."

Breakfast was the least of my cravings just then. I was on pins and needles to hear about the scheme for getting the powder through to us; but I pulled up my chair and resigned myself to blackberry-leaf tea and the rest of it. I recollect telling Ezra to sit down until I finished.

He drew a long breath. "If you don't mind, Captain Isaiah," he said, solemn as an owl, "I'll stand up. I've been straddling that mare's back for so long that anything flat underneath me, like a floor, is what Parson Samuels would call a blessed relief. It's high time I reminded my feet what they're made for."

When, ten minutes later, we were in the barn together, he told me about his Tamoset cruise. Our good friends up there had got everything fixed for the coming Friday night. The scheme was, practically, just what we had arranged in the beginning, but there was one little change which was important. The craft with the powder aboard—they had decided that one good-sized boat would be big enough and less trouble to pilot and less liable to be seen than two—was not to try and make its landing at the place we had first picked out—the one a mile above Billfish Creek—but at a point a half a mile or so below Shad Cove in the other direction. The *Gannet* was picketing Billfish, and this new landing place wasn't likely to be watched as close, or so they hoped. Our squad on shore was to be waiting there, was to stand guard all of Friday night, armed and ready to fight if there was any interference. The Tamoset folks had written it all out in detail and given the paper to Ezra, so he said.

He took the paper out of his pocket and handed it to me. I looked it through. The plan, as it was written, was just as he had told it. Having it in my own hand at last made me breathe more free, and I said so.

"Whew!" I puffed. "Well, here it is—this much, any-how—safe and sound. Ezra, the Council and I are a whole lot obliged to you. I've had enough to worry me the last few days, but, in between the other worries, I have been scared that something might happen to you on the way down, that somebody else might get his hands on this paper before I did. I am obliged to you—and all the others in our crowd had better be. A mighty good job, Ezra! Thanks again."

I looked up from the paper and at his face as I said this, and, for the first time, I noticed signs of trouble there. He shifted his tobacco from one cheek to the other before he answered.

"We-ll," he drawled, kind of hesitating, "I—I—well, I don't know as I better take them thanks yet awhile, Captain Isaiah. As a matter of fact, somebody else *has* seen that plan paper."

My mouth must have dropped open like a cellar door.

"Somebody else!" I sang out. "You mean you've shown this—this thing to somebody else before you brought it to me?"

He waved to me to hold up.

"Better wait and hear the whole of it, Captain," he cut in. "Here's how 'twas."

Along late in the afternoon of the day before—Monday, that was—he was on his way back from Tamoset and had got within a mile and a half or so of home when a man came out of the woods by the side of the horse path and called him by name. The man was Jonathan Bangs.

I broke in right there. "Jonathan! Jonathan Bangs!" I sang out. "Why—why, it couldn't be."

"That so? Well, maybe.... Only, you see, it was. Jonathan himself, as large as life—and that's plenty large enough. He told me he had been sitting there quite a spell, waiting for me to heave in sight."

"But why? *Why?*" I wanted to know. "Did he say where he came from? Of course he told you why he was there."

"He never said nothing about coming from anywhere special. He did say he knew I would be along that road and sometime that afternoon or night, and it was important that he saw me afore anybody else in Trumet did. He acted as if he was in a hurry and didn't seem to want to bother with answering questions."

"Huh! I can understand that, I guess likely."

"Um-hm. So can I—now, but I hadn't heard the Trumet news at that time."

Ezra said the reason Jonathan gave for waylaying him was that he—Jonathan, I mean—was doing some "secret work" for the Council and the *New Hope* enterprise, doing it on his own hook and without telling anyone, "even Captain Dole."

"Secret work?" I blurted. "What the nation does he mean?"

"This is about the way he put it," Ezra said. "For quite a little spell, he told me, he had been suspicious that there was somebody—perhaps more than one somebody—working against him and our privateer. 'I thought at first,' says he, 'that it was just me he was working against; thought the fellow might have a grudge against me, though I couldn't think who nor why. But since—well, since Saturday night I have begun to wonder if it isn't the whole *New Hope* game he is trying to block.' I asked him what made him think that, but he said it would take too long to tell.

"'I haven't any idea who the sneaking devil is,' he told me," went on Ezra; "'but I do think I am getting closer and closer on his track, and if I can be let alone for a little longer I hope I may run him down. You might tell Captain Dole that. Tell him that is one reason why I couldn't stay—where they put me. I couldn't work with my hands tied, so I untied them. Tell him that; perhaps he will understand.'"

I didn't understand—much—but I didn't bother to try to,

then. "About those powder plans?" I snapped. "For the Lord's sake, Ezra, are you going to tell me that he wanted to see this plan—and you let him see it?"

Ezra spread out his hands. "Why wouldn't I?" he asked. "When I left Trumet he was a Council member in good standing, high up in the *New Hope* doings, and picked to be her first officer. Didn't know of any reason why he shouldn't see 'em—not then I didn't. You want to remember, Captain Isaiah, that when he waylaid me there in them woods, *I* didn't know nothing of what had been going on in Trumet since I left here Friday morning and headed for Tamoset. It wasn't until Phoebe unloaded it all onto me that I heard the first living word of it."

And that was true, of course. I couldn't blame him and I told him so. He nodded.

"Felt certain you'd understand," he said. "Well, Jonathan said the traitor scamp mustn't get hold of that powder plan until it was too late for it to be changed or blocked off. He—Jonathan, course I mean; there's as many 'hims' and 'hes' in this yarn as there is kinks in a wet cod line—Jonathan said he wanted to look at the plans afore this traitor critter saw them. Then he—there's another darned 'he,' but it's still Jonathan—would know better just what kind of treason stuff to be ready for. Now I think it over, it don't sound like the plainest sort of explaining, does it? It sounded all right to me then, though. I wasn't looking underneath or around corners, and I'd have trusted Bangs as far as I'd have trusted myself."

"Didn't he say a word about the fire or his arrest or about Seth Black? Nothing at all?"

"Nothing. Told you the first I heard of 'em was from Phoebe after I got home here and in the house. You can bet high, Captain, that, if I had known, I wouldn't have agreed to what he asked me next: that was not to tell a soul about my meeting up with him, or his seeing the powder plan, or even to report to you that I was back from Tamoset, until this morning. 'By then,' he says, 'I may be a little closer on the heels of our friend, the British agent.' He said that and then he said one more thing."

That one thing was a private message to me about his sheath knife. Ezra was to tell me that he, Jonathan, was ready to swear on the Bible that he had not so much as laid eyes on that knife since I borrowed it of him the week before. " 'Tell Captain Dole not to believe all he sees and hears,' them was his words."

I couldn't think very clearly yet, but I did order Ezra not to show himself until I called him to report to the Council and to keep his wife from reporting that he was back—if it was possible to anchor a tongue like hers.

Council meeting—we were holding them every little while now—had been called for eleven o'clock, but I felt we ought to get busy right away on our arrangements for Friday night, so I sent a messenger around to the different houses, and the members, every one of them, dropped everything else and came. I took Ezra along, and he made his report of the session with our Tamoset friends. Then I got the floor and said my say. The powder boat must be met, and a big and competent squad must be standing by to unload that powder and transport it across town and stow it aboard the bark. Somebody—seems to me it was Captain Davies—spoke up to remind me that that boat would have to get past the *Gannet* before there could be any unloading done. "Considerable of an 'if' right there, I'm afraid," he added, shaking his head.

I agreed there was but that we must act as if there wasn't. The change in the landing place mustn't be let out to anyone. No one but us insiders must know, until the last hour or so, that there had been a change made. Somebody—Ezra, if he wasn't too used up after his Tamoset cruise—must be sent to Orham and Bayport and wherever men who had enlisted for sea duty aboard our bark were living, ordering them to report by noon on Friday.

"For," said I, "the minute the last keg is aboard that night, I mean to try to get the *New Hope* out of Trumet harbor and into blue water. Blockade or no blockade, *Hawke* or no *Hawke*, that try will be made if I have my way. The only thing that can hold us up is a flat calm. As for any other kind of weather, the worse it is the better for us. A black night and half a gale of wind would suit me to death. Fog and dark in the Bay until that powder boat makes landing—then let it blow; that would be perfect. Once out and it will take a better craft than the *Hawke* to overhaul us. My officers and men will back me, every one of them. If this Council backs me that's all I ask."

Well, the Council did. There was some uneasiness and doubt in certain quarters, which wasn't to be wondered at. Now that these two enemy vessels had camped themselves right on our front and back doorsteps, as you might call it, our risk of getting out of the harbor and a half mile or so of crooked channel without being driven back into the breakers and smashed up there was ever so much greater than we had figured it to be before those guard boats took their new stations. But the members, most of them experienced old salts themselves, stood with me. Every man Jack of them realized, of course, how desperate a chance we were taking, but they realized, too, that it had to be neck or nothing now—neck or nothing for the *New Hope* and all she meant to Trumet.

Henry Allen had to be a little mite nasty, of course. I saw Eben Fowler whispering in his ear, so it may have been Eben who gave him the idea.

"Who have you picked for your first officer, Isaiah?" he asked with a grin. "Aren't going to wait till we hang your other one, I hope. If old Holt sends him back, as we asked him to in Captain Jeremiah's letter, maybe it will be done before you clear."

Squire Bethuel Bailey asked the chairman if that letter had been sent. Captain Jeremiah said it had; a couple of men, in a boat flying a white flag, took it off to the *Gannet* as soon as it was written.

By the time the session broke up every member knew what his part in the Friday night business was to be and how he must play it. Ezra had agreed to go on the crew-calling trip. He wouldn't need to leave until tomorrow morning—Wednesday—and he vowed he would be "as spry as a greased eel" by that time.

As we were coming out of the hall I happened to be next to Squire Bailey, and I noticed he was smiling to himself, as if something amused him. I asked him to tell me the joke, because, if there was anything funny on the premises, the Lord knows I would like to make its acquaintance. His smile widened.

"I was thinking of that letter Weeks puts so much faith in, the one he sent off to the *Gannet* for the people aboard her to forward to Captain Holt of the *Terror*. I didn't vote in favor of having the thing written or sent, but I didn't vote against it because Jeremiah was so sure it was a wonderful idea. It strikes me that, if Bangs is a traitor working for the enemy, it must have been Holt he was working for. And, if that is the case, Holt could hardly go back on his own hired man, even though that man has been doing a little murdering on the side. He might wish he could, may-be—but how could he? And, besides, we don't certainly know that Jonathan has run away to the British. That is the guess, but it is only a guess, so far."

To me it wasn't even a guess. Jonathan Bangs had been right here in Trumet, or in the woods not so very far from it, hours after that letter to Holt was on its way. I didn't make much answer to the Squire, for my conscience was riding me hard. I had taken another tremendous load on my shoulders. Those shoulders were carrying enough already, and this extra bundle was liable to break my back—and serve me right, perhaps. On our way to the meeting I had ordered Ezra not to mention in his report that he and Jonathan had met in the woods and that Jonathan had asked for and looked over our powder-running plan. Ezra must have been surprised when he got those orders, but he didn't say he was. He looked at me for a few seconds and then said: "Aye, aye, Captain," and that was all, then.

After we left the hall, though, he said this much more: "Kind of betwixt and between about that sheath knife, ain't you, Captain Isaiah? Oh, I ain't asking, I was just thinking out loud. ... Um-hm ... Well betwixt and between is about where I be, myself, if you want to know. ... Say, you ain't a bad friend for a fellow in trouble to have, be you? ... Oh, all right, all right. None of *my* business, of course."

Betwixt and between. Well, that was about it. Jonathan's message to me about that knife of his was one of the oddest things in this whole crazy mess so far. What did it mean? If he was innocent, how did he know the knife had been found by Seth's body? Of course, if he was the murderer and had, all of a sudden, when it was too late to go back and get it, remembered that he left the knife there, why— why, then his message to me about it was just a sort of half-baked move to throw me and the rest off his track. If he was innocent—if what he told Ezra about not having so much as seen the thing for a week was true—then it wasn't Jonathan Bangs who killed Seth Black. Somebody else had done the killing and planted the knife to fix the blame on Bangs.

I wanted to believe that—heavens and earth, *how* I wanted to believe it! But belief wasn't proof, and, with things as they were, Jonathan's unsupported word counted for nothing—for less than nothing with Trumet in general. Oh, why hadn't he told a straight story at the Saturday night meeting? Or in the lockup when Fowler and Allen and I came there Sunday morning? Instead he had run away and had been in hiding ever since. That, even to as good a friend of his as I had been and wanted to be, didn't smell like innocence. No siree, it didn't!

And now, to cap everything, he had waylaid Ezra—the Council's messenger—got what he wanted from him, and then had cleared out to hide again. *I* might be soft-headed enough to pay attention to all his folderol about wanting to hunt traitors in secret—yes, and foolish enough to risk keeping still, and make Light keep still for a while, to help him—but what would Trumet say or do to me if it ever found *that* out?

The thoughts kept crowding in on me, each one more disturbing than the others. Who had told Jonathan about his knife being found by Seth's body? I could think of nobody but Hope Allen. Hope had told me she hadn't seen him since all our dreadfulness began, but she was lying when she said it. She had seen him, of course; that he had written to her, she owned up. Well, *I* was going to see her once more, and this time she would have to tell me what she knew. Yes, and if Jonathan had told her things, she must tell me what those things were.

So, about four that afternoon, I was hurrying again through the woods towards the Allen house. Before I got there, however, a fresh idea headed me off. It struck me that it might not be a bad notion to pay another visit to that rock where Hope had found Jonathan's letter—their private post-office, I guessed it might be. She couldn't really know that I had seen her when she took the letter from the crack in the rock; I had waited, you will recollect, until she was a good way from the rock before I spoke to her. And so there might, possibly, be another letter from one or the other of them under that sliver of stone by this time. Why not?

Well, if there was, I was going to get it and read it. The time for being finicky about reading other people's letters had gone by as far as I was concerned.

So, when I got to the big rock, I climbed up as I had seen her do, lifted the sliver, and reached into the hole under it. There was a folded paper there, sure enough. It was sealed on the back with a round splash of green wax, but the sealing had been done in a hurry, I judged, and the paper came loose in my hand even as I took it out. I unfolded it and read what was written; only, as a matter of fact, it wasn't written, it was printed out, the way a child prints before he learns to write.

This is what I read, printed there on that paper:

Dear Sir:
The powder running will be attempted Friday night, and the plans for it remain exactly as they were at first, except in regard to the slight change of landing place, which probable change I warned you in my other letter to be prepared for. My part in our arrangement therefore has been faithfully carried out. I shall count on you and our friends offshore to do the rest and to look out for me and my interests according to the terms we agreed upon.

J. B.

My eyes are pretty dependable, as a general thing, but for the first few seconds, as I stood there, hanging to that rock like a barnacle to a wharf spile and staring at the words on that piece of paper, I declare I thought they, or my brains, must be going back on me.

"J. B." ... These two letters could only mean one person. They meant that Jonathan Bangs had printed that letter, and, if he had, there wasn't any more question as to the kind of turncoat and rascal *he* was. Whether or not he had killed Black was something else, of course, but, if he could betray the town and those who had trusted him, including me—if he could do that he wouldn't be one to stick at a murder or two if the murdering would save his own hide. If he was as lowdown as all that and if Seth had found out that he was and threatened to show him up—well, it would be "good-by, Seth," no doubt about it. Elnathan Berry had said that very thing when we found the body, and, if this letter was what it looked to be, Elnathan was right.

I slid down from the rock, stumbled away to a thick bunch of trees and bushes where I wouldn't be liable to be seen, slumped to the ground, and sat there for I don't know how long, reading the devilish thing through and back, over and over. There was no name on the outside of it, but no name was needful. It was meant for Hope Allen, of course —at least it was meant for her to get and deliver—and that meant that Hope was in the game. She was a traitor, too. The fear of some such notion had been in the back of my head ever since Ezra told me his story about Jonathan's waylaying him and asking for the powder plans, but I wouldn't let myself think it through. I couldn't believe it of either of them, or wouldn't. But now—now I should have to believe—and act accordingly.

That I decided—but there was something else. It wasn't friendship or pity, nothing of that kind. If Jonathan was what this letter seemed to prove him, friendship was dead, and pity was on the way to the funeral. No, this was not either of them; it was just plain common sense.

More than once, in Council meeting and other places, I had vowed and declared that Jonathan Bangs was no fool. And who, except the most hopeless kind of fool, would sign his own initials to a letter like this? Why sign it at all? Hope wouldn't need any signature, she would know who it was from.

But wait a minute. The thing wasn't addressed to Hope.

240

It began with "Dear Sir." Who—? And what—? Oh, Lord! Where were we now?

I studied the note word by word. I knew Jonathan's handwriting well, but this wasn't handwriting, it was print, and all print looks more or less alike. I might figure it was printed for that very reason, so that the writing couldn't be recognized; but why go to that trouble and then stick down those initials at the end? Like asking a child a riddle and starting in by telling him the answer.

Nobody but an idiot would do that, and Jonathan Bangs— But why say *that* again?

Well, anyhow, I had gone as far as I could go alone. I had done all the covering up already that I would ever do —yes, and a lot more than I should have done. Jonathan, and Hope too, would have to play their own fiddles from now on. Our *New Hope* was a long way more important than any person or persons, including myself. I would go before the Council, tell them everything, and take my share of the consequences. God only knew what those consequences might be, but I would take them—yes, and even declare that I deserved to.

I headed for town as fast as I could walk. To this day I couldn't tell you what path I took. The roof had fallen in on my head, and that head was spinning. The first thing I remember plain was turning from the Point Road into the Bay Road and hearing somebody yelling my name. It was Peleg Bounderby and he came running.

"Captain Isaiah!" he sang out. "Captain Isaiah! Where you been? We've been hunting all over for you?"

"I have been all over, more or less," I told him. "What's the matter? Anything wrong at the yard?"

"No, no," he panted, for he was all out of breath. "Yard is all right. There's been another murder, that's all."

I don't know what I said, and he didn't wait to listen. "Yes, sir, murder," he puffed. And then, slowing up as if he hated to spoil his yarn but had to: "Well, no, not quite a murder, as you might say, but nigh to it. Phoebe Light's been hit on the head, and she's in bed, half dead and half crazy, and she keeps hollering for you. Come quick."

I came, breaking into a trot, with Peleg trotting and puffing alongside me. As we trotted he gasped out the story in sections. It seems that Phoebe had come to the shipyard a little after four, so excited and wrought up that she couldn't speak much plainer than a stutter, and asking all hands where I was, vowing she must see me because she had something dreadful important to tell me.

Nobody knew where I was, and nobody paid too much attention to her, calculating, I presume likely, that her notion of what was important wasn't liable to amount to a whole lot. She went off up to the village to ask for me around there. The next thing heard about her was from her husband. Ezra had found her lying on the floor of their kitchen, unconscious, and bleeding from a great bump and cut at the back of her head just aft of the temple. If it had been an inch further forward, so Doctor Blodgett said, she would have been killed then and there.

Ezra got her into bed and ran out and got help and the doctor. Now Phoebe, according to Peleg, was some better, but still a long way from sensible.

"She keeps calling your name," he went on. " 'Captain Isaiah! Captain Isaiah!' That and 'Knife! Knife!' Doctor seems to figure that she wants to tell you something and that it has to do with some sort of a knife. That's what it sounds like, anyhow. You have any notion of what she's driving at, Captain?"

I didn't bother to answer. I had been trotting before. Now I began to gallop.

5

In which Captain Dole tries to fool
the enemy and, instead, fools himself.

Told by

CAPTAIN ISAIAH DOLE

I.

WHEN WE GOT to the house there was a crowd hanging about the yard, whispering and milling around. Ezra was standing guard in the doorway, and it did my heart good to see how quiet and businesslike he was in keeping everybody but a very few from getting past him. When he saw me his leathery face lighted up a shade. What he said, though, was almost as everyday as if nothing out of the common had happened at all.

"Hello, Captain Isaiah," he hailed. "Go right along in. No, no," pushing back a couple of excited boys who would like to have followed in my wake; "that wasn't a general invitation. Children and babes with arms not admitted. That lets you out, Seth," speaking to young Seth Trotter, who was a member of the militia and had his musket over his shoulder. "Yes, yes, go in, Captain Isaiah. I'll be with you in a minute, soon as I can locate somebody to spell me here at this door."

I asked only one question. "How is she, Ezra?" I asked.

"Well, only about so-so, I'm afraid. Doctor seems to calculate she's got some concussion, or whatever they call it, but he figures she'll pull through if she can be kept in bed and quiet. He's with her now, and a couple of women neighbors are there to help him. I'll tell you all about it when I come inside. Captain Jeremiah and Captain Elnathan and two or three more of the Council crew are in the dining-room. They are full of jumps. Figure this happening

245

to Phoebe must have something to do with what happened to Seth Black. Maybe it has, but I don't know how nor why. Neither do they, fur's that goes."

In the dining-room I found Weeks and Berry and Davies and Eben Fowler. A couple of them—Captain Elnathan, you may be sure was one—were pacing the floor, and the other two were sitting in chairs by the table. They were talking together in whispers when I stepped in from the side door entry, but they stopped to look at me. I was the first to speak.

"Well?" I said. "Now maybe some of you will tell me what this all is and how it happened."

The only answer I got was a stare. Then Captain Jeremiah Weeks spoke up.

"Where have you been, Isaiah?" he asked, pretty middling sharp. I didn't like his tone any too well, and I was a little bit jumpy myself. This new surprise, following right on top of my finding and reading the J. B. letter, wasn't calming me any.

"Where I have been will keep for a spell, Jeremiah," I answered him. "Suppose you tell me what's been going on here."

Eben Fowler was, maybe, the calmest of any of them. He hadn't taken his eyes off my face since I came in. "Are we to understand you don't know, Dole?" he asked, slow and deliberate.

"Yes, Fowler," said I, "you can understand just that. All I know is that Ezra Light came into this house a little while ago and found his wife knocked on the head and unconscious. I know that much because Peleg Bounderby met me down the road just now and told me."

Elnathan Berry couldn't hold in any longer. "Didn't Peleg tell you that Phoebe had been asking for you at the shipyard and up town?" he wanted to know. "Didn't he tell you that she said she must see you because she wanted to tell you something?"

"Why, yes, he did, now that you call it to my notice. He told me that and then about her being hurt. I didn't stop to ask any particulars, thought I could get more of them right here. I'm waiting for them now."

Another little hitch, then Eben Fowler spoke again. "I suppose," he said, "you haven't any idea of what it might be she wanted to see you about?"

"Not a solitary darned idea. Have you?"

"Where were you? You haven't told us that yet." This was Captain Elnathan. I was pretty mad by this time.

"Even so," I snapped, "I have told you a mighty sight more than you've told me. What are you fellows driving at? If you are hinting that I know any more about this outrage than you do, speak out, then I can say it is a lie. I'll say it now, if it will hurry matters up any. I wouldn't mind a bit."

Elkanah Davies, who had been one of the two sitting down, got to his feet. "There, there, Isaiah," he said. "There there, Elnathan! This isn't helping us. Captain Isaiah says he doesn't know any of the particulars. Perhaps —well, well, no doubt he doesn't. Jeremiah, suppose you tell him—as much as we know, that is."

So Weeks told. Phoebe Light had been up town looking for me, at the yard, and along the main road. She was very much excited and flurried and kept saying that she must find me, she *must*, because there was something she had just remembered that she hadn't remembered before, or had forgot to remember right in the first place—a mixed-up muddle of talk that nobody who heard her could make any sense out of. And she would *not* tell anyone but me. So, as nobody knew where I was at the time, she had given it up finally and had gone back home. And then, a while later, when Ezra came home, he found—

I cut in there. "Heave to a jiffy," I ordered. "Did any of you see her while she was looking for me? Any one of you four, I mean?"

Yes, Captain Elnathan had seen her and talked with her for a minute or two. So had Eben Fowler. "I got away from her as soon as possible," Eben told us. "I had other things on my mind, as we all have just now, and, knowing Phoebe Light, I couldn't believe whatever she had to tell was really important."

"Who saw her last?" I asked. "Do you know?"

Berry grunted that the last he saw of her she had sighted Henry Allen and was chasing after him.

Henry Allen! The Allen name gave me a sort of jolt. One member of that family had been very much in my mind. Just then Ezra came into the room, and I asked him to tell me about finding his wife, when he found her, and the like of that. He had told the others before, of course.

It didn't take long in the telling. After leaving the Council meeting he had come home, eaten dinner, and gone out to the barn to look after Selah. He gave the mare a curry-combing and a rubdown and then went up to the shipyard and from there to the tavern, where he had a rum toddy with one or two of the boys—"Give you their names, if you want 'em," he said. Then, along about half-past five or so, he had drifted back home. "Cal'lated to turn in airly, so as to catch up on sleep afore I started off again on that crew-calling job you folks set for me."

Phoebe had been all right when he left her after their late dinner together. She hadn't shown any signs of being excited, no unusual signs, anyway.

"She's been in more or less of a stew ever since the fire and Seth's killing, but so has a lot of other folks, far as that goes. Talk? Lord A'mighty, yes! Course she talked, but she never mentioned you, Captain Isaiah, nor as much as hinted at having anything special to tell you."

He came into the house by the kitchen door. There was no one in the kitchen, and the first out-of-the-way thing he noticed was a kettle full of something or other which was hanging on the crane in the fireplace. The stuff, whatever it was, was boiling over and frothing and smelling at a good rate. He snatched the kettle off the hook and sung out for his wife. He didn't get any answer, so he went into the dining-room. Then he saw her, lying on the floor.

As soon as he made sure she was alive he had managed to carry, or drag, her back to their bedroom—which, considering her tonnage and his, must have been something of a job—and had run for help and Doctor Blodgett.

"And, well—I guess that's about all," he said. "Doctor, he figures she was hit from behind with something hard and heavy and was lucky not to have been killed."

He went on to say that there wasn't any doubt what the hard and heavy something was. "It was my kindling hatchet, the one we always keep nigh to the fireplace in the kitchen. The cuss hit her with the back of it instead of the edge, God knows why. Give me the chance to try it on *his* head, and I doubt if I'll be so fussy.

"And now," he finished with, "if you folks will excuse me, I'll go in and see how she's getting on."

But Captain Elnathan hadn't quite done with him. "You haven't told us what your wife said to you when you found her here on the floor. Captain Dole might be interested in that, don't you think?"

Ezra looked a little bit queer, or seemed to me he did. "Don't know's that amounts to a whole lot," he grumbled. "She didn't really say it to me, either; she was out of her head and talking to all creation in general, I judge likely. All she said was, 'Knife, knife.' Said it over two or three times. Don't ask me what she meant by it, for I don't know. Something to do with her kitchen work, I shouldn't wonder."

He went out towards the back bedroom where Phoebe and the doctor were. Captain Jeremiah Weeks looked after him and then at me.

"I wonder what knife she did mean," he said, slow. "Any idea, Isaiah?"

"No. Why should I?"

Berry and Davies swapped looks. It was Davies who put that look into words.

"It was a knife that killed Seth Black," he said, quiet. Captain Elnathan bobbed his head up and down. "Yes, and we know who that knife belonged to," he put in. "Yes, sir, we do!"

"Don't think Phoebe could be trying to tell anything about that particular knife, do you, Isaiah?" asked Weeks.

It may seem hard for you folks who read this to believe, but the notion hadn't so much as crossed my mind until they pitched it at me this way. They had had time to talk and think a little. I hadn't, for I had run every foot from the corner of the Bay Road and the Point Road. Bounderby had said something about a knife, but I hadn't paid close attention. And even when Ezra, in answer to Elnathan's suggestion, told of Phoebe's mutterings, I hadn't connected them with Jonathan Bangs's sheath knife, the knife he had lent me the week before, that I had given Phoebe to put back in his room, and that, the next time I saw it, was lying alongside poor dead and murdered Seth over there by the edge of Hornpout Pond.

But now—! I caught my breath. It might be that knife she was raving about—it might be. She had been up town hunting for me, vowing she had something important to tell me, saying she must see me. Suppose she had found out something about *that* knife.

I didn't speak, but I guess my face must have shown something of what was tumbling through my head, for Captain Jeremiah got after me again. "You see, Isaiah," he said, "we've been trying to think of a reason why anybody should hurt—yes, I'm afraid, try to kill—as harmless and good-hearted a creature as Phoebe Light. She couldn't be—knowingly, at least—mixed up in any of the devilishness that has been going on since Saturday night here in Trumet. She is—well, she is too simple-minded, for one reason."

Elkanah Davies snorted. "The devil himself couldn't make a wildcat out of a rabbit," he put in.

"True enough, Elkanah. But suppose that rabbit had learned something, or heard something, that was dangerous for a wildcat to have known. *Then* the cat might think it was a good idea to get rid of the rabbit altogether. See what I mean, Isaiah?"

I saw. It added up as plain as two and two make four. And what it was leading up to was just as plain. Captain Elnathan put it into words.

"Seth Black knew—and see what happened to him," he snorted. "Phoebe, poor soul, came to know—and she's in yonder with her head stove in. There's no doubt who killed Black. Who do you figure tried to kill Phoebe Light, Isaiah?"

I looked him straight in the eye. "If I knew I should tell you," I said.

"Humph! Well, if you were guessing who would you guess? Isaiah Dole, some of us here have a notion you know more about—er—a certain individual and his whereabouts than you've said up to now. We were pretty sure he had run off to join his British paymasters, but, in Council meeting, as I recollect, you didn't seem to be so sure. Considering this new outrage, we are beginning to believe you were right—yes, and maybe knew you were.... Oh, I realize that's pretty plain speaking, Jeremiah; but I, for one, think it is high time we spoke plain—all of us. And when I say all," looking straight at me, "I mean everybody, including the man who is supposed to be head of this company of ours. . . . There!" swinging to face the other three, "if the rest of you want to keep on with your confounded whispering you can. I've said my say and said it out loud."

He jerked forward a chair and sat down on it. The others looked everywhere except at me. Captain Jeremiah cleared his throat.

"I am quite sure," he said, "that—er—that if Captain Isaiah does know anything which—er—which—"

My mind was made up. It had been made up ever since I read the letter I took from the rock. What had happened to Phoebe had shoved it to one side, that's all.

"All right, Jeremiah, all right," I broke in. "I do know some things that no other member of our Council knows. Some of them I knew when we had our last meeting; some others—and I must say they are what seem to be clinchers—I have only just found out. Do you want to hear them now?"

Elnathan said he did, and high time, too. Weeks said, "Why—why—I guess—yes, let's hear them, Captain Dole." Fowler did not speak; he was leaning forward, staring as if he was trying to look clear through me. Elkanah Davies asked a question.

"Is what you are going to tell very important?" he asked.

"About as important as anything could be."

"Important to—to the *New Hope* enterprise?"

"Yes."

"Then I think it should be told to a full meeting of the Council."

The others would have agreed, I guess likely, but I put in an objection.

"I'm not sure it might be good judgment to have it heard by a full meeting," I said. "A few of us—yes; I'd like Squire Bailey there, for one. But not Henry Allen, not at first, anyhow."

That surprised them, of course. Berry wanted to know why I didn't want Allen.

"Because—well, because one of Henry's family is more or less mixed up in what I've learned. Just how much, or how knowingly, I'm not sure—but mixed up, that's certain."

There was a kind of rustle, as if everyone had caught his breath hard.

"Henry Allen!" gasped Elnathan. "Why—why, I don't believe—"

He didn't have time to say what he didn't believe. Eben Fowler interrupted him. He had gone white as a new top-sail.

"His family!" he choked. "You mean—? It's a damned lie!"

Even at that exciting minute it flashed across me that I had never heard him swear before. Always precise and careful about his language, Fowler was. He was on his feet now, too. Davies put a hand on his shoulder.

"Easy, easy, Eben," he said. "You don't want a full meeting, Isaiah? What would you propose?"

"My idea would be that we—just the four of us—go up to the meeting place right off, picking up Squire Bailey on the way. We'll have all the real leaders in our company there then—except Henry. I'll tell what I have to tell, and it can be talked over quietly. When you know what it is I think you'll agree it better not be spread around town."

And that is what we did. I left word with the man guarding the door where Ezra could find me, if he wanted to, and we walked down the hill to the Town House. Bailey was at home, and we took him along with us. Nobody said much. Fowler didn't speak at all. He was white and scowling, and I could understand why. He and Hope Allen were close friends; she called him "Uncle Eb" sometimes, although, of course, they weren't relations. As for me, I would have talking enough to do in a few minutes, and the

Almighty knows I wasn't looking forward to the job. What would be said or done to me I didn't even try to guess. The *New Hope* was the only thing that counted. If, in spite of my mistakes in trying to help a friend who didn't deserve help, we could still get that privateer to sea I should be satisfied.

So Captain Jeremiah unlocked the door of the room where we held our meetings, and we went in. The candles were lit and we sat down—that is, the other four sat, I kept on my feet. I was certain to be the main play-actor in the show, Lord help me.

2.

I'm not going to try to put down all that happened at that Town House talk that evening. None of us had had any supper, and nobody thought of having any; at least I am sure I didn't, and if any of the rest did they didn't say so. I made a clean breast of the whole thing, holding back nothing and making no excuses for my own actions. If they believed there was anything underhand or treasonable on my part, I wanted them to speak out. If they did that I was ready to answer them. If my answers didn't satisfy—well, then they could act as they thought best; I was ready to take whatever was coming to me.

I told it all: beginning with what Ezra Light had told of his meeting with Jonathan on his way home from Tamoset, of Jonathan's asking to see the powder-running plans and the reason he gave for making Ezra promise to tell no one but me until the next morning. I went on to explain why I had kept the story of that meeting quiet, hadn't told it to the Council. And while that explanation was being made I could see the faces of all of them—good friends of mine I had counted them to be—freezing, as you might say, getting harder and harder as I went on. I was expecting to see just that, so I wasn't surprised or hurt. I didn't blame them, either. If I had been in their places I should have felt and looked as they did.

"You don't understand how or why I could do this," I said. "There was just one reason. I believed Jonathan Bangs was square and loyal. I was willing to swear he was. I thought I was a pretty fair judge of men, and I was for Jonathan through thick and thin. You fellows heard me say so over and over. He sent word by Light that he believed he was on the track of the real traitor and that my keeping secret the fact that he was ashore—instead of, as 'most everybody thought, back with the enemy gang that hired him—would help him to find and lay hands on that traitor. I swallowed that, too, and so I did what he asked, I kept quiet. I thought then that I was doing right by him and by all of our *New Hope* company. Now—"

My breath caught in my throat. The hardest part was coming. Nobody spoke; they were still as graven images. I went on.

"Now, since then—this very afternoon, as a matter of fact—I have found out something, seen something, read something with my own eyes that—well, that—that seems to prove I was all wrong. That I have been made a fool of and catspawed into making fools of all the rest of you. You see—"

Once more there was a hitch in my breathing. Elnathan Berry leaned back in his chair; I could hear it creak. "Humph!" he grunted. If ever there was an "I told you so" in a grunt, it was in that one. It ought to have scared me, maybe, like the first grumble of thunder ahead of a tempest. It didn't though, it seemed to stiffen my backbone, if anything. I wouldn't have minded a fight just then; it was the stillness and waiting, waiting, that was the worst to face.

I talked faster. I told of my going to see Hope Allen, of her looks and actions. I told of my following her to the

rock, of watching her get the first letter, of her owning up
it was from Jonathan and her declaring it was a personal
note and that I mustn't read it.

There was another interruption there. Captain Jeremiah
Weeks was the interrupter.

"And you let her *keep* that letter!" he sang out. "Didn't
force her to show it to you?"

"That's it, Jeremiah. I was a soft-headed jackass, I suppose, but that's what I did."

Eben Fowler leaned forward. I thought he was going to
say something, but he didn't, so I kept on with my yarn.
It ended—the yarn, I mean—with how I found the second
letter under the sliver of stone. "Here it is," said I. "Addressed to 'Dear Sir,' and signed 'J. B.' I was on my way to
bring it to you, Captain Jeremiah, as Council head, when
Bounderby told me what had happened to Phoebe Light.
Read it for yourselves."

Captain Jeremiah read it first, and I could see the color
fading out of his honest, weather-roughed old face like the
tide going out over our Trumet flats. He didn't speak a
word but passed it on to the others and, one by one, they
read it. Elnathan Berry said, "Great God A'mighty!" kind
of under his breath. Squire Bailey didn't say anything, but
the look he gave me was enough. Bethuel Bailey had been
one of my best friends through all of this, but now I knew
that friendship was close to shipwreck. Eben Fowler's reaction to it came nighest of any to bring a real outbreak.
He jumped from his chair, turned towards the door, and
then stopped. Davies caught him by the arm.

"Hold on, Eben," he ordered. "What is it? Where are
you going?"

Fowler hesitated. He was looking wild. He made another
move and then stopped again. "I—I wasn't going anywhere," he stammered. "Only—only—"

Squire Bailey spoke. "Steady, Eben, steady," he said.

"We all know how you feel about the Allens, I would have sworn by Hope myself. . . . No, stay where you are. Our whole privateering scheme is tumbling."

Captain Elnathan was up now.

"Tumbling," he roared. "It has tumbled already. It has gone to Tophet, and every man, woman, and child in Trumet with it. And that fellow there," shaking his fist at me across the table, "is to blame. Yes," swinging around to the others, "and the rest of you are almost as much to blame as he is. You wouldn't listen to me. *I* told you that Bangs was no good. *I* said in the beginning that he set that fire. *I* said he killed Seth Black. *I* said—"

Bailey stopped him. "Shsh!" he ordered. "You said a lot, Elnathan. Among other things you said Bangs had run away to the British. You were certain sure of it. Well, he hadn't. This letter proves that much."

"Don't make any difference. Isaiah Dole is the one who has stood up for the damnation Bangs traitor. If he hadn't kept back what that Light scamp told about Bangs holding him up on the way home from Tamoset we would have found out—"

"Shsh!" This was the Squire again; he was keeping his head, as he always does. "What would we have found out, Elnathan? After all, the only one who has really found out much of anything is Isaiah himself. It was he who got suspicious of the Allen girl. It was he who followed her to that rock, and he who had the gumption to go there a second time and get this Bangs letter. I agree with you that he was wrong, absolutely wrong, in not telling us about the Light and Bangs meeting, but he has told us now and told a good deal we might never have known if it wasn't for him. Isaiah's getting that letter before Hope did has—humph!—well, at least it has proved what *she* is."

Captain Davies snorted. "A little mite too late for that to do any good, I'd say," he growled. "If Dole had grabbed that first letter from her, when he had the chance, and read *that*—but he didn't. He let her keep it to herself and cart it off to—to—eh? Where did she cart it?"

The Squire nodded. "I was wondering how soon that point would strike some of you," he said. "This letter begins with a 'Dear Sir.' That doesn't sound as if it was meant for Hope, herself. A fellow doesn't write that way to his girl, not as a usual thing."

It seems odd that that hadn't hit them before, but it hadn't—anybody except Bailey, that is. I presume likely the letter itself was so paralyzing that the 'Dear Sir' had slipped by. They looked at each other. Captain Jeremiah began thinking out loud.

" 'Dear Sir,' " he said, half under his breath. "Eh? . . . *Eh?* . . . Why—here, let me see the thing again, Squire."

Bailey handed him the letter, Weeks read it again. "It does begin that way, for a fact," he mumbled. "Now what on earth does that mean?"

Elnathan Berry broke out. "*Who* does it mean? you'd better say," he groaned. "Why—why, that letter couldn't be for the girl at all, according to that beginning. Do you suppose there is—is somebody else besides those two in all this? I can't believe it!"

Elkanah's brains were working, after a fashion. "She—she—Hope Allen, I mean—must be just a go-between," he choked. "Just carrying the mail, you might call it, between the Bangs cutthroat and some other man. *Another* traitor! For heaven's sake, how many of them are they?"

Squire Bailey sniffed. "If we hadn't been wooden-heads," he said, "we would have sensed that the minute Isaiah showed us the letter. It wasn't likely that that young girl was in direct touch with the people aboard those British boats all by herself. It is just possible that she might have been, I suppose, but this settles it—she wasn't—and isn't. . . .

Humph! Isaiah, I begin to see why you judged it better not to have Henry Allen here with us just now."

He had turned to look at me, and I nodded. Elnathan stared at both of us. "Henry Allen!" he gobbled. "Henry! ...Why—why, he has been at every Council meeting—except this one. He knows all our plans, every last thing about every one of them. Henry Allen! You're crazy, Bethuel! Henry wouldn't—he wouldn't—"

His face was as red as a bonfire, and his eyes were popping. He didn't finish his sentence, seemed to run hard and fast aground in the middle of it, so to say. The other faces, Weeks's and Davies's and Fowler's, were as wide-eyed and open-mouthed as his. There was a second of complete quiet, like a kind of tableau. Then everybody moved at once. Eben Fowler jumped to his feet again. So did Elkanah Davies. Captain Jeremiah started to get up and then fell—or slid—back into his chair.

I held up both hands. "Wait, wait, wait!" I ordered. I doubt if they would have paid attention if Squire Bailey hadn't grabbed the helm once more.

"Gentlemen, gentlemen!" he said. "Careful! Don't go off half-cocked. You mustn't take it for granted that I believe Henry Allen is the 'Dear Sir' in this letter. I doubt if Isaiah really thinks he is. It is just possible, though, that he and Hope and Bangs may be working with or for the fellow. Let's say that 'Dear Sir' is aboard the *Hawke* or *Gannet*, wearing a British uniform. *If* the Allens and Jonathan are working for him they would make a well-balanced team. Bangs to do most of the real dirty work; Hope to carry the mail, as you called it, Elkanah; and Henry, on the inside of everything, a member of the Council and, up to now, clear above suspicion, living near the Cove, and with a boat of his own to be used at any time without any risk, to do the errands afloat—between ship and shore, say. Well, it would be a well-balanced team, and that's a fact.

"Of course," he went on, "the idea is as full of holes as a nutmeg-grater. We haven't the least shadow of proof that Henry's hands aren't as clean as ours are. This is just another guess, and, I hope, a wild one. But I should say it did explain why Isaiah, knowing what he does now about Hope, and knowing, too, how Henry worships that adopted daughter of his and how she winds him about her finger, thought Henry had better not be with us here to learn that this letter had got into our hands. That was good judgment, Isaiah, whether it helps anything or not."

Elnathan Berry's hand slapped down on the table. "Henry Allen!" he was muttering to himself. "Henry! I knew, same as we all did, that he was cross-grained and cantankerous, generally on the off-side of everything, but I can't believe he . . . Eh? If our privateer goes under he'll go down with her, same as we all will. No, no! It's ridiculous! It don't make sense. Of course it doesn't!"

Jeremiah Weeks turned to Eben Fowler. Captain Jeremiah was a solid man, with years of tough seafaring behind him; he had faced typhoons and mutiny and had fought pirates in his day; but there was a shake in his voice when he asked Fowler a question.

"Eben," he said, "you are closer to the Allens than any of the rest of us. Have you ever suspected Henry of being on the British side?"

Eben was sitting, his elbows on his knees and his face between his hands. Now the hands dropped, and one of them clenched into a fist.

"I *never* suspected it," he vowed, the fist pounding the chair arm. "And I don't now. I don't believe it. I *don't*, I tell you! As Elnathan says, it is absurd, ridiculous! It's an outrage even to hint such a thing."

"How about Hope?" asked Bailey, quietly. "We have proof that she and Bangs have written each other and, very possibly, seen each other since he got out of the lockup.

You'll admit that Jonathan Bangs is a traitor, won't you?"

That brought Fowler out of the chair. "Admit it?" he shouted. "Certainly I'll admit it. It has been proved, just as that knife proves him a murderer. Instead of wasting time here, guessing, and slandering people who are as innocent as we are, why don't we get after the blackguard we *know* is guilty? Why don't we really try to find where he is hiding? We haven't done that yet. Instead we stay here, listening to the confessions of the man whose carelessness— if it was nothing more—has betrayed and ruined our enterprise. Not only listening, but finding excuses for him. I— I—oh, I have had enough of this! It is high time the town knew what Isaiah Dole has done to it. I'll see that it does. Let go of my arm, Bethuel."

I never would have believed that sober, straight-up-and-down Eben Fowler could get so worked up and break from his moorings this way. I knew the reason, of course—it was Hope. She was his pet. The very idea that her name was going to be dragged out and smirched was too much for him.

Once more it was level-headed Squire Bailey who pulled him and the others back to common sense. He and Davies held Fowler fast and quieted him down a little. Then he— the Squire, that is—spoke to us all.

"I agree with Eben on one point, anyhow," he said. "We *are* wasting time, and guessing won't help us just now. Is there anything that can?"

Captain Elnathan groaned. He was the most worked up of all of us. "Help!" he snorted. "What are you talking about? Help be darned! Our powder plans are in the hands of the enemy, every last item of them; that letter says that in so many words. And they can't be changed; it's miles too late to send word to Tamoset. The boat will show up Friday night, the *Gannet* will be waiting for her, and—well, that's about all, I should say. Except what comes later, when the town folks learn how we have mishandled everything. Oh, my Lord A'mighty!"

Even Squire Bailey looked pretty well sunk. He nodded. "Bad enough, Elnathan," he agreed. "About as bad as it can be. We must keep all this from being known around town as long as possible, I suppose; but what next? We might arrest Hope—and even Henry, too, but that would spill the fat into the fire without doing much good at this late day. Can anyone think of a way to save our powder from the enemy? And save our whole *New Hope* enterprise, for that depends on the powder reaching us. Has anybody got a worth-while thought in his head? If so let's hear it, for God's sake."

I had been waiting for this. "Perhaps, maybe, I have," I said.

The looks I got when I said this were a mixture of surprise, doubt, suspicion—yes, and even a little ray of hope in certain quarters, though the hope signals may have been only in my imagination. I hadn't had time to think clear, to say nothing of doing any planning, since the news about Phoebe Light came to me—but, without hardly realizing it, I guess, my mind must have been groping for light, and I had sighted a feeble glimmer, or dared to hope I had.

"First of all, let us face facts," I said. "Hope Allen and Jonathan Bangs we know—or as good as know—to be turncoats and traitors. I think you must realize how I hate to say that, but it has got to be said. Call that pair traitors, to begin with."

Eben Fowler made a move, as if to get up again, but Bailey and Davies pulled him down.

"They are double dealers," I went on, "and Henry may be another, although his part hasn't been proved. Granting as much, what can we do? As I see it, whatever we do will be about a hundred to one gamble, but we've got to gamble or haul down the flag. As Elnathan says, the British have our plans, and those plans can't be changed. They must be put through somehow. Here is the wild idea I've been playing with. See what you think of it."

I went on to give them my scheme, so far as I had it in my head. I won't set it down here, for I shall have to tell how it worked later along. I began by saying that our getting hold of the "Dear Sir" letter was, if not much real help, at least a little better than a hindrance.

"We know what they know, at any rate, and they don't know we know it. That's to our advantage, or seems as if it might be. Now they mustn't be allowed to know we know, so, with your permission, I'll put this letter back under the stone where I found it. The seal came loose of itself and can be stuck on again just as easy. Put the letter back, that's the first thing."

You can imagine how some of them—Elnathan in particular—took to that idea. "What the devil good would that do?" he wanted to know. "The fellows on the British boats know everything that counts, anyway. This letter doesn't tell them any more. If you, Isaiah Dole, hadn't let that girl lug away that other letter, *then* we might have had a chance."

Jeremiah Weeks held up his hand. "What's past and done with can't be helped, Elnathan," he said.

"Why would you put the letter back, Isaiah?" asked the Squire.

"Why, simply on the guess that it might be expected and, if it doesn't come, set the traitor gang to wondering why. Their getting it won't do any harm. Let them have it and make them sure all is going as they want it to."

Elkanah Davies spoke up. "Say, look here!" he put in, excited. "Here's a notion. Why don't we keep this letter and print one of our own? Say in it that our powder plans have been changed again and give those changes. A sham letter, I mean. Sign it J. B. and put *it* under the stone.

Mightn't that throw them off the track and set them to watching for our boat at the wrong place?"

Fowler and Berry were growing excited, too. The idea of a sham letter wasn't new to me, though. I had considered something of the sort for a minute or two and then given it up. Imitating the printing in that letter would be very hard to do. I doubted if any of us could do it and make it pass examination.

"If you will look at it," I went on, "you'll notice it is printed on an uncommon kind of paper. Suppose all the other letters—we don't know how many there may have been—were on that same kind of paper. Ours wouldn't be, and—well, there's a chance of starting suspicion there. No, if we are going to put a letter in the rock—and I think that is best—then I should say it ought to be this one."

There was whispering back and forth. Squire Bailey was studying the letter. "Hum," he said; "it *is* an odd paper and that's a fact. . . . I declare, it seems as if I had . . . Oh, well, never mind. Go on, Isaiah."

I went on with my plan. Pretty foggy it was, in spots, but it was the only hope in sight, and so, after a hogshead of objections, they agreed to let me try it out. After all, we might as well fly a kite as dig a hole, so—in a sort of desperation, I guess—they let me fly mine. I rather expected Eben Fowler to object louder than he did, on account of Hope Allen's part in it, but he said hardly a word. He looked and acted crushed, as you might call it.

Captain Jeremiah made us swear to tell nobody of our get-together, nor what had taken place in or was said at it. Then we broke up, each one so sober and worried as to scarcely remember to say good night.

My first job was to put that letter where I got it from. It was pitch dark when I got to the rock, of course, but I scrambled up best I could, lifted the stone sliver, and dropped in the paper. Fixing the seal was easy, I had done that before I left the Town House. I went home then. As for eating—well, I had forgotten that had ever been a habit of mine.

I saw Ezra before I turned in, and he told me Phoebe was no worse, even a little better, but still unconscious. I asked him if he thought he could leave his wife long enough to start early next morning on the rounding-up trip after the crew. He said he had just as soon go now, that night, if I wanted him to. "There's a good woman nursing Phoebe," he said, "and," with a one-sided twist of his mouth, "the poor old girl won't miss me, and my keeping busy will keep me from missing her." He started within an hour.

He told me that Seth Black had been buried the afternoon before—Tuesday, that was. I had had so much on my mind that I had forgotten Seth altogether.

"Quite a flock of folks went to the graveyard," Ezra said. "The heft of 'em kept away from Seth when he was walking around, but, knowing he was good and dead, they took the chance of associating with him, I presume likely. The Reverend Ichabod preached a moving sermon, according to tell. Consider'ble many tears was shed over the remains. Kind of tough on Seth, that was, when you come to think of it. Dead or alive you couldn't imagine him getting comfort from water."

I was nearer to being hungry next morning, so I got my breakfast up at the tavern, but, before I went out after it, I had a word with Hannah Badger, the woman that the doctor had hired to stay with Phoebe. "As soon as she comes to herself and can talk—the minute Doctor Blodgett will let her talk—I want to be the first one to see her," I declared. "I expect to be around town somewhere, and you send a messenger after me. Don't let me hear afterwards that I couldn't be found. I've *got* to be found. Understand?"

My next job was the one I dreaded most of all. And that

was to wait. All night long, in between catnaps, I had been mulling that precious scheme back and forth from stem to stern of my tired head. Win or lose, it was our only hand in the pack. It was already too late to get word to the Tamoset folks; no more changes could be made up there. Our only hope—and it was slim as a starved crow—was to fool the enemy from our end. I thought—and Squire Bailey agreed with me when I told him—that we'd do better to postpone putting our scheme to the test until the day before the powder was to be landed. It might make Bangs and Hope Allen feel more certain that we knew nothing of their scheming, and it would add a chance of surprise to what we all knew was a long chance at best. So, all that Wednesday, I puttered about the *New Hope*, checking stores and setting up rigging, but thinking every minute of the nasty job ahead of me and wishing it was over with.

Thursday morning I set off through the village for the Allen place. I got a glimpse of Henry Allen on his way to the shipyard. That was a little stroke of luck, for I couldn't talk with Hope, not the way I intended to talk with and to her, if her father was around. Once more I came to the back door of the Allen house and knocked. No answer. Then I knocked again. Still no answer; so I opened the door and walked in.

She wasn't in the kitchen, nor in the dining-room, nor the sitting-room. I didn't know what to do. She might have gone up to the village with her father, although he was alone when I sighted him. I walked out to the kitchen once more and stood by the back window, looking out and considering.

Then I saw her. She came out of the pine woods and was hurrying towards the house. She was bareheaded, so I judged she hadn't cruised far. Thinks I: I know what you've been up to, young woman. You've been calling for mail at your rock post-office. And I shouldn't wonder if the letter I took out of that post-office and put back last evening was inside the waist of that dress of yours this minute.

It was only a guess, but it seemed a likely one. Of course she might have got the other letter earlier and had been over to leave an answer from "Dear Sir." Or she might have been somewhere to meet "Dear Sir" himself—or even to meet Jonathan. I hardly thought it was either of the last, though. Well, anyhow, here she was—and here I was—and now for it. Lord! How I hated what was coming! I had liked that girl.

She came into the kitchen and shut the door quick astern of her. Then she swung around and saw me. And the tide went out in her face just as it had gone out in Captain Jeremiah Weeks's at our meeting when I sprung the news about the J. B. letter. She caught her breath, and her hand flew up towards the neck of her gown. I remember thinking she couldn't have been in the traitor business long or she wouldn't have made that mistake. I knew now, almost for certain, that she had been to the rock and had the letter with her.

I didn't say so, though. All I said was "Good morning, Hope."

She was breathing hard, partly from running, I judged, and partly from scare at seeing me just then.

"You're out early, aren't you?" said I.

She was fighting to pull herself together. "Early?" she stammered. "Why—why, yes, it—it is early, I suppose." She managed to pump up a smile. "You are early, yourself, Captain Isaiah," she said; "you are not early enough for Father, though. He has been gone quite a while."

I paced up and down the room a couple of times, trying to look excited and worried—which wasn't hard to do, the worried part, anyhow She didn't ask me what the matter was, she was too anxious to get me away from there, I judged. "I think Father went up to the village," she said. "Perhaps if you went there—"

I stopped her, stopping my pacing at the same time and turning to face her. "Hope," I said, very earnest.

"Yes? ... Yes, Captain Isaiah?"

"Hope, look here. I can trust you, I know."

She caught her breath. She looked, I thought, very anxious and—yes, frightened. She didn't answer me.

"This is almighty serious, Hope," I warned her. "I *can* trust you, can't I?"

She had to answer then. "Yes," she said, kind of hesitating. And then, more firmly, "Yes."

"Of course, I knew that. If your father was here I should, probably, have said my say to both of you, but he isn't here and time is short. I had rather talk with you alone first, anyhow. Hope, you believe Jonathan Bangs is straight, not a traitor nor a murderer?"

"Yes." There was no hesitation this time. "Certainly I do. I know he isn't either. I told you that before. And," with a lift of her head, "I told Captain Berry and the others."

"Certain you did. And, the last time you and I met, you as much as told me that you had seen Jonathan since he got out of that lockup. You told me that that letter you had was from him."

Another little wait. Then: "Well?"

"You said it was, and a personal and private letter, so I took your word for it and let you keep it. Proving, you'll agree, that I did trust you and him."

"Yes.... But—"

"Wait. Hope, before Jonathan was arrested, one of the last things he told me was that he was beginning to be almost sure there was a traitor here in town, somebody working against our *New Hope* enterprise. Now I am going to tell you something that only a very, very few know. Something I have just found out myself. There *is* a traitor

268

here. Who he is we don't know yet, but we mean to find out. Before we tackle that job in earnest though, we must have the powder that is coming from Tamoset safe in our hands. Now that powder is to be landed here Friday—that's tomorrow—night. Our plans were all laid for the boat to be met and the stuff got ashore."

I waited a second to see how she took this. I wondered if she would say she knew it. She didn't though; she only nodded. She was breathing fast; I could see the frill at the neck of her dress moving up and down.

"Yes," I went on. "Well, here is what I have to tell you, and I am telling you because I want you to get the word to Jonathan if you can. You can tell your father afterwards, but make him swear to keep it to himself and tell nobody else, nobody at all.

"I can't tell even you how I got the information," I went on. "That has to be secret. But I know, have absolute proof, that the officers on those two English craft, one at the inlet and one down off the harbor mouth, have learned what our landing plans are and that they will be all fixed and ready to trap and seize that Tamoset boat when she makes her try Friday night. I, and a few others, know that, and the only comforting thing is that they—the British, I mean —don't know we know it."

I went on to tell, in a few words, about the hurry-up meeting at the Town House. "If Henry—if your father had been where we could have got at him we should have had him there with us, but we didn't know where he was. We decided on some things at that meeting, but most of the responsibility for carrying out those decisions was, as usual, loaded on my shoulders. I am asking you to help me carry some of it. I am relying on you, Hope Allen. Will you help me—and the *New Hope* and all Trumet? Will you?"

She looked at me, then at the clock on the wall, and then at me again. "But—how can I?" she faltered.

"If you could get a message through to Jonathan you might be able to. If . . . Eh? What is it?"

The expression on her face made me ask that. I had to ask it again before she spoke.

"Jonathan!" She said the name after me. "Jonathan? Why he—"

"Eh? Go on. What?"

"Nothing. Only—only how can I get a message to him?"

"You and he write each other—at least he writes to you; so I wouldn't be surprised to death if you wrote him. Will you write him, or tell him—this is the very important part —that we know now the enemy has got hold of our powder plan, the plan he knows about, and that it can't be put through as it stands. And so we—a few of us in the Council, I mean—have changed that plan altogether. It won't be put into effect until a night later, Saturday night instead of Friday night, and the place picked for the landing is more than two miles from where we first agreed it was to be. Here, I've set the new plan down on this piece of paper. You can read it and then get the paper to Jonathan, if possible. You can tell your father about the change, but you musn't tell anybody else, and you must make him promise not to breathe a word to a living soul. If I see Henry, myself, I'll tell him, but you will most likely see him first.

"Now I must go. I've got a dozen things to attend to. Jonathan *must* get my message, you understand why. Good-by. And don't forget how much depends on all this."

I left her holding the paper in her hand and staring, wide-eyed and white-faced, after me. I went in a hurry so that she wouldn't ask me any more questions. This whole scheme of mine was as thin and flimsy as a cheesecloth shirt, and a few clever questions might pull it all apart. The stuff I had written for her to give Jonathan—and, perhaps, Henry, provided Henry was one of the turncoat crew—

was just stuff and nothing else. The changes of plans were all bosh. Our plans hadn't been changed at all. The powder boat would arrive Friday night and try to make its landing exactly at the location the Tamoset group had picked out and about which they had sent us word by Ezra Light. But if Hope *did* get that paper to the enemy, or the enemy's agent or agents, the British might give up expecting us on Friday and be laying for us Saturday. That was the whole of my great idea, and it all depended on her— and Jonathan—or, maybe, Henry. If one of them, or two, or all three, were in British pay it might save everything for our side.

Heaving all prejudices and earlier beliefs and liking overboard and looking square at the evidence, I couldn't honestly feel much doubt that the girl and Jonathan were playing us crooked. She, I imagined, was the most to blame. He was crazy in love with her, and she was making a monkey out of him. He was Samson, and she was the Delilah giving him a haircut. As for Henry—well, I didn't feel so sure about him, but it was a whole lot safer that he should be told about and believe in those sham powder-running plans. By the time he learned they were sham it would be too late for him to do much harm even if he wanted to.

As I passed by the dining-room window I looked in. Hope was sitting at the table, her head down on her arms and her shoulders shaking. She was crying.

It came across me that she must have some rags of conscience left, anyhow, and my telling her how I trusted her may have set them fluttering. Thinks I: Maybe playing traitor to your best friends isn't as much fun as you calculated it was going to be, Mistress. You'll earn whatever they pay you—provided you get it.

I didn't pity her any more. This, and whatever might be coming to her later, served her right. As for that poor, soft-headed fool of a lover of hers—well, I only hoped I didn't have a gun in my hand the next time he and I met.

And then, for the twentieth time, at least, the thought, conviction, certainty—whatever you want to call it—hit me hard. *In spite of his signing his initials to a hanging letter like that one, Jonathan Bangs was nobody's fool.*

But there! Neither was Samson—until Delilah got her scissors working on him.

3.

So much had been done. Now for the next entry on the list. As I look at it now, those days and nights all seem to run together, like the string of happenings in a mince-pie nightmare. No proper divisions of time; no regular hours for meals or rest or sleep; hardly any sense of light and dark. Just hurry to one place, give orders there, see that they are commencing to be carried out; then hurry to the next place—and so on. Always with the feeling of being prodded from behind; always with the indefinite notion that something has been forgotten; and, forever and ever through it all and hanging over it all and having everlastingly to be lifted off and pushed back, like a black blanket, the half-way conviction that whatever I or the rest of us might do now wouldn't amount to anything—that it was too late, too late.

I went down to the breastwork by the harbor mouth on the ocean side of town and found Major Bartlett there. When I told him what I wanted he was as near mutiny as his soldier training would allow.

"But, Captain Dole," he spluttered, red in the face and gasping like a puffing pig. "I—I *suppose* I understand you, sir. You wish me to withdraw my guards from their stations along shore tonight?"

"No, no, Major," I said. "That isn't what I want, exactly.

I want you—these are Council's orders—to hint about town this afternoon that the militia sentinels on the Bay side will be, all but a very few of them, given this night off. Make any reasonable excuse you can think of. Say that your fellows are tired after having stood watch so many nights. You might hint—remember, no more than hint and then only once or twice—that we all feel sure the landing to take the town, if one is ever tried by the British, will be from the ocean side, from the *Hawke*. She is the bigger craft of the two, more guns and more men aboard her, and she hasn't got to figure on the tide the way the *Gannet* has to. The *Gannet*, you might say you and the rest of us think, is just a guard boat, picketing the Bay shore. Got that clear, have you?"

His old back stiffened. "Yes, Captain Dole," he said, pretty average chilly. "Why, yes, sir, I understand your orders. Why those orders are given I must say I *don't* understand, but that, I judge likely, is not my business. As for the possible consequences—well, those, under the circumstances, are not my business, either. The orders shall be obeyed."

He turned his back on me. I could see I should have to tell him more if I wanted to keep his bristles down. I decided to take the risk.

"Major," I said, "I am under orders, just as you are, and my orders are not to tell anybody—anybody, mind you—more than a grain of the real truth. In strict confidence I'll give you that grain. The withdrawing of your men tonight—and only for tonight—is part of a scheme to fool the enemy. It may mean the salvation of the *New Hope* and Trumet. That is all I can say—now."

It was enough. The starch melted out of his spine like pond ice on the first warm spring day. "Thank you, Captain Isaiah," he said. "You can depend on me, sir."

Whether he dropped the hints or not I don't know, but

I do know that the news of the slackening of the watch on the Bay shore was all over town before the afternoon ended. People asked me if I knew why it was done. Henry Allen was one of the askers.

"You gone crazy, Isaiah?" he wanted to know. "What authority you got to leave half the shore unguarded? Council never told you to, not at any meeting I was at, certain. If you've taken it on yourself I want to know why. And I'm not the only one that'll want to know, either."

I gave him the same answer I had given the others. "The militia boys have been having a hard time lately," I explained. "And when the powder comes they'll have a harder one. Give as many as can be spared a full night's sleep, and they will be fitter when the powder is landed. I want every man Jack at his best then."

I walked away, leaving him staring after me. If he was straight he might fume and find fault—that was his usual habit—but he wouldn't do anything to hurt us. If he was one of the spy gang he might—Well, what could he do? Berry and Captain Weeks had undertaken to have him watched pretty careful. He hadn't said a word about the sham message I had given Hope, nothing about the pretended shift in the powder date from Friday to Saturday night. If she had told him of that make-believe shift or had shown him the paper I had left with her, I should have expected him to be all excited about it. He hadn't mentioned it, which certainly looked as if she hadn't shown it to him. Why not? Unless, of course, he wasn't in her and Jonathan's confidence at all. And that would seem to mean he wasn't "Dear Sir." But who—?

Well, I couldn't let myself get playing *that* guessing game again just now. I had other fish to fry.

If you have a map of the Trumet shore handy to look at—the shore on the Bay side, I mean—you will notice that, from the mouth of Billfish Creek stretching north for three miles, there are high sand bluffs. For most of the three the beach at the foot of those bluffs makes almost a straight line with hardly a break in it. Then there is a deep break, stretching back inland for half of a mile or so and maybe quarter of a mile across. That break is Shad Cove. Shad Cove is wide at the mouth and narrows at the southeast corner as it cuts into the land. The bluffs bordering it are as high as those along the straight stretch. North of the mouth of the Cove the bluffs stretch on again for more miles. The beach at the foot of the bluffs, inside the Cove as well as out, is flat sand.

The only building at the top of the bluffs for a stretch is the shanty that Seth Black lived in. His shack was a little way back from the inner end of the Cove. About a hundred yards from it, in the woods, is the big rock where Hope Allen got her letters. Beyond that is nothing but woods, pines and scrub oak and bushes, until you come to Henry Allen's house on the Point Road. A lonesome enough stretch, all that part of Trumet township is.

Most of the fishermen keep their boats and dories in Billfish Cove because it is nearer to town than Shad Cove; but Shad Cove makes a good harbor for small craft. At the mouth of Billfish Creek the channel has been deepened so that the fish boats can ride on an even keel at low tide. Shad Cove is pretty shallow when the tide is down. Outside both Coves, in the Bay, there is nothing, at dead low water, but sand flats and narrow channels edged with eelgrass. A ship or good-sized schooner can't get nearer than a mile and a half from shore at any time; even the little *Gannet* had to keep fairly well out. At half tide, though, rowboats could get to the beach; at dead low tide even they couldn't.

All this explaining is more or less necessary because the tide is a mighty important consideration at our part of the Cape.

At eight that evening, as soon as it began to grow dark, I was at the point I had picked out as a watching station. It was at the top of the bluff on the southern side of Shad Cove and almost at the corner where the Cove cuts in from the Bay. There is a heavy growth of pines and bushes there and a little hollow in the ground where I could lie or sit or kneel without a chance of being seen by anybody more than fifty feet off. From there, at that high place, I could, when I first got there, see all of the Cove, the bluff and the beach on the other side of it, and a stretch of shore.

Up further to the south, where Billfish Cove and Creek head in, I knew Squire Bailey would be hiding and watching, and further still, on the southern side of Billfish Cove, was Captain Jeremiah Weeks. Given a moderately clear night, such as this promised to be, we figured that one of us, at least, might be able to sight any boat that tried to come in from the *Gannet* or anybody that might be waiting for that boat on the beach. If anything of the kind was seen by any one of us he would tell the others afterwards. If no more than what we were expecting, or hoping, happened, the watcher would not hail nor interfere in any way. Of course, if it was something bigger, something we didn't expect, like a real try to land armed crews, a general alarm was to be given.

It was my contriving, the whole of this, a part of my quick-thought-up scheme to fool the enemy and the traitor —or traitors—working with them. One part of that scheme depended on another part and that on another—and so on. If Hope Allen wrote or told Jonathan Bangs, or "Dear Sir" —either or both—of the make-believe last-minute change in our powder-running date from Friday to Saturday night— he, or they, would know they must get word to the British somehow and right off. They couldn't do it in daylight, with the militia on guard everywhere; it would have to be tried after dark on the night of this very day, Thursday.

The only way such word could be sent was by a messenger from shore to boat. To send such a messenger from the ocean shore to the *Hawke* would be ten times as risky as sending him from the Bay beach to the *Gannet*. And now, with all Trumet knowing that the militia guard along the Bay was, most of it, off duty, the "Dear Sir" gang would feel pretty safe—or we hoped they would. If those fake plans got into British hands we would feel safer, too. Once make sure they had got there, and we could go ahead with our real ones.

The dark came on fast, as I sat there, scooched down in the little hollow at the top of the bluff. The night was clear, thank goodness, with plenty of stars and not a sign of fog. The flats were only partly covered when I first got there, but the tide had turned and was coming in fast. Well out, more than a mile and a half, I could see a speck of light, that was the *Gannet*, of course. From my watching place it was the only light in sight.

There was hardly any wind stirring, and it was so quiet that I could hear the wash of the little waves at the foot of the bluff. An owl set up a hooting in the pines back of me, and he sounded like Gabriel's trumpet. I could even hear myself breathe, or thought I could. The night dew began to fall, and I got damper and damper.

Nine o'clock....ten....eleven—and still nothing happened. I had to guess at the time, for I couldn't see my watch and I didn't dare strike a light. I shifted my position every once in a while, but when a twig cracked it sounded to me like a gun going off. I wondered how Bailey and Weeks were enjoying their spell of guard duty. All this dampness wouldn't help Captain Jeremiah's rheumatism. It was too bad he had to be put through this. He had insisted on it, though; said it was too important a job to trust to a foremast hand, and he was right, of course. Fine old man, Captain Jeremiah; true blue as a June sky and as full of grit as a mess of dandelion greens. As for Squire Bailey—well, I would never forget how he was standing by me. There was one debt I would pay, with interest, if I got through all this alive—and providing the getting through didn't drive me crazy.

Eh? What was that? It seemed to me I had heard something. Something besides that dratted owl and the ripples. It wasn't a loud noise, and it had come from a little way to the right and below me. I got down on my stomach and inched forward until I could look straight down the high sand bank to the Cove beach. The sound had seemed to come from there; like a footstep, or, rather, like a foot that had stumbled over a stone or a scrap of wreckage, maybe.

I looked down and I listened. The beach below me, close up to the bank, was just a puddle of blackness, as you might say, but out a little further, towards the edge of the water, things were a little plainer. I could just make out the two inshore poles of the fish weir that Sylvanus Goodspeed had set up there a dozen years ago, or so I had been told, and that he had taken up again after a spell of catching next to nothing—taken up all but those two poles, I mean. I could just see those poles, like a couple of charcoal marks against the sand and water.

And one of the poles—the one nearest the bank—looked bigger than the other, or seemed to me it did. I stared and stared and listened and listened. And then I heard another little sound, and, all at once, a light showed down there on the beach. It showed only partly at first and then clear. It was a lantern. The somebody holding it must have had that lantern covered up with a cloth or a coat or something, and now he, or she, had taken the covering off. I caught my breath and then let it out again, slow and easy. This was what I had been waiting for, hoping for.

The lantern was held up high, then lowered, then lifted again. Three times it went up, and three times it came down. I could see the arm lifting it, an arm in a coat sleeve. When it was highest I could just make out the shape of the hat and head and shoulders of the person inside the coat. I couldn't see his face, the hat brim covered that, but I saw enough to make sure the lantern person was a man and a big man at that.

A kind of twinge—I don't know what else to call it—went through me, as sharp as a pain it was. I declare I could have cried like a woman or a child, or cursed like a drunken sailor, or—yes, killed if I had had the chance. Jonathan Bangs! Jonathan! It was true then! No more hoping against hope; no more thinking it couldn't be, that there must be some explanation somewhere; no more—no more anything.

Jonathan Bangs! Oh, you dog, you dog! I am truly thankful I didn't have a gun or pistol with me just then. It would have been stark craziness, of course. It would have ruined the very scheme I was there to see go through. As a matter of fact, what I was seeing was exactly what I ought to have expected to see, what I did expect, I suppose. And yet, now that I was seeing it, I—well, I am glad I didn't have the gun, that's all.

Jonathan! Oh, you low-lived, double-dealing cur dog!

The lantern moved up and down three times more. A signal, that is what it was. I looked out over the Bay. Away out yonder, where I knew the *Gannet* was lying, a flash answered that signal. Three times that other spark out there in the water moved, up and down, up and down, up and down.

That was all for a spell. The rest was more waiting and waiting. The man below me on the beach had covered his lantern again, at least it didn't show. He was very quiet behind his weir pole, and so, you can be certain, was I, up in my lookout. Then, so close inshore that it surprised me when it came, there was another flash, just a glint, that's all. I strained my ears, and I caught the beat of oars in tholepins. They were muffled oars, moving with a regular man-of-war stroke. A minute later and the huddled bulk of a boat, filled with men, hove in sight.

I heard a low voice order: "Cease rowing." The oars stopped, the boat slid on to the beach. The same voice said: "All ready, sir." The answer from the man on shore was hardly more than a grunt. He walked out a step or two and climbed aboard. "Shove off! Give way!" The steady oar beat began again.

My watch was over. My job for that night was done. Our sham powder-running plans were on their way to the British.

And Jonathan Bangs was on his way there, too. He was, not only a traitor, but a cowardly murderer of an old man and a sneak who could club a woman. I was ready to believe even that now.

I headed off towards where Squire Bailey was on post. Things had gone as we hoped they might; my shaky scheme to fool the enemy had worked—so far. Maybe I ought to have been a happy man.

I wasn't.

4.

And I was no happier when, after a three-hour stretch of broken rest, tossings and tumblings and dreams, I looked at my watch on the chair by my bed, saw that it was half-past five, and decided that I might as well turn out. No sense in getting up so early, of course. I had a hundred things to do that day and a hundred more to see to when night came again and the real doings would begin, but I couldn't do any of them at that hour, so a sensible man would have stayed where he was a spell longer. The answer to that is that I wasn't sensible and felt as if I never would be again.

This was Friday—our Friday—what Scripture, or some-body or something, calls the day appointed. Before another morning came, our bark, powder and crew and officers aboard her, would be past the blockade ships, out at sea and off about the business we had rigged and fitted her for. I would be walking her quarter deck—Captain Isaiah Dole, commanding the privateer *New Hope*, the Stars and Stripes flying over me and fighting and profit ahead.

This is what would happen if—and what an "if"! It loomed up like an uncharted ledge, with breakers across my bows and to starboard and port. About everywhere my imagination looked I could see white foam and a ten to one chance of shipwreck. Well, in a case like that there was only one course to set—straight ahead. We had done all we could, the rest was hold the helm steady and trust to luck.

I was so fidgetty and nervous that I hurried into my clothes without bothering hardly to wash or comb my hair. Then, catching a glimpse of myself in the looking glass, I was ashamed. What was I, anyway? I might be dead, or a British prisoner with irons on my wrists, before the clock struck five twice more, but just now I was a self-respecting Yankee seaman. I took my coat off again, rolled up my shirtsleeves, and shaved as close and careful as I ever did in my life, never nicked my face once. I was rather proud of that, everything considered. As I look back at it now I don't know but I'm still a little proud of it.

While I was rummaging in the buttery for the slab of stale cornbread and mug of milk I was using as a substitute for breakfast, the Badger woman who was nursing Phoebe Light came out of the back room. She reported that Phoebe hadn't talked sensibly yet, but the doctor calculated she might at almost any time. I left the woman to clean up after me, put on my hat, and went outdoors. I recol-lect cocking that hat a little mite towards my larboard ear. I was going to *look* confident and chipper if I died for it.

I had hardly got out into the yard when Ezra Light stepped out from the side door of the barn and beckoned to me. I hadn't expected him back so early, but you can bet I didn't lose any time chasing into the barn astern of him. As soon as I got a good look at him, I knew he had something important to tell me.

Indeed he had, but, being Ezra, he didn't tell it first thing. He began by saying that he had either seen or sent word to every man of the out-of-Trumet list who had signed to sail aboard the *New Hope*. They would be on hand before mid-afternoon, dunnage and all. This was the first good news I had heard for I didn't know when, and I told him so.

He moved his head up and down. "Um-hm," he said. "There's more, though."

"More? What do you mean?"

"More to tell ye. You ain't going to believe it, neither."

"What are you talking about? Why won't I believe it?"

"'Cause it ain't one of them things anybody could believe, not first off. I didn't myself, to commence with. Fact is, I don't know as I believe it now—only I can't think of a good excuse for not believing it."

"Look here! Are you drunk?"

"Eh? Why, no, not yet. Huh! That's kind of funny, too, you asking me that. That's the very question I asked the Hosea Briggs fellow down there to North Trumet when he told me his yarn and give me the letter. 'Be you drunk, Hosy?' I says to him. He—well—ha, ha—he said he wasn't, but that he was willing to be. He's a dry-spoken rooster, that Briggs one. Ho, ho!"

"*Ezra!*" My patience was on a short cable that morning. "Ezra, for the Lord's sake—"

"Easy, Captain Isaiah. This news of mine ain't the kind

to holler through a speaking horn, like peddling fish. You'll say so when you hear it."

"If I ever do."

"You're going to now. I'm breaking it to you gentle. First off, you've got to understand more about Hosy Briggs. Lives in North Trumet, he does, has a fish boat and sets eelpots and does odd jobs alongshore—or did, in the times when there was any to be done. Well—this is just betwixt you and me, Captain Isaiah—lately he's been doing a few other things. He wouldn't want 'em generally known about, so when you tell this to the Council, as I guess likely you'll want to, keep Hosy's name out of it. I promised him you would."

"Yes, yes, yes. All right, all right! Heave ahead with the rest of it."

"Um-hm, I'm under way. Well, Hosy goes fishing in that boat of his, but he ain't supposed to go far offshore on account of the blockade. North Trumet folks figure he goes after flatfish and lobsters, 'cause that is what he fetches in when he comes. Sometimes, though, so he tells me, when the weather's a little mite thick and he can't be seen good from shore, he risks going out further after cod and mackerel. Then, every once in a while, he takes his catch into Point Town and sells it there. Point Town folks have money to spend—some of 'em."

The way he put the emphasis on "some of 'em" gave me the hint. "Humph!" I said. "That means he does business with the enemy. And they must know him well, or he and his boat would have been seized long ago. What is the fellow, a British spy?"

"Oh, now, now, Captain, don't get that notion in your head. I do some business with the enemy, myself, and you wouldn't call *me* a spy, would you?"

I couldn't help grinning. "Not a British spy—no," I said.

"Um-hm. Well, underneath the fish scales, Hosy Briggs's

politics are about the same as yours and mine, I cal'late. He don't like His R'yal Majesty any better 'n' I do, but he don't call the old boy names when he's to Point Town, that's all—except in certain quarters, that is."

"Oh, I see."

"Um-hm. Hosy's all right. He's under some obligations to me for favors I've done him, and he does one for me once in a while. For me—and you—*and* the Council folks. Understand?"

"I—well, perhaps I do."

"I wouldn't want you to understand too well, for all this about Hosy ain't to be talked about, for his sake. I know him and I trust him. That's satisfactory, ain't it?"

"Yes. But what is all this leading up to?"

"It's up abreast of it now. When I was in North Trumet yesterday I met Hosy. He had heard I was around there and was looking for me, though I didn't know that till after he told me so, himself. Seems he had been in Point Town the day before and he just got back. While he was there he met up with—well, with somebody who lives there, another good friend of our side, he is—underneath."

"And a good friend of the British overhead, I suppose. Another two-facer."

"Well, sometimes that is what you have to be—or make believe be—if you want to find out things for the side you're really on. This other man, the one Hosy met, saw Hosy on the main road nigh the wharf and told him some things. One of the things he told was that he had a letter for Hosy to take away with him, when he went in his fish boat, and be sure and get it to Trumet right away. Get it to *you*, Captain Isaiah, them was the orders."

My ears picked up. "To *me*? A letter from this Point Town man to me? I don't know him, do I?"

"You might, if I gave you his name—which I can't, for reasons. The letter wasn't from him, anyway. It was from somebody else, somebody you do know. It had been sent ashore that very afternoon—Wednesday—from the *Terror*. The man who wrote it was a prisoner aboard her, had been since early Tuesday morning. He, this prisoner one, knew Hosy's friend was a patriot—underneath, as I said—and so he found a chance to smuggle the letter to this man on shore, sent it by a fishing feller whose boat had been grabbed by the British, or something like that. It was addressed on the outside to this Point Town man, but inside that wrapping was the real letter, and that was to be got—*must* be got afore Friday—that's today—to Captain Isaiah Dole in Trumet. . . . Understand so fur, do ye, Captain?"

"I don't understand much of anything. How could I? Who is this letter from, for the Lord's sake?"

"Just a jiffy. Breaking this to you gentle, I am, remember. When you find out who it's from you'll see what I meant about not hardly believing it yet. Well, the fishing feller went to the man's house—the Point Town man's, Hosy's friend—and delivered the letter all according to orders. And the man—told you he was a good patriot, I did—was even considering some way of taking it to Trumet himself when, by grand good luck, he heard Hosy Briggs was at the wharf. Well, that—Shh!"

He stopped short, for somebody was thumping on the barn door. We had shut and bolted that door when we came in, of course. I stepped into the stall alongside of Selah, where I was out of sight, and Ezra went to see who was knocking.

It was the Hannah Badger woman, the one who was looking out for Phoebe. She was excited and flustered.

"Oh, Ezra," she cackled, "I'm so glad you're here! I was afraid you might have gone up to the village already, and I'm all alone, and somebody ought to get word to the doctor, and—"

She was crowding more words into one breath than you

would have thought possible. Ezra asked her what the fluster was all about.

"It's your wife," she panted. "It's Phoebe. She has come back to. She has—she has!"

Now—when I have time to grin in comfort—I can't help grinning whenever I think of Ezra at that minute. *He* didn't get excited.

"Back to?" he drawled. "How did she get that way? What's she back to to?"

"Back to herself. Oh, *can't* you understand? She's same as she used to be. She keeps asking for you. What do you think I'd better do? The doctor hasn't been around, and— Oh, dear!"

I stepped out of the stall. "You must go to Phoebe right off, of course, Ezra," I said.

He nodded. "Um-hm," he agreed. "Run along, Hannah, I'll be close astern of you." Then, when she had gone, he turned to me. "I'd like to have told you a little more, Captain," he said, "but I'll have to leave you to find out for yourself. Here's that letter Hosy fetched and turned over to me to give you; I don't know what's in it, but I do know who it's from. You're going to be some surprised."

He reached inside his shirt, fumbled there a jiffy, and then took out a sealed paper. He handed it to me. It was warm and damp from lying next his skin.

"I'll be with Phoebe when you want me," he said.

He went out. I looked down at the folded paper. Then I broke the seal. There were several closely written pages inside. My first glance at the handwriting made me almost jump out of my skin, as my grandmother used to tell about. *Jonathan Bangs!* It was his handwriting!

There was no doubt about it. I couldn't be mistaken. Recognizing Jonathan's writing gave me my first tremendous jolt. When I read all that was written I was past the jolting stage. I must have crossed the barn floor in my sleep, for, when I woke up—or "came back to," as the Hannah woman would have put it—I was sitting on the lid of the feed box against the further wall, and how I got there I couldn't tell you to this day.

I read the letter through again. Then I read it for the third time, and, with each reading, another set of ideas that, little by little, had come to be certainties in my mind tumbled to smash. It was like taking props, one at a time, from under a scaffolding until, at the end, the whole framework was on the ground.

A dozen points that had puzzled me for the past week were clear as spring water now. There were others left, and they were as muddy as ever, but the dozen were clear. In most ways I had been so wrong that my conscience shrivelled up like one of those sensitive plants Mother used to have in a pot in our sitting-room window. For the good Lord's sake, why hadn't I stuck to my guns? I hadn't ought ever to have let my reasoning, or any sort of evidence, even my own eyesight, bully me into believing that Jonathan Bangs was anything but honest and square and true blue.

I had kept saying to myself that he wasn't a fool. *I* was the fool for letting myself be driven into the belief that he was a traitor.

But—but if what he had written about his doings since he got out of the lockup, and before, was true—and seemed as if it must be—then what—? And who—? And how—?

Sitting there, holding my head steady with both hands— I felt as if it was spinning on my neck—I tried to think what my next move must be.

Some of those moves must be made right away. One of them in particular Jonathan had written me to attend to without wasting a minute. According to him, a British officer—Lieutenant Jermyn Forsythe, his name was—had been hiding in Trumet since before the shipyard fire on Saturday night. Slightly wounded he was, bullet scratch in the leg, and it was Jonathan himself who had put the bullet there. Forsythe and Hope Allen were in cahoots together, and it was Hope who had been hiding and feeding him.

Hope is working with the enemy [wrote Jonathan]. You can guess how I hated to believe this, but I am forced to believe it. It is true. She knows where this Forsythe fellow is, and you and the Council must make her tell, somehow. Get him, Captain Dole, and get him quick. He mustn't be allowed to escape to one of the British guard ships. If he does get to them before Friday night this more or less crazy plan of mine, the plan I have given you some idea of in this letter, will be ruined, for he and I have met and he knows I am not what— even since I got here Monday night—I have been trying to make these other *Terror* officers think I am. Everything depends on Forsythe's being kept in Trumet until after the *New Hope* clears. You see that, don't you? So get him and hold him tight.

Get him and hold him tight! Yes, of course, only—

According to Jonathan—he had accounted for every minute of his time since Saturday in the long letter—he—Jonathan, I mean—had gone down to Point Town Monday night, the night of the same day when, early in the morning, he had got out of the Trumet lockup. The letter was dated Wednesday, and he wrote that he was being held prisoner in Point Town and saw no chance of getting away unless this scheme—this wild, hundred-to-one scheme of his that he had written about in the letter he was risking sending ashore by the fisherman—should work out.

That was part of what he had written to me. Now stop and think what it meant. Jonathan Bangs was a prisoner in Point Town on Tuesday. And on Wednesday, when he wrote the letter, he was there. He expected to be—it stood to reason he had been—still a prisoner in Point Town on Thursday and was right there this minute. And yet, with my own eyes, I had seen him—or somebody I took for

288

granted was Jonathan Bangs—taken off our Shad Cove beach in a boat last night—Thursday night.

Impossible, of course. Unless everything in his letter was another string of lies; and this Hosea Briggs was another liar; and the other Point Town man who had got the letter from the British sailor was a third. Unless they were, all three, liars and traitors together.

But Ezra Light swore that Hosea Briggs was straight and loyal and that, if he could give me the name of the third man, I would recognize it and know *he* was straight and loyal, too.

In which case it was *not* Jonathan I had seen board that boat sent ashore from the *Gannet*. It was somebody else; but who?

I could think of only one possible answer. And, to make sure it was the answer, I decided to go straight to Hope Allen and put her on the gridiron. I wouldn't wait for Bailey, or anyone else, to heat that gridiron with me, I would do the grilling myself—and now.

Once more I had bad luck when I got to the Allen house. Neither Hope nor her father were there. After I had made sure of that I went out and headed back up the Point Road. I must find that girl wherever she was, find her and put her over the coals, no fooling and no soft-headed pity this time.

I hadn't gone more than fifty feet from the Allen door when I saw Hope coming up the road towards me. When she got near my first thought was: Good Lord, girl! What is the matter with you? She had looked troubled and worried the last time I talked with her, but now—well, now she looked as near like a ghost as anything I ever expect to see. Her cheeks were as white as if they had been chalked, and her eyes were like burnt holes in a blanket, as the saying is.

So, to show how consistent I am, instead of ordering her, sharp and crisp, to come with me and give me the truth or take the consequences, what I did say was: "What is it? Are you sick?"

I don't imagine she heard me. If she did she didn't answer. She looked at me almost as if *I* was the ghost. Then she said: "Oh! . . . oh, Captain Isaiah! I have been up town looking for you. I—I *must* talk with you."

I nodded. I was already beginning to pay less attention to how she looked and to remember what she was.

"Indeed you will talk with me, young woman," I said, sharp enough now. "That's what I am down this way for."

She hardly understood that, either, I judged. She hesitated. "Would you mind coming to our house?" she stammered. "We can't talk out here—in the road."

I might have said that I had been at her house already, but I didn't bother. She started towards home, and I fell into step. We walked fast. Neither of us spoke a word until we were in the Allen sitting-room again.

Then I commenced on my sermon. "Hope," I began, "it is high time you—"

But she interrupted. "Please—*please* don't talk," she begged. "Please just listen. I have so much to say, and I have waited so long to say it. . . . Oh," almost like a prayer it sounded, "I am *so* thankful to be able to say it at last!"

And then she burst out with the whole confession. To those of you who have been reading Jonathan's yarn the most of it is an old story, but to me, you must remember, it was all brand-new. After she was well under way I wouldn't have interrupted for a cargo of diamonds and a fair trade wind astern.

First of all, she told me about this Lieutenant Jermyn Forsythe: who he was, how she came to know him in her away-at-school days, what they came to be to each other—all that. And then she went on to tell of her meeting him again, down here in Trumet.

Why she had been attracted to him in the first place

wasn't hard to understand. I have never seen the fellow, but Jonathan tells me he is good-looking, very much of a gentleman, and, I rather think likely, having what they call a way with the ladies. Then, too, it must always be remembered, Hope Allen isn't American born. Having been picked up, a baby, from that English wreck, it has always been taken for granted that her folks were English. Hope is romantic, reads a whole lot, and, even as a child, was always wondering who her father and mother were, what her right name was—everything like that. She had a different feeling towards the British than that of the average Trumet person. There was no Revolutionary grudge handed down to her, you see. Sometimes she and Jonathan, so he tells me, had squabbled about these things, although Jonathan is no British hater, either—not a narrow-minded one, anyway.

So when handsome, smooth-talking Forsythe got acquainted with her in those school-day times, it is no wonder she was landed, hook, line, and sinker. As to why he took after *her* is easy to guess. Hope Allen is pretty enough and smart enough and—yes, sweet enough—to make almost any young fellow go fishing.

She told me enough of this to make it clear to me. She talked straight on, her hands in her lap, with their fingers twisting and untwisting, and her look fixed on one of the flower doodads in the hooked rug under the table. She spoke so fast and steady it sounded as if she had practiced telling it over and over to herself. As a matter of fact, I presume likely she had, poor thing. Those last few days must have been terrible ones for her.

She told me all that Jonathan has told about Jonathan's catching her at Shad Cove beach the night of the fire at the shipyard—Saturday night. She looked up and straight at me when she had finished that part.

"Captain Isaiah," she said; "what I am telling you now is true—*true*—every word of it. I want you to understand this because—because some of the things I told Jon were not true. I couldn't tell him the real truth even when he came asking for it Monday morning. I couldn't—I couldn't! By that time—oh, well, this is what really happened."

She was alone in that same sitting-room Saturday evening, when she heard the alarm bell ringing up in the village. She realized there must be a fire; in fact, she went to the door and saw the light in the sky, but she didn't go up to find out where the fire was. It didn't occur to her, she said, that it might be at the shipyard. She was tired and troubled—she and Jonathan had had a spat, you remember—and—well, she didn't go out.

Then she heard a shot. It sounded, she thought, not so very far away. The window was open a little way, and a few minutes later somebody just outside that window spoke her name. She went to the window, looked out, and saw Lieutenant Forsythe. He was wounded, a bullet in the fleshy part of the leg. I don't know what plea he made to her, she didn't tell me, but she took him in. He wouldn't let her go for the doctor. He told her about the fire at the yard and swore to her that he didn't set it but that he would certainly be accused of having done so and very likely shot, or strung up as a spy, if the militia or the town folks caught him.

Well, she was in a state, but she couldn't, she just couldn't, let him be taken. After all, he was in Trumet because of her—so he had told her at their other meetings and so she thought then.

She broke off there for a second. "You see," she stammered, "he said that was why he had come, said it when we first met—met again here in Trumet, I mean. I believed him. I was a little fool, I am not excusing myself.... Well, at any rate, there he was, wounded and in danger and all on my account. I took him in and hid him in the old storehouse out in the back lot. Father hardly ever goes up there —nobody does, it is all falling to pieces."

Forsythe told her he had expected to go aboard the *Gannet* that night. A boat from the *Gannet* was to be at Shad Cove at twelve to take him off. He couldn't go, of course, but if word could be got to the midshipman in command of the boat's crew it would help him and might prevent his presence in town being known at all. She said she would try to carry that word.

She got to the shore all right and was talking to the midshipman when the militia opened fire from the top of the bluff nearer the inner end of the Cove. Nobody was killed, and the boat shoved off and got away. She was running up the beach when Jonathan jumped out and stopped her. When he saw who she was he let her go free. She ran and reached home safely. She didn't know Jonathan had been arrested, of course.

But the next day—Sunday—she knew. Trumet was boiling. People were in and out of the house with all sorts of stories. Jonathan Bangs was a traitor; he had tried to burn up the privateer, had set fire to her and had run away to Shad Cove where a boat full of British sailors and soldiers was waiting for him. If some of the militia boys hadn't been smart enough to get to the Cove in time to grab him, he would have got clear. Now he was in the lockup, and the Lord only knew what would be done to him. Most folks favored hanging, only they figured it was too easy a death. This was some of the stuff she had to hear and exclaim over. And she had to listen to the pity and catty sympathy of some of the females who were *so* sorry for her. "I know what an awful shock this must be for *you*, dear. Well, it is better to find it out now than later on, when—"

That sort of thing. You can imagine her state of mind— knowing, as she did, that Jonathan was not a traitor, realizing what would be said of her if it were found out that she had known of the presence in Trumet of an officer in the enemy's service and that that officer was hiding, at that minute, in a building on her father's land. She didn't say much to me about those feelings of hers, but it wasn't necessary, anybody could guess what they must have been.

And she had to be so careful. There was her father to be kept out of the secret. She had to listen to his ravings against Jonathan—he was only too ready to rave because, as I have written two or three times already, Henry Allen never did take to the idea of her keeping company with young Bangs. Lucky for her, Henry was out of the house most of that day and the ones close following it, so she could take Forsythe his meals and even talk with him without a great deal of risk. His shot wound wasn't much more than a scratch, and he could attend to it himself, when she brought the cloth and things to do it with.

That was how it was on Sunday, but on Monday morning came more and worse trouble. Jonathan, having watched until Henry had gone, came to the house to see her. He had broken out of the lockup, and the hunt for him was, even then, under way. He had come to her, naturally enough, to learn why she hadn't come forward to clear him. Why she had let him stay in that jail place, called a traitor and a turncoat and all that.

"He told me," Hope said, and she was closer to breaking down than at any time during our long talk, "that he had let me go there on the beach, because—well, because I was I, and I had begged him to. All of Sunday he had refused to talk to the Council people, even to you, Captain Isaiah, because he wouldn't bring my name into it. He had been waiting, expecting me to—to come—to go to you—Oh, what can he think of me? I—I—"

I put my hand on her shoulder. "Steady as she is, Hope," I said. "Whatever he thinks won't change what was—or is. It is what is going to be that counts. Go on—and hurry."

She did go on, too. She set her teeth and squared her shoulders, so to speak, and told the rest. The explanation Jonathan had been waiting for, and had broken out of jail to come and get, she couldn't give him. She couldn't. If she told him about Forsythe's being hidden on the premises he might believe—oh, almost anything. So she told him a made-up-in-a-hurry yarn with some truth in it but the rest moonshine. She hadn't, of course, had any appointment with Forsythe at the rock that Saturday night, and she didn't go to the Shad Cove beach to see why he didn't come. She went, as she had already just told me, because Forsythe himself sent her, to carry word to the midshipman that he couldn't leave Trumet then, as he had expected to.

Well, Jonathan didn't believe her—and no wonder. She could see that he didn't, but before the talk went any further they heard people coming. She had only just time to get to the dining-room and shut the door behind her. Jonathan stayed in the sitting-room. The people who came were Elnathan Berry and Eben Fowler and me. We had, you will remember, just found Seth Black's body with Jonathan's sheath knife alongside it. And Hope had to stand there and hear Berry and Fowler call Jonathan Bangs a proved traitor and murderer and make proclamation that the hunt for him was to go on till he was found. She had to listen to this and not, by as much as the shake of an eyelash, show that she knew the man they were accusing and hunting was in the very next room.

A tough situation for her. I wonder she got through with it as well as she did.

When she, herself, went back to the sitting-room, after we left the house, the room was empty; Jonathan had cleared out, through the open window. A few minutes later Hope hurried to the old storehouse to have a straight talk with this Lieutenant Jermyn Forsythe. Jonathan Bangs, his name and his safety, was all that counted with her now. And, for the first time, there was some distrust of Forsythe growing in her mind. She was beginning to wonder—and high time, too, I must say—if he had played as straight with her as she had with him.

And Forsythe, for his part, had changed a little, too. He seemed very much surprised when she told him of Seth's killing, and she believed then, and still believed, that he had known nothing of that. But about the fire, how it had been set and who set it, she was not so sure. "I gave you my word that I did not set it," he told her. "Shall I give it to you again? Glad to oblige, of course."

"You gave me your word that you didn't set it yourself," she said; "but I don't remember your saying that you had no suspicion as to who did. Have you any such suspicion?"

He smiled. That smile was a mistake, for it made her mad. From that time on, she told me, any liking for him—remnants of a stronger feeling she used to have, I expect it was—ended. Nothing was left but pity and not too much of that.

"I believe you know who set that fire," she burst out at him. "I believe you came to Trumet in the first place, not to see me again, but to—to—oh!" as the whole idea of what that might mean came to her. "*Oh!* I—I—"

She started towards the door. He stepped in front of her. "May I ask where you are going?" he said politely.

"I am going to turn you over to Captain Dole and the others. I don't know what they will say to me, and I don't care. I took you in here because you were hurt and in trouble and I was silly enough to suppose I was responsible, partly at least. I didn't dream that I was hiding a spy and —and—Please let me go. . . . I shall scream for help."

He couldn't have been very scared on that account. Who was there to scream to? And he didn't move, either.

"I shouldn't do anything rash, Hope," he said, quiet and

polite as ever. That was, she told me, almost the most maddening thing about him; he was always polite, always the gentleman. She stamped her foot. "Don't dare to call me Hope!" she ordered.

And still he smiled. "Sorry, Miss Allen," he said. "It seems to me unnecessary, but I don't mind swearing to you once more that I didn't know of the killing of that fellow Black, or whatever his name was. As to the fire—well, perhaps the time has come when you and I should be a bit more frank with each other—for your sake quite as much as mine. We are both in a rather tight spot, don't you think? Or perhaps you haven't thought."

"I have thought enough. At least I am thinking now. And not of myself. No matter what happens to me—"

He held up his hand. "Possibly you haven't thought of one other person," he told her. "We—you and I—are in a rather tight spot, as I said, but it strikes me that your friend Bangs is in a tighter one. He *is* your friend, or so I have been told.... No, wait a minute. Here is where some of that frankness I mentioned comes in."

He went on to remind her that he was an officer in His Majesty's navy. As an officer it was his duty to take and carry out orders from his superiors. His country happened to be at war with the United States. She could suppose, if she wished—he mustn't speak plainer than that, even to her —that word had been received by his superiors that some sort of—er—enterprise directed against his country was under way here in Trumet. He had been ordered to land, get in communication with the agent who sent the word, and—

She broke in on him here. "Agent!" she said. "Then there *is* a traitor in Trumet. Who is he?"

His smile was a little broader. "I could hardly tell you that, even if I were sure," he said. "He and I have met but once and then for only a minute or two and in the dark. I will tell you this though—I owe you a great deal, Hope—sorry, Miss Allen—and I am grateful. So I shall risk telling you that I have had several—er—letters from this agent—signed letters."

Hope—so she told me—said the last two words after him. "Signed letters?" she said. "*Signed?* Then you do know who he is! You *are* sure!"

He shook his head. "The letters are signed with initials only. I'm sure of that, certainly. Whether they are the fellow's own initials or a pair he has borrowed for this particular rather—er—smelly correspondence, I can't be sure, of course."

"What are these initials? Tell me!"

Another head shake and another of those polite smiles that made her so fighting mad. "Sorry, Hope—Miss Allen—but that I can't tell you. My private opinion of the—er—rascal may be much the same as yours, but this is a matter of business, His Majesty's business, and I'm afraid I must handle it in a businesslike way. Sorry to refuse a lady—this lady especially—but—"

"Oh, *stop!*" She stamped again. "You will either tell me who wrote those letters, or I shall do what I was going to do a few minutes ago. I shall go straight to Captain Dole and tell him everything I know about you. I shall! I shall tell *him* you have the letters, and he—"

"Wait! Wait! You have forgotten one—er—rather important point. If your—What's his name? Dole, is it?—if he comes demanding letters, what do you imagine I shall tell him? That I don't know what he means, *I* have no such letters. Which will be true, because by that time I shan't have any. They will have—er—disappeared."

"But I shall tell him that you told me—"

"Pardon. And I shall be obliged to say that I told you nothing of the sort. There will be no proof on either side. We are quite alone, you know."

"Then you are a liar as well as a spy?"

"Not as a usual thing. Never on my own account, I trust. But, in His Majesty's service—why, sometimes—yes."

She was so choking angry that she couldn't speak for a minute. He could—and did. He went right on.

"It seems to me," he said, "that, now we are on—shall we say—a business basis in our affairs, we may better continue in that way. You will gain nothing by turning me over to your Trumet friends. You will have to explain why you have been in communication with an officer in His Majesty's uniform, hiding me, feeding me—"

"I don't care! I don't care what they do to me. I told you that."

"I know. But I care what they do to me. And—well, you may care what they do to your friend Bangs. *He* won't be helped by my being taken. Nothing I shall say will help him. He will still be the traitor they are looking for."

"But you *could* say things. You could tell them of those letters."

"I could—yes. But this is business now, remember. With those letters in my possession I may—I *might*—make a—er—deal is the proper word, I believe—I might make a deal with Mr. Bangs which would help us both out of our troubles. If you were able to locate Bangs and send him here to me—"

"I shall do nothing of the kind. That is, if I could, I wouldn't."

Forsythe spread out his hands and lifted his shoulders. "Too bad," he said. "Too bad for me, and for you—and particularly too bad for friend Bangs. His one big chance will have gone."

There was more of this, lots more. He wouldn't tell her what the "deal," as he called it, with Jonathan was, but he did go so far as to hint that he might be willing to tell Jonathan the traitor's initials—perhaps even his name—if

299

Jonathan would agree to do a certain unnamed favor in return.

"You see?" he said at the finish. "You see what it means for Bangs and what it may mean for—well, for you, too, if you turn me over to this Dole and the rest? The alternative is an easy way out for us all, I should say."

She saw, she had to see. And I, listening to her tell it, could see, too. Trumet was certain by that time that Jonathan Bangs was a turncoat and a traitor. As soon as the news about Seth had been spread it would be just as certain that he was a murderer. If she surrendered Forsythe it wouldn't clear Jonathan. Her story of why she had been meeting a British officer and hiding him in her own house wouldn't be believed, either. All hands would say that she was in the plot, too; that she and Jonathan were both traitors, working together. She was trapped. And, in the end, and in desperation, she agreed to find Jonathan, if she could, and send him to Forsythe.

"I know what you must think of me, Captain Isaiah," she put in. "And I deserve it."

I guess likely she did, in a way, but I couldn't tell her so. She hadn't meant to do anything treasonable or wicked, in the beginning. As she said, she had acted silly and foolish, and now, as happens to so many silly folks in this world, she was paying for her foolishness.

I didn't preach all this to her then; it was no time for sermonizing.

"That other letter?" I asked her. "That one you took from under the stone in the big rock? You told me that was from Jonathan. Where was he when he wrote it?"

She drew a long breath. "It—it wasn't from Jon at all," she said. "It was from the officer who was to meet Lieutenant Forsythe and take him away in the boat."

"How do you know that?"

"Why, because Jermyn Forsythe said so. There were

other letters there, too. Those must have been the ones signed with the initials. I carried several of them from the rock, and I carried his replies and put them there. They weren't from Jon, I *know*."

"How do you know?"

"Because—because—Oh, I know they weren't. He wouldn't—wouldn't let me—"

She was close to breaking down again. I cut in. "All right, all right," I said. "As a matter of fact, I don't think they were from Jonathan—now I don't. When did you see Jonathan last?"

"I haven't seen him since he came to this house Monday morning after he escaped from the lockup. I know he must be hiding somewhere. Father told me about his meeting Ezra Light in the woods. I have tried to find him. I wanted to find him. I had made up my mind to tell him everything I couldn't tell you or Father or the others. I *would* have told *him*. He would have understood and trusted me. And he would have told me the truth about himself. . . . Oh, do you know where he is, Captain Isaiah? *Do* you?"

I did; the letter Ezra had brought from Point Town gave me that information and a bit more. No time for all that, either. There were two all-important questions in the back of my head, and I out with them, one after the other.

"Forsythe got away in the boat from Shad Cove last night, didn't he?" I asked.

"Yes. Yes. . . . How did you know that?"

"I saw him go, that's the main reason, although I thought then it was somebody else. Now, Hope, here is what I want to be sure of: when I was here yesterday morning I left a message with you to be given to Jonathan Bangs. A message about the change in our powder-running plan, a change of date and place. I thought then that you knew where Jonathan was and that you and he met sometimes. Now you say you didn't meet, that you haven't seen him since Monday, and that none of those letters were from him at all."

"Yes. . . . Yes. . . . I told you—"

"Wait! What did you do with that message I left with you? Did you give it to Forsythe?"

She looked at me as if she couldn't believe she had heard me right. She had been very pale all the time since she began telling her story, but now the red flared into her cheeks and her eyes snapped. She got up from her chair, too.

"You—you *do* think I am a traitor!" she burst out at me. "You do! You *do!*"

I didn't exactly sense what was wrong. Should have, of course—it was plain enough—but I didn't. "Now, now, now," I began. "I didn't say you were a traitor. I just asked—"

"You asked if I gave that message about the powder to Lieutenant Forsythe. If you don't think I am a traitor how *can* you ask that? Of course I didn't give it to him. He is a British officer—an enemy. Your message was for Jon and nobody else. You said so. I didn't know where Jon was, but I couldn't tell you so then. I couldn't tell you anything until that Forsythe spy was out of the way. I have explained that. I was afraid to tell, partly for my own sake but more for Jon's. Now, this morning, I can tell and I have told. Oh, don't you see—"

"Wait, girl! For the Lord's sake wait! That message about the powder? You didn't give it to Forsythe, you say?"

"Certainly I didn't. If I had I *should* have been a traitor, shouldn't I?"

"Wait! Wait! Where is that paper I left with you?"

"Here! I was going to give it to you. Here it is."

She took it from the waist of her dress and handed it to me. I scarcely looked at it. The full consequences of all this muddle and misunderstanding were just beginning to sink into my thick head. My whole new scheme, the scheme that was about the only hope of salvation for the *New Hope* and the powder she must have, had depended on the British getting those false plans I had left with Hope Allen for her to give to Jonathan Bangs and for him to take out to the *Gannet*. He was one traitor and she was another—that we, the Council and I, had counted as proved. But now I knew it hadn't been proved at all. Jonathan was no traitor. He was in Point Town now, working hard for our side, his letter told me so. And Hope—if her story was true and I believed it was—was no traitor, either.

And our false plans had not gone to the enemy. The only plans the British had were the real ones, the plans we intended to carry out this very night. That they had those plans we knew; the "Dear Sir""J. B." letter I had taken from the rock settled that question. My "hope of salvation" was no hope at all. That was what I should have to tell the Council. And what would they tell me?

It looked to me as if this was the end of the rope. The *New Hope* and all of Trumet's fine dreams were sunk. Sunk! I groaned, I guess, for Hope asked me what was the matter.

I didn't answer her. I mumbled something about seeing her again in a little while, stumbled out of that house and along the road to the village. I didn't meet anybody—or, if I did, I don't remember it. I got to the Light place, opened the door, and went in. I was bound for the stairs and my own room. What I was going to do when I got there I had no idea. I wanted to be alone, that is all I was sure of.

Just as I got to the foot of the stairs, Ezra came hurrying after me, calling my name.

"Captain Isaiah! Captain Isaiah! Come with me, quick. Phoebe's got something to say to you, and it sounds to me as if it ought to be well wuth your hearing."

6

In which Jonathan makes an enemy, finds a friend, and is given a command.

Told by

JONATHAN BANGS

CAPTAIN DOLE HAS BEEN carrying on his part of this yarn for quite a while, telling all the things that he saw and thought and did from the time when the fire broke out near the *New Hope* Saturday night until the following Friday morning. Five and a half days isn't such a very long stretch as time goes, but a lot happened to the Captain during it.

When I look at the thick stack of paper covered with my commanding officer's hurried and impatient script, I realize, with a sense of something like disbelief, that his days were just as busy and just as frantic with worry and speculation as my own. More important, I also realize the almost complete *separateness*—if that is a good word—of his actions and mine during that identical period of time.

No more than a few miles, at the most, ever lay between us, yet we never once spoke or so much as laid eyes on each other at close range. We were working with an equal earnestness towards the same general end, but we worked apart. We might almost have been living in different worlds.

If so, I can promise—and will presently give evidence—that my personal little world was not one of idleness or peace of mind.

It was some time early in the afternoon of Monday when I left Lieutenant Jermyn Forsythe in the ruined old building near the Allen house. Forsythe was both wounded and a fugitive, but I felt, as I emerged cautiously into the blinding sunshine of that clear August day, that his case was certainly more enviable than mine. I had no pistol bullet in my leg, to be sure, but I had a number of other troubles that any sane person would have been glad to do without.

For one thing, I had a figurative price on my head as a cold-blooded and badly wanted killer. I had in my pocket a letter from one British officer to another. If I was captured, that letter would provide final proof—if more proof was needed—of my traitorous designs. My body was a dragging ache of sheer physical weariness. In my mind there was fear and anger and a despairing urgency. But above all other things there was a sense of uncertainty and confusion.

I knew that my conversation with Forsythe had been a vitally important one, but I was anything but sure whether during it I had acquitted myself like a wise man or a fool. In leaving the Lieutenant undisturbed in his hiding place and in agreeing to act as his messenger to Captain Holt, was I serving my own and my country's best interests, or was I merely being the victim of a subtle and clever mind? My knife, with my initials burned large on its leather scabbard, had been found near Seth Black's body. How had it come there—and *why?* Why was I uneasy about the letter in my pocket from Forsythe to Holt—the letter I had just watched being written and sealed?

Back in my former sanctuary among the briars and scrub oaks, I settled myself down—not for the sleep that I needed and craved—but to try to make up my mind about certain things. Using the rough, uncomfortable trunk of a small tree as a prop for my back and batting my heavy eyelids rapidly to keep them open, I drove my sluggish, unwilling mind to work.

First of all—the letter. Why did I have qualms about that? I took the thing from my inside pocket and turned it over and over in my hands, studying it closely and all but sniffing at it like a suspicious dog. I had seen that letter being written, had carefully read its contents, and had stood by while Forsythe sealed it with his massive signet ring. Obviously there could be no harm in it for me, yet it felt dangerous in my hands, like a bomb that might explode at any moment to destroy me. The feeling was so strong that my forefinger itched to break the seal, and was actually moving to do so when common sense asserted itself. I cursed myself for a superstitious fool and shoved the letter back into my pocket—out of sight if not out of mind.

The next thing on the docket was the matter of my sheath knife. According to Forsythe's story, which for some reason I implicitly believed, my knife had been lying beside Seth Black's body when Captain Dole and the other two men made their discovery. It had not been there a few hours earlier, that much I know for certain. That being so, certain inferences were plain. The knife had been planted beside the body in a deliberate attempt to lay the murder conclusively at my door. Who had planted it? Why, the actual murderer, of course. And who was the murderer? Why, he was, among other things, the man who had somehow gotten hold of my knife. But where, and how, had he been able to lay hands upon it? That, clearly, was a puzzle that I must somehow solve.

Now that I had time to think, I remembered plainly enough that I had last seen my knife and sheath nearly a week before when I had taken them from my belt down at the shipyard and had loaned them to Captain Dole. He had forgotten to return them, and I had forgotten to ask. Only the Captain would be able to answer questions about the knife's travels after it went out of my possession, and even he might know very little. There were a thousand ways, now that I came to think of it, that the murderer could have stolen my knife without anyone being the wiser.

The fact remained, I told myself doggedly, that the knife *might* be traced and the murderer thus trapped by his

309

own seeming cleverness. It was only a faint chance, as I well knew, but in my predicament faint chances could not be ignored. I made a mental note that somehow I must get a message to Captain Dole about my knife.

My last, and most important, consideration was the matter of carrying Forsythe's letter to his superior officer, Captain Holt, in Point Town. When darkness came, with its comparative security, should I set out upon my errand to the enemy, or should I first, while there was still time, change my mind and not set out at all? That decision rested, in the last analysis, upon whether I concluded that Forsythe had tricked and made a fool of me at our meeting or that he had been honest.

On the face of it, and even after the most careful examination, the Lieutenant's proposition seemed entirely reasonable. If there were flaws in the arguments he had offered me in the ruined storehouse, I could not find them. The only sure way, apparently, to save Hope from the possible consequences of shielding an enemy officer would be to aid that officer's escape. It seemed that my only means of obtaining the name of Trumet's traitor and murderer was to pay for the information by carrying a letter to Captain Holt of the *Terror*. The thing was a bargain, as Forsythe had pointed out, with the probable advantages far overbalancing the causes for hesitation.

But, I asked myself, if those things were the case, why was I so much as wavering in my mind about carrying out the agreement I had made?

My reason, of course, was that from the bottom of my heart I distrusted Jermyn Forsythe as heartily as I resented him. I distrusted his affability with its faint hint of condescension, his easy assurance in the face of his awkward situation, the readiness and plausibility of his arguments. Everything about the Lieutenant was too smooth and well oiled for my liking. Falling in with his desires might be, I felt, nearly as dangerous as thrusting my head into the mouth of a seemingly friendly but very hungry and altogether ruthless tiger. It was not a move to be taken carelessly and with a light heart.

But suppose I assumed the worst—that Forsythe was not dealing with me honestly: What deviltry could he be up to? What good could possibly come to him by sending me to Point Town on a fool's errand? Would my absence give him the opportunity for another attempt to destroy the *New Hope?* Would it give him time to get hold of, somehow, our plans for bringing in the powder from Tamoset?

Our powder-running plans!

The thought of them made me sit up, straight and tense. For I remembered that today was Monday and that sometime late this afternoon Ezra Light would be coming back from Tamoset on his mare, Selah. With Ezra would come the final word as to where and when and how the gunpowder we so desperately needed was to be landed on the Trumet shore. If an accurate report of those arrangements should reach the enemy, our goose would be royally cooked.

What would Ezra Light do as soon as he had stabled his horse in the Light barn? He would not, of course, march up and down the main street shouting the details of the powder-running plans for all the world to hear. But he would, on the other hand, see Captain Dole, have the latter call an immediate meeting of the Council members, and make his report to them. When that had happened, not only Ezra Light, but a number of others would be in possession of the secret.

If one of the Council was our traitor—as was possible, surely, if not probable—he would be anxious to sell his valuable new information to the enemy. Perhaps the traitor was fully aware of the place where Forsythe lay hidden. Perhaps Forsythe's failure to escape was due, not to his wounded leg, but to the fact that his business ashore remained unfinished. In sending me to Point Town perhaps Forsythe was merely getting out of the way a possible hindrance to his free communication with the traitor.

Perhaps here, at last, was the rat for which I had been sniffing so diligently.

I thought over all the aspects of the situation with the utmost care, and in the end I hit upon a course of action that seemed to be entirely sound. As a matter of fact, I was just a little proud of my plan, for it seemed to me that it might serve two purposes at the same time. If things worked out the way I hoped, Captain Dole would get the message I wanted him to get—the message about my sheath knife. In addition to that, I would be able to make my trip to Point Town without the fear that the enemy might lay hold of our powder-running plans in my absence.

Certain risks would be involved, to be sure, but I shrugged those aside as inevitable and struggled stiffly to my feet with a renewed vigor that had come as a result of having, at last, a fixed purpose.

The trip that I made, immediately afterwards, was risky to say the least. It was broad daylight, the cover was scant, and I knew that I was the object of a determined search by practically every able-bodied man in the village of Trumet. If I had tried to make my way towards Point Town, or towards either shore, I most certainly would have been laid by the heels, but I set off, instead, on an opposite course.

I put Point Town to my back and traveled southward on a line that ran about midway between Bay and ocean. This made it necessary for me to cross both Point and Bay Roads, but my principal hazard was the considerable stretch of open meadow that lay to the east of Hornpout Pond. No trees were there or rocks or even any grass tall enough to hide my hulking body from the least searching glances. It was a case of run for it and pray—both of which I did to the best of my ability.

I felt as naked as a skinned eel, but I must have looked more like a lumbering cart horse, as I galloped across that gently rolling field towards the safety of the thick woods on its south side. I was gasping painfully for breath, and the blood was pounding in my ears when I finally reached the sandy ruts of the Bay Road, crossed them in one jump, and plunged into the grateful thickness of the underbrush beyond.

Luck certainly had been with me on my wild dash, for if I had made it thirty seconds later I most surely would have been seen. As it was, I was still lying flat on my back, gulping in great lungfuls of cool salt air, when a squad of militia came along the Bay Road from the direction of the village.

They passed not three yards from where I was, and I could hear their excited voices clearly enough. They were talking, not unnaturally, about me, and arguing among themselves as to my probable whereabouts. "The Major," said one of them, "says we're to comb through every inch of the pine woods along the Bay shore, but *I* say that don't make sense. Just because Jonathan Bangs is a murdering turncoat, that don't make him a plain dumb fool. If he knows anything, he knows the Bay shore is the first place we'll hunt, and he'll stay away from it like pizen! Seems to me he's more likely to be hiding out in the woods some-wheres around here than he is over by Shad Cove. *I* think—"

"Militia privates ain't paid to think," said a voice which carried authority. "It's Major Bartlett's job to do the think-ing for all of us—and to give the orders. He's given us ours, and we'll stick by 'em!"

I thanked God for military discipline as the talk faded away into the distance.

My cruise after that was plain sailing. Once I had regained my breath I moved steadily due south until, a couple of miles beyond the Trumet town line, I picked up the main road that led from Orham and the other villages farther south and west. There I selected a secluded spot, but one from which I could observe at some distance the approach of any Trumet-bound traveler, and sat myself down to wait.

Inevitably, and in spite of my best efforts, I fell into an exhausted sleep that might well have claimed me until the following morning if it had not been interrupted by a lusty voice raised in song. That voice intruded itself annoyingly and persistently upon my very pleasant dream, in which Hope Allen and I were the only actors, until it finally succeeded in dragging me back to a reluctant consciousness.

I sat up, groaning, and gazed about me stupidly, unaware for the moment exactly where I was. Then I remembered, and saw—just as they were about to disappear around a curve in the road towards the village of Trumet—a man and a horse. The horse, which was ambling along in a dignified and leisurely manner, was the mare, Selah. The tuneful little man on her broad back was Ezra Light.

"Ezra!" I forgot all caution as I scrambled frantically to my feet, shouting. "Ezra Light! Wait a minute! Whoa, there!"

The mare stopped walking, and Ezra stopped singing, but otherwise they showed no signs of undue excitement as I burst out of the bushes at the roadside and came after them at a lumbering run. I must have been a surprising sight in my unshaven, bleary, and disheveled condition, but if Ezra thought so he gave no sign. His sharp, darting eyes surely missed no detail of my appearance, but he greeted me with his customary casual friendliness. "Why, hello there, Jonathan Bangs! How do you find yourself this nice afternoon?"

"I'm all right," I said briefly, panting. "I've got to talk to you for a few minutes, Ezra. It's important!"

"So?" Ezra slid easily from Selah's back and stood leaning against her as he pushed back his hat to look up at me. "Well, if you want to talk, Jonathan, I guess you've come to the right man. Even them that don't like me give in that when it comes to talking I'm up along on top of the heap. Talking comes natural to the Light family, maybe you've noticed that. Talk don't tire me, none to speak of, and it's cheap. What's on your mind?"

Captain Dole, in his part of this story, has already told about my meeting with Ezra Light on the Orham road, so I don't have to give the details of just how it went. Almost everybody in Trumet, including the Captain and Ezra, thought for a while when they heard of it—and I can't blame them—that my reason for waylaying Light was to find out the exact plans for running in the powder. That wasn't true, of course, any more than it was true that I wanted to sell the plans to the British after I had obtained them.

The powder plans, as a matter of fact, were the least of my concern in talking with Ezra. I asked about them, to be sure, but only because I was interested and because it was the natural thing to do. My real purpose was to persuade Ezra not to let a single soul know that he had returned to Trumet until the following morning, at the earliest, and not to pass on to anybody a scrap of the information he had brought with him until that time.

The reasons that I gave the peddler for making my request were essentially true. I said that there was a traitor in Trumet and that I was on his trail. I said I hoped, and had reason to believe, that within a few hours I would know the traitor's name. But until then, I asked Ezra to remember that no one in Trumet—not even any of those highest in the Council—should be trusted with any knowledge that might damage our cause if it were passed on to the British.

Ezra had claimed that he loved to talk, but on this occasion he seemed entirely content merely to listen. He did not ask me any of the thousand and one embarrassing questions that might naturally have occurred to him and which I had prepared myself to answer in one way or another. It was evident that he knew nothing about the attempt to fire the *New Hope*, about my capture and escape from the lockup, or about the murder of Seth Black. Nor did I, as can be imagined, enlighten him. I allowed him to assume that I still occupied the more or less honorable position in Trumet which had been mine when he went away, and accepted his promise to do what I asked with no more than a normal amount of gratitude.

Just before we parted I made my second request. I asked the favor casually, as though it were an after-thought, but I was quaking inside. Would Ezra, I inquired easily, give Captain Dole, when he saw him the following morning, a private message from me? Would he tell the Captain that I swore upon my solemn oath I had not seen hide or hair of my sheath knife since the moment when I had loaned it to him—the Captain—down at the shipyard nearly a week before? Would he ask the Captain, from me, not to believe a word of the story that my sheath knife seemed to tell?

Then, if ever, was the time for Ezra to be surprised and to question me, closely, if not with suspicion. I expected nothing else and was bracing myself for the ordeal, but again the little man fooled me. He merely listened gravely to my request, repeated it aloud to be sure he had it straight, and agreed to deliver it to the Captain in private.

In another minute he and the mare, Selah, were once more on their leisurely way towards Trumet, and I was staring after them with real gratitude in my heart.

It seemed to me, as I pushed my way once more into the bushes beside the road, that I had accomplished much more than I should have dared to hope. That Ezra would keep his word to me to the letter, I had not the faintest doubt. And, that being so, our powder plans would be safe from a traitor's eyes until the following morning. If the smug Mr. Jermyn Forsythe had thought to learn them while I was absent from the scene, he was due for a sad disappointment. I, in turn, was granted more than twelve hours of freedom in which to learn the name of the man I was hunting.

In twelve hours I must get to Point Town and get back again.

While waiting for darkness to fall, I pondered my best route, and found none that seemed entirely promising. It would be possible, I thought, to make the journey by foot, but the road would be long. The chances of capture would be considerable, too, since to get to my destination I would have to traverse Trumet village from one boundary line to the other. If I could borrow or steal a horse, my speed would be much greater, but secrecy would be almost impossible.

In the end I decided—wisely, I think—to try to make the trip by boat. That I had no boat, and did not know whether or where one could be found, was a somewhat disheartening state of affairs, but one which I made up my mind I must somehow overcome.

Certain factors favored the success of a journey to Point Town across the waters of the Bay. One of those was the stiff wind that was blowing out of the southeast. Given a boat with a sail, that wind at my back would send me skimming straight where I wanted to go without beating or even making a single tack. A boat with a sail? Well, in Trumet itself the close militia guard upon the shore would make stealing a sailboat practically impossible, but just now

I was not in Trumet. I was several miles south of the town line and an equal distance from the place where the beach patrol began.

For those reasons there was something approaching confidence in my heart when I set off, in the cool dusk, on my first attempt at piracy. Something told me that I should find me a craft, and something told me that it would carry me safe to Point Town. What odds the British patrol of the Bay? I should try my best, of course, to avoid prowling longboats and cutters, but even if one of them overhauled me I should merely demand to be taken at once to their Captain Holt on the Frigate, *Terror*. And Captain Holt, after all, was the man whom I must see.

I won't waste space or good ink in telling at any length about how I found my boat and about my voyage to the Point Town shore, for even if I stretched my small imagination to its limit I could make nothing dramatic or heroic out of either exploit. It was almost as though the whole thing had been carefully arranged for me in advance by a competent courier.

I merely walked westward until I came to the Bay beach, and, lo, there was my boat. No light showed in the windows of the shanty opposite which she was moored, indicating that her obliging owner was not at home. When I waded out and boarded her I found that she was small, trim, of shallow draught, and dry as a bone. All that was required of me was to cast loose, haul up the sail, take the tiller, and square away for Point Town with a brisk, fair wind on my tail.

The trip itself was as uneventful as its beginning. I kept a sharp lookout for enemy craft, but as might have been expected, since little or nothing hung in the balance, I never so much as sighted one.

I beached my stolen craft at a deserted place which was about a mile, I judged, on the Trumet side of Point Town village. In case I should want to use her again for the return trip I made everything fast, and took careful note of the landmarks, before I set off across country in the direction of the main road.

Lights in the houses on the outer fringe of the village reminded me that it was still early in the evening and that people would be abroad. Instinctively I shrank from meeting any of them, for, although my career as a marked man and a fugitive was only a few hours old, I seemed already to have acquired the habit of regarding my fellow men as natural enemies. It was necessary to tell myself quite firmly that Point Town was not Trumet and that in this latter place my appearance would arouse no more interest or curiosity than that of any other stranger.

According to my precise instructions from Forsythe, a waterfront tavern called the Gray Goose Inn was the place where I must go, and according to Forsythe again I had only to follow my nose, and my ears, to find it. Forsythe was quite right about that last. My nose soon picked up the rank aroma of aged fish, and when that perfume had become very nearly unbearable I found myself on a narrow way that led along behind the wharves. Once there, my ears did the rest. They led me straight to a weathered gray building from which emerged an astonishing medley of shouts, thumpings, laughter, and male voices raised in song. Over the door of the place hung a large bird in effigy. To my eyes it looked more like an out-sized and misshapen hen than anything else, but I had no doubt that it was intended to represent a gray goose.

Fearing to hesitate lest I lose my courage, I immediately pushed open the door and walked in.

The place proved to be, although little better, certainly no worse than many a sailor's hangout I had visited in the course of my travels about the world, but it startled me, none the less. It startled me because almost every one of the men enjoying its hospitality was dressed in the naval uniform of the country with which my own was at war. They were my enemies, one and all, yet they seemed much more thoroughly at home in their present surroundings than I was.

Captain Dole has already made plain the strange nature of the war in which we were engaged, and the sight of British sailors taking their ease in a Yankee tavern was a part and parcel of that strangeness. The British fleet, in all its arrogant power, was in complete control of the surrounding waters, and, no matter how patriotic the people of Point Town might have been, they were as helpless to prevent English sailors from drinking in their inns as they were to prevent English ships of war from using their fine harbor as a base. Thought of resistance being entirely futile, the good people of Point Town endured the situation as best they could, and even made a certain amount of profit out of it.

In any event, the Gray Goose Inn was the drinking place of British tars, and in it I was as much out of my element as a fish out of water. The noise lulled for a moment when I came into the low-ceilinged, smoke-filled common room, and faces turned to stare. As I stood, hesitant, just inside the door, a burly, red-faced man in a smudged white apron came to my side and inquired, none too cordially, what I wanted.

"This is a public house, isn't it?" Deciding that boldness was the best course, I made my voice cold and assured. "In that case you serve food and drink. I want something to drink, if you please."

"Of course. Of course, sir. Anything that you like, of course."

The fellow led me to a little table in a far corner, where he took my order. Impressed, perhaps, by the air of authority I had assumed, he was civil enough, but he still seemed to eye me with curiosity and what I thought was a certain amount of uneasiness. Just before he turned away he summoned up the courage to question me tentatively. "I don't remember seeing your face before, sir. A stranger around here, maybe?"

"A stranger. Yes." I cocked my eye at him before I glanced, with meaning, about the room. "Are strangers so rare for you? All these fine birds, for instance? Are they all chums of your boyhood?"

"What would you have me do?" He would have given something just then, I thought, to know what colors I sailed under. "A man's got to eat, even in times like these. A shilling is a shilling, no matter where it comes from."

"I'm not blaming you," I told him shortly. "English sailors have a thirst, I don't doubt, and money to pay for the stuff to quench it. For all I know, they may be noble fellows, into the bargain." I leaned towards him and spoke in a lowered tone. "As a matter of fact, Mr. Landlord, it so happens that I'm looking for one of them—an officer—a Lieutenant Harry Waterman. I'm told that he's to be found here every evening at this time. Is that true? I must see him at once on a matter of importance."

"Lieutenant Waterman?" It was obvious that the man recognized the name, and equally obvious that he was uncertain whether to admit it or not. "Lieutenant Harry Waterman? Now let me see—"

"Is he here?" I inquired sharply. "Is he here—now?"

"Why—why, yes. But—"

"Then take me to him—at once!" I pushed back my chair and got up. "My business is not the kind that will keep!"

"Take you to him? Oh, no sir, I couldn't do that! Not possibly!" The man backed away, shaking his head with emphasis. "Mr. Waterman has got a private room, and he give me strict orders that he ain't to be disturbed, no matter what. If I took you in there he'd murder me in cold blood!

You know how the Lieutenant is, sir, when he's had a bit to drink, and when—"

The landlord's coy look told me all I wanted to know. "Oh, so it's a woman, is it?" I shook my head impatiently. "No matter. I've got to see him—and at once! You can at least give him a message, can't you?"

"A message?" He hesitated and said that he didn't know about that—he wasn't sure—it might be possible.

"Of course it's possible!" I took some money out of my pocket and fingered it. "Tell the Lieutenant that there's a man out here who must see him at once. At once, understand? Never mind my name. Say that I have an important message for him from his friend Forsythe. Have you got the name straight? Lieutenant Jerry Forsythe—and hurry!"

The sight of my money ended the landlord's reluctance. He repeated my message out loud, pocketed the bribe, and disappeared from my sight for a full fifteen minutes. I had just about given him up for lost, and was about to take the search for Waterman into my own hands, when I saw the dirty apron in an open doorway on the other side of the room. The man behind the apron was beckoning me to come.

A few minutes later I was faced, at last, with Jermyn Forsythe's friend and fellow-officer, Lieutenant Harry Waterman.

Waterman's private room was entirely suitable, no doubt, as a place where an officer and gentleman might enjoy his lighter moments in comfort and without the fear that those moments might be observed by irreverent eyes. It was not, as a matter of fact, an unpleasant apartment. Small rag rugs were scattered over the spatter-painted floor, there were bright curtains at the windows, and flowers under the candles on a table set for two. The stuffiness of the air in the place was, however, almost unbearable, for, although the August night was warm, the windows remained tight shut and an open fire burned in the small hearth. The mixed odors of food, wood smoke, and tobacco were almost choking, but failed entirely to hide a faint suggestion of feminine perfume, the owner of which was, I noted with thanks, mercifully absent.

Waterman, himself, I decided immediately, was as thoroughly objectionable an individual as I had had the misfortune of encountering in many a long day, even though he failed in every detail to conform to the outward pattern of the conventional loose-living sailor. He looked more like a schoolmaster in uniform—the sort of schoolmaster who revels in his unlimited authority over defenseless small boys and who delights in using every bit of that authority to make their lot miserable, and still more miserable.

He did not rise to greet me when I came in, or so much as nod his head. With every detail of his uniform as correct as though he were on parade, he observed me with cold contempt out of close-set, beady black eyes. Those eyes gave me the shivers, for something about their expression revealed a very mean man, and one who was, at the same time, more than half drunk.

"State your business and get out." The syllables were not even slightly blurred. To the contrary, they were clipped, and almost meaningless in their lack of intonation. "This is an impudent intrusion."

"I'll do that, Mr. Waterman." Aside from my refusal to give the man his official title, I think I gave no indication of my impulse to slap some expression into that narrow gray face. "The matter is urgent. I come from Lieutenant Jermyn Forsythe, who is wounded and is hidden in the village of Trumet, near here. He sent me to you with a message."

"The message?"

"Lieutenant Forsythe asks that you take me, with the least possible delay, to your commanding officer, Captain

Holt of the *Terror*. There is something that Captain Holt must be told—and told within an hour!"

"So?" Waterman moved nothing but his eyes. He dropped those and surveyed me from boots to hair as dispassionately as though I were a thoroughly undesirable horse offered for sale. "Suppose you let me be the judge as to whether or not Captain Holt is to be disturbed. And I will be the one to disturb him if necessary—not you. What must Captain Holt be told?"

I thought I saw, without any need for pondering the matter, what shape events would have if Lieutenant Waterman should have his way. I was all too familiar with men of Waterman's stamp. If he thought that any credit would reflect upon himself by delivering Forsythe's message to Holt, he would deliver it. The glory, if any, must be his alone. It seemed certain also that he would never, in any case, lift a finger to take me to his commander unless he was convinced that it was to his own personal interest to do so.

"I'm sorry." I shook my head firmly. "I can give Lieutenant Forsythe's message to nobody but Captain Holt himself. Perhaps, Mr. Waterman, I did wrong in bothering you. I shouldn't have done it if your brother officer hadn't urged that I do so. I can remember Lieutenant Forsythe's almost exact words. 'Harry Waterman's your man,' he told me. 'Go straight to Lieutenant Waterman at the Gray Goose Inn. Tell him from me that if he wants to do himself a bit of real good—if he wants a string of medals on his chest, and perhaps a handle on the Waterman name—he'll take you to old Holt-Holt at the double and without bothering to ask questions.'" I shrugged. "That's why I came to you, but I see that I came at an—er—well, inconvenient time. I won't trouble you any further. Probably someone else will be willing to help me."

"Wait." Waterman's voice did not change, but there

was some faint difference in the expression of his face that made me guess that I had judged the man correctly. Perhaps the bait I had offered in the form of the imaginary quotation from Forsythe had proved tempting to the fish. "I remember saying nothing about not taking you to Captain Holt. I shall do so if it appears in the line of my duty."

"I wouldn't, of course, presume to try to tell you your duty." My bow was ironically polite. "But I can promise that, if you do what Lieutenant Forsythe asks, you will please Captain Holt and interest him very much. The sooner your commander learns what I have to tell him, the more pleased he will be—and grateful, I imagine."

"Perhaps." My fish, I thought, was on the hook. If he flopped about a bit now, in the bottom of the boat, it would be only for show. "You will realize, on the other hand"—how much of his dignity was natural and how much due to the liquor he had aboard I couldn't be sure—"that, as Captain Holt's personal aide it is part of my responsibility to protect him from unnecessary annoyance, as well as from—hum—impostors. You say that you have come from Lieutenant Forsythe, but how am I to know you are telling the truth? Can you describe him? Is he lean or plump, short or tall? Is he redheaded or as bald as a round-shot? Come!" He chuckled for the first time, but almost as if it hurt him to do so.

My remembrance of Forsythe was vivid, and my word picture of him must have been convincing, for Waterman halted me almost at once. "That will do." He shrugged. "You appear to know the Lieutenant by sight—but that may mean little or nothing. Where and how did you meet him? What—not that it matters particularly—is your name?"

Trying to keep my fists unclenched, I told him that I had stumbled upon Forsythe, more or less by accident, at the place where he was hidden in Trumet. "My name," I concluded shortly, "is Jonathan Bangs."

"Jonathan Bangs!" As he carefully repeated the syllables of my name after me, I thought I saw a flicker of almost human expression pass across his face. He seemed actually interested. "Did I hear correctly?" he inquired very softly. "Did you say that your name was—er—Bangs? Jon-a-than Bangs?"

"You did." I could have choked the puffed-up bullfrog. Forsythe was, at least, a gentleman; it was hard to believe this thing was a friend of his. "Jonathan Bangs is my name —not, as you say, that it matters particularly."

"But it does. Oh, yes, it does indeed! Well, well! It in-terests me immensely, Mr. Jon-a-than Bangs."

There could be no doubt that the fellow was telling the truth. For the first time there was a gleam of light in his hard eyes, and he was chuckling again. "Jonathan Bangs—humph! And with a message of importance for Cap-tain Holt! . . . Oh, I say!"

Lieutenant Waterman was actually laughing now. It was silent laughter, but it shook his stiff body, and it seemed as if it would never stop. It was, at the same time, the most insulting laughter I have ever heard—or rather watched. My blood was boiling. I had to use all my will power to keep from knocking him across the room.

"I'm glad my name amuses you," I said, between my teeth. "It is always gratifying to be able to give pleasure so easily! Now, will you take me to Captain Holt at once, or must I find someone else to do it?"

To my surprise, the Lieutenant was suddenly out of his chair. He was bowing to me. "No, no, Mr. Bangs! You have come to just the right man! I give you my word you shall be taken before Captain Holt—and that nothing on God's earth shall stop that very thing. If you will excuse me for a moment I will make the arrangements."

He went out. I was left alone for about five minutes in that stewpot of a room, but the heat of the place was not the reason for the discomfort and uneasiness that I felt while he was gone. If ever I sensed anything, I sensed danger just then, but I could not give myself a sensible reason for the feeling. What was the meaning of the sudden change in the uniformed bully? Why the amusement and evident satisfaction he had felt when he heard my name? It seemed impossible to believe that he had learned of my trouble in Trumet or to understand what possible benefit the news could have for him, even if he *had* learned it. There was nothing to be afraid of, I told myself firmly— but I was still afraid. Only the common-sense knowledge that running away would get me into worse trouble kept me from getting out of that place at top speed.

When the door of the private room opened once more, Waterman returned to me, alone. He seemed in better spirits even than before and continued to treat me with the same ironical deference.

"Everything is arranged, Mr. Bangs of—er—Trumet, is it? You will be gratified to know that you are to see Captain Holt. I swear you shall see him! Aren't you grateful to me, Bangs? You should be!"

"Oh, certainly. Much obliged." I looked at him keenly. "From what you say, I gather that you have asked someone else to take me to the Captain."

"Exactly! An escort, no less!" Again there was that silent, apparently jubilant, laughter. "I've arranged an escort suitable to your—er—rank!"

"Thank you. Then I'll be going." I was still fighting the temptation to slam my fist into his mocking mouth. "I hope you've told whoever is to take me that there is no time to be lost. I must see Captain Holt at once. You understand that?"

"One moment, Bangs!" The Lieutenant had seated himself once more at his table and was holding up a restraining hand. "I have given you my word that you shall see Captain Holt, and so you shall, but that is as far as I can go. Your request to see him immediately is regretfully denied. Your interview with the commander will take place tomorrow morning at about four bells."

"Tomorrow morning! Ten o'clock tomorrow morning! You're mad! Why, damn you, didn't you hear me say that my business was urgent? It won't wait an hour—much less until tomorrow morning! Tomorrow morning will be too late!"

"Too bad, too bad!" The cat was playing with the mouse and thoroughly enjoying the game. "The fact remains that ten o'clock tomorrow is the appointed time. You can't see Captain Holt before ten. But don't worry, you shall see him then. I hope to have the pleasure of being present."

"I can't wait until tomorrow! I told you my business couldn't wait. Why can't I see him now?"

"Because the commander is asleep," said Waterman very softly. "Nor," with a swift change from chuckle to snarl, "would I think of waking him to trade words with a stinking provincial traitor—a traitor who happens to be a filthy murderer as well!"

I began to understand at last. Somehow or other the British *had* heard from Trumet.

"So." I was suddenly quite steady and composed, as I took a step towards him. "So that lying yarn has reached Point Town already!"

"Quite so," said Waterman with venomous satisfaction, "and it might interest you to know that the citizens of your own charming village were the ones to acquaint us with it, in the form of a petition to Captain Holt." He laughed. "Really, this is devilish amusing. Your friends assumed that, being in our pay, you would flee to us for refuge. They petitioned Captain Holt, as a man of honor, to return you to them for hanging—not as a traitor, of course—but as a particularly dirty murderer!"

"I see." I forced myself to be calm while I tried desperately to think of some way out of this new trap. "And what about Captain Holt? Is he going to grant the petition?"

"He would like to, of course," Waterman nodded judicially. "Under normal circumstances he would do so immediately, but it so happens that he is somewhat worried about Lieutenant Forsythe. The Lieutenant apparently met with some misadventure on his—er—mission to Trumet, and there is still a possibility that he might be captured there. In that case—"

"That's enough," I said bitterly. "I see the trick. If Forsythe is captured and Holt has me in his hands, he will offer to trade!"

"Damned generous of him, too, don't you think?" Waterman raised an insulting eyebrow. "Although if I were Forsythe I should consider it a slap in the face to exchange me for a murderer. Still, that is Captain Holt's affair, and he has given strict orders that, if a provincial named Bangs appears in Point Town, said Bangs is to be placed under close arrest!" He laughed. "You can see what has happened. You *have* appeared—you *are* arrested!"

"Not yet, I'm not." The words were hardly out of my mouth before I had leaped for the door. "You've got to take me first."

"Quite right." Waterman's mocking words came to me clearly—just as they must have come to the group of British sailors that was crowded in the corridor outside. "Hold him, men! Don't let him get away.... *Hold* him, you fools!"

I think I can say, in all modesty, that I put up a respectable fight.

There must have been a half dozen of the sailors waiting for me when I flung out of that door and straight into their arms, but at least three of that number went out of action before I did. I remember the keen satisfaction of feeling a nose crack under the swing of my right fist. I heard a man howl when I brought my knee up into his groin. I picked up one little fellow bodily and slammed him against the wall so hard that it shook.

It is just possible that I might have got clear in spite of all, if it had not been for a heavy log of firewood that was swung as a club. I caught a glimpse of the thing as it came down towards my head, and I tried belatedly to duck.

The pain of the blow was not great. There was just a sharp stab of hurt, a flash of white lights in front of my eyes, and—well, I was asleep before I hit the floor.

2.

When I came back again to a state of knowing, the first thoughts that came to me were the ones that, from all accounts, come first to all men under similar conditions. I wondered where I was, and I wondered what hour it might be of what day.

There was a throbbing, persistent pain in the back of my head that robbed me of all inclination to move so much as my little finger. I realized that I was lying, flat on my back and fully clothed, on some sort of narrow and much too short bed. When I tried, tentatively, to open my eyes, the light stabbed them so shrewdly that I must have groaned a little.

"Gently there, gently," said a gruff but kindly voice from somewhere close by. "Don't try too much, too soon. Lie still, and if you must think, think you are grateful to be alive. Being allowed to live is supposed to be a privilege, God knows why."

Masculine fingers lightly touched my forehead, without hurting it, and I felt an inclination to whimper—as a child will when it receives unexpected sympathy. Taking the advice that had been given me, I made no attempt to move other than to run my tongue over lips that were as dry as paper. "Tell me," I heard my own voice saying, as though from a distance. "Please tell me."

"Yes, yes, of course." The man with the kindly voice seemed to find nothing surprising in my plea or to have any difficulty in understanding it. "You have been laid out with a whack on the cranium that would have killed an ordinary sized chap. I am, God save the mark, the surgeon who is supposed to be helping your recovery. Shall I go on? Want to hear any more?"

"Yes."

"Very well, then I'll try to answer the questions that you either are, or soon will be, asking yourself. Where are you? You are aboard His Britannic Majesty's ship *Terror*, which is lying at anchor in Point Town Harbor. Why are you here? As I understand it from that half-tight maggot—humph!—I should say from Lieutenant Waterman—you are here because he brought you here by boat in a condition no more limp than that of three of his own plug-uglies whom you stove in while attempting to resist arrest. Why are you snug in Lieutenant Forsythe's cabin instead of in the brig, where Waterman wanted you thrown? The answer to that, my friend, is that your obedient servant is much too soft-hearted for his own good. I insisted; and Waterman let me have my way. You see, my uncle happens to be a member of the House of Lords, and such matters carry weight with the Watermans of this world. . . . Let me see, have I told you everything? I think so, except—oh, yes! It is now three bells—nine-thirty o'clock—of a beautiful August morning. The day is Tuesday."

It was nine-thirty on Tuesday morning! That knowledge made me ignore the blinding pain in my head and caused me to throw my feet out of my bunk and to roll groaning into an upright position.

I remembered everything now, clearly and vividly. The most urgent of my memories was that long before now I should have learned the name of our traitor from Captain Holt and have carried it back to the people of Trumet. By this time I should have convinced the Council of my innocence and have put them on the trail of the man who was actually guilty of treason and murder.

Nine-thirty o'clock Tuesday morning!

I had asked Ezra Light to conceal the fact of his return to Trumet until Tuesday morning, but only until his breakfast should have been eaten. Long before this, Ezra would have lived up to his promise to me and have handed the powder-running plans over to the Council. If my guess about the traitor and Jermyn Forsythe had been sound, it was possible that our precious plans were already in British hands.

"I must go! I must get out of here at once!" I made a feeble effort to get to my feet. "I haven't a second to lose!"

"Gently, my friend! Gently." The plump, bald little naval surgeon, whose name I later learned to be Eric Cobble, pushed me back, without much difficulty, into a sitting position on the bunk. "You are still groggy—and small wonder. You forget you are a prisoner on this ship—a valuable prisoner if Waterman isn't lying. Two marines with loaded muskets are on guard just outside this door, and they'll never let you run for it. I'm sorry, Bangs, but you aren't going anywhere just now—except to a talk with our commander, Captain Holt. That talk was originally arranged for four bells, but I said you wouldn't be in your right mind so soon. Consequently you have two hours' grace, and I think I will best be doing my job if I leave you to rest alone. If you should need anything in the meantime, ask one of your guards to send for me."

I don't think that I even had the sense to thank the little man for all his kindness, so deep was the dejection in my mind. It seemed to me then that I had reached, at last, a place in my travels where any further struggles would be a waste of time. Staring dizzily at the floor of Jermyn Forsythe's cabin, I admitted defeat. I had fought as hard as I could—and lost. Let them hang me if they wanted to. I almost wished they would.

Looking back, I can see how much I really owe to the surgeon, Cobble. It was his unselfish interest—coupled perhaps with his dislike of Waterman—which gave me the two-hour delay before I was brought before Captain Holt, and it was that delay which gave me a chance to gather myself together and to bring back to life my nearly dead courage.

It was during that delay, also, that an accidental movement of my arm caused a piece of paper to crackle in my inside pocket; which crackle, in turn, made me remember Forsythe's letter to Captain Holt.

I pulled the thing out into the light without any sense of excitement and with only a sort of dull surprise that it had not been taken from me while I was dead to the world. Apparently Waterman, perhaps because of the liquor he had drunk, had neglected to have me searched after my capture, for, not only was the letter still in my possession, but Forsythe's seal on the back of it remained intact.

My first reaction was of spiteful satisfaction in the knowledge that, if my plans had entirely miscarried, so had those of Jermyn Forsythe. Captain Holt was still, at this moment, completely ignorant of the predicament, whereabouts, and plans of his missing lieutenant. Because of the stupidity of another of his officers, this Waterman ass, he was likely to remain so, for I would never ease his mind.

Almost as quickly as I had it, however, I stifled my impulse to tear Forsythe's letter into tiny little bits. My pain-dulled wits beginning to quicken, I found myself wondering if, as a matter of fact, the bit of writing might not be valuable. Could I use it, in some way, to my own advantage? Could I possibly employ it as a lever to pry myself out of the tight corner I was in?

I was turning the thing over and over in my hands, deep in thought, when I remembered my earlier misgivings as to its contents. This time I did not hesitate to act. Taking a thin-bladed ivory paper cutter from among the untidy litter of Forsythe's belongings, I sat myself down to prod delicately at the edges of the big blob of wax that formed the letter's seal. After only a moment it came free, practically unbroken.

Flattening the paper and raising it so that I could read, I suddenly found that my big hands were trembling. For I needed no more than a glance to know that this was not the letter I had watched Forsythe pen in the abandoned storehouse. The text was longer, and the wording entirely different. I had been neatly hoaxed, and the manner of the hoaxing was explained by Forsythe, himself, in the very first paragraph under his respectful salutation to Captain Holt of the *Terror*.

If things fall out as I hope [penned Forsythe in his almost illegible script, sprinkled with badly spelled words, which bad spelling I am correcting here] the man who hands you this letter, sir, will be wholly ignorant of its contents. He will think that he is delivering a harmless note which I shall write and seal under his inspection. He will be wrong. I hope to be able to substitute this one in its place without his knowledge. So if you read this letter at all, Captain Holt, that fact will be ample proof that my messenger knows nothing of what I have to say to you, sir. Perhaps you will decide that he should remain so, since I am informed that Mr. Bangs is entirely loyal to the Yankee cause.

It is my duty to report to you two unpleasant facts. The first is that the vessel in Trumet Harbor remains undestroyed, since a change of wind drove our prettily arranged fire in the direction opposite from the one intended. The second is that I was clumsy enough to get myself pinked in the leg by a pistol bullet which was fired, I believe, by the very man who will bring you this letter.

I beg you, sir, to be in no way concerned about either my health or my security. My wound is nothing but a scratch. I find myself securely hid, tenderly nursed, regally fed, and diligently served throughout this business by none other than the young American lady of whom you have heard me speak. So, you see, I am a man not to be pitied.

In deadly earnestness, sir, I ask you to make *no* inquiry in any quarter, concerning me, and to take no step of any kind with the view of hastening my return to the ship. By remaining where I am for two or three days, I hope to be of very real service to His Majesty's interests.

I am informed that the Americans plan, some time this week, to bring powder for their privateer across the Bay by boat. The details of the precise arrangements for landing the powder—the day, the hour, the exact spot on the Trumet shore—will be brought to this town by a messenger whose arrival is expected Monday night. As soon as this messenger makes his report, the two-faced Yankee who is my agent will report, in turn, to me. There can be no slip-up about this last, since the lady who takes care of me is acting most efficiently as our go-between. My only danger is the man Bangs, who will—I hope—bring this letter. He is dangerous, indeed, and must be dealt with by you.

Forsythe then honored me, in the next two or three paragraphs, by giving Holt an outline of my recent misfortunes and present predicament. He reaffirmed my loyalty to the American cause and warned his commander to make very sure that I remained a prisoner aboard the *Terror* until he, Forsythe, was safely aboard once more, with the powder-running plans in his possession.

Then came a final paragraph that capped everything which had gone before.

Bangs is anxious, naturally, to track down the actual traitor and murderer, and I am hoping to profit from his anxiety. I propose to offer Bangs, as payment for bringing you this letter —perhaps I should more accurately say for bringing you *a* letter—my word of honor that you, sir, will give to him the name that was signed at the bottom of the original communication which came to us from the Yankee agent in Trumet. I have no doubt you will uphold my honor. But if by any chance you should have forgotten the name, or if the letter has been mislaid, I will repeat it here. In repeating it I'm not sure whether I should be amused or a trifle ashamed of myself as a sharp-dealing spy—which, I suppose, as a matter of fact, I am. In any event, you can tell Mr. Jonathan Bangs that the name signed to the letter from the traitor—and, incidentally, the name which I have addressed said traitor in all our dealings —is nothing else than Jonathan Bangs! I imagine that the real Mr. Bangs may find pleasure—surprise, certainly—in the knowledge.

My hands were no longer trembling when I finished Forsythe's letter, and I myself was cold as ice.

There was fierce anger in me, of course, and a humiliating bitterness that is past describing. I saw how I, and my country, too, had been deceived and tricked and betrayed—not only by Jermyn Forsythe but by Hope Allen, the girl I had once loved and had thought to marry. I was raging, but I no longer gave any thought to despair.

As I sat there, slowly tearing Forsythe's letter into minute bits, my mind was already at work—making plans. I was filled with a cold, hard determination that somehow I should have my revenge. I had been used, and used again, as a credulous and sentimental fool.

Somehow I would show Lieutenant Jermyn Forsythe— yes, and Hope Allen, too—that I had been so used just one time too often.

3.

It seems to me that it must be a rare thing for a man to stand before a court, no matter how informal, and to plead with all earnestness and all the skill at his command that he should be judged guilty as charged. But that, to all intents and purposes, was exactly what I did when I was brought before Captain Holt in his cabin on the *Terror* shortly after high noon of that same Tuesday.

Captain Holt believed me to be a traitor to my country, and I strove to the best of my ability to confirm his judgment.

If the British Admiralty desires a scapegoat to take the blame for what I did, I will give them gladly, and with my compliments, Lieutenant Harry Waterman. It was Waterman, with his alcoholic, glory-seeking officiousness, who had refused the night before to honor Forsythe's request that I be taken immediately to Captain Holt. It was Waterman, again, who had caused me to be knocked on the head and brought unconscious to the *Terror*, my errand still undone. It was Waterman, finally, who neglected to find in my pocket the precious letter from Forsythe to his commander.

All in all, I should, I suppose, be grateful to friend Waterman—and the alcohol. Without them I probably should have found my way to Captain Holt sometime the night previous, and have given him the letter Forsythe had palmed off upon my innocence. As a reward for my pains and for the risks of my journey, I'd have been held in close arrest as a hostage, and have been permitted to enjoy what slim comfort I could find in the knowledge that the name used by the traitor in all his dealings with the British had not been his own—but mine! But, most important of all, Captain Holt would have read Forsythe's letter. From that he would have learned that his lieutenant was hidden safe in Trumet under Hope Allen's care; that, with Hope's aid, Forsythe expected soon to come into possession of the powder-running plans; that I—Jonathan Bangs—far from being a traitor, was a person likely to be very dangerous indeed to the British cause.

Once more, and in all reverence, I thank God for the nincompoop Waterman. Because of him, Captain Holt did not have the information that would have made my position completely hopeless.

When the time finally came and I was led into Captain Holt's comparatively spacious cabin, I found that our talk was to be anything but private. Behind the chair that held their commander stood a group of uniformed men which included, I noticed, both the scowling, gray-faced Waterman—who looked as if he was suffering from a "morning after" headache—and the genial ship's surgeon, Cobble. I paid little attention to the satellites, however, and fixed my attention upon the human planet about which they revolved.

Captain Holt was what might justly be called, to my way of thinking, a fine figure of a man. Even though he was seated it was obvious that he was tall and slim, with the broad square shoulders that are suitable for carrying responsibility. His eyes were the clear slate gray of his hair and eyebrows, and the features of his somewhat long face showed the sensitiveness of breeding. He would have been handsome except for the fact that what appeared to be a heavy cold made the tip of his nose a dull angry red and made his eyes water. Just now those eyes were regarding me with an expression of involuntary distaste, as though they did not like what they saw.

"You are Jonathan Bangs," stated Holt in a quiet voice, "the man with whom we have had dealings in Trumet. Lieutenant Waterman tells me that you have a message from another of my officers—Lieutenant Forsythe. What is the message, and what do you know of Lieutenant Forsythe's situation at this time?"

"In all honesty, Captain Holt," I told him respectfully

but with the bold confidence I had previously determined to assume, "I don't quite know how to answer your questions—or whether, in point of fact, I had better answer them at all."

There was an astonished, angry buzzing from the group of officers in the background, and I heard someone mutter something about "infernal damned impudence." Captain Holt, however, merely continued to look at me, the corners of his mouth more tightly compressed. "I advise you, Bangs," he said at last, still quietly, "to remember your present position. It might be most unwise for you to forget it."

"I can promise you I meant no offense of any kind," I said earnestly. "I'm as fully aware of my position as I am at a loss to understand it. You just asked me two questions about your officer—Lieutenant Forsythe. May I point out that I came to Point Town last night, at some risk and in great haste, simply so that I might answer those questions even before they were asked? I begged Lieutenant Waterman to let me see you at once so that I could deliver a report and an important message from Forsythe, but all I got for my trouble was the information that I was under arrest—that and a knock on the head. Forgetting the possible damage to my wits, do you wonder that I'm confused?"

"Your cracked head is your own fault." Holt smiled grimly. "You resisted arrest."

"That isn't quite true." I shook my head. "I wasn't trying to get away from you, Captain Holt, but the reverse. What I tried to resist was Lieutenant Waterman's determination that I shouldn't see you, to give you my report and message, until late this morning. I felt that, in His Majesty's interest, neither could wait that long. Lieutenant Waterman will tell you, I'm sure, that I begged him to take me to you last night without the loss of a moment."

"Is that true, Lieutenant?" Holt did not turn his head,

but there was an edge to his voice. "Did this man tell you that he had pressing word for me from Forsythe—and did you refuse to let him deliver it?"

Waterman glared at me, and I knew that if looks could kill I should be very dead indeed. "He may have said something of the sort, Captain, but I didn't believe him. He refused to give his message to me, and I didn't believe he had any—not taking much stock in a cowardly murderer's word! I had no desire to drag you from your bed on a fool's errand." Waterman looked hurt and almost holy. "Besides, I had your strict orders to arrest the man, Bangs, on sight. I felt that I should obey the orders, sir."

"Ah, yes. My orders!" The tall man sighed. "I expect my officers to obey my orders, Lieutenant Waterman, but there are times— Never mind." He shrugged and turned his attention back to me. "It is possible, Bangs, that because of circumstances you were badly used. If so, we are sorry. The fact remains that you and I are, at last, face to face. I am waiting for Lieutenant Forsythe's report and also for his message."

Things were going very much in the way I wanted them to go, and I thought that the time had come to toss overboard a little unimportant information in the way of bait. To that end I told about what I termed the unfortunate change of wind that had spoiled Forsythe's and my plans for destroying the *New Hope*. I told the story of Forsythe's wound and of how he was safely and comfortably hidden in the tumbledown storehouse. I did not even flinch from saying that Hope Allen was shielding, nursing, and feeding him. I stressed Forsythe's earnest request that Holt make no move towards freeing him, lest Hope Allen suffer the consequences of her treasonable acts.

In the end, and after countless interruptions, I came to the important part of my tale.

I said that, in spite of the annoyance and humiliation of

Forsythe's and my failure to destroy the *New Hope* by fire, there was still a good chance that Holt might not be forced to send a risky and costly landing party in order to prevent the vessel from ever gaining the high seas as a privateer. "You already know," I pointed out, "that there is no gunpowder in Trumet and that without it their raider can never fight her way free through your blockade. The *New Hope* is in desperate need of powder, and, to get it, her people have decided to take the risk of running a boat from Tamoset, some time this week, across the Bay to the Trumet shore. The powder will be aboard her."

"She'll never land," said Captain Holt softly, never taking his eyes from my face. "I'll bottle up that coast so tight that not even a piece of driftwood can get through! We shall blow their powder—and their impudence—to smithereens!"

"I beg pardon, sir." I shook my head in denial, while speaking with respect. "It's my belief that no patrol—no matter how tight—would turn the trick. You must remember to give the devil his due. Trumet men are fine sailors, and they know the tides, currents, shoals, every inch of the Bay, better than you can. They aren't fools, either. Their need for speed in getting their vessel away before you send a landing party against her is great—but not so great that they would risk their precious powder on the Bay unless they felt sure it would come safely through. Waiting for the slow ox-carts would be better than losing the powder to your patrol. At the risk of displeasing you I must respectfully say what I believe—that, as things stand now, the powder will come safely to Trumet."

"So?" The Captain drew his gray brows together in a frown. "Then you believe that, if I'm not to let these farmers make a fool of me, I must spill good English blood on a raiding party?"

"No, sir. You perhaps forget that I have served you before and will gladly do so again if that way I can hurt the Americans. I hate them, but luckily they don't know it. To the contrary I've fooled them so neatly that I'm even a member of their inner council. That way I've been able to learn the details of all their plans. I know the exact day set for the powder landing, the precise spot on the shore, the hour, and the state of the tide. With what I know, Captain Holt, you could capture the powder with no trouble at all. That was why, since Lieutenant Forsythe was laid up and couldn't come himself, I came to Point Town in such a hurry last night. That was why I was so anxious to see you immediately. I would have handed you the details of the powder-running plans early last night —if Lieutenant Waterman hadn't decided to interfere."

"So?" A light came into the Captain's eyes, and he half turned as though to speak to his gray-faced scowling lieutenant. But just then a fit of sneezing overtook him—a fit which shook his body for nearly a minute and which left him dabbing wearily at his eyes. By that time he had forgotten Waterman, apparently, and had returned his attention to me. "Never mind. The incidents of last night were unfortunate—and will be dealt with later. The fact remains, Mr. Bangs, that little has been lost but time. You can give me Lieutenant Forsythe's message now. Just what *are* these powder-running plans?"

I felt a little quaking weakness inside me, then, for this was to be the test. I hoped, however, that none of my nervousness showed in my face. I merely looked him squarely in the eyes, and said, "Last night, Captain Holt, I'd have told you everything you want to know with the greatest pleasure. This morning? Well, sir, this morning I'm not so sure that, in the interests of my own safety, I should say a word."

"Why not?" The Captain's broad hand slapping down on the table quieted the buzz of angry ejaculations and whispers from the men behind. As he looked at me I had a feeling that, no matter how gentle his appearance, Captain Holt would be a hard man to cross. "Just what difference, Bangs," he asked, icily, "do you find in your mind between last night and this morning?"

I shrugged. "Last night I felt sure that I could rely on British protection. This morning, I am not so sure. I'm told that you have received a petition from the people of Trumet asking my return. I'm told that you're inclined to grant this petition—for a price. If Lieutenant Forsythe is released to come back to his ship, Jonathan Bangs will be duly returned to face a lying charge of murder, in Trumet, as well as to pay the penalty for having served the British cause. You can understand, sir, that I don't see anything pleasant in such a prospect."

There was a long, strained silence in the room while the Captain stared at me. There was a hint of color in his long, aristocratic face, but if an explosion was indicated it did not come. "It would seem," he said evenly at last, "that you have obtained a lot of information that you might better have done without. I infer that it was supplied you by Lieutenant Waterman. But never mind that—for now. I take it you are hoping to bargain with me. If I guarantee your safety, you in turn will tell me what I need to know in order to capture this powder. Is that your proposition?"

"In effect, sir. Yes." I nodded, relieved that I would not be required baldly to state my own case. "You will understand that I have always hated Americans and that this petition they have sent you makes me hate them that much more. Nothing would please me more than to have a hand in capturing or destroying their powder." I drew a long breath. "If, when I give the word, you will put me—as pilot—aboard one of your armed vessels, I will undertake to steer that vessel to a point where the powder cannot fail to be captured."

"I see." He drummed his fingers on the arm of the chair. "Just how am I to know, Bangs, that you aren't lying to me? How do I know that there *are* any plans for running in powder? How do I know that you know them? What assurance have I that, once aboard one of my vessels, you won't take her away from the scene of the powder landing, instead of towards it?"

"I'll be unarmed and in your hands." I shrugged and smiled wryly. "If I'm lying, or if I should try any dirty work, I imagine it would go hard with me. If I'm honest, on the other hand, and the venture succeeds, I'm hoping that you'll pay me by offering me real protection from the people of Trumet. May I remind you that I now have no value as a hostage, since Lieutenant Forsythe hasn't been captured and since it is his particular request that you make no move to set him free? Perhaps you dislike the thought of harboring a murderer—and won't believe my oath that I am not one. In that case, I am willing to accept the verdict of Lieutenant Forsythe. If, on his return to this ship, the Lieutenant says that I'm a murderer, I will neither ask nor expect further protection. If, on the other hand, he clears me of the charge—"

"Suppose I offer you my protection, here and now." Holt interrupted me, with an upraised hand. "In that case, will you tell me what you know without any further delay?"

"I'm sorry." I shook my head stubbornly. "The truth is that a burnt child fears the fire, and that I have been burnt." I tenderly fingered the back of my skull. "I dare do exactly what I have said, Captain Holt, and nothing more."

"I see." He eyed me. "You remember, of course, that you are a prisoner on this ship—and entirely at my mercy. There might be ways—"

"No, sir." I spoke with confidence. "I've never heard that the British use torture—and don't believe they will this time. In any event, I can promise you I had rather die under the cat than be sent back to Trumet."

"That is enough." Captain Holt halted the proceedings by getting to his feet. "I have heard all that I need to know for now. I will consider the matter and let you know my decision. Guard! Take the prisoner back where he came from and see that he doesn't escape!"

Half an hour later, I learned from the surgeon, Doctor Cobble, that it had been decided to accept my proposition. "You did well up there, my big son," he said, eyeing me shrewdly, even as his light fingers questioned the sore, ugly lump on the back of my skull. "You stood up to Captain Holt, and to the rest of us mere mortals in his court, and you made all hands listen to what you were saying. I marveled, I can tell you, knowing that only a few hours before you had been as senseless as so much cold meat on a butcher's block. You acted, and argued, more like a shrewd tradesman driving a sharp bargain than you did like a—"

"Like a murderer and traitor in fear of his life." I finished the sentence for him. "Well, Mr. Cobble, I will tell you this much—I am no murderer."

"Any fool," said Cobble contemptuously, "would know that."

"Perhaps." I smiled. "But that doesn't alter the fact that if I go back to Trumet, I'll come to a murderer's end. Perhaps that knowledge helped me to plead my case a little better than I might otherwise have done."

"You pleaded it well. At last accounts Captain Holt had decided to accept your conditions—each and every one. He feels that he has no alternative and is acting wisely." The little surgeon stepped back and observed me, half smiling and with his head cocked. "I should very much like, just now," he said slowly, "to make a remark that would be considered as highly treasonable."

"Say it," I told him honestly. "Anything that you say will be safe with me. I owe you a lot."

"Very well." He nodded briskly. "I should like to say that, in my opinion, Captain Holt, if he trusts you and accepts your conditions, will be a fool! In his position, I had rather handle the business end of a red-hot toasting fork than you, Mr. Jonathan Bangs!"

I laughed out loud. "I hope you'll keep that feeling to yourself, Mr. Cobble! Mind telling me what inspires it?"

"It's inspired," he said soberly, "by the feeling I have for people. I know that captains in His Majesty's navy are supposed to be good judges of men, but I believe that, in this particular case, I am a better judge than Captain Holt. I told you just now that anyone would be a howling jackass who thought you a murderer. I meant it. You might kill in a fair fight, or, perhaps, in self-defense, but that's all. I also tell you that anybody is a fool who believes you are a traitor to your country! Knowing men, I'll stake my year's pay that you're no traitor! And if Captain Holt accepts you as one, he is headed for trouble just as surely as I am now headed for my afternoon nap! That's my conviction. What do you think of it?"

"I don't like it," I told him swiftly, still smiling, "and I hope that Captain Holt doesn't like it either."

"He won't ever hear it." The surgeon shrugged his shoulders. "For one thing, I know better than to urge my unasked opinion upon Captain Holt. For another, I haven't the inclination. I fancy myself as loyal a British subject as the next man, but this time I'm not interested. I consider that you've been ill-used. I consider Waterman a pig, and I hope he gets what's coming to him. I like you, Bangs, and I hope you succeed in whatever foul work you undoubtedly have in mind. How's that for treason? I'll cap it by wishing you luck!"

346

"Thanks, Mr. Cobble," I said very slowly. "Thanks a lot. Luck is what I'm surely going to need!"

4.

Only a little while later I was once more summoned before Captain Holt, but this time we talked alone. The Captain, sneezing and blowing his nose at frequent intervals, was obviously a man who should have been in his bed, but he did not let his physical discomforts distract his attention from the business in hand. He told me, making no bones about his distaste for the whole thing, that he had determined to let me have my way. "I am not accustomed," he said coldly, "to accepting terms dictated to me by another on my own quarter deck. I don't like it any better than I like placing a number of my men and one of my vessels under the orders of a man of your somewhat—if you will pardon the plain speaking—somewhat dubious character. Englishmen are sometimes forced to make use of traitors, but that doesn't change their dislike for them. If I followed the advice of some of my officers, as well as my own feelings, I should tell you, Bangs, to go straight to hell and fry there! Being a practical man, to whom results are of more importance than injured sensibilities, I have decided to let you have your way."

"Thank you, Captain Holt." I bowed stiffly. "I hope you won't have cause for regret. I clearly understand that, if the matter in hand should turn out badly, it will be much worse for me than for you. Some part of your dignity, Captain Holt, may be at stake in this affair, but I'm risking my life!"

"I'm glad you understand that." Captain Holt's glance was coldly dispassionate. "If you are as good as your word you need have no fear of getting your reward—perhaps more. Even if you should fail, through no fault of your

347

own, you won't necessarily suffer. But if, on the other hand, you should dare to try some trickery—!" The effect of the menacing scowl he directed at me was somewhat spoiled by a series of rapid violent sneezes which shook him from stem to stern. "Damn this cold!" he said in parentheses, weakly, wiping his eyes. Then, in sharp conclusion, "I advise you to try no dirty work, Bangs, if you value your skin!"

The Captain's temper did not improve in the discussion that followed concerning details and arrangements. He persistently tried to worm from me some bit of precise information about the Americans' plans for landing their powder, and I just as persistently evaded him. In describing the craft I should require for my venture I described to the best of my ability the pink-stern sloop, *Gannet,* which I knew to be anchored in the Bay off Trumet at the mouth of Billfish Creek, and felt a deep relief when Holt offered to put that same vessel at my disposal. I refused to give any satisfaction to leading questions as to whether I proposed to sail north or south or east or west; as to how long I should be gone or when I should want to leave. This last refusal irritated the British commander almost beyond all bounds.

He declared, with heat, that there were limits beyond which my obstinacy could not carry me. He demanded to know if I thought he would be able, or willing, to put the *Gannet* at my disposal at any moment of day or night when the whim seized me to ask for it. Having no intention of letting him know, until the last possible minute, the day on which the powder was to arrive, I countered by asking how much notice would be required to make the *Gannet* ready. Learning, after considerable sharp bickering, the answer to that question, I said I was satisfied. I told him that when the time came I would give him the necessary notice and that, once I was aboard his armed sloop, the responsibility, as well as the risk, of the adventure would be entirely mine.

"Things are going very much to your liking, I imagine, young fellow," said Captain Holt, at last, with an angry sniffle. "You are doubtless pleased with yourself. In that case, let me give you a warning. I am going just so far along the road you point and not one step further! When you go aboard the *Gannet* you will be totally unarmed, and helpless as a baby among twenty men, any one of whom had rather toss you overboard than not! In your post as pilot, the vessel will sail the course you order—but there your authority ends. One of my officers will be at your shoulder every second with a loaded pistol in his hand. If that officer should decide, at any time, that you are attempting treachery he will shoot you dead. I advise you to take care!"

"I shall do that, never fear." I tried to make my smile easy. "I can only hope that the officer guarding me will be just as careful. An itching trigger finger is apt to be a dangerous thing."

"Quite right," said Holt grimly, "but the danger, Bangs, will be entirely to you!"

"May I differ, sir?" I inquired respectfully. "If I am shot dead simply because I glance at the sky when some nervous officer happens to think that I should be looking at my toes, the American powder will never be captured. The officer who goes with me on the *Gannet* will have a heavy responsibility."

"I need no advice from you, sir, on that score," said Captain Holt unpleasantly, "or on any other. The officer I am detailing to the *Gannet* knows he will have *me* to deal with if he should shoot you carelessly. He'll tread extra softly, since he knows that this trip will be his last chance to get back in my good graces. Lieutenant Waterman will be careful, Bangs, have no doubts about that!"

"Lieutenant Waterman!" Some of the dismay that I felt must have shown in my face. "I beg you, Captain, to send any other officer with me but him! Lieutenant Waterman hates me out of all reason, sir. I haven't a doubt that he'll drill me through the head with the greatest of pleasure, the moment he finds even a half-way excuse."

"I think not." Holt smiled grimly. "Waterman knows that my concern is the capture or destruction of that powder and that it will be unhealthy for him to face me if it escapes him. If, on the other hand, he hates you, as you say, so much the better. His hate will make him watch you all the better."

"But, Captain—"

"That's enough!" He slapped his open hand sharply down on the table and resolutely stifled a budding sneeze. "I've had enough insolence. If Lieutenant Waterman doesn't please you, so much the better. Perhaps you will discover that this enterprise you have forced on me will not turn out to be the pleasant outing in the country that you had planned!"

Pleasant outing in the country, indeed!

Captain Holt having reluctantly given me the comparative freedom of the ship, I sought the shadow of a long gun and sat myself down to consider what lay ahead. Insofar as I could see, any picture that I could draw for myself of the immediate future would resemble a pleasant outing in the country about as much as Lieutenant Harry Waterman resembled a gentleman—which was not at all.

Doctor Cobble had done me the compliment of suggesting that I had in mind what he referred to as "foul work." Well, to a certain degree he was right, in that I had every intention of doing some real damage to the interests of His Britannic Majesty.

The reading of Forsythe's letter to Holt had filled me with an anger, bitterness, and reckless determination of which I would not have believed myself capable. As a result, and as a result of the circumstances in which I found myself, I was able to form a plan and to put it into successful operation during my first interview with Holt.

But where did I stand now? Having been able to convince the British commander that I was a traitor to my country, and having persuaded him to put me aboard the *Gannet* as pilot in an expedition against the landing of the powder, I had surely struck a telling blow for the cause of the *New Hope*. For, once I was safely aboard the British sloop, and away, I would see to it that the craft I was piloting was a long, long way from the scene of action when the barge from Tamoset poked her nose against the Trumet shore.

Unless things sadly miscarried, the *New Hope's* powder would come safely at last to her hold—but what about Jonathan Bangs? What would happen to him when Waterman or Captain Holt discovered the treachery? It seemed as though there could be but one answer to that question. Jonathan Bangs would be very, very dead.

Heroics are all very well in theory and at a distance. In my first rage after reading Forsythe's letter I asked nothing better than death, if in dying I could take some revenge for the injuries done to me and my country. But, now that events had brought me several long strides closer to the actual event, I found that I took no pleasure at all in the prospect of ceasing to exist.

I spent quite a bit of time that afternoon in trying to cook up a scheme for escaping the fate I had brought upon myself, but, in the end, the best that my slow brain could produce seemed unlikely to succeed. I would be, as Captain Holt had been careful to point out, a lone, unarmed man in the midst of twenty who were my enemies. Worst of all, I would have Lieutenant Waterman to deal with, and, unless I greatly misjudged the vindictiveness of the man's character, I would have to be both clever and lucky to escape his attentions without a couple of lead slugs in my body.

In the end I shrugged my mental shoulders, deciding that I had no choice but to let the future take care of itself. For all I knew, I might never sail the *Gannet* on a wild-goose chase across the Bay with Waterman as my nurse-maid. My plans to that end had been carefully laid, but I very well knew that they might be blown to atoms at any moment by a double event—the escape of Jermyn Forsythe from Trumet and his return to the *Terror*.

The thought of Forsythe made me shudder. Long before this, as he had predicted in his letter to Holt, Hope Allen would have brought to him from the traitor—whoever that traitor was—the exact details of our powder-running plans. Having those, his object in remaining in the abandoned storehouse would be attained, and he would be eager to escape. If he was able to do so before Friday and to return to his post in Point Town, all my hard work would have been wasted. In my unhappy mind I could hear Forsythe's mocking laughter if he was told that I had been chosen to pilot the *Gannet* in her venture against the American powder.

Would Hope's British lover succeed in getting safely away from the Trumet shore? He had time enough, heaven knew, for today was only Tuesday and the powder barge from Tamoset would not make her attempt until Friday night. On the other hand, the man was wounded and might find it difficult, if not impossible, to travel. Nor would the hunt for me, which still must be going on in Trumet, work to his advantage. Because of me, the militia would be every-where on the alert, and it was possible that they might catch the British officer in their net. If they only would! My worst worry would be over if only Forsythe could be captured—either in his hideout or as he made his way towards a boat on the shore.

It was just about then, I think, that the thought took root in my mind of writing, and somehow sending, a warning letter to Captain Dole in Trumet. In my present position, the chances of such a letter reaching its destination seemed remote indeed, but I determined, nevertheless, to write it. I felt that the taking of *any* action would be more tolerable than merely sitting still, with my hands folded, waiting for the worst.

There was little sleep for me that night. During most of its small, dark hours, I was busy with pen and ink in the insecure privacy of Jermyn Forsythe's cabin.

In spite of the faint, flickering light of a carefully shaded candle and in spite of my alertness for the sound of an approaching footstep, my letter to Captain Dole was a long one. It contained the information that a British officer lay hidden in the old storehouse near the Allen clearing, together with an urgent plea that he be immediately arrested and held prisoner. Those were the important things I had to say, but I wrote much more. Feeling that perhaps I should never see Captain Dole again and wanting him, should that be the case, to remember me with some degree of kindness, I told him everything that there was to tell. I gave him an exact account of every little thing I had done from the time when disaster first threatened up to the time of writing, and gave my reasons for doing them. I told him what I had in mind for Friday, if Forsythe did not spoil everything by returning first to the *Terror*, and I even outlined my vague and half-formed plans for trying to save my own skin and, perhaps, save the *New Hope* and her backers from total failure.

When all was done and the thick letter tucked into my jacket pocket, I said a silent but earnest prayer that it might somehow reach its destination. Nor was that prayer entirely inspired by my desire to have Forsythe made a prisoner. Captain Dole was my friend and the person I cared most about—now that I was done with Hope—in all the world. If it should happen that I must die, I wanted Isaiah Dole to know that he had not trusted me entirely in vain.

All Wednesday morning I was on pins and needles. For one thing, I knew that the letter in my pocket was as dangerous as many times its weight in gunpowder. If it should fall into Captain Holt's hands by some piece of bad luck, the British would know almost as much about me as I knew about myself. I was on edge, too, to find some means of sending my letter on its way. Not only was every minute precious, but I had no messenger of any kind at my command. I had thought I might possibly bribe a member of the *Terror's* crew to deliver my letter to some patriotic American in the village of Point Town, but when I came to the point of taking such a step I realized how very dangerous it would be. The amount of money I could offer as a bribe was small. The danger to whatever British seaman I approached would be great. What was to prevent such a sailor from taking my money and then handing over my fatal confession to one of his superiors?

I hesitated to gamble so recklessly, except as a last resort, and while I was trying to screw up my courage, my prayer of the night before was wonderfully answered—at least, in part. I found a messenger.

So deep was my own preoccupation that I hardly noticed the man and surely would have passed him by but for his own actions. Strolling along the deck, I was vaguely aware of a wiry, red-faced little man in shabby fisherman's clothes who was walking rapidly back and forth just ahead of me and muttering angrily to himself. As I was about to pass him by, I carelessly and without any particular thought wished him a civil good afternoon.

"Good afternoon, is it?" From the way the fellow spun

354

about and flung the words back at me, you might have thought I had offered some insult to the good character of his mother. "Don't try to soft-soap me, you mealy-mouthed Lobster-back! I've stood all I will stand from your breed of cats! You and your cutters and longboats! You and your damned patrol! What harm have I ever done to you? Not a mite! I'm just a hard-working fisherman with a wife and six hungry young ones to feed—leastways, that's what I *was*, before you pirates stole my schooner away from me! Said I was too far out, contrary to regulations. Now I ain't *anything*, and my children'll starve, most likely. Good morning be darned!" He looked for a moment as though he were about to spit on the sacred cleanliness of the *Terror's* deck. "Let me tell you something, mister! The only mornin' that'll be a good one for me will be the one when there ain't a single live Britisher within a thousand miles of this here port. I just pray I live to see it—and to help it happen!"

"Hush! Wait a minute!" I was at his side in an instant and had his thin elbow tight in my hand. "I'm no more British than you are," I told him in a low urgent tone. "I'm an American and a prisoner aboard this tub! Will you help me out? Will you do something for me that will help me get away—and that will be a crack in the eye for the Redcoats at the same time?"

He gave me a sharp looking over. Then his teeth clicked together.

"Mister, just name it!" Quick to understand, the little man's voice was just as fierce as ever, but he lowered it almost to a whisper. "I'd do anything short of murder—maybe I'd do that—to get even with these swabs! What do you want? Just name it quick!"

I named it fast enough, and in less than thirty seconds my business with the fisherman was done. He had my fat letter to Captain Dole, and I had his profane but earnest promise that it would get to the right place with the least possible delay. As I watched him pull his small boat away from the *Terror*, not five minutes later, and saw him pause in his rowing to shake a vindictive fist at the Union Jack, I felt an impulse to dance a jig of triumph.

It seemed almost as though this miracle had been granted to me as a sign that, in spite of all the misfortunes of the past and the dangers of the future, I must not falter or lose heart. Such a sign was needed, heaven knows, for without it I doubt if I should have been able to endure the complete inactivity of the next two days.

To my mind there is no torture like that of waiting, in complete helplessness, while fate makes up its mind whether or not to strike.

It was early Wednesday afternoon when the fisherman departed with my letter to Captain Dole, and it was noon on Friday before I could lift a hand to do something for my own cause. In between I fretted in my tiny cabin or paced back and forth above decks, never free for a moment from the fear and expectation that Jermyn Forsythe might suddenly show his arrogant handsome face aboard the *Terror*.

Dr. Cobble sensed my intense nervousness, and tried his best to soothe me with conversation and with offers of games of chess. But, as much as I liked the man, I found his company tolerable only in comparison with that of Lieutenant Waterman, who seemed to find pleasure in haunting me.

Waterman left no doubts in my mind that he was keenly looking forward to our cruise together on the *Gannet*, or that, once he had me securely under his thumb, he would take sweet revenge for the trouble I had got him into with Captain Holt. He hunted me up almost every hour to ask if the time had not yet come for us to set off on our venture, and each time that I shook my head, asking him civilly to have patience, he regarded me with scowling suspicion.

"I'll wait, Bangs," he told me unpleasantly, late Thursday afternoon; "but some time or other the waiting will have to come to an end. Remember that. Going to this tea party was your own idea, and I intend to see that you don't miss it! Captain Holt tells me that you aren't precisely charmed with the idea of having me for chaperone, but I can promise you that there's no alternative." He laughed in a way I didn't like. "We'll have fine sport together, my two-faced Yankee, on our little cruise. I look forward to it with a great deal of pleasure."

Waterman's intense hatred of me was so plain to be read in his face that I seriously considered pleading once more with Captain Holt that he appoint some other officer as my guard. But when I mentioned the idea to Dr. Cobble, the surgeon shook his head soberly. "You'd gain nothing by attempting to talk to Captain Holt today about Waterman—or about anything else, for that matter. The Captain is in no fit state for conversation. To be perfectly frank with you, Bangs, Captain Holt is a very ill man. He's so ill that, if he gets any worse, I shall fear for his life."

"Captain Holt sick?" I was surprised for a moment, until I remembered the sniffles and sneezings that had accompanied our earlier talks. "Oh, you mean his cold has grown worse?"

"Yes." Cobble nodded. "So much worse, in fact, that it can no longer be called a cold. He is in his bunk with a raging fever and a sound in his left lung that I don't like at all. Such infections can be, as you know, both swift and —devilishly dangerous. . . . You are not to repeat that remark, of course."

"Too bad." I was genuinely sorry for the British commander, who seemed to be a decent sort. At the same time, my own selfish interests were uppermost, and I found myself wondering just what, if anything, his illness might mean for me. "If he's in such a bad way," I said, thinking aloud, "he must have been forced to hand over his command to someone else! Perhaps I could persuade whoever is in charge here now that that fellow Waterman is not the man to send with me on the *Gannet*."

"There's no hope there, either," said Cobble flatly. "We're short-handed aboard here. Captain Holt's second in command has temporarily been put in charge of the *Hawke*, which is guarding the mouth of Trumet Harbor, on the ocean side. Lieutenant Forsythe is absent, and Holt, perhaps wisely, is unwilling to place heavy responsibility on any of the rest. In any event, he insists on keeping actively in command. Since the high fever makes his mind wander from time to time, the situation isn't a pretty one for any of us—including you. As things stand now, I'm afraid your only court of appeal is Waterman himself. I'm sorry—and I wish you luck."

But there was to be no luck. I hoped that, during the interminable hours of Thursday night, Captain Holt's condition might take a turn for the better, but I needed no more than a glance at Dr. Cobble's anxious face at breakfast time to know that the reverse had happened. Captain Holt would be of no use to me this day, and I could wait no longer. I must throw myself upon the tender mercies of Lieutenant Waterman.

"So!" A gleam came into Waterman's expressionless eyes when I sought him out and said that I should like to be put aboard the *Gannet* early that afternoon. "And on a Friday, too! Haven't you ever heard, Bangs, that it is bad luck to begin any enterprise on that day?" He smiled thinly. "Never mind. You have made your request, and it will be granted. A cutter will be ready at high noon to take you and me down the Bay! See to it that you are ready, too, for I dislike being kept waiting. The prospect of our little expedition pleases me no end, and nothing shall prevent or delay it. Understand? Nothing!"

"I imagine nothing *will* prevent it," I told him, with a shrug, "unless Captain Holt should suddenly decide to change his mind—or unless Lieutenant Forsythe should return with fresh news."

"Did you hear me, Bangs?" inquired Waterman icily. "I said that nothing would prevent—and I meant what I said! Captain Holt will not—in view of his condition—change the orders he has given me, and I shall carry them out. As for Lieutenant Forsythe, that gentleman happens to be my junior. If Forsythe should return this morning with the news that there *was* no powder, it would make no difference to me! You and I would still leave this ship at high noon." His face was hard and grim. "I have my orders, and, by God, I'll carry 'em through!"

What he meant, of course, was that he had his score to settle with me and intended to settle it. I wondered if the man wasn't just a little bit insane. It seemed impossible that he could have conjured up such an intense hatred of me, simply because he fancied I had injured his precious dignity.

In any event, I made it my business to stay out of his way the rest of the morning, and was surprised when, about eleven o'clock, he condescended to come to me with the information that he was going ashore for a brief, but "important" errand. From something both boastful and sheepish in his manner I had a suspicion that his purpose was to say good-by to the bit of fluff he had been entertaining at the Gray Goose Inn on the evening of my arrival in Point Town; but I had sense enough not to let him see what was in my mind.

"I've left orders for a cutter to be manned and alongside when I get back," he said coldly as he turned away. "I expect you to be ready, Bangs. If you know what's good for you, you won't keep me waiting. In spite of all hell you and I are leaving this ship on the stroke of eight bells! Nothing is to stop that!"

It was just about eleven o'clock when Waterman left for shore, and it couldn't have been more than twenty minutes later that a sloop appeared at the mouth of the harbor. She was just coming to anchor at a point at some distance from the *Terror* when I first caught sight of her, and one glance at her sharp stern was all that it took to send my heart plunging down towards my boots.

I didn't need the astonished identification of the very young officer, Smythe, beside me on the quarter deck to know her name. She was the vessel which now should be at her station in the Bay off Billfish Creek, unknowingly waiting the arrival of Lieutenant Waterman and myself. She was the pink-stern vessel *Gannet!*

If the consternation that I felt showed in my face, the deck officer of the *Terror* did not see it, for he was busy peering through his glass at the new arrival and muttering to himself in the process. "It's the *Gannet*, by gad! What's she doing off station? Something important must have happened. I must report this at once!"

"There isn't any use in that," I managed to remind him. "Captain Holt is too sick to care about anything, and Waterman's ashore. You're in command here for the moment, and you'll know what's happened in a few minutes. They're sending a boat, aren't they?"

"Eh? Why, so they are!" Smythe raised the glass again. "Who's that in the stern of her? Doesn't look like Hawley. 'Tisn't either. Looks like— Why, by gad, it is! It's old Jerry! It's no less than Jerry Forsythe himself, and in the flesh! By gad, if it isn't!"

I stood silent, not listening to the excited "by gad's" of the man beside me and not really seeing the little gig on which he trained his glass. With very stroke of that gig's oars, Forsythe was coming closer—and riding with Forsythe was disaster.

I remember trying desperately to think, in the very few minutes of grace that were left to me, but I can't remember making any decision of importance. All I can remember is a sensation of intense anger—as though I had been cheated at cards just as I was at the very point of winning the game.

Even when the boat from the *Gannet* had come alongside and I could hear Forsythe's hearty tones, I had still made no kind of plan as to what I might possibly do in order to save the situation and myself. Luckily, I had sense enough not to go to the head of the gangway with young Smythe, but retreated instead to a place just inside a nearby companionway, where I could hear what was said without being seen.

A moment later Forsythe came into view, just as smiling and arrogant and at ease as when I had seen him last and walking with only a barely noticeable limp.

He greeted his brother officer as casually as though he had seen him only an hour ago, but it seemed to me that there was a businesslike briskness about it that was not quite in character. He showed also a frank disinclination for stopping to chat. "Sorry, old boy," he said in a friendly, apologetic way, "but I can't spare the time just now to tell you about my adventures among the savages. 'More later,' as my mother always says in her letters. Fact is, I'm in a tearing rush to have a bit of a gab with the old man on a matter that won't keep."

"Don't know if you can do that, Jerry," said Smythe, shaking his head. "The skipper's ill. Damned ill, by gad, so Cobble says. Doubt if he'll be able to talk to you, by gad!"

"Holt off his feed? That's a crying shame!" Forsythe didn't seem to be greatly worried by the news. "I fancy he'll pull himself together, all the same, when he hears what

I have to tell. I'll just brush up a bit in my cabin before I have a go at him."

Smythe was full of curiosity and would have liked to ask a dozen questions, but Forsythe wouldn't have it. He turned away with a hasty apology and came rapidly in my direction.

I fled before him, in the direction of his cabin, and as I did so I suddenly had a very clear understanding of what I must do. I knew that I must give Jermyn Forsythe, when he entered his private quarters, a greeting that would be both unexpected and rude.

I dislike to attack a defenseless and unsuspecting man without giving him so much as a word of warning, but I felt that I had no choice. When Forsythe opened his cabin door, I was behind it. When he closed the door again he saw me, and his eyes widened. But just at that moment I swung my fist, with all the power that I could put behind it, straight for the point of his astonished jaw.

The blow went home, and Forsythe crumpled to the floor, as dead to the world as though he had taken a pistol bullet through the heart.

After that I worked just as fast as I could move. Grabbing one of the Lieutenant's own spare linen shirts from the place where he kept them, I rudely ripped it into strips. With those I trussed up the limp body on the floor so tightly that when the officer came back to his senses he would find it very difficult even to wriggle. Nor did I forget the important detail of a gag. A bright red silk scarf with white polka dots served admirably for this purpose—admirably enough, I felt, so that the charming Forsythe voice would be completely lost in its folds.

In the end I dragged my neatly wrapped bundle into a corner, where I hoped it would be out of the way of a casual glance, and got myself out of that cabin as hastily as though it were plague-infested. As a final precaution I locked the door from the outside and thrust the key into my breeches pocket.

My temptation was to run at full speed back to the quarter deck, but I forced myself to walk slowly so that my heavy breathing would have a chance to slow down to something like its normal rate of speed. Young Smythe apparently noticed nothing out of the ordinary when I found him again and had done nothing in my absence to spread the word of Forsythe's arrival.

"I feel as though I ought to be doing something special to celebrate old Jerry's return to the fold, but, by gad, I don't know what to do! Can't very well leave my post, you see. If Holt-Holt should catch me off station he'd slice off both my ears, by gad!"

"It's just as well you've done nothing," I told him swiftly. "I just saw Lieutenant Forsythe in his cabin, and he asked me to bring you a message. Since Captain Holt is so ill, Forsythe has decided that he won't try to talk to him. He's made up his mind to put the whole thing in writing— thinks that a written report will be better, in any case, since his story is so long and complicated."

"That's a rum one!" Smythe laughed. "Can't imagine Jerry writing anything. Fellow can't spell. When he wants to set down the word 'kitten' he has to write 'small cat' so there'll be only two spelling mistakes instead of three. That's a fact, by gad! It is, 'pon my honor."

"Well, he's writing now, make no mistake about that." I spoke with emphasis. "He has his door locked and is scratching away for dear life. He told me to ask you not to let anybody know he's back aboard ship. He said that the job might take two hours—or six—but that he doesn't want to be disturbed until it's done. He implied that if you let anybody so much as knock on his door, he'd not only slice off your ears but your nose as well!"

"So? Old Jerry said that?" Young Smythe scratched his

blond curls in puzzlement but produced nothing new in the way of expletives. "Well, by gad!"

"Ahoy, the *Terror!*"

The loud voice came from alongside, and I realized that Waterman had returned from his trip ashore. With a quick-beating heart I followed Smythe to the head of the gang-way and looked down.

"What's the *Gannet* doing in this harbor?" Waterman was still seated in the stern of his small boat and seemed to be making no move to leave it. It was evident, too, that he was in a temper. "Why has Hawley disobeyed orders and left his station? He'll be court-martialed for this, the fool."

"Old Jerry's come home, that's why, sir." In his excite-ment Smythe forgot all about keeping the return a secret. "He's tired of bedding down with Indians and has come home to mother, by gad! Says that he's brought some im-portant news with him. He's down in his cabin, just now, sir, writing it all out for the skipper."

"So?" Waterman seemed hardly to be listening. He glanced upward, scowling, at the sun and said sharply, "Where's the Bangs fellow?"

"I'm here, sir." I stepped forward to show myself. "What did you want?"

"What do you think I want? I want you!" He shoved himself over in the stern sheets as though to make room. "It's eight bells exactly, and time for us to be shoving off. Come down here, and step lively!"

I hardly believed my ears or my good fortune, but I would have obeyed the order quickly enough, no fear, if Smythe hadn't interfered. He stepped in front of me and waved his telescope incredulously in Waterman's direction. "Oh, I say, sir, you can't seriously mean that you're going to pop off on this trip down the Bay without so much as a word with Forsythe! Jerry's just come back aboard with important news! You'll want to hear what it is before you go anywhere, sir, I'm sure. Why—"

"That's enough, Smythe! When I want advice from a subordinate I ask for it!" Quite evidently Waterman was boiling with anger. "I'll ask you also to keep your mouth shut! I heard what you said about Forsythe, and I'm not interested. All that interests me is my orders, which are that I'm to leave this ship for the *Gannet* at eight bells. It's eight bells, and I intend to obey those orders!" He beckoned with his closed fist in my direction. "Did you hear me, Bangs? Come down here, and step lively!"

I didn't wait for anything more. In a matter of seconds I was seated beside him in the stern sheets of the gig, and the *Terror* was falling away to the starboard. I wanted to pinch myself to make sure of my incredible luck, for it didn't seem possible that Waterman, of all the people in the world, should have come to my aid.

A rich odor of rum that came strong from the man himself to my nostrils gave me a partial explanation for the turn of events. Waterman himself supplied the rest. "I suppose you thought Forsythe's coming back would save you from this!" His eyes were no longer cold. Although a trifle bleary, they were hot with excitement. "Well, in that case you don't know me. I told you that all hell wouldn't be enough to stop our taking this little honeymoon, Bangs, and I meant it! We're alone together at last, with no one to spoil our fun."

Ahead of me, over the bow of our gig, and coming closer, I could see the hull and rigging of the pink-stern sloop, *Gannet*. Ahead of me, also, lay an immediate future that I could not see. Glancing at the surely half-drunk, and possibly half-mad, officer on the thwart beside me, I found myself thinking that it was perhaps a blessing that the future must remain obscure.

7

In which Captain Dole and Squire Bailey
find the answer to a riddle.

Told by

CAPTAIN ISAIAH DOLE

Phoebe Light was in her bedroom, hers and Ezra's, which opened off the kitchen at the back of the Light place, when Ezra and I got there. She was in bed, of course, propped up on pillows, her head tied up in bandages, and Hannah Badger, the nurse woman, was with her.

This was Friday morning, you may remember. I had just come back from the Allen house. In my pocket was the letter from Jonathan—the one Ezra had brought me— and my head was buzzing with the amazing things he had written and with the words of Hope Allen's story about herself and the Forsythe man.

If I was to believe what I had read and heard—and so far it seemed more reasonable to believe than not to—Jonathan Bangs was not, nor had ever been, the renegade and traitor that all hands, I included, had come to feel certain he must be. Instead he was as true blue and loyal to the United States as I was, myself. And as for Hope—well, I could have mastheaded her for having been such a ninny as to let herself be caught in this snarl with the Redcoat lieutenant, but, at least, she hadn't cried baby or offered excuses. As soon as, according to her thinking, she honorably could, she had come of her own accord to me, made full confession, and was standing ready to take whatever punishment was coming to her.

All of which, while it cleared up a lot of the fog I had been trying to navigate through, didn't alter the paralyzing fact that my false plans had *not* been carried to the enemy and that tonight—the night of this very day—our powder was due to arrive from Tamoset, and with that same enemy not fooled at all, but knowing just exactly how, when, and where it was to arrive.

So perhaps it isn't much wonder that, as I followed in Ezra's wake to see his wife and hear what she had to tell me, I wasn't as excited and interested in her or her story as, maybe, I should have been. In fact, if Ezra hadn't been so heated up, himself, and so sure Phoebe had something very worth while to tell, I doubt if I should have gone to her just then. I had to see Weeks and Bailey. They must be shown Jonathan's letter. They must see Hope and hear her story at first hand. There must be some sort of decision made as to what was to be done now.

But Ezra was so persistent that I did follow him to the bedroom. Even before his finger lifted the latch of the bedroom door I could hear his wife's tongue clacking and the Badger woman trying to tell her not to talk now but to save her strength—that sort of thing. Of course she might as well have tried to coax the tide not to come in, but she kept on trying. Hannah Badger is one of those conscientious souls who are so uplifting to read about and so everlasting hard to live with.

The arguing mill shut down when we walked in, but it started up again the second afterwards.

"Oh, Ezry, I thought you'd *never* get here. I—"

"Now, now, Phoebe, dearie." This was from Hannah, you understand. "You mustn't get so upset. Now, dearie—"

"I *do* wish you wouldn't call me 'dearie.' I told you not to. I just can't seem to stand that word. My great-aunt Huldy—she was my great-uncle Ziby's half-sister on my mother's side when I was a child—of course she was afterwards, too, but, oh, you know what I mean—Uncle Ziby was her half-brother and they lived way down to Poke

370

Neck. Well, she used to call me 'dearie' when she wanted me to run errands or something, and I got so-o sick of it! You remember great-aunt Huldy, don't you, Ezra? Course you do. And great-uncle Ziby—you remember *him*. He was so-o funny. Used to wear his Sunday shirt buttoned on hind side to, so as he could get air on his chest. That's what he said—air on his chest. Well, anyhow—"

Ezra cut in and took charge. "Sure and sartin, Phoebe," he said. "I remember it all. Wait until we have a little more time, and I'll remember Methusalem when he was a little shaver and him and me went to school together. Just now, though, here's Captain Isaiah, came to hear what you've got to tell him. Hannah, suppose you go into the sitting-room and stand watch there till we come out. Don't let anybody else in here, you understand."

The Badger woman went, though it was plain to see she didn't want to. After the door was shut astern of her, Ezra turned to me.

"Got to make this as short as we can, Captain," he whispered. "She's a long ten fathom from being clear of the shock yet. Now, Phoebe, old girl, you tell Captain Isaiah what you've told me. About the knife, I mean."

Getting that story from Phoebe Light, in the state she was in just then, was like pulling a back tooth with a woolen string—just about when you thought you'd got a good purchase on it the string broke and you had to start all over again. If Ezra hadn't been there I don't know that I should have ever got through with the job.

What she had to tell me was about that sheath knife of Jonathan Bang's, the one I had borrowed of him a fortnight or so ago and had left with her—Phoebe—to put back in Jonathan's room. I had left it with her, you will remember, on the Friday morning of the week before this one, and the next time I saw it was when Captain Elnathan and Eben Fowler and I found it lying beside Seth Black's body

at the edge of Hornpout Pond, which was early in the forenoon of the following Monday. That knife, with Jonathan's initials on its sheath, was the main proof that damned
him as the killer of poor old Seth.

You will recollect, too, that when the committee picked
by the Council to search Jonathan's room for anything—
papers or letters or whatever, which might show him to be
in British pay—when that committee did their searching on
Sunday, the day after the fire, they were perfectly sure
there was no knife on the bureau or anywhere else in the
room. And yet Phoebe, when they—and I later—questioned
her, was just as sure she had put it on that bureau the very
Friday morning I left it with her. She knew the day was
Friday because Friday was her "sweeping day" and
she remembered laying the knife, after I handed it to her,
on the shelf of the kitchen closet where she kept the broom.
She put it there so as to be certain to see it and take it with
her when she went into Jonathan's room to do her regular
weekly sweeping, dusting, and general overhauling.

Now, in the light of that statement, the case stood this
way: The knife was put on Jonathan's bureau Friday
morning. It was not there when the committee came on
Sunday. The room had been locked all the time, with the
key hanging in its private hiding place by the dining-room
mantelpiece. And yet, sometime between Friday and
Sunday, the knife had been taken. Who could have taken
it? Nobody *but* Jonathan; that seemed to be the answer. *I*
hadn't been in that room. Phoebe hadn't, except when she
went in to make the bed and sweep and leave the knife,
and she swore she locked the door when she came out and
hung the key on the hook. Ezra—well, Ezra was off on his
Tamoset cruise from Friday to Monday afternoon, and
Seth Black was alive and drunk on Saturday and found
dead Monday morning. Jonathan was in and out on Friday
afternoon and once or twice Saturday forenoon. He had

taken it on himself to stand watch aboard the *New Hope* nights, but he could have come back to the house at any time during the days. Yes, even I had considered it settled that Jonathan had taken the knife from his room, though that he had done a murder with it I had never really believed.

And now Phoebe Light was telling things that made the murder case against Jonathan Bangs fall to pieces like a house built by children with plaything blocks. She was saying now that she had *not* put the knife on Jonathan's bureau on Friday. She had not taken it in there until around twelve o'clock Saturday night, after she came home from running to the fire at the shipyard.

Saturday night! Just stop and think what *that* meant. Saturday night, even before the fire was completely put out, Jonathan was arrested by the militia over at Shad Cove beach and taken to the Town House and from there to the lockup. He was in that lockup the rest of that night, all day Sunday, and a good-sized part of Sunday night. Now then, if Phoebe did not put the knife in his room until after twelve Saturday night—as she was now vowing and declaring was the truth—and that search committee found no knife there Sunday forenoon, then—

Well, then, if these things were so, the time when the knife could have been taken from the room had narrowed down from the stretch from Friday morning to Saturday night—which was what we had been figuring on— to from midnight of Saturday to noon Sunday. And Jonathan Bangs was in the custody of the militia or in the Trumet lockup every minute of that time—and a lot more besides. Whoever had taken the knife and left it by Seth Black's body, it was not Jonathan.

Not Jonathan—but who? And with the door locked and the key hidden in a place nobody knew of but Phoebe and Ezra and I!

Impossible. That was what I was saying to myself. Unless Phoebe's new yarn was all nonsense, something that had got into her poor cracked head while she was lying unconscious; a part of her delirium dreamings that she was mixing up with realities.

I whispered as much to Ezra, but he shook his head. "Cal'lated so, myself, fust along, at the beginning," he said; "but, when I stopped to think, seemed as if it must be more than that. Recollect, Captain, she was up to the village last Tuesday afternoon, hunting for you and saying she had something important to tell you, something she *must* tell you, about a knife. Couldn't be any knife but that one of Jonathan's, fur's I can see, and you want to remember she hadn't been hit on the head then. It wa'n't until she came back home here, *after* her cruise up town and her 'knife' talk, that she was thumped with that kindling hatchet. Seems almost as if somebody wanted to fix her so she couldn't talk any more about it, don't it? Looks that way to me."

It did to me, too, when he put it that way. As a matter of fact, a hint of some such idea had been in the back of my head all along, but I had had so many other puzzles and troubles in that same head that I hadn't given much thought to this one. Now, though, it sounded like at least the outside edge of the truth. Provided, of course, that Phoebe's new story *was* the truth.

Ezra was certain it was.

"Ask her how she knows it was Saturday she put back the knife, Captain Isaiah," he said to me.

Before I put that question, however, it struck me that it might be well to have somebody besides Ezra and myself on hand to hear the answers. If she could really give convincing proof of that Friday-to-Saturday shift it might do more than clear Jonathan. It might possibly put us on the track of the real traitor and murderer, the fellow who had written the "Dear Sir" letter and signed it "J. B." That Jonathan hadn't written it I knew already, for he was in Point Town at the time. I wanted a clear head and wide-awake brains to help tackle this new twist, and I didn't know any head or brains that filled the bill better than Bethuel Bailey's. So I sent Ezra up to the Bailey house with orders to get hold of the Squire and bring him back with him right away, if possible.

Ezra wasn't gone but a few minutes. As good luck would have it he met Bailey on the road before he got to the house, and the Squire didn't argue, but came. Acting under my orders, Ezra had told him what was going on, so I didn't have to do any explaining after he got there. "Shall I do the questioning, Squire, or will you?" I asked. He told me to begin and he would cut in if, or when, he thought it needful.

"Now, Phoebe," said I, walking over to the side of the bed and speaking gentle, so as not to excite her any more than I could help. "Now, Phoebe," I said, "first of all I wish you would tell us what makes you so certain you didn't put that knife of Mr. Bangs's in his room until after you came home from going to the fire Saturday night. You meant to put it there the very day I gave it to you. You say, yourself, you did. You told Ezra and me that you laid it on the shelf in the kitchen closet so as to take it with you when you went in to Mr. Bangs's room to sweep, as you always did every Friday. Now, why didn't you take it?"

Phoebe's answer to that was just—well, it was just Phoebe Light, that's all I can say. It was a jumble of kitchen closet and broom and this on the floor and that on the shelf and the shipyard fire and being all alone in the house and "scared pretty nigh out of my ten senses or is it nine, I don't remember" and—oh, never mind. Put into something besides Phoebe-talk it added up this way:

She had laid the sheath knife on the closet shelf after I gave it to her on Friday, but she "guessed likely" she couldn't have put it on "all the way," and so it fell off and down behind the mop pail on the closet floor. When she went to get the broom she had forgotten the knife altogether and went in Jonathan's room and did her sweeping without remembering it. In fact, it wasn't until Saturday, after doing her supper dishes, that she went to that closet, moved the pail by accident, and heard something "go clink." She looked to see what was clinking, and there was the knife, sheath and all. She took at least three minutes to explain what a mercy it was that the pail had hit against the knife handle instead of the sheath, otherwise she didn't know when she might have found it.

She laid it on the table so as to be sure and not forget it again, and then somebody—Patience Atwood I believe it was—came in and "stayed and stayed," and they "talked and talked." "Pashy is *such* a talker," she said, and didn't see anything funny in her saying it, either. Soon after the Atwood woman went, the Town House bell began to ring, and Phoebe looked out of the door and saw the sky "red as one of Ezra's under-flannels." She rushed off to the fire, of course, and didn't come back until the last spark was out, you may be sure.

"And there was that dratted knife right on the table afore my eyes," she crowed. " '*Well*,' says I, 'I won't let you get lost again, I declare for it!' and I marched right into the dining-room, took the key of Mr. Bangs's room from the place where we always kept it hanging, unlocked his door, and went in and laid it right on his bureau. There! *That's* how I know 'twas Saturday night when I done it," she finished, in a cackle of vainglory.

I looked at Squire Bailey and he at me. Then he asked a question.

"Plain enough, Phoebe," he said. "Only, when—Tuesday,

I think it was—Captain Isaiah, or some of the rest of us, asked you when you put the knife in that room, why didn't you say it was Saturday night instead of Friday morning?"

That really did fuss her. She fidgeted, kind of picked at the bed clothes with her fingers, started to speak and stopped—and, at last, came out with it.

"I—I—I—" she stammered. "Well, I was so—so shook all to pieces, as you might say, what with the fire and—and Mr. Jonathan's being took up and all, and then Seth Black's being murdered in his bed—well, no, not in his bed, but murdered to death anyhow—that—that when they asked me I—well, I just couldn't seem to remember anything straight. I knew 'twas Friday, sweeping day, I *meant* to put that awful knife back so I—I just said 'twas, I suppose likely. And I *thought* 'twas, too—then. I honestly did. I'm *so* sorry."

What could we say? For anybody else it would have been a lame enough excuse, but from Phoebe Light it wasn't so surprising. She had about as much mind as a hen and about the same kind, too. I glanced over my shoulder at Bailey, and he lifted his shoulders and smiled, as much as to say: "Oh, well, what's the use?"

What he did say, though, was to Phoebe, not to me.

"I see," he said. "Well, you remembered afterwards, anyhow, didn't you? How did you happen to do that?"

Another half hogshead of words. Out of that collection we managed to sift enough sense to make out that once more it was the mop pail that put her on the right track. By and large, that mop pail deserves a vote of thanks, seems to me. Tuesday afternoon, when she went to the closet again, she stubbed her toe against the pail, and "all at once," as she said, it "come acrost her" how she had found the knife on the floor behind it and that it was Saturday, not Friday, when she found it there and, later on in the evening, took it to Jonathan's room.

As soon as all this had really "come acrost" her, she dropped everything and raced off up town to locate me and tell me of the mistake she had made.

"I felt perfectly dreadful about having told you a wrong story, Captain Isaiah. As you know, I do pride myself on being a truth-speaking woman. I never *meant* to lie—as I hope for everlasting salvation, I didn't. It was just—well, oh, dear me, dear me!"

"There, there, Phoebe," I said. "Anybody that knows you knows you wouldn't deliberately lie. You hurried up to the village to tell me. What then?"

She couldn't find me anywhere. She went to the ship-yard and the Town House and to the James Otis and all around and asked this one and that, but nobody knew where I was. So, after a while, she gave up and came back home. The fire in the kitchen fireplace was almost out, so she went to the shed, got an armful of wood, and came in again. Then she started to go into the dining-room when she heard a little noise behind her, began to turn around, and—well, that was as far as she could remember anything. The next thing she knew she was in her own bedroom and in her own bed, same as she was this minute.

"That was when the blackguard, whoever he was, thumped her with the back of the kindling hatchet," growled Ezra under his breath. Then he leaned towards me and whispered: "Don't you think likely that's about all she ought to stand just now, Captain?"

I nodded to Bailey, and we got up to go. Before we reached the door, though, the Squire had one more question to ask.

"Phoebe," he said, "when you were up in the village, asking those people if they knew where Captain Dole was, did you tell any of them what you wanted to see him about? Did you mention the knife, I mean?"

Eh? Why, she didn't know but she did. Her head was

so full of it she might have said something. She wasn't sure.

I, for one, was sure. Peleg Bounderby, when he met me there on the Point Road, had said that Phoebe Light was hunting me. "Something to do with a knife," I remembered his saying. I was dying to ask her what people she had met up town, but Ezra was shaking his head at me, so I took the Squire by the arm, and we went out of the bedroom together.

In the dining-room I found out that he had been thinking along with me all the way, for the first thing he said was: "She told everybody she met, probably. And one of them must have realized what it meant."

I nodded. "What it might mean to him, if her whole story was told, I should say. He realized it, followed her home here, waited his chance, and—"

"Put her out of the world for the time, and himself out of danger. Yes, I should say you were right, Isaiah. This puts a new light on Jonathan Bangs, too. If that knife wasn't in his room until Saturday night, after the fire, *he* couldn't have used it on Black."

"You bet he couldn't! Well, by the everlasting, I never could believe he did!"

"This situation is a queer one. *If* she put it on his bureau Saturday night and nobody went into that locked room until Sunday forenoon, when our committee came to search, why didn't they see it? They said they didn't, you'll remember."

"Um-hm. Look here, Squire, either somebody did get into that room between twelve o'clock Saturday night and noon on Sunday, or somebody is lying hard."

He nodded. "Isaiah," he asked, "who was on that search committee? Elkanah Davies and—Henry Allen, wasn't it?"

"Eh? That's right. . . . I had forgotten Henry."

Neither of us spoke for a little while; both thinking, I

379

guess likely. Then he said: "Isaiah, whoever took that knife took it and used it on poor Seth and then—"

"Then left it there so that the murder would be pinned on Jonathan. Of course he did."

"Humph! Why Jonathan in particular, I wonder? Of course, Bangs has been proved to be in British pay, so perhaps—"

I held up my hand. "Avast heaving, Squire!" I ordered. "In British pay, eh? Proved to be, you say? I want to know! Well, read that."

I took the letter Ezra had brought me—the one Jonathan had written me from Point Town and handed it to him. He settled his specs on his nose and read it through. Then he read it again.

"Good Lord Almighty!" he muttered. "Good *Lord!*"

It sounded almost as if he was in prayer-meeting, so I followed on in the same way.

"Amen!" said I. "And now what?"

2.

Squire Bailey didn't answer me. With Jonathan's letter in his hand he started for the outside door. I caught him by the arm.

"Just another jiffy, Squire," I said. "Where are you bound?"

He turned on me like a flash. His jaw was set, and his eyebrows drawn together. "Bound!" he snapped, impatiently. "Bound? Why to Jeremiah Weeks's, of course. We must have some sort of Council meeting—now. Good heavens, man, do you realize that tonight—*this* night— Eh? Isaiah, how long have you had this letter? How did you get it? Are you sure it isn't another trick?"

I told him how Ezra had got it and how he brought it to me. "And the handwriting is Jonathan's own, I'll swear to that. Besides, who but Jonathan could know all those things?"

His mind was working clearly enough now. Phoebe's story was pushed to one side for the time. "But I can't understand," he said. "If Bangs *is* loyal and has been from the first, then—"

I interrupted again. Even minutes were too scarce and too precious to be wasted. "Hold on!" I ordered. "There is a lot more the Council has got to hear, but I want you to hear it first. I want somebody besides myself to know it all and be ready to shut off unnecessary talk at the meeting. I have learned an amazing lot, Bethuel. Now listen."

I told him about Hope Allen, of her coming to me of her own free will and confirming everything, from the beginning of her renewing acquaintance with this Lieutenant Forsythe to how and why she had tricked me into letting Forsythe—I thinking at the time, of course, that he was Bangs—get away in the British boat. "She has been a very foolish girl," I said, "but—"

He broke in there, for the first time. "Never mind that," he said, brisk. "She can tell that to the Council—if she will."

"Oh, she will! She will do anything to help us now. In her talk with me she didn't spare herself at all."

"Humph! Well, better late than never, perhaps, although I am afraid it may be *too* late. Then those false plans of yours didn't go to the enemy at all, Isaiah?"

"No. Makes me look like a good deal of a fool; I realize it full as much as anybody."

"We all belong to the same lodge, so far as that goes. And the British know our real plans, and those can't be changed now."

"Right."

"I see. Well, then we haven't got to worry about trying to change them. Somehow or other we must put them through—or go under. Our chance is about one in a hundred. Even that may be an exaggeration."

"Unless Jonathan can put this wild notion of his through. Then I'd call them a little better than that."

He shrugged his shoulders. "You don't really believe he can, do you?" he asked.

"If it was anybody but Jonathan Bangs I'd say no. As it is—" It was my turn to shrug.

He smiled a little and slapped me on the back. "That young fellow has one good friend anyhow," he told me. "All right, if he pulls Trumet and the *New Hope* out of this he will have plenty more. If what he writes in this letter is all true—"

I was on edge. "Hang it all, Bailey," I snapped. "We've got to *act* as if it was true, haven't we? And begin to act this minute."

He jerked the door open. "Thanks, Isaiah," he said. "That is sense. I'll see Captain Weeks at once."

"And I've got to see Major Bartlett about having the militia ready for tonight. Yes, and every other able-bodied man, old and young. I'll have him set a picket guard at the tavern, too. Mustn't be any rum-selling done there today, I want a sober crew under me when I leave the harbor. ... Oh, by the way, Squire: What about this yarn of Phoebe's? Unless she is crazy somebody got that knife and—"

"I know, I know. Perhaps you and I better keep that part to ourselves for a little while. I want to think it over. See you at the Town House in a little while, Isaiah. I'll take the Bangs letter with me, if that is all right with you."

He hurried off. I headed for the harbor breastwork and Major Bartlett.

I found the Major a good deal upset by some news that one of his men had brought him from the watch station on the Bay shore. There had been a light fog over the Bay through the early morning, not much more than a haze, but enough to make it next to impossible to see out more than a mile or so from the beach. That haze had blown clear later on, and, when it did, the lookouts along by Billfish Cove and Shad Cove couldn't see hide nor hair of the *Gannet*. She wasn't at the anchorage where she had been for a week and where she was lying at dark the night before. She wasn't cruising further out. She wasn't in sight anywhere—she had gone.

Now where had she gone—and why? The Major was worried about it. He had just got the news himself and was going to send it on to me, but my coming had saved him the trouble.

Well, I was a whole lot worried, myself, although I didn't tell him so. The *Gannet* was at her anchorage when she sent in the boat that picked up Lieutenant Forsythe. I saw that boat, and I saw the *Gannet's* riding lights. Why had she gone? Well, the only reason I could think of was that Forsythe had news to carry to Captain Holt—news so important that it couldn't wait—and he had ordered the sloop to take it and him to Point Town. If that was so— well, I didn't dare think beyond that. Jonathan's whole scheme—the one he had written about in his letter to me— depended on his getting aboard the *Gannet*, and the one person who could surely block it was this same Forsythe. And I—I—nobody else but me—was responsible for letting Forsythe get away from Trumet. I had helped him get away!

I could have wrung my hands and howled, if wringing and howling would have done any good. They wouldn't— and what had to be, would be. I must try to believe that the *Gannet's* leaving had nothing to do with Forsythe. I mustn't lose my head. I must go on just as I had intended. There was nothing else *to* do.

So I told Major Bartlett that the enemy craft might have

gone off station for any one of a dozen reasons and that she would probably be back at any minute. Then I gave him the orders and instructions I had come there to give him.

The old boy was all business when I told him what I wanted. He agreed to have every one of his company armed, ready, and on hand for the night's work and to get as many volunteers from the old men and half-grown boys as he could, to help them out.

"No excuse except being sick a-bed will keep them off duty," he vowed. "This is what most of us have been waiting for, Captain. I'll have that Otis Tavern picketed, too. Anybody that drinks too much today will wish his rum had been poisoned before I get through with him. I'll see to it that the harbor and the Bay shore are watched, and if anything out of the common run happens I'll let you know right off. You can depend on me, Captain Isaiah."

I knew I could, bless his plucky old heart. He died a few months later, and on his gravestone now in the Trumet cemetery is the epitaph he had written for himself.

"The battle fought,
The victory won.
I enlisted under
Washington."

An honest, able man and a patriot, little old Major Ebenezer Bartlett.

After seeing him I went back to Ezra. He said Phoebe was asleep and the Badger woman was with her, so he could go anywhere and do anything I wanted him to. I told him his job was to keep a general eye on the *New Hope's* enlisted crew. See that their dunnage was stowed aboard and that they, themselves, were on board, too, by nightfall. Then I went to the yard, myself, and gave the bark a sort of last-minute inspection. Every rope was in place and every gun. She could head for sea on a ten-minute notice. I left Doane, my second officer, in charge there and, at last, hurried off to the Allen house to get Hope. I intended for her to go to the Council meeting with me. Her story, coming from her own lips, was bound to be more convincing than if I told it for her.

She met me at the door, looking just as white and tired-eyed as when I left her, but quiet and with a sort of desperate determination about her that was proof enough she meant to face whatever was ahead of her, face it and go through with it without a whimper. She said Henry Allen was up in the village somewhere, she didn't know where.

I asked her if she had told Henry her true story, same as she had told it to me. She said she intended to but had not had the chance yet. "I meant to, and shall, but I wanted to tell it to you first, for you were the one I had deceived most and lied to—and—"

She had to stop there for a minute or so, pulling herself together, so to say. Then she went on: "So I went up town to find you. Father, as you know, was not here when we came in, but he came a little while after you had gone. He was very nervous and disturbed, said he couldn't bother to listen to any chatter now, with all sorts of stories going around town, and so on. I told him he *must* listen, but he wouldn't and hurried out again. And now I shall have to tell all those other people and—and him at the same time. He will be— Oh, how *can* I! But I must, of course. And I will. I am ready, Captain Isaiah."

She had the grit, that girl. The things that Trumet would soon be saying about her I knew she realized full as keen as I did. I tried to tell her the Council would be easy with her, that maybe the whole story needn't even be made public—that sort of thing; but it didn't ring true, even to me, as I was saying it. She was in for a hard, hard time, knew it, and was ready for it. I did all the talking on the way to the Town House. She didn't speak a word.

The main road was, for Trumet, a pretty lively place that morning. Clumps of people talking and whispering together; a considerable number of out-of-towners—*New Hope* foremast hands, they were—among them; a notice tacked on the James Otis Tavern door, saying that no liquor would be sold there that day, and a couple of militia men, with guns on their shoulders, pacing up and down in front. A half-dozen times I was stopped to be questioned, but each time I said: "Don't bother me now."

Worried and anxious as I was, I couldn't help but be struck by the ridiculousness of it all—ridiculous in a way, I mean. There wasn't a man, woman, or child inside the town limits who didn't know something big was going to happen. We Council members had tried to keep our powder plans a secret, but a secret like that is bound to get out. Every grown-up must know that the *New Hope* was ready for sea, and today they must know that she was going to try to run for it as soon as that powder was aboard. Every one of the crew and every yard workman and militia man had sworn on the Bible not to tell what he knew and not to gossip about what he might guess—but, when guessing gets to be a practical certainty, who can head it off? No, so far as this night being the big night it had been working and waiting for, all Trumet knew.

And the British knew, that was the staggering thought. I for one—in fact, all the active leaders in our privateering enterprise—had realized from the beginning that, no matter how tight the blockade and how close shut we Trumeters might keep our mouths, the enemy was bound to learn or guess something of what was going on. That is why we had primed Ezra Light to tell around Point Town all his yarns about outfitting a vessel to be used for coasting trade after the war ended. They might believe or they might not, but, even if they suspected a try to run the blockade some-time or other, we counted on their getting no details, learn-ing nothing of our real how and when plans, until it was too late. We calculated we *had* fooled them too—until we learned, on what seemed to be full proof, that they knew about as many of the facts as we did.

We had taken account of every important thing, we thought. What we hadn't taken account of was treason among ourselves, in our own little inside circle. Impossible as it seemed, the traitor was one of us, an insider. We had followed trails leading to Jonathan Bangs and Hope Allen —with the base chance of Henry's being mixed up in it— but, so far as Jonathan and Hope were concerned, it looked as if we had been wasting time.

And now our time was shortened down to a few hours. This was Friday. Before Saturday's sun rose it would have been make or break with us. Well, one thing I swore to myself, swore it over again on that walk to the Town House: Whether the *New Hope* got past the blockade or not, whether I was to be a Yankee captain of a Yankee pri-vateer or a prisoner of war, some day, somehow—if I lived— I would dig that traitor snake out of his hole and stamp my heel down on his head. I would, I would!

There was an excited huddle of whisperers on the Town House steps, but no larger or more excited than the other huddles along the main road. I judged that the word of the holding of another Council meeting hadn't been spread around. I was a little surprised to find a militia guard posted by the door of the meeting room, but I judged that was one of the Squire's good ideas. We certainly didn't want any outsiders pushing in uninvited to hear what went on. All hands would have to know about it later, but not until we were ready to tell them.

The guard—he was one of the Major's seventeen-year-old boys and feeling and looking as important as a dog alongside his master on the front seat of a chaise—gave me a fine regulation salute and stood to one side as Hope and I came up.

"You two are to go in, Captain Isaiah," he said. "Captain Weeks said you was allowed to."

"Now that was real nice of him, wasn't it?" said I. "Much obliged—and to you, too, General."

I rapped on the door with my knuckles. The door opened a crack, and Captain Elnathan Berry peeked out. He looked at me and at Hope. Then he motioned with his hand, opened the door wider, and we squeezed past him and into the room.

You would think I ought to have been past surprising long before this, but I got what the doctor would most likely call another slight seizure when I looked around that room. I had expected to find a full meeting of the Council, with every member in his place. Instead there were only three people there, Captain Weeks, Elnathan Berry, and Squire Bailey. I couldn't understand it.

"What's the matter?" I asked. "Where are all hands?"

It was Captain Jeremiah who answered. He was looking pretty shaken and upset, but his looks were nothing compared to Captain Elnathan's. Elnathan looked as if a chair had been kicked from under him.

"Well, Isaiah," began Weeks. "Well, you see—Bethuel, maybe you better tell him.... er—er. Sit down, Isaiah. Sit down—er—both of you."

Hope and I sat. Squire Bailey spoke up. "When I left you, Isaiah, it was with the idea of seeing Jeremiah and having a full Council meeting called at once. You know that, I told you so; but, as I was on my way, another thought struck me. We have had the Lord knows how many meetings with everyone present, and, in spite of the fact that every soul at those meetings was sworn to secrecy, the news of what went on in this room got out—

and"—he was emphatic here—"somehow or other got to the British. We thought—most of us—that Bangs was the turncoat who was selling us out, and, later on, we began to think—those who knew what was going on—that he was being helped by—well, by Hope Allen here. It certainly looked as if he was, and what we thought was proof was so strong that even you, Captain Dole, were pretty well convinced. That was the way things stood at the adjournment of our last meeting. Your finding that letter beginning with 'Dear Sir' and signed 'J. B.' we figured to be the final, absolute proof. That's correctly stated, so far, I think."

Jeremiah Weeks said "Yes, yes." Elnathan Berry started to speak and then gave it up. I didn't say anything. The Squire went on.

"That letter, and all we thought it meant, were the reasons why we agreed to let Isaiah try out his scheme for sending the false plans for the powder landing—by Jonathan, as we thought—to the enemy. That was why Isaiah let the man that he thought was Bangs get away on that boat last night. I have already told Captain Weeks and Captain Berry about that, Isaiah, and I have taken the liberty of telling them all that you told me an hour or so ago. I have shown them the letter from Bangs that Light brought you from Point Town, and I have reported, as well as I could, Hope's story about Forsythe. We shall ask her to tell it again here, of course, but first I want to explain to you, Isaiah, why, after consideration, it seemed to me wiser to have only us four members hear these things now, instead of bringing them before a full meeting."

He leaned across the table. "We know now—and I honestly believe we are justified in taking it as truth—that Bangs is not a traitor and never has been one . . . oh, I know your feelings, Elnathan, but, in spite of prejudices—"

Captain Elnathan broke in. "Prejudices be damned!" he growled. "If that Bangs fellow isn't a traitor then—then—

well, confound it, he isn't, I suppose. But, if he isn't, who is? There's a traitor *somewhere*. You'll give in to that much, won't you, Bethuel?"

Squire Bailey nodded. "I will, indeed," he said. "Somebody sent word of our enterprise to Holt, and that was why Holt sent Forsythe to Trumet. Seth Black may have—must have, I should say—found out enough to make him dangerous to our treasonable friend, and that friend killed Seth to keep him quiet. Somebody set the fire. Somebody wrote the 'Dear Sir' letter, or letters. 'Dear Sir' was Forsythe, that seems certain, but who signed himself 'J. B.'? Not Jonathan Bangs, for he was a prisoner in Point Town when the letter was written."

"Or says he was," grumbled Berry.

"Oh, he was, he was!" snapped Weeks impatiently. "There's proof enough of that. Don't waste time, Elnathan. Heave ahead, Squire, and lively."

"There isn't much more for me to say—except this: Bangs is not the traitor we must find. Who is? That we don't know; but that he is a member of this inside circle of ours is now as sure as death and taxes. And to hold more meetings and discuss further plans before him is simply playing the fool. That is why, Captain Dole, I asked no one but Jeremiah and Elnathan to be here now. That *they* aren't traitors we *know*. . . . Now, Hope, if you will tell us the story you told Captain Isaiah."

Hope told it. She told it just as she had told it to me, only even more businesslike, adding nothing and skipping nothing. Before she began it, however, she asked a question that I had been wondering if she would ask.

"Why didn't you call my father here, Squire Bailey? Surely you don't suspect *him* of being a turncoat and a murderer."

Now, knowing that Bailey's mind had been working along about the same lines as mine, I could understand why he hadn't asked Henry Allen to be present. Some of us *had* suspected Henry, in a half-way sort of fashion, at the time when there was a chance that Jonathan and Hope and he might be in the treason plot together. Hope and Jonathan had cleared themselves—or we were acting on the notion that they had—but Henry hadn't yet, and in the little light we were working by, he showed up as about the only candidate. I was sure that was why the Squire hadn't asked him to meet with us now.

"I am sorry he isn't here," said Hope, "I haven't told him yet, and I should have liked him to hear it at least as soon as anyone else—except Captain Dole, of course."

If Bailey was the least bit fussed by her question, he didn't show it. His explanation was prompt. Henry would have been summoned, and so, for that matter, would Captain Davies and Eben Fowler, but they weren't, any of them, findable in the short time he felt we had at our disposal. "They will be told later, of course," he said, "either in private or, with the others, at the full meeting—provided one can be held."

I don't know whether Hope was satisfied with this or not, but she didn't say she wasn't. She told her story, all of it, as I have said. There was some questioning by the Squire and Captain Jeremiah and some pretty sharp badgering by Elnathan Berry; not as much, though, as I had expected. Elnathan seemed to be floundering around in circles, as you might call it. The plank he had been clinging to was labelled Jonathan Bangs. Now that plank had been snatched away from him, and he was all adrift.

When they were finished with Hope, the letter from Jonathan to me was read aloud by the Squire. He had read it to the others before Hope and I came, so it wasn't new to anyone except her. I watched her face while the reading was going on, and it was interesting to see the changes move across it every now and again, like cloud shadows and sunshine moving across a sand shoal where the water is only a foot or so deep. Sometimes, as she realized how her Forsythe chum had tricked Jonathan and how Jonathan had been forced into believing, and no doubt still believed, that she, herself, was working with Forsythe against him and Trumet, the shadows were black enough. And when Jonathan told of his plan to trick the enemy that had tricked him and, if the trick *should* drive the *Gannet* aground, give the *New Hope* the clearance for her getaway, the sunshine flooded up over her cheeks and shone in her eyes.

She didn't interrupt from the beginning of the reading to the end. Then she burst out with: "Oh, but it is so—so *desperate*. So dreadfully dangerous! Can he do it, Captain Isaiah? Do you think there is the slightest real chance?"

If I had answered honestly I should have said no, I suppose. Desperate and dangerous were too mild words for Jonathan's scheme. What I did say was: "Well, there is always *a* chance."

She asked if she might read the letter herself. Squire Bailey handed it to her. She went over to a chair in the corner. While she was reading the rest of us whispered together, trying to work out what to do at our end, ashore. Captain Elnathan was to see Major Bartlett and emphasize the orders I had given him. Bailey was to arrange for the necessary money, which he was to get from the safe where it had been kept, and deliver it into my hands just before I stepped aboard the *New Hope* as her commander. As for me—well, I had plenty to do without any special orders.

Captain Jeremiah Weeks had something else on his mind. "There will have to be some sort of town meeting late this afternoon, it seems to me," he said. "Practically every man and woman in Trumet has his or her stake in our vessel, and they ought to know something of the real whys and wherefores. What about all this we have learned from the Allen girl and that letter? I should like to keep Hope out of all the gabble if possible, for her sake; but it does seem as if Trumet must understand that Jonathan Bangs is cleared of being the traitor and murderer all hands thought he was.

"As it looks now," he went on, "he is about the squarest and bravest friend we've got instead of being the meanest and most cowardly enemy. He's risking everything to pull us through, and, if he fails, no matter what may happen to the rest of us, *his* goose is cooked. More than that, he is going to need the help of every man Jack of us here ashore. The minute the *Gannet* shows up again and near the shoals —*if* she does—our boats, loaded with armed crews, must be ready to head for her. Now the average human works a whole lot better with his eyes open than he does with 'em shut. There'll have to be some explaining done to fill those boats with men ready and glad to fight. The question is, how much shall we tell at that town meeting—or before?"

Elnathan Berry grunted. "If I was dead certain sure that Bangs was straight—" he began. Squire Bailey broke in on him.

"That we must take for granted," he declared. "If he isn't, then—well, we're gone anyhow. Call your town meeting, Jeremiah. Send a crier out asking as many men as can be spared from other duties to be here at the Town House at—say four o'clock. Then have someone—you for preference, because everyone trusts and relies on you—stand up and tell them what we have learned from Jonathan. Don't mention the Forsythe fellow. Don't drag in Hope's name. Just state that you, and other members of their Council, have been put in possession of what seems absolute proof that Jonathan Bangs is not, and never has been, in British pay and that he did not kill Black."

Berry cut in here. "They'll want to know who did, of course," he said. "What answer can Jeremiah make to that?"

"He can tell them the truth. Say we don't know—yet—

who is guilty but that we do know who isn't. Then he can go on to tell how Bangs has been a prisoner in Point Town ever since Monday night, how he is plotting and planning there to save our ship and our enterprise, and how he needs the help of every loyal Trumet citizen. Trowel it on thick, Jeremiah. Don't let them ask questions; don't let them catechize you. Promise them plenty of explanations later, but keep emphasizing that what is needed now is fire and pluck and enthusiasm and whole-hearted Yankee loyalty. I'll back you, if you need backing, and so will Elnathan and Isaiah. I don't think you will need it, though—not after they hear you read parts of the Bangs letter. Set them in a blaze, Jeremiah, and then adjourn. They'll have no time to cool down before the real night's work begins."

That is the way we left it. Game old Jeremiah said he would do his best, but it was plain that he, like the rest of us, knew what a job was ahead of him.

Elnathan had one more word. "What was it Bangs wrote about wishing he had a gun or something? Said he didn't have so much as a jackknife with him, didn't he?"

Hope had heard nothing of our whisperings, for she had been in her corner reading Jonathan's letter over and over. She did hear Elnathan's question, though, and she answered it. "He says," she was reading from the letter: " 'If I can only get hold of some sort of weapon. Perhaps I can while I am aboard the sloop, but I don't see how without exciting more suspicion. The trust these fellows may have in me isn't likely to be whole-hearted. If I only had a pair of pistols handy I should feel a lot more confident.'

"That is what he says," Hope went on.

I grinned. "Well, a loaded pistol in each fist are a couple of powerful arguments sometimes, and that's a fact," I agreed. "But I guess he'll have to do without them so far as we are concerned."

Captain Elnathan snorted. "He'll need a cannon in each

of his breeches beckets to win *this* argument.... Oh, well, we've had talk enough. Let's get going. I'd rather be shot than hung, anyhow. Is your will made out to suit you, Jeremiah?"

As we were coming out of the Town House Bailey touched my arm and motioned with his head. I judged that he had something private to say to me, so I hung back. He waited till the others were well ahead, and then he said it.

"Isaiah," he asked, "what were you intending to do next?"

"I? Why, I've got so many things to do that I couldn't tell you which was next. It must be pretty near noon, so perhaps I may as well get a mouthful to eat. Get it while I can. Lord knows when there'll be another chance."

"For any of us. You're right there. Well, why not come home with me? We'll eat together and talk together. I think there are some things you and I ought to talk about."

I was doubtful. "They'll have to be pretty important things," I told him.

He looked me straight in the eye. "In my opinion," he said, "these things *are* important—very."

"Well.... Oh, all right, Squire, I'll go with you, but I can't stay long.... Hope, I—"

But Hope wasn't there. She wasn't outside on the steps or anywhere in sight. I took it she had gone home, so the Squire and I hurried away together.

3.

Bethuel Bailey was a widower. His house was one of the nicest places in town, not large—not near as large as Captain Weeks's or Berry's or Fowler's, for instance—but a homey, comfortable place with big chairs made to sit in and crickets to put your feet up on and no tidies on the chair backs to rumple up and come unpinned when you leaned your head against them. One of the front parlors he had fitted up for his law office, and, in spite of the shelves of law books and the desk, even it was homey and comfortable. It didn't *smell* like a front parlor, either, if you know what I mean.

It was into this office room that he took me, and he gave his housekeeping woman—Betsy Draper, her name is—orders to bring us something simple to eat and the bottle of Madeira from the locked closet.

"It isn't a full bottle," he told me, "and it is the only one left. I can't give you coffee, Isaiah. You know why and will excuse me, I'm sure."

"I'll excuse anything but blackberry-leaf tea," I told him—and meant it.

The woman brought the food and the bottle and glasses in on a big tray and set the tray on the center table, after she had cleared away the piles of papers and the inkstand and quills and the sand-shaker and hour glass that had been there. We pulled up chairs, and the Squire filled our glasses.

"We must talk as we eat," he said; "but, to begin with, here's luck to the *New Hope*."

"God knows she is going to need it," I vowed, and we drank. He ordered me to help myself to the eatables and then he began to say what was in his mind. I had been so busy and so full of cares and worries that morning, to say nothing of the Town House session we had just finished, that Phoebe Light's story of the change in the day and hour when she put the sheath knife in Jonathan's room had been crowded out of my thoughts. I hadn't forgotten it, by any manner of means, and I realized that it was likely to be mighty important when I found the time to think it through, but I hadn't had that time since I heard it. Bailey had been busy, too, but he had done some thinking, not only after the talk with Phoebe, but before, and now he began to speak his thoughts.

"Isaiah," he said, "Phoebe put that knife of Bangs's back

on his bureau late Saturday night or very early Sunday morning, so she says now. Assuming that she is right this time—and you and I and Ezra believe she is—and the committee, Davies and Allen, both swear it wasn't in the room when they searched it Sunday morning, then—well then, where was it? It was found beside Black's body Monday forenoon. You saw it there, yourself."

"Yes." All this was old stuff, nothing new in it all. I didn't see why he was going over it again.

"Yes. Well, according to Doctor Blodgett's estimate, Seth was killed sometime that same Saturday night. Of course, it looks now as if he wasn't killed with that knife."

This was brand-new, for certain. "What!" I cried out. "Not killed with it? Why, it was there, alongside him, and all bloody, too."

"I know. It was there then, and, whether it was used for the actual killing or not, it was left there for only one purpose, to prove Bangs the killer. He wasn't the killer, of course. The only time *he* could have killed Black was *before* the fire broke out in the yard. And—here is the point —Phoebe had possession of that knife, it was in her broom closet, until *after* the fire, when she put it in Bangs's room. Which not only makes it impossible for Bangs to have used it but seems to prove it just as impossible that Seth was killed with it. Do you see?"

I did see. Perhaps I ought to have seen before, but I'm no lawyer, the Lord knows, and my brain for such things isn't one-two-three compared to the Squire's. I leaned back and stared at him.

"Well!" I puffed. "*Well!* ... And where on earth does that leave us?"

"Just about where we were before. I have always been suspicious about that knife. It was so obvious. If Jonathan left it there he was—"

"A complete fool. Which is exactly what I've said from the beginning."

"I know you have. And you said, too, that he wasn't a fool. All right, no argument between us on that point. Now let's get on to the next one. Whoever did put it beside the body went to a tremendous lot of trouble and took a big risk to get that particular knife. Of all the knives of all kinds in Trumet at least half of them would have been easier to get hold of than that one, I should say. Why, just think what this murdering scoundrel, whoever he was, did! He kills old Seth sometime Saturday night—either before the fire or afterwards, we can't be certain which. If he is our traitor—and I should say he must be—he set the fire. Then came Bangs's arrest by the militia and the big pow-wow at the Town House. What time did you get home that night, Isaiah?"

"Somewhere around two. Yes, it was five minutes to two when I looked at my watch upstairs in my room."

"Phoebe was there before that, wasn't she? ... Never mind, she just told us she was. Did you go right to sleep, Isaiah?"

"Yes, or pretty soon afterwards, I was tired out."

"Naturally; so were most of us. But our murderer wasn't. Or, if he was, he didn't let it interfere with business.... Look here, can you remember one member of our Council who was not in the Town House when they were questioning Jonathan?"

I thought for half a minute. Then I shook my head. "We were all there, every last one of us," I told him.

"I am sure of it, myself. Now our traitor *and* killer—what does he do? He leaves that Town House, after the pow-wow is over and Bangs is on his way to the lockup, and heads for home, as we all do. Very likely he goes home. But he doesn't stay there the rest of the night. My guess would be that, having heard Jonathan satisfactorily damned as a double-dealing traitor and, as he well knows, likely to be branded as a murderer when Black's body is found, it strikes him how completely damning it would be if some piece of personal property belonging to Bangs was found by that same body. And so he goes to the Light place, gets inside, goes to Jonathan's room, sees that sheath knife on the bureau, thinks, I presume, there is truth in the saying that the Devil will always help his own, takes the knife, and hurries back to the edge of Hornpout Pond. After which he really goes home—to stay. How does that guess strike you, Isaiah?"

I drew a long breath. "If he did that he is a cool one," I said. "Cool and—yes, close to crazy, to take such a chance. Phoebe says she put the knife on the bureau—when? Around twelve or so. I came in at two. I got up at six; I don't know when Phoebe got up, I ... Eh? ... By the Lord Harry, I forgot that!"

"What did you forget? Don't forget any more than you can help."

"I remember now—I *had* forgotten it—that when I went out next morning, I found our side door, the one leading to the yard, swinging part-way open. I was almost certain I had shut it when I came in at two. Thought then I was mistaken, of course, but now—"

"Now you wonder who made the mistake. That door hadn't been locked?"

"No, no. Do you lock your doors, Bethuel?"

"No, certainly not. Humph! Well, that guess of mine is one—er—theory. There is another."

"Wait, Squire. Go back to something you said a minute or so ago. It wasn't absolutely needful for the cutthroat to leave a knife alongside the man he had killed. If your guess is the right one he didn't leave it there in the beginning. Instead he thought of it afterwards and risked everything to get Jonathan Bangs's knife, even sneaking in to our house at three o'clock in the morning to get it. And how did he know it was in that room at all? According to Phoebe it wasn't there till an hour or so before he did his sneaking."

"Good point, Isaiah. That struck me, too. The only answer I can think of is that he didn't go there for the knife. He went to Bangs's room to get something, some piece of personal property, that a lot of people would know belonged to Jonathan and nobody else. The knife was there, and nothing could be better for his purpose, so he took that."

"Whew! That makes it look as if he must hate Jonathan the way Cain hated Abel. As if it wasn't alone wrecking the *New Hope* enterprise that would satisfy him, he was risking everything to hang Jonathan."

"That is how I figure it. Bangs had been having troubles at the shipyard for a week or so before the fire, hadn't he?"

I nodded. "Yes. He told me he was as good as sure that somebody was doing little things there to make him look incompetent and careless at his job, hold up the work and get the men down on him. I thought it was his imagination."

"We can bet it was more than that, considering what followed...but we'll leave that train for just now. It is my favorite, but there is another we shouldn't pass by. That room-searching committee from the Council. Davies and Allen were the committee."

"Yes. Captain Elkanah was head, and Henry served with him. What of it? The knife wasn't in the room when they ransacked it. They both said so."

"So they did. But have you thought to wonder if they both went into that room at the same time? Suppose one of them went in ahead of the other and had a half minute alone, by himself, in there. If the sheath knife was in plain sight on the bureau—why—"

We looked at each other. So far as Captain Elkanah was concerned, he was as above suspicion as the Angel Gabriel. But Henry Allen—well, here was Henry bobbing up again. He was one of the members the Squire hadn't been able to locate when he got Weeks and Berry to the Town House this very morning. I was as good as certain at the time that Bailey had tried harder not to find him. Although, of course, there were others he hadn't found.

"Huh!" I grunted. "Yes, I see what you mean. All the same, though, I can't seem to make myself believe it of Henry."

"I know. Neither can I. But is there anybody in our crowd you can believe it of?"

I shook my head. "No." I said.

"But somebody is guilty.... Isaiah, after you and I separated, following our talk with Phoebe and listening to her new story about the knife—"

"This morning, you mean?"

"Yes. After I left you, this thought I have mentioned came to me, and I went back to your house, saw Ezra again, and got him to ask his wife two more questions. The first was if she remembered whether Elkanah and Henry went into the Bangs room Sunday forenoon together or separately. And what do you suppose she said?"

"Lord A'mighty, Bethuel! You don't mean— What did she say?"

"She says that she asked Captain Elkanah some questions about the fire, and, while he was answering them, Allen took the key—she had already taken it from under the mantelpiece and given it to him—and went into the Bangs room alone. Elkanah went in a minute or two later."

He let that sink in. Then, before I could pull myself together enough to say anything, he spoke again. "We mustn't let that prejudice us too much, Isaiah. It is possible, remember, that the knife had already gone from the bureau and the room; that someone had taken it earlier; which would explain why you found the outside door partly open that morning. But I think you will agree that Henry Allen ought to answer a few questions."

"Yes. . . . Yes, indeed."

"He is going to have his chance to answer them. I have ordered Betsy to try and find him, wherever he is, around town or at home, and ask him to come here right away. I think I heard someone come in at the kitchen door a minute ago ... Yes, I thought so. Easy now, Isaiah. Better let me handle it at first."

Betsy was knocking on the office door.

"It's Henry—Mr. Allen, I mean," she said from the other side of the door. "I found him and he's here. Shall I let him in?"

It was Allen, himself, who had the answer to that. He opened the door, pushed past the woman, and stepped into the room.

"Let me in!" he snorted. "Why the devil shouldn't I be let in? Asked me to come here, didn't he? Don't have to have a password to get by, do I? ... Hello, Squire! What—Oh, you're here, Dole, eh? Should cal'late you'd have enough to do this day without sitting round visiting ... Eh? Why, yes, *and* drinking. What you got in that bottle?"

Bailey told him to sit down. There was a little of the Madeira left, and the Squire ordered Betsy to bring an extra glass. She did, and, after she had gone again, the Squire filled it and handed it to Henry, who tasted the wine and smacked his lips.

"I'd have bit sooner if I'd known you used this kind of bait," he chuckled. "Well, what's up? What do you two want of me?"

"Just want answers to a question or two, that's all, Henry. Here's the first one."

It wasn't at all the question I had expected to hear.

"Henry," said the Squire, "when Phoebe Light was up in the village hunting Captain Isaiah, the other afternoon, just before she went back home and somebody hit her over the head—"

"Somebody! Before Jonathan Bangs hit her, you mean. Don't try to tell me there's any doubt in your mind he was the somebody. Two-faced, sneaking, murdering devil! Good God! Why—"

"All right, all right. Let me finish my question. When Phoebe was up there that afternoon, did you see her? Did she talk with you?"

"Eh? Certain sure I saw her. She was flying around like a pullet scared off the roost. I didn't talk with her, though, had something better to do. She would have talked to me, if I'd given her the chance. She'd talk to anybody any time, that woman."

"She didn't say anything to you about wanting to tell Isaiah about some knife or other?"

"No. Maybe she would if I'd have listened. I understand she was cackling about a knife she'd lost or hadn't found or had found—or something like it. From what I hear she wouldn't say enough to make sense. Wouldn't talk straight to anybody but you, Isaiah. Special message for you, she had. Pity you wasn't on hand to get it. You missed a treat, I'll bet."

He chuckled again. Bailey went on.

"Did you see her talking with anyone else? After she left you—or before?"

"Saw her tackle Bounderby and Ike Atwood. All she did was ask where Captain Dole was—or so they say. Last I saw of her she was chasing Eben Fowler. *He* wouldn't bother with her, you can bet on that.... Say, what is all this, anyhow? Has she come to and started to talk again? I heard last night that she was some better."

The Squire dodged that. "Where were you the rest of

that afternoon, Henry?" he asked. "After you talked with Phoebe, I mean."

"Told you I didn't talk with her. . . . Here, come up into the wind a minute! What are you driving at? Are you trying—"

"Shh! All we are trying to do is to find out who Phoebe Light saw and talked with at that time and, if we can, what she said to them. Because, not so very long after she said it—probably *because* she said it—some person in this town tried to kill her."

"What's that got to do with me?"

"Nothing more than it has to do with any decent man or woman. If we can learn just who Phoebe talked with, and what each one of them did immediately after that talk, then we might be able to scratch them off the list, one by one, till we got to the person whose story of what he did doesn't sound straight. Then we could check up on *that* story. That's what we're driving at, Henry. It doesn't mean that we are gunning for you. We don't suspect anybody in particular—yet."

Allen's face was as red as an old-time grenadier's jacket. He jumped from his chair.

"Suspect!" he bellowed. "If you start in heaving your hints at me, I'll—I'll— Look here, you want to know what I did that afternoon, you say? All right, I'll tell you. And, after I get through with that, I'll tell you a few other things. You, Isaiah Dole, in particular, for you're behind all this and all hands know why. That afternoon—Tuesday, it was—I was up town with my horse and truck wagon doing a little carting down to the shipyard. I was helping haul away some of the burnt trash from what was left of the storehouse. Solomon Fletcher will tell you I was there, for he was working with me. After I dumped my last load —there were only two—I asked Sol to come on up to the James Otis and have a dram. He said he would and got up on the cart seat alongside me. . . . That's straight enough so far, ain't it?"

"Certainly, certainly. Captain Isaiah and I are only—"

"Shut up! Well, I hitched my horse to the post outside the tavern; and just then the Light woman came flapping along. She got after us to know if we'd seen Dole anywhere. We said no, and she flapped off after somebody else. Then Sol and I went into the James Otis and had our dram. That was just five minutes past four. I know that because Sol looked at the clock over the counter when we went past it. We sat down at one of the tables and had one rum and molasses and then another. We were sitting there when somebody—Asaph Cahoon, seems to me 'twas—came rampaging in with the news that the Light woman had been killed, or next door to it. Sol said he guessed he'd go out and find out some of the particulars. I was tired, and so I went out and hitched up my horse and drove home. I don't know where Sol went, and I don't give a darn. . . . Now then, that accounts for my time, don't it?"

Bailey nodded. "It does. Much obliged, Henry."

"Much obliged, hell! What do you mean by picking *me* out to get after this way? Why me more than the next fellow? Course I know what Dole here is up to—everybody does. He can't get reconciled to the idea that that Bangs doll baby of his is what we all know he is. Dole knows it, too, only he can't bear to have the town realize that he, himself, was as fooled as the rest of us. Jonathan Bangs, First Officer of the *New Hope!* Gosh Almighty! Well, he didn't fool *me* long. I was suspicious of him from the start. The big, hulking, butter-talking—"

He called Jonathan everything he could think of, and he thought of a lot. I was on the point of stopping him, but Bailey motioned to me to keep still. The Squire let him run down, then he said: "You are pretty bitter against Bangs, aren't you?"

405

"Eh? Bitter? Who wouldn't be bitter against a renegade that would sell out this town the way he did, and kill an old man, and use a hatchet on a woman?"

"From what I hear you were down on him long before any of those things happened. You never did like him, have been talking against him for a long time. That's odd, considering that we all thought he and your daughter—"

"Shut up!" Allen's fist banged the table. "You keep Hope's name out of this, do you hear?"

"Just as you say. But you won't deny that Hope liked Jonathan. Yes, and likes him yet. *She* doesn't believe he is a traitor and a killer. I have heard her say so, and so have you, I imagine."

"She's a soft-headed little fool. Got her head full of notions of story books. Partly my fault for letting her go away to that dratted academy. By the everlasting!"—Henry was so hot that his tongue was running away with him—"why, by the everlasting, I do believe she'd have married that—that bloodsucker, in spite of me or her Uncle Eb or anybody else, if this new devilishness hadn't come along to show him up for what he is. I—I vow to man I don't know that she won't yet—unless he's caught and hung in time to stop her!"

My, but he was raging mad! "Just think of it," he sputtered. "Just think of it! A girl that could have had her pick of some of the best men in Trumet. Ain't it *crazy?*"

Squire Bailey seemed to be thinking.

"Does sound so, as you tell it, Henry, that's a fact. Of course I knew that Atwood and Peleg Bounderby and one or two other young squirts were chasing in that direction a while ago. I don't know that I should call them the best men in town, exactly, but they are all right enough, I suppose."

Henry Allen snorted like a horse with his nose in the feed bucket. "Atwood! Bounderby!" he blurted. "I tell you that girl of mine could have married a man with money, a lot of money. A man who owns the biggest saltworks from Ostable down—and that's only part of what he owns. He's looked up to and respected by everybody. She could have had him by just turning her hand over. Young squirts—nothing! You don't know what you're talking about, Bailey."

The Squire smiled, "I certainly don't—if that's true," he said. "But you are exaggerating a little, aren't you, Henry? The biggest saltworks owner in this section is Eben Fowler."

"Well, what of it? What's wrong with that?"

Bailey's smile broke out into a chuckle.

"Considering that Hope calls him 'Uncle' and that he is old enough to be just that, I should say something was wrong. Speaking as a lawyer I advise you to be more careful with your statements, Henry."

Instead of making him more careful this seemed to make Henry Allen even madder—which may have been the Squire's idea when he said it.

"Uncle! You know darned well Eben ain't her uncle. He ain't any relation to her, course he ain't. She used to call him 'Uncle Eb' when she was little, and she teases him by calling him that once in a while now, that's all. As for being older than she is, what difference does that make? He's got plenty of money and he'd make her a fine husband, and that would give her the place in this town and county a girl like her ought to be thankful to get. . . . Little fool! Throwing it away for a—a state's prison cutthroat!"

My ears were open. They were hearing things I never once suspected. The Squire, though, was still chuckling.

"So you think Eben would like to marry her, eh?" he asked, as if he didn't believe it.

"Think! I tell you I know. He's crazy about her. He's told me so more than a dozen times."

"Has he told her?"

"Yes—or as good as told. But she just laughs and won't listen. She—"

He pulled up short and stood, scowling, first at one and then the other of us.

"What in thunder are we talking about Hope for, anyway?" he growled. "She's nobody's business but her own—and mine—as I know of.... Well, are you two satisfied? Don't want any more of me, do you? If you want to check up on my story of where I was Tuesday afternoon you can ask Sol Fletcher. Yes and the others that were there in the James Otis."

He got up and stamped to the door. Then he turned to glance at me. "And I'm going to say this, too, Dole," he said. "I understand a Council meeting was held a couple of days ago, and I wasn't notified. I was left out, and, from what I can gather from the hint or two that's come my way, you were responsible for my not being there. Afraid I'd ask some things that would be troublesome to answer, I shouldn't wonder. I'm a member of that Council—and an honest one. Full as honest as—well, as some I could name. So don't try that game again."

Before he could shut the door Squire Bailey spoke. "When Fowler told you that I'm sure he didn't tell you Captain Dole was responsible. That part is just your imagination, Henry."

Henry Allen was set back, that was plain.

"I never said Eben told me," he began. "I—well, what if he did? A man is entitled to one square friend."

He slammed out. Bailey leaned back in his chair. "An interesting interview, Isaiah," he said. "Yes—very interesting."

I was trying to hold my head together. There were ideas running through it that I knew just shouldn't be there. They were *too* impossible—and too silly.

"Eben Fowler swore, just as the rest of us did," I said, slowly, and as much to myself as to him, "that he wouldn't tell one word of that meeting where we left Henry out. He knew why Henry was left out, too."

The Squire nodded. "He did," he agreed. "Well, Isaiah," he went on. "Shall we check up on Allen's testimony at the tavern or take it as true? We haven't much time. *I* believe it *is* true."

"Eh? ... Yes, so do I. But—but that about Eben and Hope—Why—"

"Isaiah, we know Fowler has never liked Jonathan Bangs. Perhaps now we can see why.... And I have always—er—fancied that he doesn't like you very well. You and he were after the same girl years ago, weren't you?"

"Yes. He got her, though, finally."

"Why?"

"Oh, I don't know. Yes, I do, too, but we won't talk about it. Probably she thought she would be happier with him than with me."

"I see. Well, from some things I have heard, she wasn't so very happy. Possibly Eben may have realized she wasn't and known—or guessed—the reason why."

I wouldn't say any more on that subject. I told him I must be getting on about my other business.

"That business is important, the Lord knows," said the Squire, "but we haven't finished with this yet, and it, to my mind, is about as important as anything. Isaiah, just before Henry came in here I told you how I went back to the Light home this morning and got Ezra to ask his wife two questions. One of them was whether the search committee went into Jonathan's room separately or together. You know the answer to that—Allen went in alone first. The second question Ezra asked Phoebe was about the hiding place of the key to that room. You have told me that no one but you, Phoebe, and Ezra, and Jonathan himself, knew where that key was kept. That was what you said, wasn't it?"

"Yes. And it is true, nobody else did know."

"Well, when Ezra asked Phoebe about it this morning, she remembered that somebody came to the house—about a week or ten days ago, she thinks it was—looking for you on some business connected with the *New Hope*. She had been in the Bangs room and had left the key on the dining-room table when she went in. When she came out this caller saw her lock the Bangs door and—she doesn't say this, but if he was there of course he did—saw her hang the key on the hook under the mantelpiece. Now, going back to my guess that the knife was taken from that room sometime between two and, say, five last Sunday morning—and I told you that was my favored guess—it could only have been taken by a person who knew, not only that that was the key to Jonathan's room, but where that key was always kept. You say that you found the outside door of the house partly open when you went out Sunday morning. So—"

"Wait, Squire, wait! Who was this fellow who saw Phoebe hang up that key? You don't—you can't mean it was—"

"Wait! I'll tell you that in a minute. I am certain—and I am sure you will agree—that the person who hit Phoebe must be the same villain who stabbed Seth Black."

"Of course, of course." A law training fits a man for picking the bones out of a puzzle and getting at the meat, but it does seem to make him long-winded. "Of course," I said impatiently. "He had to do away with the chance of her remembering the knife couldn't have been used by Jonathan because it wasn't where he could get it until after Seth was killed. We've been over all that."

"I am hurrying as fast as I can. Henry Allen did not attack Phoebe Light. If he was at the tavern with Fletcher he couldn't have."

"Bethuel, *will* you tell me who saw Phoebe put that key under the mantelpiece? If you are going to say it was Eben Fowler—"

"Phoebe declares that is just who it was."

I didn't say anything for a spell, how long a spell I don't know. The temptation was to say "rot" and get up and go away. Eben Fowler! Why, Eben Fowler, of all the solid men in Trumet, was about the solidest. Well off, straight up and down, dignified, trustee on the First Church board, a good-sized shareholder in the *New Hope* enterprise, a patriot. I didn't especially like him, and it might be true that he didn't like me and hated Jonathan, but . . . Oh, bosh!

When I did speak it was to say just that, or what amounts to the same thing.

"Well," I said, "that ends that part of your guessing, Squire. You'll have to call it a dead-end channel and try some other way out—if you can think of one."

He was looking at me as steadily as ever, and he was as earnest. "Isaiah," he said, "you remember the letter you found under the stone on that rock near Shad Cove? The printed letter which began with 'Dear Sir' and was signed 'J. B.'?"

"Did you think I was liable to forget it?"

"Well, when you brought that letter to our Council meeting you may remember that I said something about its being written—or printed—on a rather unusual kind of paper? You do? Good! And do you recollect my saying to you that I had the feeling I had seen that paper, or paper like it, somewhere before? Do you remember that?"

"Why—now you remind me—seems to me I do."

"Well, here is something I think you nor anyone else noticed. I was the last one of our Council to read that letter, and, when I had read it, I folded it and gave it back to you. What you didn't notice was that I didn't give you back the whole of it. I tore off a strip at the lower fold, below the signature, and kept it. You didn't notice that? No? Well, I didn't mean for you to. Here is the strip I kept."

He took it from his pocketbook. It was about an inch one way and three the other. Blank, of course, nothing written on it. It *was* a kind of odd paper, thicker and of better quality than the usual run, and it wasn't lined across, as most writing paper you buy in Trumet is.

"Hold it up to the light," he said. I held it between my eyes and the window, and the sunshine through it showed it was thicker in some places than in others, if you understand what I mean. The thick places looked like flats beginning to show near the top of the water at half ebb.

"That paper didn't come from any store around here," the Squire went on. "It is what we might call a fussy man's paper. Whoever orders and uses paper like this is particular, knows he amounts to something, and intends to have other people know it, too, even if it costs him money. You agree with me so far?"

"I guess so. Sounds reasonable. But, Bethuel, you said you thought you had seen paper like it before. Had you? Do you know where you saw it? Was it here—in Trumet?"

"I had the feeling that it was, but, at the time, I couldn't remember where or when. This morning it came to me. I have done some legal work, not important nor very much, for a business man in this town. He has written me a few letters. Here is one of them. . . . No, no, don't look at the top of the sheet yet. Hold the lower part up to the light as you did the other."

It took all my will power to keep from looking at the top, but I did as he told me. There were the thick spots scattered around. It was the same identical kind of paper, no doubt of that.

"Now look at the printed heading," he ordered. I did that in a hurry. Printed across the top of the sheet was this:

FOWLER SALT WORKS

Eben G. Fowler, PROPRIETOR.

Makers and Wholesalers of Fine and Coarse Salt."

4.

Yes, there it was! And still I couldn't believe it. The Squire went on talking. "It looks—well, at least probably," he said, "as if the Dear Sir, J. B. letter was written on paper torn from a sheet like that one in your hand. Of course there may be some other person in Trumet who uses paper of that kind, but I don't know one other who would be likely to."

I am guessing that was what he said. I didn't hear it plain. The absolute impossibility of the idea—of the idea that must be in his head—was too strong for me to shake. It was like running bows on against a rock where you knew a rock couldn't be.

Eben Fowler! Eben—Oh, no, no!

"But, Bethuel," I sputtered; "but Bethuel, I—Oh, you can't mean it! Why should a man like Eben Fowler turn renegade and sell out his country, to say nothing of murdering an old man? *Why?* He doesn't need the money. He's rich—or, at least, we all suppose he is."

Bailey shook his head. "I don't know much about his money affairs," he said; "but I hear that he has been landed with a lot of bad debts since the blockade. That isn't material, anyhow, as I see it. If this idea of mine has any truth in it at all, money, one way or the other, doesn't play much part in it. Isaiah, have you noticed anything—er—peculiar about Eben lately?"

"Eh? Peculiar? I've noticed that he acts pretty nervous,

413

in Council meeting especially—nervous and, maybe, touchy when you cross him; but that's nothing to wonder at. We're all nervous these days."

"I have begun to think it is more than nervousness. Besides that letter of his you have there, I have three or four others that he has written me in the last few months. Some of them—well, they aren't very clear. They emphasize matters of no importance and slur important ones. They are impatient, crotchety—sometimes so much so that I was tempted to write him he had better get another lawyer, for I didn't care to act for him any longer. And—Isaiah, do you remember Sarah Hutchings, who was his housekeeper for so long?"

"Certainly. She left a couple of months ago and went to live with her sister in Orham. He's got somebody else now."

"He had yesterday; whether or not he has today I don't know. Sarah Hutchings didn't leave; Eben pitched her out, bag and baggage. He owed her wages, and she came to me about it. Crying, she was. According to her no decent self-respecting woman could work for a man like Mr. Fowler. He has changed altogether in the last year, so she says. Ugly and glum some of the time, speaking hardly a word for days, and, every once in a while, flying in a rage over next to nothing. She told me some of the names he called her when he gave her her walking papers. If she didn't exaggerate—well, I wonder she didn't get after him with the poker. And, Isaiah—"

"Yes, yes. Go on. This is the—well, heave ahead."

"Isaiah, Doctor Blodgett was here at dinner with me last week. He told me that he was worried about one of his patients. After a little it came out that this patient was Fowler. He said Fowler's nerves were in a wretched state, that he couldn't sleep without drugs, that he was so irritable—Wait, what's that?"

I hadn't heard anything, but I had something in my head that couldn't wait.

"Bethuel," said I, "you are trying to tell me you believe Eben Fowler is crazy. Well, *I* don't—I can't. And, anyhow, could a crazy man plan out all this cussedness as carefully as it must have been planned, and carry it through? You know he couldn't."

"I didn't say he was completely crazy. I said he might not be altogether sane. He is a peculiar man, always has been, and a proud one. He broods over things. Well, if what Henry Allen told us a few minutes ago is true—that about Hope's refusing to listen to him as a possible husband—it must be a blow to his pride, a hard one. . . . Yes? Who is it?"

It was the Betsy woman knocking. She opened the door. "Mr. Bailey," she said, "Caleb Fisher is here, and he says Major Bartlett sent him. He wants to find Captain Isaiah, came here looking for him."

Young Fisher—he was about eighteen or so—was all rigged up in his militia uniform. His face was red and his forehead wet, as if he had been running. He didn't forget to salute, though—every man and boy that attended militia drill had the saluting trick down pat—and he spoke to me the second he was across the door sill.

"Captain Dole," he said, "Major Bartlett is up to Mr. Eben Fowler's house, and he wants to see you there right off. I've been hunting for you all over."

I looked at the Squire and found he was looking at me. What was the old saying? Talk about angels and you would hear their wings flap, something like that. Coming at this particular time it must have struck Bethuel as strange, just as it did me.

"The Major wants me to come up to Fowler's?" I asked. "What for? What is he doing there?"

Young Caleb looked as if he wanted to say a good deal

but had orders not to say anything. "Don't know," was his answer. "Major Bartlett, he asked you to please come, that's all."

"Is Mr. Fowler there, himself?"

"Yes, sir, he's there."

I turned to the Squire. "Better go, hadn't I," I said. "You'll come with me, won't you, Bethuel?"

He said he would, and we started along with Caleb. On the way Bailey fell into step with the boy, and I heard them whispering together. I didn't listen. What with the things I had just heard and wondering what was coming next, my mind was a whirligig. One thing I do recollect was passing Sylvanus Tiddett, the town crier, ringing his bell and calling all hands to the special meeting at the Town House. People were hurrying that way already.

Fowler's good-sized white house was on the little hill the other side of the Bay Road. A private driveway led from the road up to the front door. The yard was neat as a man-of-war's quarter deck, and so was the side door and the step in front of it. Eben's newest housekeeper let us in. She looked frightened and upset, I thought.

She said Mr. Fowler was with Major Bartlett in the sitting-room and she would tell them we were here. Bailey took the chance, while she was gone, to tell me a word or two. The Fisher lad hadn't come into the house with us.

"An odd thing has happened," whispered the Squire, speaking fast. "It seems that the guard at the harbor mouth saw a rowboat put out from the beach near them a little while ago. They had orders from Bartlett—your orders, I suppose, Isaiah—not to permit anyone, no matter who, to leave town today, so they got after this boat, three or four of them, in a dory of their own. There was only one man in the other boat, and they caught him easily. They think he was bound for the *Hawke*, although he didn't say so. Fisher says he didn't say anything except to rage at them for daring to interfere with him and cursing the Major and the militia up hill and down dale.

"They hung on to him, though—and, considering what an important man he is, they deserve a medal for sticking by their orders—brought him to this house and sent for Bartlett. And Bartlett sent for you. I got all of this from Caleb. He was afraid to tell, but I vowed I would take all the responsibility and square him with the Major. The man in the boat, Isaiah, was—Eben Fowler."

I had seen it coming, but it hit me pretty near as hard as if I hadn't. I mumbled something, it doesn't matter what. Bailey had time for a word more.

"According to Fisher," he said, "Fowler was in a furious state. 'Acted wild-like,' those were Caleb's words for it."

The woman came back then, and we followed her to the sitting-room. Before the door of that room was open I could hear voices behind it, Major Bartlett's crisp crackle and Eben's heavy bass. Usually that bass was deliberate and dignified. Now it sounded like a bull's bellowing, a bull that had bellowed so much already that he was hoarse. I squared my shoulders and set myself for trouble.

I wish I could give you a little idea of how that room looked when we went into it. A good-sized room it was, fine carpet on the floor, mahogany furniture, mahogany spinet in one corner, two silver candlesticks on the mantelpiece, gilt-framed portraits on the walls—pictures of Elijah Fowler, Eben's father, and Temperance Fowler, his mother, she that was Martha Allen, Henry's sister, the girl I had meant to marry and that Eben did marry. The artist who painted that picture was a good hand at his work. He had made her look just as I remembered her—young and pretty and with the little smile at the corners of her mouth. . . . Oh, well! I didn't have much chance to look at pictures. There were other things to catch my attention.

The two men in the room were standing facing each

other when Bailey and I came in. Little Major Bartlett's back was as straight up and down as a flag pole. He was nearest the door. Eben Fowler was at the other side of the room, and, after one sight of him, I didn't look at anything else.

He was dressed in black, same as he usually wore. The coat was splashed and muddy in places, and it and his figured waistcoat were unbuttoned, showing the fine white linen shirt underneath. The shirt had a high collar with a black neckcloth, or stock, as they call it now, folded around it. The collar was crumpled, and one end of the neckcloth hung loose. His hair, which he always kept so carefully brushed, was standing every which way. These things I noticed first because they were, for him, so unusual. The average run of Trumet was liable to be fairly careless about clothes, except when it dressed up for church meetings, but Eben Fowler was always carefully rigged from main truck to keelson, weekdays as well as Sundays.

As I say, I noticed the things I have mentioned first, but I forgot them when I looked at his face. It was bright red—no, more than red—it was purple. His eyes were sunken, they looked as if he hadn't slept for nights and nights; but they blazed as he glared at the Squire and me. He didn't waste time on how-d'you-dos or good afternoons. His first word was a question to me, and he was so raging mad that he could hardly hold his voice straight in the course. And yet you could see he was fighting to keep it dignified.

"Ah, there you are—at last," he snarled. "And time, too, I should say. Look here, Dole, are you responsible for this outrage? This—this brass-buttoned little upstart"— pointing at Bartlett—"tells me you are. Says it is by your orders that I have been manhandled by his—his ridiculous clam-diggers playing at soldiers. I ask you again—*are* you responsible? Because if you are—"

I don't know how much further he would have gone on,

but I stopped him. I had to speak twice and raise my voice to make him hold up, but I did, finally.

"I can't answer anything, Eben," I said, "until I know what is going on and what it is all about. Suppose we let Major Bartlett have his say first. Go on, Major."

The Major's face was red, too, but he didn't hesitate a second. His story was just what the Fisher boy had told Bailey. The guard at the breastwork by the harbor mouth had seen a boat leaving the shore, had hailed the man in it and ordered him to turn back. When he paid no attention, four of the guard got into a dory, chased and caught the other boat, and brought the man back to shore with them. Then they sent for the Major, and he had taken charge. While the Major was telling this, Eben kept trying to interrupt, but I wouldn't let him.

"Of course," ended Bartlett, "my men were surprised when they recognized Mr. Fowler, but they had their orders to let nobody—*nobody*—leave this town today, and they obeyed those orders. I am pleased with them, and I told them so; they behaved like good soldiers. I told Mr. Fowler I didn't doubt that he had a good reason for going out in that boat but that my men weren't supposed to ask for or consider reasons. Their business was to carry out the orders of their superior officer, and that is what they did. I told him, too"—it was fine to see the little man's back bristles rise—"that I was that officer and the orders were mine. He demanded to go to his own house, and I saw no reason why he shouldn't, so a couple of my men and I brought him here. I sent for you, Captain Dole, because it was you who gave me *my* orders. That is all, sir."

Again Fowler started to bellow, but this time it was the Squire who headed him off. It was the first word Bailey had spoken since we came into that room.

"One moment," he said. "Wait, Eben; let him finish.

Major Bartlett, has Mr. Fowler explained to you why he was in that boat and where he was going?"

Major Bartlett's spine curved backwards. "Squire Bailey," he snapped, "I gave Mr. Fowler every chance to explain; although, of course, I told him that he must make the same explanation to Captain Isaiah Dole, he being in command of us all at the present time. Instead of explaining, Mr. Fowler chose to call me—to—well, never mind. The only thing I care to hear from him after this is an apology to me, personally. *That* I *shall* expect."

There was no shake in *his* voice, it was all hot iron. He turned to me.

"With your permission, Captain Dole," he said, "I shall leave the—er—prisoner in your hands and go about my other duties. I have a lot to attend to."

I looked at the Squire and he nodded. "You may go, of course, Major," I said. "And thank you and your men. I'll see you again in a little while."

Bartlett turned on his heel, bowed to both of us, and marched out. He didn't bow to Eben, didn't so much as look at him. The door had already shut when Fowler was raging once more. It was me he was raging at—he seemed to pay no attention to Bailey.

What the devil did I mean? Did I realize who he was? Who gave me authority to interfere with him? And so on—a lot of it. As soon as I could, which was when he ran out of breath, I tried to soothe him.

"Come, come, Eben," I said. "There is no need of all this; I am in charge of such things here in Trumet, and I did give Bartlett strict orders to keep everybody inside town limits. Naturally he and his men had to treat you like anyone else. Now let's sit down and talk it over. You can tell us why you—"

. "I'll tell you nothing. And who are you to invite yourself to sit in this house? This is *my* house, and you, Isaiah

420

Dole, or any—er—parasite of yours, shall not sit in it while I am alive."

The Squire was the particular parasite he was shooting at just then, I presume likely, but it didn't bother the Squire any. "There, there, Eben," he coaxed. "Don't excite yourself this way. We are all friends here."

"Friends!" Fowler fairly screamed it. It was then that I began to believe in the Squire's theory that he was going crazy. "Friends!" he yelled. "Do you dare call that—that damned villain, Dole, a friend of mine?"

He leaned towards me, his fists clenched tight. "You, Isaiah Dole!" he snarled. "I have hated you for thirty years. For thirty years I have been waiting to get even, and now I'm going to do it."

He swung around and pointed at Martha's portrait on the wall. "Do you see that?" he croaked, his hoarseness catching him again. "Do you see her? I saw you look at her when you came in. You *dared* to look at her! You took her away from me. She married me—yes; but it was you she cared for. She told me so before she died. Said it in so many words, by God! She—Stand back there, both of you!"

The Squire and I must have made a move towards him, I guess. Something had to be done, the man was stark mad. His face was working, the sweat was running down his forehead, and he was twitching all over. He jumped back behind the big center table and motioned, as if he was pushing us away from him with both hands. We stayed where we were.

"I vowed then I'd get you, Dole, if ever you came near me again. I swore that. And then, years afterwards when I began to forget and someone else was—was taking her place—you *did* come. And you brought that Bangs devil with you. Oh—"

The names he called Jonathan would have made a

drunken fishboat crew ashamed to hear. There was no stopping him, and the table was between us, besides.

"And *he* took *her* away," he raved. "He hasn't got her, though. I may not, but he shan't. He'll hang—hang—hang! And so will some of the rest of you, if I have my way. You and your fool privateer! Where will your *New Hope* be before this time tomorrow? Oh, I planned it well! I let nothing or nobody stand in my way They're saying—old Jerry Weeks told me so, himself, an hour ago—that it looked now as if Bangs wasn't a traitor or a murderer, either. He says the town will learn that he isn't at the meeting in the Town House. 'But who *can* it be, Eben?' he said. I almost laughed in his face. *I* could have told him! *I*—Back there, I tell you! *Back!*"

We must have made another move, for he reached down, jerked open a drawer in the table before him, took out a pair of pistols, and was pointing them at us, one in each hand.

Nobody moved for a breath, and then we all did. "Grab him, Bethuel!" I shouted and started around the table.

There was a big flash of fire before my eyes and a roar like a clap of thunder. The next thing I knew was that I was on the carpet, my head in the Squire's lap, and he was asking me if I was dead.

I wasn't. I had a—well, you might call it a furrow—along my scalp, and my hair was bloody when I reached up to feel of it. It was as close as that, but I wasn't hurt a pennyworth. I lifted myself on one elbow and looked around. There was nobody but us two in the room. Outside, in the other part of the house somewhere, a woman was screaming.

"Where is he? Where is Eben?" I asked.

Squire Bailey drew a big breath. "Whew!" he panted. "Eben? Oh, he's gone—somewhere. We'll catch him later, he can't get away.... Whew! ... Good Lord, Isaiah! I was just thinking that our *New Hope* had turned to *no* hope. When I saw you go down, I. ... Well, I should say we had answered our riddle, shouldn't you?"

I shook my sore head. "I should," I agreed. "And what do you suppose Trumet will say when it hears what that answer is? As for myself—well, if I didn't smell powder smoke I should think I had been dreaming. Come on! This is no time for naps. Give me a hand up, and we'll get going."

5.

We hurried out of that place and set sail for the Town House. As we raced through the kitchen to the back door we passed the Fowler housekeeping woman. She was still screaming and crying, frightened half to death. Seems that she had heard the shot and seen Eben rush out of the sitting-room, waving his pistols. She wasn't hurt, so we didn't waste but a minute on her.

When we got to the Town House the meeting had been under way quite a while. Squire Bailey was bound I should see the doctor and have my furrowed topknot attended to, but Doctor Blodgett had gone to the meeting, like everybody else. The Squire—he can be obstinate when he sets out to be—sent word in for him to come into the entry and have a look at me before we went in.

When he did come he was all excitement. Captain Jeremiah and Captain Elnathan, between them, had broken the news of Jonathan Bangs's innocence and were explaining what Jonathan had been up to in Point Town and what he hoped to do to help us with the *Gannet*. Captain Elnathan was speaking now, and, judging by the cheers and yells, he was doing a good job at poking the fire. As near as we could learn by the few careful questions we asked Doctor Blodgett, no mention of Hope Allen's name had been made —so far, at least. I was glad to hear that.

The doctor would have asked a hundred questions of his own about how my head got hurt, what it all meant, and what was really going on, but we told him all explaining would have to wait. Yes, we did know who our traitor was and who had killed Seth Black and knocked over Phoebe Light, but that would have to wait, too.

We asked him if Henry Allen was at the meeting. He said he was and would have made trouble—at the beginning, anyhow—but the crowd was so excited and anxious to hear Weeks that it howled Henry down every time he opened his mouth. I couldn't help grinning to myself when he told that. Poor old Henry! I thought. *He* is in for some revelations—a whole book of them. His little mud god has crumbled, and that's a fact.

As soon as the doctor got the last plaster battened down on my skull, I pushed him to one side and headed for the door of the meeting hall. The place was jammed; Bailey and I had to fight to get through the bunch at the outside end of the main aisle. As soon as the people saw us pushing our way along there was, first a rustle, then a rumble, and then a roar. All hands stood up.

Considering how I must have looked, with all that doctor padding on my head, I wasn't surprised that my entrance caused a sensation, as the newspapers tell about; but I *was* surprised when somebody astern of me yelled for three cheers for Captain Isaiah Dole. They gave those cheers, too. I could hardly believe they were for me. It was only such a little while ago that, when I went down the main road, I felt as if I was wearing an "unclean" sign, like a leper in the Bible.

Oh, well! Crowds are like that. It doesn't take much to switch them from larboard to starboard. And this particular crowd, you must remember, was all wrought up anyhow. They knew, of course, that this night was to be live or die, so far as all they had worked and hoped for for months was concerned. The "live" part had been getting to be pretty dubious in the minds of most of them. Now that Jeremiah and Elnathan had pumped a little pepper into their hope buckets they were more cheered up than they had any right to be—a whole lot more, as I saw it.

Captain Elnathan Berry saw me pushing up the aisle and motioned—there was so much noise he couldn't make me hear—to come on the platform. I got up there, somehow, and the whooping then was louder than ever, if that was possible.

"Talk to them, Isaiah," he yelled in my ear. "Now is the time. Jeremiah and I have got them going. Now is your chance. You and the Squire talk to them."

I'm no Fourth of July speechmaker, Lord knows, and you better believe I didn't hanker for the job. However, now *was* our chance, just as he said. I stepped to the front of the platform.

There was another thunder of cheering, but they were noticing my bandaged main truck now, and the clap died down to a buzz like a dozen upset hornets' nests. Somebody yelled: "What ails your head, Isaiah?"

I held up my hands. "Just the first shot in the war, that's all," I called back. "You'll hear all about it later, but we can't bother with little things now. The inside of the head is all right, I hope—and ready for work. Much obliged for all those cheers, but I don't deserve them half as much as somebody else does. That somebody has been called a murderer and a traitor—that's what we all called him—but, as Captain Weeks has just told you, we know now that he is the best and bravest friend we've got, and, if what we expect and believe he is doing at this minute goes through, it will be he, more than all the rest of us put together, who sends our privateer into clear water. So *I* say, let's give three cheers for Jonathan Bangs, First Officer of the *New Hope*."

That set them off. Only that morning they were all for

hanging Jonathan—most of them would have come to the hanging and brought their dinners—and now they were cheering their heads off for him. And they didn't really *know* much more than they knew before; just took Weeks's and Berry's word that Bangs was all right and planning to help them, that's all. Human nature is a good deal of a disgrace when you get a lot of it together in a bundle.

As soon as I could hear my own voice I stepped to the front of the platform again. Before I could begin, though, there was a disturbance at the back of the hall. It got louder and louder. A man—one of the militia men, it was—was shoving and being shoved down the aisle.

"Captain Isaiah! Captain Isaiah!" he was shouting. I held up my hands once more.

"All right, Jonas, what is it?" I shouted back. "Shsh! Quiet, all hands, please.... What is it, Jonas?"

The man was wet and out of breath from running. "Major Bartlett, he sent me," he panted. "He says to tell you that the *Gannet* has been sighted in the Bay, and it looks as if she was heading straight for Horse Mackerel Bar."

Elnathan Berry jumped up. Jeremiah Weeks jumped up. Everybody in that hall—they had begun to sit down after the cheers for Jonathan—stood up again. It was my chance and I took it.

"Here we go, boys!" I sang out. "This is what we've been waiting for. All hands to your stations!"

8

In which a pinky and a brigantine
run into trouble.

Told by

JONATHAN BANGS

1

CAPTAIN DOLE HAS made it clear enough, I think, that life in the village of Trumet on that pleasant Friday afternoon in August 1814, was anything but tranquil. With its streets thronged with the rapidly assembling crew of the *New Hope*, together with those who had come to bid them good-by; with the intense excitement attending the knowledge that the risky attempt to land the powder would be made that night; with the grim hunt for a murderer and traitor still going on, Trumet was certainly not the place that a man badly in need of rest for his jangled nerves and tired body would be likely to pick out.

Yet pick it out I did, and with longing, for from my place on the deck of the sloop, *Gannet*, which was at the time cruising far out on the waters of the Bay, the long, low, snow-white line of its sandy shore was deceptively peaceful in appearance. If I could have been granted one single wish just then, it would have been to be set down anywhere within Trumet's boundaries.

Yet, so far as appearances went, I realized that to the casual onlooker there was no visible reason why a berth aboard the *Gannet* should have been sneered at. The day was a fine one for sailing, with a fresh southwest wind no more than ruffling the dark blue waters of the Bay. The sky overhead was clear, with a great pile of fluffy white clouds towering up from the horizon in the direction of the mainland. The sloop herself was trim, with clean sharp lines and a snowy expanse of canvas that stretched against the wind as smooth and unwrinkled as the head of a drum. To a sea gull, for instance, sailing overhead, the *Gannet* might well have appeared a pleasant craft, pleasure bound, on a pleasant afternoon.

But there, again, appearances would have been deceptive.

The man at the wheel, acting under my orders as pilot, was setting a course that would lead us to nowhere in particular and then bring us back again, much in the manner of a craft that is being sailed merely for the fun of sailing it. Our objective, however, was not pleasure, but merely to waste time.

It had been shortly after noon when Lieutenant Waterman and I boarded the *Gannet* in Point Town Harbor. On that occasion, if we never did so again, the Lieutenant and I saw eye to eye on the subject of what had best be done next. We both were anxious, almost frantic, to get away as quickly as possible from Point Town and the *Terror*. My fear, of course, was that Jermyn Forsythe might escape from his stateroom and from the strips of linen with which I had bound him in time to give the warning that I was no traitor to my country.

Waterman, of course, had no knowledge of what was in Forsythe's mind, but was equally anxious to get out of his way. It was easy enough to read Waterman's thoughts. He was afraid that, if Forsythe talked, our trip on the *Gannet* might be postponed—or even cancelled altogether.

Waterman had said in so many words that "all hell" would not serve to prevent him from having his revenge upon me, and his first act as we came over the *Gannet's* rail showed that he meant what he said. He met young Hawley, the officer who had been in charge of the sloop at her post off the mouth of Billfish Creek, with the curt announcement that he was hereby relieved of his command. Almost in the same breath he said that the three young midshipmen on duty aboard were to go back with Hawley to the *Terror.*

The last part of that order surprised me, and I'm frank to say that it frightened me a little, for it showed the lengths to which Waterman was willing to go to make sure that I should be entirely at his mercy, once we put out into the loneliness of the Bay. It was evident from the puzzled expression on Hawley's face that it surprised him, too—if for different reasons.

"Aye, aye, sir. We'll leave at once." He was wholly respectful, but there was hesitance in his voice. "May I ask if you intend to take the sloop out again—alone—without another officer?"

"Exactly." Waterman frowned. "Those are Captain Holt's orders. Have you any objections?"

"None at all, sir, of course." Hawley shook his head hastily, denying any such impertinence. But he was still genuinely troubled, and unable to refrain from expressing what was on his mind. "It just occurs to me, sir, to wonder if you will be entirely safe—being the only officer among a crew of more than twenty. Not that the crew isn't well disciplined—it is. But they're a rough lot—and if they found out that you and one other were the only—"

"Don't worry, Hawley! My pilot, Bangs, and I will be quite safe. I'm armed, and the crew is not." Waterman laughed shortly, patting two ugly pistols that were tucked conspicuously into the front of his belt. "I'm taking it for granted that there are no arms among the crew."

"Certainly not, sir." Hawley shook his head. "We never issue small arms to the crew until the last moment before an action. All the rest of the time they're locked up safe in the arms chest. Here, by the way, is the key to that." He handed it over. "But still, sir—"

"That's enough! You've heard your orders, Mr. Hawley. Obey 'em at once."

Waterman had turned away and was issuing orders to get the sloop under way before Hawley and the three midshipmen had had time to scramble over the side into the dinghy. The anchor and the mainsail both came up as smartly as could be asked, and in no time at all the *Gannet* was running for the mouth of Point Town Harbor and the open Bay beyond.

I heaved a sigh as the silhouette of the *Terror*, astern, grew smaller in size, under my anxious gaze. Part of that sigh was relief at having been permitted to come safely so far along the road, and part of it was an acknowledgment that the path ahead was certain to be strewn with anything but roses. Unless I missed my guess it would be, for me, strewn with Waterman's hatred and his two vicious pistols.

Waterman, himself, lost no time in letting me know exactly where I stood. He came up to me with both hands lovingly on the butts of his weapons and spoke quietly, but without being able to keep his satisfaction out of his voice. "Well, Mr. Bangs, you did your impudent damnedest to get me into trouble with my captain. Enjoyed it, too, no doubt. Very good and very clever—but where did it get you? Well, I'll tell you just where!" He laughed. "It got you aboard the *Gannet*, under me as your commanding officer, *and* bosom companion. You needn't fear that I'll be anything but a loving one, for I swear I'll never leave your side. Every moment of every hour you'll find me, and my pistols, at your shoulder—and at your service! Do you understand?"

"Yes, sir." I understood only too well, but I refused to give him the satisfaction of knowing it. "I'm grateful for your help, and I assure you that I'll do everything I can to put you and your men in the right place at the right time. If trying has anything to do with it, not many hours will pass before you'll have the pleasure of blowing the American powder barge into a million bits!"

"For your sake, Bangs, I surely hope so." He scowled. "Captain Holt, being soft-hearted, told you that you might not suffer for it if the American powder should escape your best efforts. I doubt if *I* will be able to make myself quite so agreeable. I advise you to see that nothing goes wrong. Otherwise—eh?" he patted the pistols suggestively. "Well, so much for that. I wanted you to understand what will happen if I see anything that is even faintly suspicious about your actions. I give you my oath that I'll shoot first and investigate afterwards! Is that clear? Good! Then, you may give the helmsman the course you want sailed. Being always at your service, I'll see that he sails it!"

The course that we sailed was unimportant at that time, as I pointed out, since we had considerable time to waste. I had not asked to be put aboard the *Gannet* until mid-afternoon, while it was not yet one o'clock. In addition to that, I said, it had been my intention to take the *Gannet* away from her station off Billfish Creek for the sole purpose of trying to persuade the people of Trumet that the coast might be clear for their powder landing. Since the sloop was already off her station, there would be nothing for us to do—as I informed Lieutenant Waterman—but to cruise aimlessly in the deep water of the Bay, at some distance from the Trumet shore.

I fretted, of course, under the necessary inaction of the next few hours, but it gave me ample opportunity to study my chances of finding a way out of the trap I had so carefully built for myself. My general plan, which I had set down in outline in my letter to Captain Dole, was simple enough. I intended to run the *Gannet* hard aground, high and dry, on some sand bar close to the mouth of Billfish Creek, at about half-past five o'clock that afternoon. The tide in the Bay would be about three quarters of the way out at that time, and I knew if I did my job well, no power on earth would be able to float the sloop again for a matter of hours.

Once the *Gannet* was firmly aground, what happened next would depend largely upon Captain Dole. If the Point Town fisherman had lived up to his promise to see that my letter reached Trumet safely and promptly, the Captain would be ready to act at the proper time. Small boats full of armed men would be lying hidden in Billfish Creek, and at the signal would swarm out to overwhelm Waterman and his crew. At least, I devoutedly hoped they would.

And even if my letter had altogether miscarried, it seemed to me that events should rightfully go in much the same way. Major Bartlett's militia guard could not fail to see the kind of trouble the *Gannet* was in, and, seeing it, they would know—unless I sadly misjudged their commander—exactly what to do. The tide would give them plenty of time in which to gather men and boats for a boarding party.

Yes, my plan, which had seemed neat enough when I wrote it down in Jermyn Forsythe's cabin on the *Terror*, seemed neat enough still. If it succeeded, the *Gannet* would be in American hands long before the tide floated her again at about nine o'clock that night. Once afloat, under the Stars and Stripes and the command of Captain Dole, her brass cannon would provide enough protection for our powder barge so that they could ignore any attempts the British might make to prevent a landing.

Oh, yes, I thought grimly to myself, the whole affair seemed very neat to the superficial eye. From my point of view, however, there were things about it that promised to be anything but neat.

Of those things, Lieutenant Harry Waterman was undoubtedly the most important, and most unpleasant. I felt a cold, creeping sensation along my spine when I thought of how the Lieutenant was almost certain to act when the time for action arrived. I already had his solemn assurance that he and his pistols would never leave my side for so much as an instant, and so far it seemed that he intended to keep his promise. I also had his word for it that on the first suspicion of trickery he would drill me through the head with a pistol bullet first and think about it later. Knowing very well the nature and intensity of his dislike for me, I didn't even pause to question the sincerity of that statement. Waterman would shoot as quick as a wink if I gave him a half-way excuse for pulling the trigger.

Forcing myself to face the fact that unless I had incredible luck I should be very dead a moment after the *Gannet's* keel touched sand, I wondered further if Waterman would be stupid enough to let me accomplish even that much. I decided that the odds were decidedly against, but, trying to be as critical and disinterested as though it was somebody else's perfectly good blood that was likely to be splattered about the surrounding scenery, I also decided that a few omens were favorable instead of the reverse.

I knew that Waterman had been drinking more than a little while he was ashore at Point Town that morning. If he continued to drink during the rest of the day, he might possibly get himself into a state where his watchfulness might momentarily slacken. If that happened I must take advantage of it instantly. I knew, too, that Waterman was wholly ignorant of the treacherous and unexpected sand bars of the Bay. Not knowing them, and having sent away Hawley and the midshipmen, who would have given him warning, perhaps he would not wake up to what I was doing until it was too late to prevent it. A third cause for hope was my knowledge that Waterman, of all the twenty-odd men aboard the *Gannet*, was the only one who was armed. If, therefore, I could somehow throw him off guard long enough to snatch those two pistols from his belt, I ought to be able to have things very much my own way.

Just how I was to accomplish such a thing, in the face of Waterman's suspicious and alert watchfulness, I could not make up my mind—nor had I made it up at four o'clock when our aimless meandering about the Bay was interrupted by a call from the lookout in the bow.

"Small boat ahead, sir—just off the starboard bow! Looks as if she's in trouble, sir! Her sail is down, and she's rolling in the trough. Man aboard her's waving for help, sir!"

"Let him wave!" Waterman was angrily impatient. "What does he think this navy is—a life-saving charity? What's a boat doing way out here, anyhow?" He turned to me, his eyes narrowing at the thought. "Damned odd, it strikes me! How do you account for it, Bangs?"

"I can't, sir." I was genuinely as much puzzled as he was. "Not many craft dare come out in the Bay, these days, on account of your patrol. A fisherman, or a man with business in Boston important enough to make him take the risk, might try it—but only at night or in a thick fog. No American in his senses would poke his nose out here on a clear day like this."

"Damned odd!" Waterman tried to catch a glimpse of the boat in question without letting me out of his sight. "The trouble is, I'm not just sure what my duty is. Prizes and prisoners aren't part of my business just now. Still, the thing's odd, and perhaps I'd better have a look." He turned to the helmsman. "Run close enough to that craft so that I can speak to her, but don't lay her alongside. For all we know, this may be a piece of Provincial dirty work!" He eyed me coldly. "It isn't a part of *your* scheming, is it, Bangs?"

"No, sir, it's not." I was thoroughly sick of the fellow and his silly suspicions. "How could I possibly have arranged anything like this—and what good would it do me? You may think I'm a fool, Lieutenant, but I'm not such a fool that I'd try any tricks on a man with two pistols that he wouldn't hesitate to use!"

"Good, Bangs. I'm relieved to hear it." He made me a mocking little bow. "It would be a sad day, indeed, for me if I was forced to—er—dispense with the pleasure of your company! Lookout!" He raised his voice to shout. "Can you make out that craft any better now? Is she armed?"

"No, sir, she ain't. She's just a tiny little tub, more'n 'arf full of water. Looks as though her main sheet had parted, sir, the canvas is piled up round the feet of the bloke aboard her. He—Well, by God!" The lookout's oath showed his complete astonishment. "Begging your pardon, sir, it ain't a *he* aboard her—it's a *she!*"

"What?" Waterman cupped a hand behind one ear. "Speak louder, you fool! What are you trying to say?"

"I'm saying, sir, that it ain't a man that's waving to us— it's a woman! I can see her skirts, now, just as plain as not!"

"A woman! Well, I'm damned! Can't a man get away from petticoats even in mid-ocean?" Waterman laughed shortly at his own joke and spoke again to the man at the wheel. "Heave to, when you get close enough, and we'll have a word with this seafaring charmer!"

A moment or two later the wheel was spun sharply, and the *Gannet* came smoothly up into the wind. As she hung there, trembling, I heard, over the slatting of the canvas, a cool, clear, unperturbed woman's voice giving us a hail.

"Ahoy, the *Gannet!* Can you lend me a hand, here? I'm in trouble!"

The voice was one I would have recognized anywhere in the world. It belonged to Hope Allen.

2.

Only a few minutes later Hope and I were face to face again, but we were a long, long way—in more ways than one—from the pine-scented warmth of Doane's Hollow where we had faced each other as lovers. We were strangers instead of lovers, now, and enemies instead of friends. Since fate had ruled that this reunion must take place at all, it seemed to me, in my bitterness, that the deck of a British armed sloop of war was as suitable a place as any.

I use the words "in my bitterness" deliberately, for bitterness was the strongest of all the sensations that swept over me when I recognized Hope's voice and looked down from the *Gannet's* deck to see her slight, straight figure swaying easily with the wallowings of her half-swamped cockleshell of a boat. I remember thinking, as I gazed dumbly at the glinting mahogany of her tumbled spray-soaked hair, that, of all the foul tricks that had been played upon me in the past few days, this last was the foulest and most unbearable.

It never occurred to me that Waterman might not take her aboard the *Gannet*, for he really had no choice. If he left her where she was she would surely drown, and thoroughly as I detested Waterman, I never went so far as to think him totally devoid of normal human feelings.

There was nothing inhuman about the Lieutenant on this occasion, in any event. If a man had been in Hope's place he probably would have been loaded aboard with scant ceremony and less welcome, but one look at Hope, even from that considerable distance, was enough to inspire Waterman to something that was as close to gallantry as he was ever likely to be able to come.

In response to his sharply barked orders the *Gannet's* crew lost no time in getting Hope's sinking little sailboat alongside. And in another moment Hope herself was standing on our deck with the water dripping from her skirts and her blue eyes as full of laughter as though she had just had the good luck to drop in upon an unexpected but thoroughly delightful party.

She prettily thanked the goggle-eyed seaman who had salvaged her from the Bay and walked straight to Waterman, who, as I did not fail to note, had not moved from my side. She dropped him a little curtsey and looked only at him, ignoring me as completely as if I had been invisible. "I'm sorry, sir, to have made such a nuisance of myself. I realize that you in His Majesty's navy are busy men, these days, with important business to do. Saving silly females from the results of their own silliness is no part of it, and I wouldn't have blamed you if you'd left me to drift to the Tamoset shore—or even to Davy Jones's locker. Anyhow, I'm sorry and I'm grateful."

"Don't mention it, Miss." I could see Waterman's hard little eyes taking in every detail of Hope's appearance, and finding the process anything but unpleasant. I shared his appreciation in spite of myself, for, even though she was soaking wet and wind-blown and wearing a man's dark blue heavy peajacket that was many sizes too large, she met the test of close inspection and passed it with ease. She brought to mind a young, eager boy, in some ways, but her very slim boyishness only served to drive home the fact that she was all woman. Waterman liked what he saw, no doubt of that, and tried clumsily to express his liking. "I can assure you," he told her, talking like the hero of a sentimental love story, "that the pleasure is entirely ours. We sailors are accustomed to picking rare things from the sea, but it is seldom our privilege to pluck so fragile and beautiful a blossom as you."

I almost laughed out loud, wondering where on earth Waterman had picked up that mouthful of silly twaddle. But, as for Hope, she acted as though she had just been

439

paid the most delicate of tributes. "You are kind, sir." She glanced downwards, demurely, but only so that she could glance up again to give the Lieutenant the full blaze of her suddenly wide blue eyes. "But somehow—the moment I saw you—I knew that you would be kind."

I wanted to slap her then. In spite of my deep dejection and my dread of what certainly must happen within the next few minutes, I wanted to slap her lovely impudent mouth in payment for the thing she was doing. She might at least, I thought bitterly, have chosen a more worthy target than this for her arrows. Waterman was already groggy under her attack. In a few more minutes he would be sitting up on his hind legs and begging prettily for sweets.

I turned away, disgusted, and walked to the opposite rail where Waterman would not have to follow in order to keep me under guard but where I hoped to be able to escape the more nauseating details of their talk. Most of it still came to me, however, and I writhed inwardly until the conversation finally turned to a matter of real interest.

"May I ask you how you happened to be in the extremely dangerous place where we found you?" asked Waterman in the manner of a parent waving a fondly admonishing finger. "Don't you know that it's dangerous for a lovely and inexperienced young lady like yourself to go sailing alone? Don't you know that this is war time and that the coast is closely patrolled by our vessels? How did you know that you wouldn't be captured by a British officer far less—er—sympathetic and gentle than myself?"

Hope ignored the first part of the question and began her answer to the second with a laugh. "Why, Lieutenant, I'm not afraid of the British for a moment! To confess the honest truth, one of my reasons for going sailing was the hope that I might come across a British ship. It's fun—

or at least *I* think it is—to be able to talk my own language once in a while, with my own people."

"Your own people?" Waterman gasped. "Why—why, you mean that you're English? You're one of *us?*"

"Did you think I was an American?" Hope's tone implied faint resentment. "Far from it, Lieutenant Waterman, and God forbid! I'm English to the bone—merely caught in this savage country by the war. Tell me, do you know Nottingham?"

"Nottingham? I'm afraid not." Waterman's delight in Hope's professed nationality was unmixed. "Do you live there?"

"Oh, yes. I'm Alice Caldwell, and I hoped that you might know my father, the Bishop."

"Bishop Caldwell? I'm afraid not." I could imagine Waterman looking owlish. "But my brother, Ronald, probably does. Ronald goes to Nottingham quite a bit to visit the Albert Springleys. You know them, of course."

"The Springleys! Why, of *course!* They and the Croxstons—"

Oh, well, they went on that way for quite a time, playing the old game of "do you know?" As for me, I was busy asking myself if I had gone completely mad, and if not, what this nonsense was all about. I knew, or thought I did, that Hope was an American who was a traitor to her country, and one who was very busy in the British cause, as well as in the cause of her lover, Jermyn Forsythe. That being the case, I asked myself in bewilderment, why all this bosh about Nottingham and the rest? Why didn't she tell Waterman the exact truth, and why didn't she question him about me? Ever since she had come on board I had been waiting for just such questions and waiting—almost with resignation—for the swift disaster they would bring to all my plans.

The whole business was inexplicable, and destined to

become more so, for upon Hope's casual remark that she was an unwilling visitor in Trumet, Waterman laughed unpleasantly and pointed in my direction. "You're staying in Trumet? In that case, although I doubt it, you may have had the honor of meeting Mr. Bangs. Mr. Bangs, I believe, lives in Trumet."

"Bangs?" Hope wrinkled her brow and studied me as attentively as though she never in her life had laid eyes on me before. For my part, I turned—determined to get the unpleasant business over with as quickly as possible—and looked her squarely in the eyes. All that I got for my pains was a look completely blank of recognition. "Why, no. I don't think I've ever seen Mr. Bangs before. Strange, too, for I thought I had met everyone in the village."

"No doubt," said Waterman nastily, for my benefit, "Mr. Bangs does not move in the circle you would be familiar with. He is, nevertheless, from Trumet."

"An American? Indeed?" Hope looked puzzled. "But, in that case, what is he doing aboard a British ship? Is he a prisoner?"

"Not at all. He's aboard the *Gannet* quite willingly." Waterman took pleasure in talking about me to my face as though I were an inanimate object. "The truth is, Miss Caldwell, that, although an American, Bangs prefers to work for us."

"Oh. I see. A traitor!" Hope's expression as she looked at me was as though I were repulsive to see but fascinating at the same time. "I've never seen a traitor before. I've always thought that they would be ugly brutes—as well as dangerous."

"This one isn't dangerous at all. At least he isn't dangerous for you. You shall see." He took her by the elbow and brought her over to where I was standing. "Miss Caldwell, this is Jonathan Bangs. Bangs, this is Miss Alice Caldwell, of Nottingham, *England*." He bore down heavily upon the last word, as though in saying it he was placing upon Hope the ultimate in stamps of approval. "At the moment she is visiting in your rustic—or should I perhaps say sandy?—village of Trumet, but she tells me that for some strange reason she hasn't the honor of your acquaintance."

Hope laughed, nervously, and when she spoke her assumed voice was as artificial and silly as her real one was honest. "Our not meeting just goes to show, doesn't it, Mr. Bangs, that the world is really a much larger place than people like to make out? It really *is!* Lieutenant Waterman tells me that you—that you are—"

"He tells you," I said coldly emphasizing each word so that she could have no doubt as to the exact position I had taken for myself aboard the *Gannet,* "that I'm an American, working as a British agent. In other words, Miss Caldwell —that's the name, isn't it?—I'm a traitor. I hate Americans, and I'll do anything that I can to harm them! I'm busy at that very job this minute!"

"Really? You're *really* a *traitor?*" Hope actually had the impertinence to simper and act girlish—in front of me—me, of all persons. "I never thought that I should live to see the day when I should be able to say that I had seen a real, *live* traitor!"

"I'm alive enough," I told her grimly, "at the moment. It's a question how long I shall be able to stay that way."

"Oh!" Hope shuddered in an exaggerated fashion. "You mean that you might be captured by your own countrymen, and—and be hanged? How awful! How can you bring yourself to be a traitor, Mr. Bangs? It isn't really such a *nice* thing to be, is it? Please, please don't misunderstand me!" She raised a hand in delicate protest. "It isn't that I don't *approve* of everything that you're doing! I think it's *wonderful,* of course! It's just the idea of your being a *traitor.* I should think—"

She babbled on like that for a while, in a way that would have fooled no one who knew her, and wouldn't have fooled even Waterman, I felt, if he hadn't thought she was making fun of me. At any rate, Waterman enjoyed the farce thoroughly, grinning with delight at each inane phrase. He was standing directly behind Hope, and could not see that she was busily at work, as she talked, unknotting a red silk scarf that was tied around her neck under the upturned collar of the peajacket.

At length the scarf was dangling in her hand, and even while I was wondering what she was up to, she raised the hand that held it into the air as a casual gesture. The stiff breeze caught the piece of silk, of course, and in an instant had blown it out of Hope's hand and away—a bright blob of color that danced along the deck towards the bow.

"My scarf!" Hope screamed as though she had stepped on a snake. "My beautiful scarf!"

Lieutenant Waterman, I am glad to say, acted as a gentleman should when faced with a lady in trouble. He darted after the bit of material without even giving me a single thought, pursuing its erratic course with all the concentrated agility of a man chasing his hat in a March blow.

I was watching him, and wanting to laugh, when suddenly I felt something hard pushed against my chest and heard Hope's low, urgent voice. "Hide it quick, Jon! Quick! Inside your jacket! Remember that I'm with you and have another just like it! Be quick!"

Automatically, and almost before understanding came, I had hidden the thing she thrust upon me safe inside my jacket. When Waterman returned, panting from his triumphant quest, he found Hope still lecturing me upon the evils of being a traitor, and me listening with submission.

I could only pray that none of my bewildered tumult of emotions showed in my face, but it would have been a miracle if they had not. Inside my jacket there was now a bulky object. Its hard coldness pressing against my skin was the most welcome feeling I have ever known, for the thing that Hope had given me was a pistol. It was just as ugly and just as businesslike and just as efficient a pistol, I had no doubt, as either of those that were stuck in the front of Waterman's belt.

3.

It was about an hour later—about half-past five, as near as I can judge—when Major Bartlett's militia guard caught sight of the *Gannet* as she cruised on a southerly tack across the mouth of Billfish Cove and about a mile out in the Bay. The meeting in the Town House must have been in full swing with Captain Weeks, or Berry, at the very moment speaking in my interests from the platform.

In my mind, however, there was no thought of meetings or Town Houses or even, just then, of Captain Dole. Instead, there was intense concentration on the business in hand, together with a new exultation and a new courage that made me almost eager to face the danger that was coming closer every moment.

Other than the words that Hope had said to me, in haste, as she passed me the pistol, we had had no further private conversation together. To the contrary, once the weapon had changed hands, Hope immediately went back to playing her part of the flighty and brainless young female who was showing her wares for the benefit of an officer in His Britannic Majesty's navy. She soon tired of taunting me for being a traitor to my country and resumed her vigorous flirtation with Waterman.

The coy and langorous glances that she bestowed on the Lieutenant, together with the sugary and worshipful compliments that she paid him in my hearing, would have made me, at any other time, either violently jealous or actively ill. Just now, however, they didn't even serve to temper my desire to dance a jig of triumph on the *Gannet's* deck. For instead of going to my death, as helpless as a pig to the slaughter, I was armed and would be able to give a decent account of myself. Every time I breathed I could feel against my ribs—miracle of all miracles—the cool metal of the loaded pistol Hope had brought to me. Each breath brought me the promise that I might yet live to draw many others.

It is small wonder, I think, that I felt as though, being already dead, I had been brought back to life again. Nor was the pistol in my jacket the sole reason—or even the main one—for my feeling. For dreary days I had been living with what I thought was the sure knowledge that Hope not only did not love me, but that she had been playing false to me and her country since the very beginning. Jermyn Forsythe, in his letter to Holt, had stated baldly that Hope was not only sheltering him, but was acting most efficiently as his messenger to the British agent in Trumet. The very fact that Forsythe's letter had been written with the intent that I should never read its contents had seemed to clinch the fact of Hope's faithlessness. At the same time it had finally taken from me, I thought, any purpose or joy that I might have found in continuing to live.

Yet not five minutes ago Hope had handed me a pistol! While that fact did not alter my inability to explain away Forsythe's letter, it did much better. It made the need for such an explanation totally unimportant.

Facts were facts—and the things that Hope had just done were facts. She had taken a small boat and had sailed it far out into the Bay for the deliberate purpose of putting herself in a position where she would be sighted and picked up by the *Gannet*. When this purpose, in which she surely

446

risked her life, had been accomplished, she pretended that she and I were complete strangers. She had manufactured an incident to take Waterman out of the way and during his absence had handed me a loaded weapon.

Those were the facts—and they were more than enough for me. Explanations could wait. In addition to my pistol I had the glowing knowledge that Hope was not false, but true. In my new strength I felt as though I could twirl an elephant about. my head by his abbreviated tail and toss him over the moon.

I felt like singing but restrained myself. Instead I turned to Waterman with the remark that it was time for the *Gannet* to quit her aimless wandering about the Bay and to go to work. Speaking quietly, but distinctly enough so that Hope could not fail to hear and understand every word I said, I asked that the helmsman be ordered to run squarely before the wind towards a point on the Trumet shore just north of Shad Cove.

If Waterman was sorry to leave so soon the conquest he undoubtedly thought he had already made, his actions did not show it. He immediately passed on my order to the man at the wheel, bowed briefly to Hope in apology, and came to my side with a multitude of suspicious questions.

He wanted to know exactly what I intended and when and why. Did I expect him to believe that the Americans would be fools enough to try to land their powder in broad daylight under the noses of the British patrol? Why was I setting a course for Shad Cove? Was that to be the landing place? At what time was the powder barge to be expected? From what direction would it come? Did I remember that at the first sign of intended trickery I should promptly be shot dead?

Firmly, but as respectfully as I could make my words sound, I refused to give him much satisfaction. Repeating the words that I had used to Captain Holt aboard the

Terror, and eyeing the pistols in his belt by way of explanation, I said that I would pass on to no one the details of what I knew about the powder. Pointing out that Captain Holt had been content to accept my assurance that I would have the *Gannet* at the right place at the right time, I asked that his lieutenant be similarly content.

"Damn your impudence!" Waterman, in a temper, swore softly. "You'll pay dearly for it before you're done—mark my words! Do you think you can keep me entirely in the dark as to what's going on? You'll tell me instantly, if you're wise, the meaning of this order you've just given! Why are we running for the Trumet shore?"

"I'll explain that gladly." It was a relief to be able to say anything that might help to soothe the obvious itching of his trigger fingers. I was anxious, moreover, to have Hope—who had managed to edge close behind Waterman's back without attracting his attention—get some idea of what was in my mind. "I want the guard on the Trumet shore, and everybody in the village, for that matter, to know exactly where the *Gannet* is just now and where she seems to be bound. She left her station off Billfish Cove this morning, you remember, for the first time in many days. They'll be worried about that, ashore, and I want to ease their minds. To that end, we'll swing to a southerly course when we get within a mile of the Shad Cove beach. We'll cruise, just about that far off shore, from one end of Trumet to the other."

"And then?" Waterman was acid. "What is to follow that brilliant bit of strategy?"

"Then we'll come about and sail back again," I told him easily, "until we reach the *Gannet's* usual station off Billfish Creek."

"You intend to anchor there?"

"I think not." Waterman may have thought that my eyes were on him, but in point of fact I was staring straight past him at Hope, trying to will her with all my strength to listen carefully to what I said next. "I think we'll maneuver in that vicinity long enough to make the Trumet militia thoroughly aware of us and very much on the alert. Perhaps they'll think we're going to try a landing. Then, at the last moment, we'll haul off and set a beeline course for Point Town, which is the last place we'd supposedly be bound for if we knew anything about the powder landing. The Americans will certainly be relieved to see us go. Perhaps, if we hold the Point Town course until nightfall, they'll be fooled into thinking they've shaken us completely. If so, they'll be wrong." I looked mysterious and knowing. "You can be sure that the minute it grows dark we'll be off in a different direction altogether."

Lieutenant Waterman had no more liking for my plans than he had for me and surely would have cancelled them had he dared. In the back of his mind, however, there must have been the knowledge that he'd get little mercy from Captain Holt if he failed to capture the powder as a result of refusing to obey my instructions as pilot. Hope's being aboard must have been cause for thought, too, since he might feel that, with her as a witness, he would need more genuine cause for shooting me than he otherwise would.

In any event, he finally let me have my way and fell back a few paces—scowling and very much on the watch, with both hands on the butts of his pistols. As for me, I tried to act as confident and at ease as though I were walking the deck of my own ship without a care in the world.

In the manner of captains I kept my own counsel, and paced back and forth in silence until the *Gannet* reached the desired point off the Shad Cove beach, when I abruptly ordered the vessel on a southerly course. In giving the order I was careful to speak directly to the helmsman, without so much as a glance in Waterman's direction, and was relieved when he made no objection. So far so good! I heaved a sigh, praying that I had succeeded in my object of setting a precedent.

We cruised, as I had promised, the Trumet shore from one end to the other. As we did so, there passed by in slow review, and in full sight at this distance, many of the places and objects that had loomed so large in my troubled life of the past week. First there was Shad Cove, with its narrow beach and the steep sandy cliff behind. It was on that beach that I had first seen the British longboat, and there that I had waited in ambush to catch the British agent who had tried to fire our privateer. My prisoner, instead, had been Hope Allen. From the top of the cliff, just above, Major Bartlett's militia had fired their volley and had captured me only a few minutes later. Back of that was the big rock where Forsythe and Hope had met to talk.

A little further along I caught a glimpse, as we passed it, of the gray shingles of Seth Black's deserted and now ownerless shack. Next came a view of the clearing in which stood the Allen house with its outbuildings. I could even spy, above a tangle of scrub oaks, a corner of the old storehouse where Jermyn Forsythe had been hidden.

It was all there, I thought grimly, and it all brought back memories that would be slow to dim.

As the *Gannet* crossed her old station off the mouth of Billfish Creek, I spared time to satisfy myself that the militia guard at the entrance to Hornpout Pond was awake to its duty. There could be no doubt of that, for I saw groups of men obviously watching us closely, and I thought I saw a single figure start off at a dead run for the Point Road and the village. He would be a messenger, or so I hoped, sent off to warn Trumet of our arrival.

But I had no time just then to worry about messengers, or even try to catch a hoped-for glimpse of the small boats filled with armed men that I had asked Captain Dole to have waiting in the shelter of the creek. My business, at the moment, lay closer at hand.

Between me and the shore, from which the tide had already ebbed a long way, there was nothing but a broad smooth stretch of blue-green water. To the eye it looked serene and deep, and safe for the passage of a craft of considerable size. But I knew—what I devoutly hoped that Waterman did not—that it was anything but safe. Between me and the shore stretched the long sandy shoal known as Horse Mackerel Bar. Just now, because of the way the light came from the afternoon sun, the Bar was invisible. But, unless my calculations were far astray, the water covering it was no more than two feet deep and destined to grow more shallow with every minute that the tide continued to ebb. Peering intently, I thought I could make out the telltale line of lighter colored water marking the place where the deep water ended and the shoal began.

The rest of our reach to the south seemed to last forever, but I continued it doggedly as far as the Trumet boundary, so that Captain Dole and his men would surely have time to be ready for our return. But finally I gave the order to come about, and the *Gannet's* bow swung as the steersman spun the wheel. I remember drawing a long breath in that moment of pause before the wind again bellied the canvas taut, aware that the moment I had worried about for so many long hours could not be much longer delayed. In a very few minutes the issue would be settled—one way or the other.

When Billfish Cove had come back to view again, after painful waiting, and the militia emplacement was directly opposite to starboard, I took a final glance at Hope. I don't know whether I meant that look to be one of warning or of farewell, but in any event I saw Hope look back, straight into my eyes, and saw her briefly nod the dark red head that I loved.

Over my shoulder I spoke abruptly to the helmsman, but without excitement. "Hard a starboard! Run straight before the wind towards the shore. Carry on until I give the word to come about! Look sharp, now!"

The man at the wheel obeyed without a word. In another moment we were running fair and free, straight for the middle of Horse Mackerel Bar. So far as I was concerned, Horse Mackerel Bar would be the *Gannet's* resting place, for I hadn't the slightest intention of giving an order to sheer off.

"Look here, Bangs!" Waterman's face, as he suddenly stepped closer to me, was definitely worried. "Are you sure you know what you're doing?"

"Perfectly sure." I managed to keep my voice calm in spite of the heavy beating of my heart. "I'm just maneuvering the way I told you I would. There's plenty of water hereabouts."

"Begging your pardon, sir!" A chill went down my back when I heard the helmsman's hesitant, greatly daring words. "I know it's not my place to speak, sir, but I must tell you, sir, that I think the gentleman's mistaken!"

"What!" Waterman had dragged both pistols out of his belt and cocked them in a single gesture. "What's that you say?"

"There's a sand bar dead ahead, sir!" The sailor was confident now, and greatly urgent. "I've seen it often! It's bone dry at the full ebb!"

"Nonsense!" I tried to make my urgency the greater of the two. At the same time, my hand was about the butt of the pistol inside my jacket, and my thumb was pulling back the hammer. "There's no sand bar within a mile of here, Lieutenant! Who knows these waters better—an English sailor or a man who's lived here all his life?"

"He's wrong, sir!" The man at the wheel was almost

dancing up and down in his excitement. "I swear it! We'll be hard aground in ten seconds!"

"Come about!" Waterman must have been convinced, for there wasn't the slightest hesitation before he roared his order. Nor was there the slightest doubt in my mind as to what he intended to do next. "So you tried to make a fool of me, after all! You dared, damn you!" His eyes were cold with almost fanatical hate as he glared at me, slowly raising his pistol. "Well, you two-faced dog, here's where you pay!"

It is against my nature to shoot a man in cold blood, but I had no choice. Knowing that it must be the end of either him or me, I whipped the pistol Hope had given me out of my jacket, pointed it full in his scowling face, and pulled the trigger.

I expected the man to drop dead, then, at my feet, but nothing of the sort happened. My pistol misfired. There was a sickening little click as the hammer fell, and that was all.

If a man within a second or two of violent death can look foolish, I must have looked foolish indeed, for surprise completely robbed me of the ability to move. I was standing perfectly still, staring dumbly at the useless weapon in my hand and stupidly waiting to die, when there came the sharp bark of a pistol that was not aimed at me.

From somewhere close behind, and at the last split second, Hope had fired her own weapon—and hers had not misfired. Nor had the bullet in it flown wild. For Waterman, even as I stared at him, crumpled grotesquely at the knees and fell.

I'm not sure if it was the man at the wheel who shouted hoarsely or if it was I. At any event, there was a shout, and at the same time the *Gannet* suddenly dragged—as though a giant hand had seized her stern to pull her backwards. She lurched violently to starboard, too, so that I was thrown bodily down the suddenly steep hill of her deck, to fetch up with a crash against the bulwark.

I was dazed for a moment but managed to scramble to my feet. Shaking my head to clear it, I realized what had happened. The efforts of the helmsman to come about, or sheer off, had been made too late, and the *Gannet* was now where I had prayed for days that I might be able to put her. She was high and dry on Horse Mackerel Bar.

4.

My first concern naturally, as soon as I was able to think with even a moderate amount of coherence, was for Hope, but, even as I looked wildly about, I saw her struggle to her feet at a little distance and come, running swiftly, in my direction. "His pistols!" She was shouting at me urgently but without the slightest sign of terror or panic. "Find his pistols quickly, Jon! We've still got the crew to deal with. Quick, Jon, please! *Quick!*"

Once more I think Hope was responsible for saving my life, for I was obeying her orders even before I fully grasped what they implied. And it was finding Waterman's pistols, still unfired, in the scuppers that enabled us to handle the *Gannet's* crew. For, with those in my hands, I was, as Hope had probably realized, the only armed man on the entire vessel.

The *Gannet*, after her dizzy lurch to starboard on going aground, had heeled back again so that her deck was almost level. As a result I was able to run to the prone body of the helmsman and to cover him with my pistols before he could make any move to get to his feet. But that sailor, as a matter of fact, was not likely to give much trouble, for he was groaning from the effects of a blow on the head that had laid open an ugly three-inch wound just above his right eye.

454

I motioned Hope to me and handed her one of the two pistols. "Don't let this fellow move from where he is," I said quickly. "You stay here with him while I go forward to attend to the rest."

"Oh, Jon, be careful!" She took the pistol I offered her readily enough, but her tone was frightened. "There are thousands of them, and they can easily drag you down in spite of your pistol!"

"I don't think so." My confidence wasn't pretended but real. "The crew doesn't know anything about me except that I've been giving orders aboard a British vessel—and with Waterman's consent! I might be an admiral in their own navy, so they won't dare question me. Wait here!"

The plan in my mind wasn't half-formed but very definite, for I had considered this exact situation at least a dozen times during my long days of waiting on the *Terror* and had made up my mind exactly what I must do if it arrived. I hadn't run more than half a dozen steps towards the bow when I met a group of men coming from the other direction.

"Avast there!" Waterman's pistol in my outstretched hand was enough to command instant respect, and I put all the cold authority I could summon into my voice. "Stop! Where do you men think you're going?"

"We thought we heard a shot, sir!" The bos'n at the head of the group was already regretting that he had dared to think for himself. "We thought there might be trouble aft! We thought—"

"Who asked you to think?" I roared. "Your job is to obey orders when they're given—and I'm giving them! I'm in command here, do you understand?"

"Yes, sir!" The bos'n didn't question my authority by so much as a blink. He cast one frightened glance, which told him nothing, towards the stern and then retreated under my threatening advance. "Aye, aye, sir!"

"Then get about your business! Let go the anchor. Drop all sail. When that's done, get all hands below on the jump!" I stamped my foot. "Don't stand there staring at me, you fool! Give the orders!"

"Aye, aye, sir!"

The bos'n swung about, shouting to his men, and they, being disciplined members of the British navy, instantly obeyed. Badly knocked about as the crew must have been when the *Gannet* went aground, they scrambled quickly to their stations and to work.

"Drive 'em, Bos'n!" I said urgently to the man at my side. "It's our only chance! If the Yankees see the fix we're in, we'll all rot in one of their jails for the rest of this war! If we can fool them into thinking we've just anchored here, they'll never dare come near us before the flood tide floats us again! Get those men below decks in a hurry. Look alive!"

There was to be no real use for Waterman's pistol, for the bos'n no more questioned my authority than he would have if I'd been the First Lord of the Admiralty, himself. He drove his crew savagely, as I had commanded, and in an incredibly short space of time the thing had been done.

No more than five minutes could have passed, surely, before the *Gannet's* anchor was down and her canvas brought in and secured. Except for a slight cant to starboard, the sloop must have appeared from the shore very much as she had all during her vigil of the previous week. More important still, the crew was rapidly disappearing, man by man, out of sight into the hold through the forward hatch.

"Look here, sir! Look!" The bos'n in his excitement was forgetful enough to tug at my arm. "There's boats putting out from the shore—dozens of them! The Yankees have seen us and are sending out a boarding party! Shall I order the men back to their stations, sir? Will you issue arms?"

"No." One glance was enough to tell me that my letter had safely reached Captain Dole, for a swarm of small boats were already spewing out from the mouth of Billfish Creek and coming towards us at speed. I felt that there was no time, or need, for any further deception. Raising my pistol in a way that couldn't be misunderstood, and looking the bos'n coldly in the eye, I said, "You'll order nobody to do anything! If you want to keep on living, you'll get down in that hold and pull the hatch cover shut over you! I mean just what I say. No talk! Get moving or I'll shoot!"

I could see understanding come into the fellow's eyes. Bewilderment was replaced by furious chagrin and desperation, and that in turn—as I slowly raised the barrel of my pistol—by fear. Without another word the bos'n turned and vanished into the hold, not forgetting to pull the hatch closed behind him.

To someone in the mood to appreciate it, the arrival of the Trumet boarding party aboard the *Gannet* would have been genuinely amusing. It seemed to me that dozens and dozens of my former friends came pouring over the bulwarks. Each and every one of them was heavily armed and spoiling for a fight, but they found no excuse for so much as pulling a single trigger.

The decks of the British sloop of war were, as a matter of fact, about as peaceful a place at the moment as could be imagined. The boarding party found me resting my two-hundred-odd pounds of flesh and bone solidly on the edge of the forward hatch. In the starboard scuppers, aft, lay Lieutenant Harry Waterman, more dead than alive from his wound. Nearby knelt an injured and only half-conscious British sailor, who groaned as he nursed his broken head. Over him, to complete our odd complement, stood Hope Allen, faithfully on guard. When Henry Allen gently took the pistol out of her unresisting hand he found that she was crying—quietly, but as though her heart would break.

Her tears at that moment were something that I can very well understand. The reaction to the intense excitement of everything that had gone before, together with the sudden and complete relief from intolerable suspense and anxiety, were enough to make even a supposedly nerveless brute like myself feel that a brief fit of hysteria would be a luxury.

Under the circumstances, however, I was allowed to indulge in nothing of the kind. It seemed as if there were at least a thousand and one things to be explained, understood, planned, and done, all without the loss of an instant of time. In looking back I don't wonder so much that some important things were forgotten as I do that we were able to accomplish as much as we did. I know that I, for one, was in a state of such complete confusion that if things finally straightened themselves out—even partially—I deserve no credit for it. Even now I remember very little, in any detail, of what happened for the first half hour after Captain Dole's boarding party took charge of the *Gannet*.

I remember, for one thing, being cheered and pounded on the back by the very men who had been cursing and hunting me as a turncoat and murderer only a few days before. I couldn't understand their change of attitude any more than I could understand Hope's risking her life to bring me a pistol aboard the *Gannet*, but, wisely, I didn't even try. I merely accepted my inexplicable new standing in Trumet as a gift from God and asked no questions about it, even from Captain Dole—when I found myself shaking his hand.

There wasn't any doubt about the nature of the Captain's welcome. His eyes were bright with triumphant excitement, and he seemed to be mixing his congratulations to me with curses at himself for being such a fool as ever to believe I might be a traitor. "That grapeshot that busted my bones aboard the *Strong Arm* a year or so ago must have nicked my wits," he said sorrowfully, shaking his head. "If I'd been sane I'd never have believed *you'd* sell us out—no matter what anybody said, or how black the evidence against you was! Why, Jonathan, boy—"

"Let's talk it all over later, shall we, Captain?" I held up my hand to stop him. "There are a lot of things to think about, and do, and we haven't got any time to waste if we want to get that powder in tonight!" I pointed. "For one thing, there are twenty-odd British sailors in that forward hold. They're harmless enough—not being armed— but they ought to be taken ashore right way. The point is that we may have to fight to keep this craft, now that we've got her. That British lieutenant, Forsythe, that I wrote you about, got back to the *Terror* this morning, and he's sure to make trouble sooner or later. He not only knows our powder plans, but he must know that I'll have done my best by this time to put this sloop out of action! I tied him up before I left Point Town this morning, but the minute he gets loose hell is going to pop! The British will be down here in short order to find out what's happened to the *Gannet,* and when they find she's in our hands there's sure to be a fight. We'd better be ready for it!"

I rattled off all that long rigmarole just as fast as I could talk, and while a lot of it must have been Greek to the Captain, he understood the part that mattered. "We'll be ready for them!" he promised grimly. "They'll never get this sloop back—no matter how soon they show up or how many of them come! We need the *Gannet* in our business, as a convoy for the powder!" He glanced anxiously at the expanse of Horse Mackerel Shoal, which was now almost dry. "How soon do you figure the tide will float her again?"

"About eight-thirty or nine tonight." I was able to

answer that question promptly because I had worked out the problem of tides very carefully in my mind when I laid my original plans. "A lot of small boats with tow lines might be able to yank her off a little earlier—but not more than a few minutes."

"No matter!" Captain Dole grinned. "Even if she doesn't float till nine o'clock, that'll still give us two hours' leeway. She'll be cruising under the Stars and Stripes when those powder barges heave into sight—and that's all that counts. The British haven't got an armed craft in Point Town Harbor that doesn't draw too much water to navigate in these parts. All they can send against us will be cutters and longboats, and the *Gannet* will take care of *them* in short order!" In his delight he slapped me hard on the back. "Capturing this vessel has changed the job of running in the powder from a risky, dangerous business into something that ought to be as pleasant and peaceful as a tea party! The *Gannet* had just about turned the trick, Jonathan, boy, and all Trumet knows who's to be thanked for it!"

"No they don't—not if they want to thank me!" I took him by the arm and shook it to make sure I had his full attention. "I'd have been helpless to do a thing if it hadn't been for Hope Allen. Hope's the one to be thanked—and don't think she isn't! She risked her life out there in the Bay to bring me a pistol, and just at the last she saved my life when it didn't look to be worth a brass farthing! Hope's the one who deserves the cheers, and she can't deny it. Where is she?"

I flung myself about, looking for her—ashamed that even in the excitement of rapid events I hadn't done so before. But nowhere could I spy her dark red head, for the very good reason that it wasn't there.

"Hope's gone ashore." I had opened my mouth to shout her name when one of the boarding party stepped forward with his news. "She was brave enough when we first found her, aft by the wheel. She was cool as a cucumber till she saw her father, but then she kind of busted down. Cried considerable, she did, claiming that she'd just shot a man dead. Well, it turned out that her Redcoat in the scuppers ain't dead by a long sight, but we didn't find that out till after Henry Allen had packed her into a boat and ordered one of the boys to row her ashore. Hope's safe at home by this time, I cal'late."

"But—but I've got to see her! I must!" In my dismay I swung back to Captain Dole. "I must thank her for everything she did. There are a thousand things I must tell her! Why—"

"Just right, Jonathan, boy!" Captain Dole nodded swiftly. "You've got to see Hope, and there's no time like the present to do it. Take a boat and go ashore after her."

"No." I shook my head. "I guess I'll have to wait. You need me here."

"Did you hear what I said?" The Captain spoke sharply. "I said you were to go ashore—and I meant it. Your job here is done—and mighty well done, too. There won't be a living thing for you to do for another two hours at the earliest, and I don't want to lay eyes on your face before then. You may not realize it, boy, but this may be your last chance to talk to Hope for a year or more! I say that you go talk to her—*now*. It's an order!"

Well, an order is an order, and I generally obey one, even when it doesn't take me to the one place in the world I really want to be. In this case I imagine that I did what I was told fast enough to suit even such a stickler for discipline as Captain Dole.

A couple of men in militia uniform were waiting for me when I jumped ashore on the sandy beach just north of the entrance to Billfish Creek. They were grinning with excitement, and full of congratulations and questions, but

I was in no mood to be delayed. "Tell you all about it later," I said hurriedly. "Just now I'm on important business! Did Hope Allen come ashore here just now?"

"Hope? Hope *Allen?* Now let me see." One of the men, thinking himself very funny, put on an exaggerated scowl and scratched his head as though in deep thought. "Seems as though I did see a young lady around here. Had kind of reddish hair, as I recollect. Would that be the one you was asking about, Jonathan?"

"Where did she go?" I asked impatiently. "Did she start for her house?"

"No."

Assuming that the answer would surely be in the affirmative I had already taken a step or two in the direction of the Allen clearing before the man's single syllable brought me up short. "No? Then where did she start for?"

"We don't know." The fellow's delighted grin was even broader. "We only know the message she told us to give you if you happened to come along this way."

"Message! She left me a message?" I could cheerfully have choked him. "What did she say, you idiot? Spit it out, or—"

"There, there, Jonathan, don't get riled!" The man backed hastily away from my threatening advance. "I'll tell you what Hope said—even if it don't make much sense. She said to tell you that she was tired of picking blueberries without any help. Them were the very words she said, and Nathan, here, will back me up!"

"Yup. That's what she said." Nathan shook his head. "Seems to me like a fool thing for a girl to say. Don't make *no* sense!"

Well, it made sense enough to suit me, and I'd have been off on my travels in another two seconds if the sound of a musket shot and of excited shouting had not drifted to our ears from the direction of the *Gannet*. It caused us to turn about, naturally enough, and to peer out across the Bay, shielding our eyes against the afternoon sun that was low in the west.

I understood, at first glance, just what was going on and remember a feeling of surprise that nobody had earlier considered the probability of such an event. A British longboat had appeared from the north and had headed, in all innocence, straight for the *Gannet's* side.

For the young midshipman in charge of the patrol boat, it must have been something of a shock when, instead of the friendly greeting he so confidently expected, he was met, the moment his craft came within range, with angry shouts and a ragged volley of musket fire. But, shocked or not, the officer used his wits. He immediately ordered his crew to back water while he studied the *Gannet* and, I should imagine, pondered this strange reception from a vessel that he had every reason to believe was a unit of his own navy.

Nor did it take him very long to reach the correct conclusion. Even as I watched, the longboat's prow swung around in the direction from which it had come, and in another moment the fast, many-oared craft was making all speed in the direction of Point Town.

In my mind's eye I could imagine the angry strides with which Captain Dole must have been pacing the *Gannet's* deck at that moment. For, if the boarding party had not been overeager, the longboat would have been allowed to come alongside before she was advised of her mistake, and where she surely would have been captured. As it was, not many hours would now pass before Captain Holt on the *Terror* had been warned that his armed sloop had fallen into enemy hands.

At any other time I would have been deeply concerned over such a serious blunder, but just then it did not seem very important. All that seemed important to me at the moment was the message from Hope. In leaving word that she was tired of picking blueberries alone, she told me, just as clearly as if she had drawn a map, exactly where she would be waiting.

I set off at a fast dog-trot in the direction of Doane's Hollow.

Out on the Bay that afternoon the stiff breeze out of the west had kicked up quite a little chop that was flecked with whitecaps, but inland among the close-growing pines of Doane's Hollow, there was hardly a breath of air stirring. As I walked into it, the place was just as cool and hushed and silent as a church, and, I thought, just as beautiful.

I found Hope exactly where I knew I should find her— in the shadow of the big boulder where we had first spoken our love. She was waiting for me, just as she had waited on that other summer afternoon. And how much had happened to both of us in the time between!

On that first occasion I had been full of the exciting knowledge that my dream for a privateer was to be made into a reality, and full also, as a result of my knowledge, of young enthusiasm and self-confidence. I felt that I held the world in the palm of my hand, and not even Hope's fierce anger at my lateness in keeping our appointment had served to dampen my spirits for very long. Once my apologies had been made, I had rushed to an account of my good fortune, and then quickly to a realization of love.

But today was another day, and as Hope and I stood looking at each other gravely and in silence, I felt that she and I were truly other people. Never again, for either of us, could life be quite the carelessly played and light-hearted, exciting game that it had seemed only a few weeks back. The events in between had had their effect. I, for my part, felt older—older in the sense that I no longer had any serene assurance that the future would obediently mould itself to my will. I had learned to expect trouble as a part of living, and I think I had learned to look trouble more or less calmly in the eye.

If Hope seemed more mature, it was not because she had lost any of her zest for life. The spark still glowed hotly in the back of her deep blue eyes—as I hope it always will —but she gave me the impression that she had learned there are times when the playing of games must be put aside. There was now no hint of impending feminine sword play in either her manner or her voice.

"I'm glad you got my message and came here." She spoke quietly, almost shyly. "It seemed the right place—somehow."

"Yes." I nodded. "Doane's Hollow is ours. It belongs to you and me."

"Yes." She suddenly put one small hand over her mouth, her eyes darkening. "The British officer, Jon? Lieutenant Waterman. Did I—? Is he dead?"

I wanted to take her in my arms then, but she hadn't yet given me the right. "No, he isn't dead." I spoke swiftly, trying to be matter of fact. "Before I left the *Gannet* someone told me that there was little chance of his dying."

"I'm glad." Her body relaxed. "I wouldn't like to have to remember that I'd killed a man."

"You won't have to do that." I spoke jerkily, blurting out my words. "You can remember, instead, that you saved a man's life. Except for you, *I'd* be dead. I have so much to thank you for, Hope, that I don't know where to begin. You were brave to sail out into the Bay that way, and to—"

"I surprised you, Jon, didn't I? But I know I did, for I saw your face. Poor Jon!" She smiled then, and there was a hint of the familiar sparkle in her eyes. "You thought

465

I was a traitor, working with Jermyn Forsythe against my country. You thought—"

"Whatever I thought, Hope, was wrong—completely wrong!"

"You've talked with Captain Dole, then? You know the truth?"

"No." I shook my head. "There hasn't been time to talk with anyone. I don't know anything except the facts. If you'd been what I thought you were, you'd never have brought me that pistol. You'd never have pulled a trigger to save my life. I was wrong about you—and I'm sorry. Can you forgive me?"

"Of course." She shrugged her shoulders as though there was nothing to forgive. "It was only natural for you to think what you did. I suppose it was only natural for you to think another thing—that I wasn't in love with you but with Jermyn Forsythe? You thought that, didn't you, Jon?"

I could only nod, dumbly.

"Well, you were wrong about that, too, and I forgive you." She smiled at me gently. "Jermyn Forsythe means nothing to me, while you mean everything. I love you, Jon, and always will. Do you believe me?"

"Yes." I felt incapable of much speech. "And I love you."

"I'm glad." She sighed, nodding her little head. "And now, Jon, would you mind holding me close for a little while? It's been a long, horrible time, and I—I've been lonely."

She cried quietly for quite a little while in my arms, but at last I felt her body stop its shivering. When she leaned back to look up at me, freeing one hand to brush her eyes, she spoke seriously and with pleading. "Please don't go away from me again, Jon. It frightens me. Please don't leave me. Not ever!"

Hope knew as well as I that, if the powder came in safely that night, the *New Hope* would sail at once and I would be aboard her. But she was not thinking just then of that sort of long physical parting. Knowing quite well what she meant, I nodded before I bent my head to kiss her gently. "No, Hope, you don't have to think about that. I've come back to you—and this time it's for always."

Two hours isn't such a very long time, after all.

To Hope and me, with our knowledge of what must lie immediately ahead, our time together was almost unbearable in its shortness. Each time we kissed it was with the pain of knowing that we were that much closer to our parting kiss, and each companionable silence was broken by the realization that it wasted precious seconds. Perhaps it was a mercy to both of us that there was so much between us that must be explained and understood.

Sitting close beside me in the deepening shadow of our boulder in Doane's Hollow, Hope, carefully and in detail, filled in the wide gaps in my knowledge of what had happened in Trumet while I was in exile. Her story was so long and so difficult to tell clearly that it was dark before she came to an end. It was dark, and my two hours of leave were almost up.

"And so," I said slowly at last, knowing the truth but hardly able to believe it, "in Trumet's eyes I'm no longer a traitor and a murderer, to be hanged as soon as caught!"

"It's just the other way round!" said Hope gladly. "Everybody knows that you've been called wicked names and been hunted like an animal—for no good reason! They're anxious to make it up to you, Jon. You'd be treated like a hero, even if this *Gannet* business hadn't happened. As it is—!"

"And you say that the man who *really* did all this dirty work is still running around loose?" I scowled. "It doesn't seem possible, and it doesn't seem safe. He might be dangerous still! Doesn't the Captain have even an idea who the fellow might be?"

"If so, he hasn't told me." Hope shrugged. "But perhaps he isn't telling everything he knows. You can ask him about it when—when—"

"When I go back to work." I finished the sentence for her as casually as I could. "Well, I'm afraid that that must be right now. My two hours are up, and, unless I miss my guess, there's a big night's work ahead for us all."

"Yes, Jon." She accepted quietly what had to be. "You can walk with me as far as the house, can't you? I'll walk fast, I promise you, but I'm selfish enough to want every last minute that we can have."

"There'll come a time, young lady," in a feeble attempt to make a hard thing easier by joking, "when you'll wonder how you ever said a thing like that. After we've been married five or ten years you'll be wishing that I'd get out of the house once in a while, so that you wouldn't have to look at my ugly face!"

"Perhaps." She didn't even try to laugh. "Just now I'd be happy if I could know that you were right!"

I should have hurried but could not, linking her arm through mine and walking slowly at her side through the quiet peace of the pine woods. I don't think we spoke a word to each other from the time we left Doane's Hollow until we came to the clearing and to Henry Allen's lonely, unlighted house. My heart, I know, was much too full for words.

At the doorstep Hope turned to say good-by, gently but firmly refusing my request that I come inside with her while she made some light. "I'd rather you left me here, Jon," she said quietly, standing on tiptoe so that she could slip her arms about my neck. "If I should let myself see your face again, I'm afraid what I might say or do. It's better this way. If the *New Hope* should sail tonight, of course I'll be on the dock with the rest of us women who must stay behind. But this, Jon, must be our real good-by. The dark is a nice place to say it, don't you think? It makes me feel as though we were so very much alone. We might be the only two people in all the world."

But Hope was wrong. We were not the only two people in the world, or anything like it, for just as I bent my head to kiss her, the kitchen door at her back swung silently open. There was a black rectangle instead of its dim whiteness. There was also a man's heavy voice. It was nothing but a voice, after all, but it sent shivers down my back.

"Hope Allen! Come inside, Hope—you and the man with you. I want to talk to you both. Come inside!"

Hope, having no warning at all, must have been even more startled than I. With a gasp she twisted about in my arms and stood facing the kitchen door. "Who is it? What are you doing here? What do you want?"

"You'll hear if you come inside."

The voice sounded more human, now, and more recognizable. The hearing of it brought relief to Hope, at any rate, for I felt her body go limp against mine. "Uncle Eb!" she cried. "Why, you nearly scared me out of my wits with your—well, not very funny joke! I honestly don't think it was a very nice thing for you to do—or very like you either. How long have you been sitting here in the dark? What were you waiting for?"

"I was waiting for you." By this time I, too, could recognize the dignified measured voice of Eben Fowler, and I could even make out the outline of his solid figure as he stood in the dark doorway in his dark clothes. "Will you come inside?"

"I should say I *would!*" Hope sounded half indignant and half reproachful, and as she took my hand I could feel that hers was still trembling from her fright. "We'll both come inside, and, as soon as we've lighted a candle or two, we'll give you a real tongue-lashing, Uncle Eb, don't think we won't! Don't you really think you ought to be a little sorry for scaring me like this? Don't you know that you ought to say so?"

Still scolding, Hope dragged me into her kitchen past Fowler, who stood to one side without saying a word. At the fireplace she knelt and carefully raked the ashes until she had exposed a core of coals that still glowed red. Two long pine splinters, from a jar of them on the hearth, almost instantly burst into cheerful flame when she presented their frayed ends to the hot coals.

"There!" She handed me one of the little torches and got swiftly to her feet. "Light some candles, will you, Jon? Light lots of them! I seem to be afraid of the dark for just about the first time in my life, and I know who's fault it is! Aren't you ashamed, Uncle Eb, to have done this to your almost best girl?"

Fowler did not answer, as Hope and I set to work lighting candles, nor did he make any move to help.

The light in the Allen kitchen rapidly grew brighter as we moved about with our splinters, and before long it was again homelike and cheerful. Obeying my orders to set flame to every stick of tallow in sight, I was stretching to reach a final, seldom-used one on the top of a cupboard in the corner, when I suddenly heard Hope gasp and cry out.

"Uncle Eb!" There wasn't any doubt of the real fear in her voice now. "Why—why, Uncle Eb!"

I spun about to find Hope motionless, staring towards the door through which we had just come in. I stared, too, and as I did so the sliver of wood I was holding fell from my hand to the floor. I snuffed out its flame with my heel without even glancing down.

The kitchen door had been closed again, and, with his back firmly pressed against its panels, stood Eben Fowler, holding a pistol in each hand. I don't think I needed more than that one glance to know that the saltworks owner was stark, raving mad.

The man was a sight to see. He was wearing his customary, formal dark clothes, but they looked as though he had taken them through a taproom brawl. The black coat was covered with stains and dirt, and most of its buttons were gone. One leg of the trousers was ripped, so that the white flesh showed through. The black stock was gone altogether from around his neck, and the once white linen shirt underneath had been torn open at the collar. Fowler's usually neat hair was tumbled, and there was a smear of mud across his forehead. His black eyes gave the impression of glowing hotly from deep in their sockets.

"Stay where you are!" Fowler's deep voice was no longer dignified, but cracked and hoarse. "Stand still while I say what I have to say—keep back, I tell you!"

Hope would have gone to his side, I think, but the fierce gesture of his weapons stopped her. Instead, she turned and ran swiftly to me.

"That's better!" Fowler laughed as I put my arm about Hope's trembling shoulders. "Hug the little red-headed trollop while you can! Hug her well, Jonathan Bangs, you miserable bootlicker of Isaiah Dole! Isaiah Dole!"

He began then to curse Captain Dole and me with a vicious thoroughness and rising fury that made my blood run cold. It was not the foulness or the senselessness of the names that he dragged out of the gutter to throw at us that affected me, so much as it was my realization that only a hatred so violent as to be insane could have inspired such a tirade. Eben Fowler loathed both of us, I realized then and there, in a way that was beyond belief.

"You thought you'd got away from me, didn't you, Bangs?" His cursing over for the moment, Fowler was immediately off on another tack. "Well, you haven't got away from me, and you're not going to! Maybe you're not going to hang by the neck the way I'd planned, but all the same you're going to die!" He laughed. "You're going to die, here and now, and your red-headed ladylove is going to sit by and watch!"

By that time I knew everything of importance, of course, that there was to know. I knew that Eben Fowler was not only insane but that he must be the traitor and murderer I had been hunting for days. I knew that he hated me with the same unexplainable madness that he hated Captain Dole. I knew that he intended to kill me, as soon as his raving was done, and that I would be helpless to resist.

As sometimes happens to me in moments of excitement, I suddenly wanted to laugh. Would I never, I wondered, be armed when the event demanded it? I had walked in on the man Forsythe without even a stick for a weapon. I had been even more harmless when I boarded the *Gannet*. And here I was, defenseless, on the third and most dangerous occasion of all! And this time I had trusted my luck too far.

"This is another of your jokes, Uncle Eb. It is, of course!" Hope must have realized, as well as I, that Fowler was completely out of his mind, for she spoke to him in the calm, soothing, pleading tone that she might have used to a child. "I love Jonathan Bangs, and you wouldn't think of harming somebody I love. Why, Uncle Eb, think! You've been father's friend for years—and mine. You've known me since I was a baby. You've always called me your best girl! Why, you like me a *lot*, Uncle Eb, don't you remember? It wasn't so very long ago that you—"

"That I wanted to marry you! Why, so I did!" There wasn't the slightest softening of his tone or expression as he turned to her. "I'd have done it, too, if Isaiah Dole hadn't taken you from me! Isaiah Dole! May his soul burn forever in the fires of hell! He stole Martha's love away

472

from me, even before I married her. She hated me till she died—all because of Dole! And now he's stolen you!"

"Tell me this, Mr. Fowler," I broke in, sharply. "Just what has Captain Dole got to do with Hope and me?"

"Everything!" His face worked. "Dole brought you here to wreck my life for a second time! He told you to steal Hope Allen away from me, and you did! When I saw what was happening I swore on the Bible I'd have my revenge. I swore nothing would stop me from having it— and nothing will!" He laughed again. "Seth Black thought he could stop me, didn't he, and where is Seth? He's up in the graveyard where I put him—and where I'll put you and the skunk that owns you—Isaiah Dole!" He waved the pistols dangerously. "There's a bullet in these for both of you!"

"No." Hope shook her head in a sort of dazed disbelief. "You *can't* hate Jonathan so much—or Captain Dole."

"No?" Fowler's deep red face had turned almost purple. "I hated Dole enough, didn't I, to throw away everything I have in the world? When the *New Hope* is burned up, or sunk, I won't have a penny to my name, but I hate Dole enough so that I don't care. I fixed it with the British so they could destroy the vessel I've put my own money in! Is that hate, or isn't it? Who do you think made a fool of Bangs at the shipyard? *I* did! Who set the fire down there? *I* did! Who killed Seth Black when he got in my way? Who's going to kill Jonathan Bangs this very minute? *I* am—that's who—the man that hates Isaiah Dole!"

Fowler was shouting, by this time, so loud that he could have been heard a quarter of a mile away. He had come farther into the room, too, and was waving the pistols in my direction. I was just gathering myself together to make some desperate gesture towards saving my life when in the window to the right of the kitchen door I suddenly saw a white face that was pressed against the glass.

Someone had heard the uproar that Fowler was making and had come to investigate! There was still hope if only I could gain a little more time!

"I don't believe a word of it!" It was my turn to shout now, hoping that the noise would cover up a squeak from the kitchen door if and when it opened. "You're just bragging! You couldn't have done all those things!"

"No? Well, I *did*—and a lot more, too! Did you know that the British know all about your powder-running plans, and that they'll blow it sky high when it comes in to-night?"

"I don't believe that, either!" The latch of the kitchen door had been lifted, and I could see that the door itself was slowly opening. I kept on talking at random, just for the sake of gaining time. "How could you possibly have got word to the British about the powder?"

"Easy!" His cracked, mad voice was full of triumph. "I fooled Hope into carrying my letter to a British officer who was hid right on this place. I fooled her just the way I fooled Dole!"

The door was open all the way now, and I could see the figure of Ezra Light, as the little peddler cautiously put one foot after the other up on the sill. As Ezra intended, Fowler did not hear him. I doubt, as a matter of fact, if Fowler could have heard anything just then, for he was completely lost in his moment of triumph.

"Dole thinks he's smart!" The crazy saltworks owner steadied the pistols and began to raise them. "Dole thinks his pet, Bangs, is going to live—just because they aren't going to hang him on the gallows. But Dole is wrong! Bangs isn't going to live. He's—"

At that moment Ezra Light dived for the back of Eben Fowler's knees, and his dive was not a moment too soon. Ezra's frail body hit Fowler's sturdy one just as both pistols went off and jarred it enough so that the bullets flew wild.

Fowler, however, did not fall. He staggered heavily away from Light's clutching hands and brought up against a wall with a crash that shook it. I lunged forward as quickly as I could, but not quickly enough. With a bellow of crazy rage Eben Fowler jumped for the open door and disappeared into the darkness outside.

5.

About a half hour after that—no later, certainly—I was again walking the deck of the *Gannet* in earnest talk with Captain Dole and two or three of his advisors.

It makes me shake my head even now, as I write that fact, for it seems as though by that time I had already done enough work for one day, and, by all that was fair, ought to have been allowed to sit down to rest and to think things over. But rest and thought weren't even a small part of the program on that jammed-full Friday, for there wasn't *time*. *Time* was the precious thing that day, and there wasn't enough of it to go around. There wasn't even enough of it so that a man could completely finish one thing before he had to begin another.

Just take, for an example, what happened after Hope and I and crazy Eben Fowler had had our nightmare party in Henry Allen's kitchen, and after the madman who had given the party rushed away into the outside darkness.

It doesn't take much imagination to picture what I was feeling immediately after *that*.

I had just had an almost miraculous escape from being shot down in cold blood, and the man who had had every intention of killing me was still free to try again. Added to that I had just heard an amazing and full confession, from the man's own lips, that he was the traitor and murderer Trumet and I had been hunting for so long and so hard. Is it any wonder that the sole notion in my head just

475

then was to dash after Eben Fowler and to lay him by the heels without a moment's delay? I don't think so. I think my intent was entirely reasonable and sensible, but Ezra Light—the man who had come to my aid just in the nick of time—wouldn't hear of it. In so many words, he said that there wasn't time!

"No, Jonathan! No! Whoa, there! There ain't time for you to go chasing Eb Fowler. Listen to me! Something important has happened, and Isaiah Dole sent me to fetch you aboard the *Gannet* right away! Eb Fowler'll have to wait. There ain't time for him now!"

"Don't *you* be crazy!" I was half way out of the Allen door, and would have been the whole way out if the little peddler hadn't been hanging on the back of my jacket with a bulldog grip. "Don't be a fool! You don't know about Fowler! Lord above, Ezra! He's the traitor—and murderer, too! *Fowler* is, I tell you!"

"I know all about Fowler," panted Ezra, grimly resisting my efforts to shake him off. "Isaiah Dole just finished telling me all about him—and I still say he'll keep! He'll *have* to! Will you listen to what I've got to say, you pesky young hothead?"

I listened in spite of myself, and, when I had heard his tale, I realized that, for all of me, Eben Fowler must be free, for the time being at least, to go his own mad way. My obvious duty was to get to Captain Dole aboard the *Gannet* at the first possible moment.

"You win," I admitted, shortly. "I'll come with you, Ezra, but only on the condition that Hope comes along too. I'm not leaving her here for that crazy murderer to find if he should take it into his head to come back this way!"

"Glad to have her!" Ezra grinned, obviously relieved because I was, at last, showing some sense. "She can stay at the militia camp while we're off on the *Gannet*. She'll be safe as a meeting-house there. Heave ahead, you two. There ain't no time to lose!"

We left the Allen house without even bothering to blow out the candles we had lit and hurried down to the shore. On the way there, and on the way out to the sloop in a small boat, Ezra and I discussed the news that had sent him running to fetch me.

The news was that the British armed brigantine, *Hawke*, had left her station off the mouth of Trumet Harbor on the ocean side. Some little time back a lookout had seen a rowboat come alongside her, and, a few minutes later, seen the *Hawke* heave anchor, crack on all her canvas, and set off on a northerly course. The natural inference was that she would round the tip of the Cape at Point Town, and sail into the Bay. If nothing delayed her, it looked as if she would reach a point off Shad Cove at almost the exact hour our powder barges from Tamoset were due there.

"Looks bad to me," I shook my head grimly as I realized the full significance of this new change in the situation. "But we should have known it was almost sure to happen. Forsythe is loose by this time, so the British know our powder-running plans in just as much detail as we do. By this time, too, they know that the *Gannet* isn't theirs any more. That longboat we were fools enough to drive off a while back will have told them that. Sending for the *Hawke* to come around to this side is just about the only thing, when you come to think of it, that Holt or Forsythe *could* do. She's the only craft they have that doesn't draw too much water and is armed heavily enough to tackle the *Gannet* after we float her. It looks to me as if we're in for a fight—and a tough one."

"Think so?" Ezra nodded. "I was just asking myself about that, and I had sort of a notion about it, as you might say. I was just wondering—but no matter." He laughed. "I won't bother you with my crazy notion, but, if I can raise the spunk, I'll ask Isaiah Dole what he thinks of it. He'll probably tell me to go fish. A peddler ain't supposed to know about fighting wars and battles and such. His business is nailing down every copper he can lay eyes on—and that's job enough, these days! So you cal'late the *Hawke* and the *Gannet* are due for a tussle, do you, Jonathan? Who do you figure to win?"

"Captain Dole hasn't ever failed to give a good account of himself in a sea battle yet, and he won't this time," I declared. "But the odds, as well as the weight of metal, are all on the *Hawke*. Don't forget that the British will be handling a vessel they know, while we won't. The *Gannet*'s a stranger to us. No." I shook my head dubiously. "I confess, Ezra, I can't see anything good about this news you've brought me."

"Can't ye? Then I'll tell you something." He chuckled. "I ain't a sea-faring man, none to speak of, but folks that know me—especially customers—admit that I know how to add on and take away. See here, Jonathan, boy! According to the way I was larnt in school, one from one leaves nawthing. If you have one thing, and it's took away, what you have left is *no* thing. I ain't wrong there, be I?"

"Stop being funny," I said impatiently. "What are you getting at?"

"Just this." Ezra chuckled again. "This afternoon them Redcoats had one vessel—the brigantine, *Hawke*—standing guard just outside Trumet Harbor. Tonight she was took away. What have they got left out there now? What's one took away from one?"

"By God!" I swore with delight as I caught his meaning. "The answer is *nothing*, of course! The *New Hope* can walk out of Trumet Harbor whenever she wants to—and nobody is there even to try and stop her!"

"That's the answer, Jonathan, boy; unless my arithmetic is away further off than I think 'tis!" I could imagine him grinning to himself in the darkness. "I've heard it said that you can't have your cash and spend it, too. Well, the British have risked theirs on a bet that they'll capture the powder. To me, it don't sound like such an awful good bet. If they lose, they'll lose the powder *and* the *New Hope*. If they win, all they'll have is the powder. You boys'll still be able to take the bark to sea, powder or no powder. You won't need powder, so far as getting free is concerned —not if there ain't nobody to fight you when you clear the harbor."

"There might be, though." I had a sudden chilling thought. "There's no reason why the *Terror* herself can't come around to take the *Hawke*'s place on the ocean side. There's plenty of water there."

"Gosh a'mighty! That's so, too!" Ezra groaned as though I had kicked him in the ribs. "If that happens our meat will be burnt for good and all!"

"Well, there's no use worrying," I told him. "There isn't anything that we can do about it. Anyhow, something tells me that it won't happen. Forsythe, I'll bet, is on the *Hawke* —or soon will be. Waterman is a prisoner here. Holt is a very sick man. I don't think there's an officer left on the *Terror* who would take the responsibility of ordering the frigate to make sail—even if he should think of it."

"I hope to the Lord Harry you're right, Jonathan, boy!" Ezra didn't seem to be particularly comforted. "Because, if you're wrong, here's one shareholder in a privateering scheme that's going to feel mighty sick. . . . Well, anyhow, I'll have lots of company!"

When we got out to the *Gannet* we found that she was still aground on Horse Mackerel Bar. The flood tide had just passed the point where I had thought the sloop would float again, but apparently my calculations were wrong. She was still fast, in spite of the sweating efforts of six or eight boats' crews, who were trying to yank her off bodily by means of ropes made fast to her stern.

One of the group of men peering intently over the side, when I came aboard, was Captain Dole. When he turned to speak to me I was relieved to see that he didn't seem greatly worried. "She'll ride clear again in a little while," he said confidently in answer to my query. "That's the least of my troubles. I've got others that are real ones—which is one of the reasons I'm glad you're here. If ever a man needed good sound advice—and needed it quick—I'm the man!"

Well, I was ready and willing to give him the best advice I could, but, as a matter of fact, it didn't seem to me that we had much choice. "I can't see anything for it, Captain Dole," I said, "but a fight. True enough, the *Gannet* hasn't got anything to fight with but one little popgun of a brass cannon, while the *Hawke* has real guns. If we let her keep her distance she'll blow us to splinters in short order; but we'd be fools to do that. I happen to know that this craft is fast and handles like a dream. We ought to be able to out-sail the *Hawke* well enough to close with her and board before she blows our ears off." I shrugged. "Maybe we'll get licked, even then, but we ought to be able to keep the Britishers' hands full long enough for the powder to get safe ashore. That's the best we can hope for—the way I look at it."

"I know, son." The Captain sighed. "I knew you'd feel that way, and I don't blame you a bit. When I was your age and saw as good a chance for a knock-down and drag-out fight as this one, I'd have jumped at it." He laughed. "The fact is, even now, in my doddering old age, I don't exactly hanker to run away from a good scrap. Maybe you know that."

I knew it, all right. I had sailed under him, on the *Strong Arm*, and I knew that there wasn't a skipper in all the American privateering service that liked to fight any

480

better than he did. When the hot shot were flying Captain Dole was cool, reckless, clever, and happy as he never was any other time. I guess the answer was that he thrived on gunfire—the way a baby thrives on milk.

"The thing is," he went on, "that as head of this *New Hope* enterprise I'm being paid, as you might say, as much to use my head as I am to fight. And my head tells me, this time, that I'll be a fool if I fight!" He slapped a fist into his open palm. "Yes sir-ee, a plain damn fool! Listen to me, Jonathan. If we should decide to tangle with the *Hawke*, we'll have to take a chance of boarding her, as you already said. To do that we'll have to have a big crew and a good one. We'll have to take the pick of my hands from the *New Hope*. You know what will happen, then, Jonathan, as well as I do. Heads or tails, we'll lose a lot of good men. Too many! Yes sir, the way I look at it, we can't *afford* to fight tonight. There's a price for everything, and this time the price is too high!"

"But—" I stammered. "But, Captain Dole—"

"I know you don't like that idea." He patted me on the arm. "Well, maybe I don't like it any better than you do. But I've thought it all over a dozen times while I've been waiting for this pesky tide to rise, and I've practically made up my mind. I'm going to leave this craft just where she is, to float when she gets ready. Every man Jack of our crowd is needed ashore—and that's where we'll go—and go now."

"But, Captain Dole!" I couldn't believe he was in earnest. "The powder!"

"I know." He shrugged. "We've been saying the powder is all that counts. But now, with this devilish *Hawke* complicating things, we can't wait any longer for the *Gannet* to float and then use her to help us get it in. If that powder gets ashore—all to the good. If it's captured or blown up by the *Hawke*—well, in that case we'll have to make out the best we can. Do you realize that now, tonight, for the first time, we've got clearance way to take the *New Hope* to sea with nobody so much as trying to stop us? We'd be flying in the face of Providence if we turned down this chance that the good Lord and the British have given us. We may be able to get powder somewhere else, if we have to, but we'll never get another *New Hope!*"

It was true—perfectly true. And yet I was so sick at heart in the knowledge that all my efforts in capturing the *Gannet* had been wasted that I felt disappointment rather than elation. I said nothing, but Ezra Light spoke up. The little peddler's suggestion was offered somewhat sheepishly but without hesitation. "Captain Isaiah," he said, "a while back you said you'd be glad for some advice. Mind if I put in *my* two cents' worth? It probably won't be wuth that much, but, on t'other hand, it might be."

"Eh? ... Why, certain sure, Ezra. You've got a good head on your shoulders. What's your idea? Let's have it. Heave ahead."

"Well, first off, I'd like to ask you something." Now that Ezra had the floor—or rather the deck—he was brisk enough. "If you wanted to sail this vessel—the craft we're on now —from some place to some place else, what would be the smallest number of men that could get her there? I'm not talking about fighting on the way, or anything fancy like that. I'm just asking how many men it would take to plain *sail* her."

"Not many." The Captain shrugged. "She isn't so almighty big. A man at the wheel, and one other, could do it, I guess, in a pinch."

"That's how I cal'lated. And, if that's the case, I don't see why my notion mightn't work. Anyhow, it couldn't do no harm. Listen." Ezra was talking eagerly now, and with growing confidence. "You want to keep your *New Hope* crew from being smashed up, but you'd like to save the Tamoset powder, too, if you can. Now *I* think you can."

"How?"

"By letting two or three men sail this *Gannet* thing the way you said they could." He held up a hand. "Now, wait a minute before you laugh. What I mean is that, soon as the *Gannet* floats, you have the sails h'isted. Then take everybody off except a couple of men—say Jonathan and me. We'll sail her for you, won't we, boy? We'll kite her up to the north'ard to meet the *Hawke*, and what's more we'll keep those Britishers so busy for a while that they might be late keeping their appointment with our powder!"

"Bosh!" Captain Dole started to laugh but immediately thought better of it. "Two men might be able to sail this craft, but they couldn't fight her."

"Who said anything about fighting?" Ezra was more eager than ever. "There won't be any of that—not if I'm on board and have my way! I'm a peaceable man, and cannon balls sour my stomach. No, sir, no fighting! We'll just *find* the *Hawke* and then tease the daylights out of her. We'll come close enough so that we're almost in range, but not quite. The John Bull captain will go crazy, if he's human. Sooner or later he'll turn around and chase us."

"And then?" I could see that Captain Dole was thinking intently. "What next?"

"Nothing next!" Ezra chuckled. "When he chases us we'll run straight for the coast of Maine, or anywhere that's a long way from Shad Cove. We'll run just as long as he chases. If he gives it up as a bad job and comes about, we'll come about, too, and tanterlize him some more!"

"What? . . . Why, say! . . . By the Lord, I think that's a good idea!" I was suddenly excited. "I think it might work!"

"Maybe." I could see that Captain Dole was impressed, even though he shook his head. "Humph! It might hold up the *Hawke* for a little while; but, if the officer aboard her is worth his salt, he won't be fooled long enough. He'll see what you're up to, and go about his business—which is blowing up the powder or grabbing it."

"Maybe he won't be wuth his salt," Ezra insisted, refusing to be downed; "and maybe we'll be able to fool him anyhow. I've got one more shot in my locker. Pass the word for Nate Braddock, will you, Isaiah? He's aboard here, and he knows more about the Bay than anybody in Trumet. I want him to pass judgment on the rest of my scheme."

Nate Braddock was a good pilot in the Bay, all right, as I was soon to learn, but he didn't look like a good anything. He was a leathery-skinned hulk of a man with a face on which there wasn't a trace of expression. He was chewing on a long piece of grass when Ezra started to talk, and was still chewing on it, wordless, at the end.

"Well?" demanded Captain Dole, excited now in spite of himself. "What do you think of that idea, Nate? Could the thing be done?"

Nate continued to chew on his piece of grass for so long that I thought he must be in a trance. . . . Then, just as he was opening his mouth to speak, the *Gannet* suddenly floated free of Horse Mackerel Bar.

A moment before her deck felt solid and unnatural underfoot, but all at once that feeling was gone. No sailor would have needed the exultant cheering of the men in the small boats to tell him that the tide had done its work at last.

"Um-hm," said Nate Braddock, morosely, in the midst of the hubbub. "If *I* did it, it could be did."

"You hear?" Ezra Light, hewing to the line, grabbed Captain Dole by the arm. "Nate says my notion might work! How about it, Captain Isaiah? Do I win?"

Well, the long and the short of it was that Ezra won. Captain Dole was a man who was quick to make up his mind and quicker still to act, once it was made up. I don't believe more than fifteen more minutes had passed before I was, for the second time that day, cruising the Bay on the deck of the *Gannet*. But this time my company was very different, and much smaller. All told there were three of us aboard. Nate Braddock, still morose and still chewing hay, was at the wheel. Ezra Light, humming to himself in his satisfaction, was tinkering with the small brass cannon amidships. I, in my new post as foremast hand, was conning the sails. Somewhere over our bow, from the Point Town direction, we fondly hoped that the British armed brigantine, *Hawke*, was hustling towards us.

Ezra's plan, as he had outlined it to Captain Dole, worked out so like what actually happened that the happening itself needs little telling.

We met the *Hawke* just about where we thought we would, about half way between Billfish Cove and the entrance to Point Town Harbor. She was boiling along as close to the shoals as she dared to go, and we passed to windward at no great distance. The night was clear and starlit, though there were clouds piling up towards the mainland which gave a promise of overcast weather to come, and the British lookout must surely have seen us.

Ezra, however, was taking no chances. The moment he caught a glimpse of the brigantine's silhouette to the eastward he set about making as much clatter as one small man could possibly be expected to make. Shouting rude insults at the top of his lungs through a speaking trumpet held in one hand, he used the other to beat furiously with a belaying pin on the bottom of a tin pan. If the British heard him, and didn't think he was crazy, Nate Braddock certainly did.

Nate looked at Ezra's goings-on stolidly for a few seconds before a quiver of feeling crossed his wooden face. "Durn fool," he observed with disgust, spitting heavily on the deck and rubbing the place with his boot. "Durn, dumb fool!"

Ezra hadn't, by any means, forgotten his brass cannon. At what he evidently deemed the correct time he plucked a slow match from its bucket of sand and applied it where it would do the most good. The little gun went off with a satisfactory bang, considering its size, but Ezra was not pleased. He kicked at it angrily and swore. "If the Johnnies hear that pipsqueak noise, they've got ears as sharp as a fox's. Why—"

Boom!

The single gun the *Hawke* fired didn't do any damage, except perhaps to Ezra's nerves, but it served notice that we weren't to be scorned. Peering astern I could see that the brigantine was swinging to come about.

"They've seen us! They're going to follow!" I spoke sharply to Nate Braddock. "Don't run away from them too fast, or they'll give up! Don't let them get within range, either, or we may be sorry for it!"

That was the beginning of a game that must have been as maddening for the British officer commanding the *Hawke*—I only hope his name was Forsythe—as it was pleasurable for us. By seeing to it that the distance between the two vessels never widened—but lessened, instead, with painful slowness—we were able to lure the brigantine into pursuing us for precious minutes in a direction opposite from Shad Cove and the powder landing.

When, at last, the game was up and the *Hawke* gave up the useless chase, we followed Ezra's plan exactly as he had laid it down. Coming about, we became the hunter instead of the hunted, and, having much the more speed, were soon back at our game of trying to tease our opponent into chasing us once again.

The temptation to Forsythe, or whoever was the enemy commander, must have been great, but I soon realized that he had no intention of being fooled for a second time. Ignoring us to the extent of refusing even to fire a single hopeful gun in our direction, the *Hawke* set and held a course straight for the mouth of Shad Cove.

"It's no use," I said at last. "He's had enough, so we'll have to pull our last rabbit out of the hat! It's your show, Nate, from now on. Think you can do it?"

Nate didn't answer, or even look at me. He merely moved the wheel a bare inch and continued to chew his grass stem.

There was nothing for Ezra and me to do but stand by and wait with whatever patience we could muster. Ezra did most of the talking, while I peered at the *Hawke*, which, by now, was directly astern and on the same course. "It'll work," said Ezra nervously. "It's got to work! I'll bet my last dollar them Redcoat officers never heard of Hammonds's Shoal! Even if they have, they'll never believe we'd do what we're going to do! They know we know these waters, and they know we're headed straight for Shad Cove. They'll trust us. They have to. They'll follow straight on our tail as meek as a lamb. Wait and see if they don't!"

It was wishful thinking on Ezra's part, but it turned out that he was right. The *Hawke* followed where Nate Braddock led, which was squarely towards and over Hammonds's Shoal—a sandspit thrust up treacherously in the deep water where no such thing had any right to be. Nor can I blame the brigantine's navigating officer for doing so. His incomplete chart probably made no mention of the little known and newly formed sand bar, and it would have taken a very clever man indeed to have reasoned that we might do what we did.

"Better take aholt of something," said Nate calmly and without warning. "We'll fetch up any second now."

Ezra gasped. "We're on the shoal already?"

487

"Yup. Been on it quite a little spell. *Hawke*'s just coming on now. She might fetch aground afore us, drawing a lot more water, the way she does."

But, in that last, Nate was wrong. The two vessels "fetched up" at almost exactly the same instant. I felt a little grinding shudder. Then—the next instant—I just missed being thrown entirely off my feet as the *Gannet* came to grief, and to earth, for the second time that day.

"Look, Jonathan, boy, look!" Before I could gather myself together Ezra was jumping up and down in hilarious excitement. "Look at that darned *Hawke!* She's high and dry, by glory! She can't stop our powder from coming in now! Not this night she can't!"

The next thing I knew, he had picked up his tin pan and was thumping upon it again in triumphant celebration.

"Durn fool!" Nate Braddock, having satisfied himself that everything was to his satisfaction, so far as both the *Hawke* and the *Gannet* were concerned, was already turning towards the stern. We had been towing a small boat there, and Nate began pulling on the tow rope. He paused only to spit once more on deck and to give Ezra his final blessing. "That's you, Ez Light—just a plain, durn, dumb fool! Banging on a skillet! What in time do you think you be—cook aboard a flatfish boat?"

9

In which the New Hope
spreads her wings.

Told by

CAPTAIN ISAIAH DOLE

I DO WISH I could give a real, worth-while idea of what our little town of Trumet was like that night. I can navigate a ship and boss a crew, but when it comes to writing —well, by this time, if anybody has had the patience to cruise through all these pages with me, he or she must realize that, when it comes to handling a pen, I am a long way from rating A. B.

Trumet was a crazy town, and, if a stranger could have dropped in on us, he would have been willing to lift his right hand and swear that every man, woman, and child in it was a lunatic. This was the end of the long waiting. The powder barge had signalled to shore, our watchers had answered those signals, and boats had been out to meet the barge and pilot her in. The precious gunpowder was here at last, and, out in the Bay, still stuck hard and fast on the shoals, were the two vessels that the enemy had ordered to take stations and keep especial watch to stop it ever getting to us.

Not only the *Gannet* pinky, which had been in the Bay for weeks, but the brigantine *Hawke*, which had been guarding our harbor on the ocean side. They were both there, and there they would have to stay until Captain Holt found a way to float them again. And, for a little while, at least, our harbor mouth was open and unwatched, and the *New Hope's* road to blue water was as clear of trouble as a pigpen is of soap. Every Trumetite older than a baby knew that, and every one that could walk was out of doors and busy in one way or another.

Every house, big or little, was lighted up, and the Bay Road and the Point Road and the main road, all the way to the wharf where the *New Hope* lay, were ablaze with lanterns and torches and bonfires. We didn't have to be afraid of the enemy's seeing the illumination and guessing what was going on. Those in the Bay must have guessed it already, and those in Point Town would know it pretty soon. On our shoulders was the responsibility of seeing that our own job was done before the news got to the *Terror* and the big frigate came out of Point Town Harbor and around to where she could head us off.

As for the *Hawke* and *Gannet* sending armed boats to fight on their own account, we weren't much worried. Those boats, we were sure, could be beaten off. As I said at the beginning of this yarn, we had never been really afraid of a raiding party landing from boats. It would cost the landers altogether too many men, before and after they set foot on our Bay beach. And such an important expedition would hardly be ordered by anybody but Captain Holt—and Captain Holt, so Jonathan Bangs reported, was dangerously sick. And—well, no matter, whether or no, this was our chance, our wonderful chance, and we were taking it.

Every horse-drawn cart, every oxcart,—yes, every hand cart and wheelbarrow—were loaded with powder kegs and sent rattling and rumbling and squeaking from the shore where the powder was being unloaded to the wharf on the other side of town. Men were sweating and swearing and heaving and tugging; some women—the younger ones— were working, too; children were shouting and screaming, some at the beach, some at the wharf, and some running back and forth alongside the carts and wheelbarrows.

Quiet old Trumet had never known a night like this, and, I guess likely, never will again.

I was aboard the bark, superintending the storing of the powder. Jonathan was at the Bay shore, bossing the unloading, and Hope was—well, I don't know where she was just then—but I should imagine she was nigh enough to Jonathan, at least, to look at him. If there wasn't a halo around his head that night there ought to have been. The news of how he had bamboozled and tricked the Britishers into the pickle they were in just then had spread all over town. He hadn't done any more than just tell me and a few others about it, not giving many particulars and talking as if what he had done didn't amount to much. It was all Hope, so he said. If it hadn't been for her—

Which was just like him, of course. But Hope didn't talk that way. She declared it was every bit Jonathan. Between the two of them, Weeks and Berry and Davies and Bailey and I got a pretty clear idea of the facts, and you can be certain we did our best to light up that halo I mentioned and keep it shining where it belonged. It did me good to say "I told you so" to Captain Elnathan Berry. And, to give the old boy his due, he didn't so much as put up the shadow of an excuse for the way he had been damning Jonathan for almost a week. Instead he owned up that he had been a fool.

"It isn't the first time by a long shot," he told me. "I wanted to hang the boy, certain I did. Now I want to kiss him. Maybe I would, only I judge he's got somebody who'll do the job better. I made my apologies to him—or tried to. He was so everlasting busy he wouldn't listen, so I'll have to send 'em by you, Isaiah. Tell him I'm going to have the doctor take soundings in my head, soon as I have time. When a man gets so that he chums around with a murdering loony like that Fowler and is all for stringing up the one person that has pulled the *New Hope* out of the fire—

493

well, all I can say is that Eben's craziness must be catching. As for you, Isaiah, the whole town is—"

But I was busy, too. I cut in to ask him if Fowler had been caught yet. He said not so far as he had heard.

"He will be, pretty soon, of course," he told me. "Only a few of us know that he is the traitor we've been hunting. Jerry Weeks broke the news to Henry Allen a little while ago. Poor Henry! He was knocked into the lee scuppers by it. He just about worshipped Eben. Eben, with his money and his dignity and all, was Henry's idea of the Lord A'mighty on earth. Jeremiah says Henry couldn't speak a word after he was convinced it was true. Well, a speechless Henry Allen is another miracle, that's all."

Finally—and in a surprisingly short time—the last keg was stowed aboard the *New Hope*. The last member of the crew had kissed his wife or mother or best girl, or all hands of them, one after the other. Everyone but the militia guards—who were still at their stations, with Major Bartlett to keep them there—was on or close to the wharf. Jonathan Bangs was the last person to report to me; he had been the last to leave the Bay shore, when the powder landing was over.

I saw him, by the light of the torches and lanterns, coming down the pier. Hope was with him. I couldn't forbear taking just a final minute to speak to Hope, so I walked down the gangplank and pushed my way through the crowd to meet them. Hope's eyes were wet, but she was brave. Not a word to me that Jonathan might be starting his last cruise, that there was a chance she might never see him again. No sir-ee! She even managed to pump up a pretty fair imitation of a smile. As for Jonathan, he was smiling, too—not with both sides of his mouth, but doing pretty fair with one. Neither he nor I, not any other officer, was in uniform, of course. There hadn't been time for that.

Hope and I shook hands. "Take good care of him for me, won't you, Captain Isaiah?" she said. I told her I'd keep him under glass just as long as I could. "He shan't wilt if I can help it," I said. "And you've got to keep yourself in first class, A-Number-One condition, young woman. Can't have a pale, sick-looking bride at the wedding I hope to be invited to right after I get back here. Don't forget to eat your three meals a day."

She promised not to forget. She and Jonathan looked in each other's faces. "Good-by, Jon," she said. "Good-by, Hope," said he, and stooped and kissed her. I was scared that the crowd might start cheering them, but, for some reason, they had sense enough not to. Hope shook hands with me once more.

"A lucky voyage, Captain Isaiah," she said. "And come back to us soon—all of you."

That was all. She turned then and moved away. Jonathan looked after her; then he hurried up the gangplank. I was following him, but someone caught my arm. I turned and saw it was Squire Bailey. He and I had said our good-bys before, and I had had a chance to thank him for all he had done to back and help me. I—yes, and all of Trumet —owed him more than we could ever pay, and I told him that, too.

What he said this time had nothing to do with that.

"News, Isaiah," he said. "Thought you ought to hear it before you sailed. They have found Eben Fowler."

He didn't say "caught," and I noticed that. "Found!" I repeated. "Found? You mean—"

He nodded. "Yes," he told me. "They found his body in the woods just back of the Allen house. He had shot himself through the head. The best way out for him, I suppose."

I sighed. "Yes," I agreed. "Poor devil!"

We didn't either of us say any more. It wasn't a thing

to talk about. Eben Fowler had been a big man in Trumet. As for what he had done lately—well, nobody can hold an insane man responsible for his actions.

The last person to shake hands with me was Ezra Light. I asked him about Phoebe.

"Oh, she's getting along fine," he said. "Beginning to relish her vittles and talking all the time between mouthfuls. The Hannah Badger woman's ears are beginning to show signs of wear. Just afore I left the house Hannah asked me if I didn't think 'twould be a good notion for her to look up somebody to set along with Phoebe times when she—Hannah, I mean—had to leave long enough to sleep or eat or something. I said I cal'lated maybe 'twould, and I asked her if she had any likely candidate in mind. She said she wouldn't wonder if her Aunt Dorcas would take the job if she asked her to. Said Aunt Dorcas, so she figured, would be just the one for Phoebe. Only special thing I can recollect about Aunt Dorcas is that the old woman is stone deaf. Don't cal'late that had anything to do with Hannah's recommend, do ye, Captain Isaiah?"

I had a word or two to say to Ezra about what he had already done for Trumet and the *New Hope,* and told him I imagined he would be asked to do more pretty soon.

He grinned. "Yus, yus," he agreed. "I shouldn't wonder. All according to Scriptur'. 'Well done, good and faithful servant. You've risked your neck half a dozen times, now we'll give you a chance to risk it a dozen more.' All right. 'Tain't much of a neck, anyhow; my shirt collar size is middling small."

What I had in mind was his getting down to Point Town before very long—on a peddling cruise, of course—to listen to the talk there and see if there were any hints of reprisals on the part of the British. "We have tricked them pretty bad," I said, "and it may be they will be for making Trumet pay the bill. A good stiff ransom or a real house-burning landing party, that's what I mean. Keep your ears open, Ezra, and report whatever you hear to Squire Bailey and the Council."

He promised he would. As a matter of fact, I wasn't very much disturbed. As I have said over and over again, I was pretty sure that kind of a party would cost the raiders more than any ransom Trumet could pay. I believe Holt, provided he was well again, would figure it that way, too.

The time came to cast off. The last picture of Trumet that I had to carry to sea with me was of the crowd on the pier and in the boats alongside and on the deck of our bark, waiting, bareheaded and quiet, while the Reverend Ichabod Samuels prayed for the blessing of the Almighty upon our enterprise, our vessel, and those aboard her.

I can see that picture now, when I shut my eyes and call it back—see it plain as plain. The bared heads of the people, showing, now shadowy and then clear, in the red light of the torches blowing in the wind. I can see the old minister standing there by the wharf edge, his white hair fluttering and his thin hands held high. I can hear the amens coming from the pier and the boats and our own deck. I said one myself, so did Jonathan—so did about everybody, I think. God had certainly been good to us so far, whether we deserved it or not.

And then it was time to go. I gave the orders, and Jonathan and Abijah Doane jumped to pass them on to the hands. The cables were cast off, the crews in the rowboats —the boats that were to tow us out into the channel—laid to their oars, and the bark turned her nose away from Trumet. One more big cheer came from the folks we were leaving behind.

The wind was fair, thank goodness—fair and steady. The sky was overcast, and, although there was no fog, the night was black dark. Just the night I would have picked if I had had my way. We showed no light, of course, below or

497

aloft. The oars in the boats were muffled. We had just enough canvas set to give us steerage way. Steady and at a fair rate we moved down towards the harbor mouth.

And, at last, outside in the deep water, the boats left us. I turned to Jonathan, standing there alongside me. His hand reached across and squeezed mine. I squeezed back. We didn't, either of us, say anything: we didn't need to.

When I did speak it was to give an order.

"Mr. Bangs," I said, "you may get full sail on her."

"Aye, aye, sir."

The sails were set and filled. The deck tilted as she began to feel the pressure. The water bubbled and splashed under the bow. The wake showed ghostly white astern. The *New Hope* spread her wings and flew.

————————